J-HORROR

J-HORROR

THE DEFINITIVE GUIDE TO
THE RING, THE GRUDGE AND BEYOND

DAVID KALAT

VERTICAL.

Published by Vertical, Inc., New York

Layout by Hiroko Mizuno

ISBN 978-1-932234-08-4 / 1-932234-08-4

Manufactured in the United States of America

First Edition

Vertical, Inc.
www.vertical-inc.com

Dedicated to my beloved son, Max.
May he never run out of burrets.

TABLE OF CONTENTS

ACKNOWLEDGEMENTS

Acknowledgements are too often just a private communiqué between the author and the people whose names are (or should have been) on the list. I hope that you will treat this particular acknowledgements page differently, if only out of your own self-interest: J-Horror is still a living thing, and you will need to know where to look for information about all the movies that surface *after* this book went to press.

For that, your best starting point will be the sites to which I turned as my most important sources: www.midnighteye.com, www.twitchfilm.net, www.koreanfilm.org, www.theringworld.com, www.mandiapple.com/snowblood, www.fjmovie.com/horror. With almost no exceptions, the quotes used in this book were not obtained by me, but rather were sourced from these sites and others. Please consult the bibliography for full details, but know here and now that this book exists thanks to the invaluable research done by the likes of Tom Mes, Jasper Sharp, Darcy Parquet, Mark Schilling, Art Black, J. Lopez, and all the other J-Horror fans around the world who have made the web their home.

I lack the proper words with which to thank Norio Tsuruta and Koji Suzuki: they showed me more patience than I deserved and gave me more of their insights than I'd dared hope for. I only hope that they are not too displeased with what they will find here.

Stephen Stratman translated a treasure trove of Japanese-language material for me that proved essential in shaping several chapters. Without him I would have been lost at sea, since the only thing I can read in Japanese is the word "Japan," which is essentially useless.

I also need to thank Tim and Donna Lucas, who gave me my first public platform on which to start talking about J-Horror. I hope every reader of this book rushes out and buys a subscription to Video Watchdog immediately. In an age where the internet is rapidly co-opting the world of information and pushing many print magazines into oblivion, Video Watchdog stands as a shining example of the enduring merits of print—each issue is worth waiting for, and contains more meaty substance than a dozen websites combined.

I am profoundly grateful to my family and friends—especially Julie Stapel, Ann Stapel-Kalat, Sam Kalat, Sheila Denn, David Landis, James Maysonett, Kristen Gustafson, Elissa Preheim, and Jonathan Wilan—

for putting up with my most insufferable character traits as I hashed out these ideas. I am also indebted to my publisher, Ioannis Mentzas, whose personal commitment and enthusiasm for this project can be seen on every page.

Finally, but in no way least, I struggle to find the words with which to thank my agent, Janet Rosen. For nearly ten years she has been my loyal advocate, even though I have given her precious little reason to be and sometimes ample reason not to be. She remains unflagging and dedicated in my service. More so: she rejected an earlier version of this book, and in face of my petulant complaints, patiently explained her reasons why she wanted me to go back and try again. She was right, I was wrong, and without her thoughtful guidance I would never have found the right track. This book is as much hers as mine.

A NOTE ON THE TEXT

This is a book about Japanese cinema intended for use by non-specialists, casual fans, and people who don't speak a lick of Japanese. I can't help the fact that most of the names I'll be discussing will be foreign, and to untrained ears will likely blend together. I hope that when you're done reading this book you'll be able to distinguish the biggies, such as Hideo Nakata, Norio Tsuruta, Masayuki Ochiai, Kiyoshi Kurosawa, Hiroshi Takahashi, Taka Ichise, and Takashi Shimizu, even if the other names become foggy. The convention in Japan is for family names to go first, followed by the individual's given name—exactly the reverse of Western conventions. For the convenience of the Western reader, I've taken the liberty of switching the name order in this book, so that, for example, the man called Ito Junji in his native land is referred to as Junji Ito here.

As for movie titles, I faced a more curious challenge. The prevailing trend in film scholarship when discussing foreign movies is to use the original language title. I did not wish to do this because I know that even more than people's names, Japanese movie titles would become quickly incomprehensible to English speakers. Additionally, one of the principle aims of this book is to aid you when you go to the video store. It does me no good then to recommend you seek out ***Nagai Yume***, ***Joyurei***, or ***Saimin*** if all you see on the shelf are ***Long Dream***, ***Don't Look Up***, or ***The Hypnotist***. So I chose to discuss the films by their English language release titles.

In this regard I was greatly helped by the fact that most of the films have official English language titles that are consistent around the world. Many feature the English title onscreen with the Japanese one on the original release prints. Some of the movies, such as ***Ring*** or ***Tomie: Another Face***, use English words as their Japanese titles, merely written in katakana. Some, such as ***Cure*** or ***Doppelganger***, don't even bother transcribing the titles into Japanese and actually use the English word as the sole onscreen title. A few, such as ***Inugami*** or ***Uzumaki***, are marketed in the United States under their Japanese name. However, a few of the films—especially those made prior to the J-Horror boom—never anticipated an international audience and do not have official, consistent English titles. In these cases, when I introduce the film for discussion I will give its Japanese title, provide an English alternative and go from there. It has already happened that, while writing this book, some of these more obscure films are picked up for DVD release in this country and are therefore assigned a new English title. Sometimes the official release uses the same name I did, sometimes I've gone back and changed the name in my text—but there may well be instances I cannot catch because the release happened after this book went to print. As a stopgap measure, the filmography in the back is listed by original Japanese title and offers all known English variants, so with a little elbow grease you can match up any discrepant titles.

CHAPTER 1

DEAD WET GIRLS

When I heard that the Pope had died, a guilty fear flashed through my mind: how much of this is my fault? Halloweaster, I mean. Had he heard what I was up to?

You see, I had the good fortune to have been born before the advent of DVDs and VCRs, before satellite TVs and digital cable and Tivo conspired to make sure we had hundreds of options of nothing worth watching. Back in my day, we got a mere handful of channels, which we had to dial by hand and tune in on rabbit ears, but man were they entertaining! This isn't just the rantings of a grumpy old man. There's some of that, I'll admit, but I can prove to you things were better back then: horror hosts.

Sure, my youth was on the tail end of the horror host heyday, but still. These were guys (or gals, depending on where you lived) who dressed up like vampires to present screenings of old black-and-white monster movies on late-night TV. I was too young to remember the name of my local horror host, but I do remember the impact he had on my young mind. Since my father believed these shows were as important to my cultural edification as the symphony or the art museum, he would dutifully wake me up each Friday night to join him on the couch, with pizza and popcorn, to learn about Boris Karloff, Bela Lugosi, and Vincent Price. One sad day, we tuned in and found his show replaced by a variety program starring Soupy Sales.

I grieved the loss, but by then the bug was in my system. I've had a jones for gothic chillers ever since. Even as a responsible grownup with a house and a wife and kids, I'm still wasting my time watching Frankenstein's monster waving his cold dead fist at a crowd of angry villagers.

Every year at Halloween my brother would drive across state lines to join me for a daylong marathon of old school horror movies. But as time went on we found our Octobers too crowded and busy to maintain the ritual, and bumped our plans back to the spring. Watching movies about the reanimated dead on Easter was an appealing idea, and not as blasphemous as it sounds. Once and only once in human history came a story in which returning from the dead wasn't a Really Bad Idea. It helped celebrate that distinction to point out the contrasts—the times when resurrection didn't turn out well at all.

Gradually, Halloweaster took root as a ritual in itself, and every year a crowd of like-minded friends would join us to develop bedsores while watching horror movies. It didn't always land on Easter weekend precisely, but on April 2, 2005 it managed to coincide with the passing of Pope John Paul II, a portentous omen if there ever was one.

Lightning hasn't struck me yet, so I don't think I caused the death of the Pope. But if word of our day's activities filtered back to Rome I doubt it would have made him smile. Even people who know me well get the wrong idea when I tell them I spend my time watching horror movies with my kids. One year, my daughter Ann, who was maybe three at the time, sat rapturously in front of the TV holding a stuffed Dracula doll and pumping her fists excitedly in the air whenever Christopher Lee bared his fangs. This is what I mean when I talk about horror movies—the kind of fun/scary that rollercoasters offer. A chance to confront your fears, to indulge in feeling terror, but to know in your heart you'll be just fine. Scary but safe.

But when you tell the average person that you let your little kids watch horror movies, they think something altogether else. Most of the moms in my neighborhood already think I'm too lenient about what my kids watch. I was taking five year olds to ***Spider-Man*** (2002) when my neighbors had decreed ***Finding Nemo*** (2003) too intense for youngsters. But setting aside the arguments in my defense (we live in a media-saturated culture and it's good parenting to teach your kids critical-viewing skills, teach them not to be manipulated or dominated by what they see, blah blah blah), the point here is that the term "horror movie" has been hijacked and redefined since I grew up watching my local horror host.

Like any extinct animal, the old-time gothic chiller was hounded off the earth by a combination punch of losing its traditional habitat and the arrival of a ruthless predator. The habitat of the Gothicus Chillerus included drive-ins, revival houses, independent TV stations, and other places where niche market movies were screened to audiences. As the Me Decade progressed, these venues closed down. But the advent of the MPAA ratings system was like Global Warming to the movie-world's habitat. Ostensibly, Jack Valenti conceived the ratings system as a mechanism for parents and other concerned moviegoers to control what they watched, but the end result was to profoundly coarsen the content of American movies.

Prior to the implementation of the MPAA ratings in 1968, movies in the United States were expected to be suitable for all ages, all audiences. If you wanted to make a movie that dealt with racy or problematic subject matter, you had to be discreet about it. An excellent case in point is the 1942 thriller ***Cat People***, by producer Val Lewton and director Jacques Tourneur. Working with a low budget at RKO Studios, an also-ran movie company specializing in B pictures, Lewton and Tourneur were so clever at milking the most screen values out of the least resources that ***Cat People*** stood as a benchmark for efficient filmmaking for generations to come. For a film about a chick who turns into a were-cat and mauls people to death, ***Cat People*** has no special effects. No shots of Simone Simon transforming into a panther-lady, no panther-lady make-up, no spilt blood or dismembered corpses—it was all handled with atmosphere and suggestion.

The filmmakers were so good at planting suggestions in the audience's minds, they were able to handle a storyline that ought to have been too hot for the censors of the day: our panther-lady heroine, played by Simon, is a Serbian immigrant who has the curious idea that sexual arousal will cause her to turn into a monster. She meets a man, takes him back to her place for the night, and within a few short days they are married. But she won't let him act on the intense sexual chemistry they've built up because she fears it will trigger her dark side. She sleeps alone in a locked bedroom, her husband forlornly waiting outside her door, denied even a kiss. Eventually their sexless marriage takes its inevitable toll, and he falls for a coworker. When Simon's character discovers the other woman, her sexual jealousy is aroused and turns her into a beast. Hubby tries to get her back under control by taking her to a psychiatrist, but the quack gets it into his head that if he rapes the wife she'll be forced to realize her monstrous fantasies are untrue. Things go downhill from there.

Now, bear in mind that at no point in the movie is the word "sex" even uttered. An average rerun of ***The Simpsons*** broadcast during dinnertime has more overtly sexual content than ***Cat People***, which danced expertly around its sex-fueled horror story decades before Kinsey issued his famous report. By the time an unnecessary remake was mounted in 1982, the ratings system had wrought its destructive effect upon the film industry. The modern ***Cat People*** showcases plenty of nudity and gore, minus the drama.

It made sense that filmmakers creating movies aimed at adult audiences shouldn't have to tame their stories down for children, that the film market ought to be large enough for serious grownup films that could comfortably assume that only serious grownups would attend. And from that logic, the ratings system made sense: slap an R on something, exclude the kiddies, and let the filmmakers follow their own uncensored visions. But anytime you make something rare you make it valuable. Tell a teenager he or she is not allowed to go see an R-rated film and you've pretty much insured that is exactly what they will want most to do. If the R was designed to create a safe place for movies like ***Ordinary People*** (1980), it also perversely created an entirely new kind of movie—the splatter flick.

This is the predator I mentioned before: a new kind of horror movie that was driven first and foremost by its graphic violence. If the gore effects were shocking enough, the film would earn an R, making it that much more marketable to the teenage audience that was supposed to be excluded by the R. It was a Catch-22 situation, but one that made for fat profits to gore flicks. Movies like ***Friday the 13th*** (1980) and ***Halloween*** (1978) and their many sequels and imitators were R-rated, but were clearly aimed at youngsters. Fangoria magazine appeared, its glossy pages dedicated to advertising which movie had the most extreme violence.

The horror movies I fell in love with as a child were films about dread, free-floating fear, and abstract ideas. Fear of sex, fear that science was reaching hubristically too far, fear of the foreign, fear of one's own inner demons—these were the themes underlying the best of the gothic chillers. Modern slasher movies reduced it all down to the simplest, dumbest element: fear of being killed. There was little need to write anything more sophisticated, or to hire particularly talented people to realize those scripts, because the real point was special effects. Spend your money on Tom Savini instead.

The change in horror movies is not all to be blamed on Valenti's ratings system. In Peter Bogdanovich's ***Targets*** (1968), Boris Karloff plays himself, more or less, an aging star of monsterrific B-movies whose personal appearance at a drive-in is rendered tragic by the arrival of a gun-toting madman who takes to killing the audience for no clear reason. In the 1960s and 70s, the real-life horrors of assassinations and riots and wars made it impossible to feel the same shivers from monsters of a more innocent age.

The summer after September 11, 2001 I was at a monster movie convention. The attendees, all of them fans of gothic chillers and creepy monsters, shared a dazed bewilderment at the unutterable horror the real world had too recently become. If the traumas of the late 1960s had rendered Frankenstein and Dracula obsolete, then how could Jason and Freddy and Leatherface possibly compete with real-life madmen who could vaporize thousands of innocent people in an instant?

I was in the dealer's room, where I was selling my own line of DVDs of forgotten classics and lost gems, "movies that fell through the cracks." A collection of Frankenstein ephemera on one disc, a surrealistic silent version of ***Fall of the House of Usher***, a pulpy spy thriller by

Fritz Lang—but I could tell by the listless look in my customers' eyes and the low sales that the spark had gone out of the convention, compared to innocent years past. A colleague stopped by the table to wish me well, and urged me to seek out a Japanese horror movie called ***Ring*** (1998). I smiled and nodded politely, but he might as well have advised me to farm goats for a living for all the intention I had of listening to him.

You see, my booth was directly opposite a table proffering bootlegs of various Japanese shockers such as the ***Guinea Pig*** films (1985-91), and ***Guts of a Virgin*** (1986). If you don't recognize those titles, then you're a happy lucky person. These are sadistic exercises in video cruelty that even gorehounds find extreme. In my mind, that's what Japanese horror was: everything that was wrong with modern American horror films, but even more vicious, misogynistic, and depressing. Even some Japanese horrors I kind of enjoyed, like ***Tetsuo: the Iron Man*** (1988) and ***Versus*** (2000) had a mean-spiritedness that was sure to alienate all but the most stout of viewers.

I had heard raves about ***Ring*** before. I had seen an import disc at a neighboring table, adorned with an image of a diseased, distended eye peering through a curtain of stringy wet hair. Connecting the gruesome cover art with my preconceived notions of what modern Japanese horror had to offer, I wrongly judged ***Ring*** to be something gaudy and rough. I almost missed the fact that, halfway around the world, the suspense-driven gothic thriller had been brought back from extinction.

Meanwhile, the ***Ring*** spread. At that point, Hideo Nakata's 1998 motion picture had not yet been officially released in the United States. So it circulated instead through an underground subculture of fans who made copies for each other. "Here, ya gotta see this!" Ironically, that's the same thing that happens in the movie: people make copies of a scary video for each other. Reportedly, if you watch this cursed videotape, exactly seven days later you drop dead. When a group of teenagers simultaneously die of unknown causes at different places around Tokyo, an investigative reporter traces their lives back to a common point when they watched a scary video together. She watches it herself, and realizes in horror she now has just one week to solve the mystery of the tape and save her own life.

Ring deftly mixed the clichés of modern slasher movies (urban legends, postmodern self-referentiality, threatening phone calls, doomed teenagers) with old Japanese folklore and traditional ghost story motifs, in a film that relied on suggestion and atmosphere instead of shock effects or gore. Inexpensively made for $1.2 million, it earned $15.5 million in Japan alone, before rippling across the world as an international phenomenon, sparking remakes and imitators everywhere it hit theaters.

One of the underground copies wound up in the hands of a man named Roy Lee, whose destiny was soon to become intertwined with Hideo Nakata's. Lee was overwhelmed by the movie—no surprise, really, since everybody who saw it responded by a) loving the movie, b) recommending it to a friend, c) trying to make their own version, or d) some combination of the above. Since Lee worked in Hollywood, his ability to take action was substantially more advanced than the average fan. He made a copy for a development executive at Dreamworks Pictures, Mark Sourian. "Here, ya gotta see this."

Sourian immediately phoned producers Walter F. Parkes and Laurie MacDonald to gush, "I've just seen the scariest movie I have ever seen in my life. You have to see it right away." Sourian copied the tape and sent it along to his producers. They watched it, and had the same reaction. They then copied the tape and mailed it to up-and-coming director Gore Verbinski (whose major credit at that time was ***Mousehunt***, *1997*).

"It was really poor quality," Verbinski recalls of the dupe he received, a copy of a copy of a copy of who knows how many grades down, "But actually that added to the mystique."

Hollywood has a habit of eating the pop culture of other countries and regurgitating the results to American audiences as if we were baby birds. The sad fact is American audiences don't much like subtitles, but also don't much like dubbing, and basically are hostile towards movies that don't have English-speaking stars whose faces are familiar from grocery-store checkout-aisle tabloids. And so, Dreamworks mounted a remake, with Verbinski vowing to maintain as much of Nakata's original atmosphere as possible. ***The Ring*** would be Americanized, but no more than necessary. It arrived in theaters around Halloween-time 2002, and sported a decidedly low-key marketing campaign. Whatever I had mis-expected of the original, the remake was obviously aimed at—and attracting—a crowd of serious adults, who didn't come out talking about the splatter FX but instead made comparisons to the early films of Luis Buñuel. My interest was piqued, and off to the theater I went.

I kept my expectations low—it was a Hollywood remake after all. Time and again I'd seen superb films made in other countries (***The Vanishing***, ***Nightwatch***, ***Open Your Eyes***) diminished and degraded by their Hollywood replacements. But as the film unspooled, I was enthralled, mystified, intrigued, and yes scared out of my wits.

There is a moment towards the end when the entire cramped auditorium erupted in simultaneous shrieking. It's been a long time since I was genuinely shaken by a movie, but ***The Ring*** is the real deal. I'll let my kiddies watch ***Dracula*** to their hearts' content, but they'll have to get older before they can see ***The Ring***, in any of its versions. There's no blood, no severed heads or impaled breasts, but it's awfully strong stuff for a quiet, slow-paced, minimalist suspense thriller.

Emboldened by its enormous success, Roy Lee went back for seconds. He started buying and selling remake rights to a slew of Japanese (and other Asian) horror flicks, brokering an entire remake genre all on his lonesome only. There was plenty to choose from, since the Asian film industry had responded to ***Ring*** by flooding theaters with similar ghost stories. One of the most popular of these was the haunted house movie ***Ju-On: The Grudge*** (2003), by a gifted young filmmaker named Takashi Shimizu. With Lee's intermediary help, Shimizu was invited to come to Hollywood to direct an American remake of his own film. Shimizu did them one better: he hired an American cast including Sarah Michelle Gellar, and brought them out to Tokyo to remake the film on the same sets as the original.

The Grudge turned out to be one of the major theatrical successes of 2004. Its cost was so low, yet its box office returns so large, that it outperformed many expected blockbusters that had bigger stars and heftier promotion. ***The Grudge*** was so big, in fact, it caused industry observers to remark that Sarah Michelle Gellar was now a "real" star (forget that ***Buffy the Vampire Slayer*** stuff, that's just TV).

Shimizu started preparing a sequel... Which brings us to a point of some confusion. As of this writing, Takashi Shimizu has directed five ***Ju-On*** movies, with the following titles: ***Ju-On: The Grudge*** (2000), ***Ju-On: The Grudge 2*** (2000), ***Ju-On: The Grudge*** (2003), ***Ju-On: The Grudge 2*** (2003), and ***The Grudge*** (2004). This last one is marketed in Japan as... ***Ju-On: The Grudge***. He has two more in the works: ***Ju-On: The Grudge 3***, and ***The Grudge 2***.

Meanwhile, Roy Lee brokered more work for Hideo Nakata, including directing the Hollywood sequel to Verbinski's remake of Nakata's film. This movie was released on March 18, 2005 as ***The Ring Two***. It bears no relation to the Japanese film ***Ring 2***, which was also directed by Hideo Nakata.

Confused yet?

I haven't even broached the fact that in Japan the first attempt to sequelize ***Ring*** wasn't Nakata's ***Ring 2*** at all, but a film called ***Spiral*** (1998). This movie flopped so thoroughly, the producers tried to pretend it never existed, and commissioned Nakata to direct an entirely unrelated sequel.

Gore Verbinski's 2002 film was not the first remake of ***Ring***: Korea had already produced a very fine version called ***The Ring Virus***, which had been prepared almost immediately upon the Korean release of Nakata's version. And for that matter, Nakata's was not the first version, either. The earliest appearance of the story was Koji Suzuki's novel, published in 1991. That was then adapted for a 1995 TV version ***Ring: The Complete Edition***. Produced by Fuji TV with a cast of soft-porn starlets, it managed to adhere very closely to the novel while adding as much nudity as possible. For a film with so many bare breasts, ***Ring: The Complete Edition*** is staggeringly dull and uninspired. I am told it was popular in its original run, but I don't know how to believe that. Nakata's take on the material, from a screenplay adaptation by Hiroshi Takahashi, works so very many improvements it is tempting to forget about the TV version altogether.

While the TV version of ***Ring*** is a washout, and the various sequels suffer a bit, the three major film versions are all extremely well-made. Each of these versions can be said to be a remake of someone else's prior work, yet each once has its own visionary strength. And despite sharing a very high percentage of their filmic DNA (these three cousins differ in only minor ways) they managed to be huge successes and inspirational influences in the different cultures and film industries of Japan, Korea, and the United States.

In each of these three countries, the local variant of ***Ring*** made a huge splash that sent out ever-widening ripples. Japanese, Korean, and American filmmakers rushed to mimic the success with similar follow-ups. A consistent aesthetic sensibility developed, with a common set of storytelling themes and visual ideas that linked the movies together in a single sub-genre. This much is to be expected. What is startling—puzzling, even—is that the films made in the wake of ***Ring*** not only maintain a uniform set of ingredients (dead wet girls, ghosts, urban legends, female heroes, viral curses) but a uniform quality as well.

Consider a more typical scenario. When George Lucas' ***Star Wars*** broke into theaters in 1977 it sent a similar shock wave, inspiring imitators and knock-offs to try to duplicate its success. A few of these ***Star Wars*** wanna-be's managed to get enough traction to hold on as moderately popular TV series—***Battlestar Galactica*** (1978), for example, or ***Buck Rogers in the 25th Century*** (1979). Far more common were the likes of ***Message From Space*** (1978). I remember being a kid and reading Starlog Magazine. There was an announcement for something called ***Message From Space***, and a picture or two of its spaceships. I knew it was striving to be as much like ***Star Wars*** as possible, but I was too young and naïve to recognize that as probably a bad sign. Anyway, this

Japanese-made ripoff never got a wide release in this country and never played in my area. I didn't get a chance to see it until I was thirty-two years old, by which time I had become much more jaded. ***Message From Space*** may have been directed by one of Japan's more interesting and storied filmmakers, the late great Kinji Fukasaku, but it's a mess of a movie and insufferable to watch. As is ***Star Crash*** (1979), ***Cosmos: War of the Planets*** (1977), ***Star Odyssey*** (1978), ***Beast in Space*** (1978), ***Battle of the Stars*** (1979)... If you're a ***Star Wars*** fan, you might as well not bother trying to find an imitator that can justify itself on its own merits.

By stark contrast, ***Ring*** (choose one) set in motion a cycle that produced films of actual quality, worth watching, discrete and independent of one another. It is a subgenre that for lack of a better term is called J-Horror.

I wish we didn't lack a better term. I don't like the label "J-Horror" and use it myself only under protest. For one thing, I think the name fails to provide adequate distinction from the gorier, shock-driven films that continue to come out of Japan, or from the grand tradition of Japanese ghost stories made long before ***Ring***. The movies covered in this book share features in common with one another that separate them from, say, Takashi Miike's cruel nightmare ***Audition*** (1999), or Nobuo Nakagawa's elegant classic ***Ghost Story of Yotsuya*** (1959). If we are to talk about these movies as a coherent body of work, they deserve a characteristic name.

Another reason I object to the term "J-Horror" is the J part. It must stand for Japanese (nothing else makes much sense) but the genre is not exclusively Japanese. It was American remakes of these films that sparked my interest—and maybe yours as well. More to the point, of the movies I cover in this book, a third of them hail from Korea. They are so close in style and content to the Japanese ones there's no good reason to coin a new term (K-Horror—why bother?), and for that matter there a handful of titles from Hong Kong as well.[1]

Hoping for an alternative to "J-Horror," I turned to the Mobius Film and Video discussion group (www.mhvf.net) for suggestions on what to call this genre. Suggestions ranged from "Nu-Kaidan" to "Dead Wet Girls." I toyed with calling this book "Dead Wet Girls," but as you can see (flip back to the cover if you don't remember) that idea didn't last long.[2]

As I began to examine the genre, though, I continued to ruminate over the uniform set of thematic and visual ingredients, and the unusual consistency of overall quality. It struck me that in the credits for these films I kept finding the same names. Perhaps the various ***Star***

Sadako...

The Complete Edition *poster*

Wars rip-offs would have turned out differently if they had actually been made by the same people who made ***Star Wars***.

Instead of thinking of J-Horror as a traditional kind of movie genre, then, I think it is more akin to an art movement, like surrealism or impressionism, where a group of like-minded people come together at the right moment to inspire each other to explore the same set of artistic concepts in the same fundamental way. Let's call our school of art, then, the Haunted School, after one of its earliest examples.

The artists of the Haunted School are a select group of influential creative people and savvy businessmen (I'm not trying to be sexist here—but for all the strong and interesting women on screen in these movies, few of them played much of a role behind the scenes). A variety of circumstances brought various people into one another's orbit, forming a new constellation of creative forces that would shape the genre. You should start learning the following names: novelist Koji Suzuki, manga artist Junji Ito, producer-director Kiyoshi Kurosawa, director Hideo Nakata, director Takashi Shimizu, screenwriter Hiroshi Takahashi, director Masayuki Ochiai, director Norio Tsuruta, producer Takashige Ichise, to name a few.

It is then quite natural that the same imagery and thematic concerns recur over and over again throughout the cycle. What makes these few people tick is what makes their movies tick. What we find in the recurring visions of ghostly schoolgirls, dark water, viral curses, and disrupted families is a common iconographic language. The written language of Japan is ideograms (kanji, katakana, hiragana). Kanji characters don't represent isolated sounds as in our alphabet but are symbols representing ideas. Depending on context, the meaning and pronunciation of a kanji character will change. The imagery of the Haunted School is a sort of cinematic kanji, using an alphabet of phantoms to symbolize larger issues. Sure, this book catalogs over four dozen films of almost identical visual substance, but in each film the respective context gives those ideograms a different meaning and effect.

Of this symbolic alphabet, certain symbols are especially common, and their relationship to modern Japanese fears are fairly easy to trace. For example, suicides feature prominently in these films, while suicide rates in Japan happen to be alarmingly on the rise. The hauntings and curses of these films tend to spread in a viral fashion, an epidemic of spookiness: after the deadly Sarin gas attack on a Tokyo subway in 1995, fears of bioterrorism and plagues are quite naturally weighing on the Japanese mind. The prevalence of water imagery is also striking (here's a drinking game for you: slam a shot every time one of these films shows a bathtub filled with some dark murky liquid).

As an island nation whose fate is linked with the sea's bounties, threatened by tidal waves and tsunamis, Japan's longstanding awe of water goes back farther and deeper than any fear of nasty microbes.

By far the most recurrent image in the Haunted School is the dead wet girl herself. Nothin' says scary like a chick with her hair hanging in front of her face. It's tempting to write this off as obvious mimicry of ***Ring***. In Hideo Nakata's landmark, the monster is the ghost of a girl drowned in a well, so everyone following in his footsteps feels honor-bound to include a drowned girl somewhere in the plot. But we're missing something if we leave it at that.

Legends of *hannya*, female demons, are part of ancient Japanese folklore. More recent (20th century) art forms have popularized stories of Oiwa (a murdered woman who returns from the grave to avenge her death), and Okiku (a girl drowned in a well who then haunts the place of her death—sound familiar?). Nakata has gone on record that the film that most directly influenced his style…well, it was Robert Wise's ***The Haunting*** (1963). OK, bad example, but the Japanese film that most influenced him was Nobuo Nakagawa's 1959 ***Ghost Story of Yotsuya***. Since this highly regarded Japanese classic is not well known outside their country, chances are you've never heard of it, much less seen it, so a quick refresher is in order. It's set in the same feudal Japan as many of Akira Kurosawa's samurai pictures, but the samurai in this picture is no noble hero. This guy is a Grade A bastard, whose approach to wooing his lady love is to kill her father, kill her friends, kidnap her sister, steal her money, frame her for adultery, poison her and dump her corpse into the river. Her ghost returns with an eye towards meting out some justice, poltergeist-style. Along the way the audience is treated to scenes of a pallid ghostly woman, and water clogged with clumps of black hair.

Ghostly schoolkids feature in such pre-Ring J-Horrors as 1995's ***The Haunted School*** and ***Phantom of the Toilet*** (yes, you read that correctly, *phantom of the toilet*). The evil ghost girl with hair combed in front of her face and a viral curse in plan shows up in Masayuki Ochiai's ***Parasite Eve*** (1997), made a year before ***Ring*** made its impression. So what gives?

Notice how the ghostly schoolgirls are ghosts in the first place because they were once victims of some terrible crime, returning as phantoms to threaten other children, and confronted by (in most cases) female heroes. The victims and villains of ghostly curses intertwine, with women and girls presented as both vulnerable and powerful at the same time. The Haunted School is not so much about monsters, not in the literal sense. Instead, the monsters serve to highlight alienation, how modern society disrupts traditional family structures and leaves the most vulnerable of us alone in an unfriendly world.

The connective tissue that links the many symbols of J-Horror together is sexual deviancy and violation of traditional family structures. The Haunted School consistently invokes incest, rape, homosexuality, abortion, divorce, adultery, the irredeemable trauma of child abuse. In each of these films we find some departure from established traditions of how men and women are "supposed" to relate to one another and form families. These departures threaten the existing order, and lead to anxious, uncertain futures. The modern world with all its progressive ideas gives women the power and opportunity to break away from their traditionally circumscribed roles in society, but as women increasingly turn away from established orthodoxy they threaten the social order—something these films represent with monsters and ghosts. What else are ghosts but the revenge of the past on the present?

When I asked Norio Tsuruta (director of ***Ring 0: Birthday***, and arguably the creator of J-Horror's visual style) what it was about long black hair Japanese folk found so unsettling, he explained that in feudal Japan the custom was for men to wear their hair very long, in a style called *Chon-mage*. As a contrast, women were expected to have their hair neatly closed up. So, a woman whose hair was lengthy like a man's, and wildly unkempt, signaled deviance—perhaps madness or even demonic possession. At the very least, it signified a woman who was...non-conformist.

Let's look at the three major J-Horror franchises—***Ring***, ***Tomie***, and ***Ju-On*** (these alone account for twenty-two of the movies discussed in this book). In the original novel of ***Ring***, the evil ghost Sadako is a girl with unusual properties. I don't just mean her powerful psychic gifts, or her antisocial hostility. What really sets Sadako apart is her ambiguous gender identity. She has "Testicular Feminization Syndrome," which is a fancy way of saying she has both male and female genitalia. Outwardly she appears to be a woman, a pretty one even, but she lacks a uterus or the ability to conceive a child. She lives a life of disappointment and quiet despair that culminates in a moment of profound suffering: raped by a man infected with smallpox, drowned in a well to conceal his crime. The smallpox virus' infectious potency commingles with her own psychic ability to create a new "lifeform," the ring virus, which she projects up the well into the world above as both a curse and a desperate bid for survival.

Sadako is victimized by men: her feminine side, if you will. But she is powerful, aggressive, and her will ultimately dominates: her male side. The threat to the world, the ring virus she creates, is her "child," the offspring of a woman who became too much like a man.

The best known film iterations of ***Ring*** omit this curious detail. Only the misguided TV movie of 1995 and the Korean ***Ring Virus*** version include Sadako's hermaphroditic qualities in their storylines. However, when director Hideo Nakata and screenwriter Hiroshi Takahashi came to their 1998 adaptation, they performed a sex-change operation of their own on the source material. Koji Suzuki's book (and the TV movie) involved milquetoasty male reporter Asakawa investigating Sadako's curse to protect himself and his shy, mousy housewife; the 1998 film recasts Asakawa as a forceful career woman and single mother trying to shield her child from the ring virus. A woman who is a man, that's too arcane to connect with the average viewer, but divorcees and women intruding into historically male professions had a wider cultural resonance. All subsequent ***Ring*** variants maintained Nakata and Takahashi's female hero.

Or consider Tomie Kawakami, the murderous teenager whose rampages are chronicled in seven films adapted from an influential graphic novel by artist Junji Ito. Obsessed with boys and steered by overpowering crushes, Tomie could be any oversexed teenage girl if not for the trail of corpses in her wake. For over a hundred years, this doomed young lady has cycled through a self-destructive pattern: her uncontrolled sexuality compels the boys around her into jealous rages so intense they end up killing and dismembering her. She regenerates from her mangled body parts and moves on to the next boy.

Tomie is a familiar Jezebel figure, with the addition of supernatural powers. Just about every culture shares the same myth about female sexuality being something dangerous, a temptation destined to ruin the lives of men unless kept in check. Tomie is a sex bomb, a maneater, a strange woman. It's an ironic twist on the Black Widow image that it is Tomie who gets her head lopped off by a lover in passion, but there is no denying she is the destructive force behind all the carnage and lust.

As with Sadako and Asakawa, the ***Tomie*** films pit the ghost girl against a heroine. In Junji Ito's comics, Tomie's nemesis is her onetime friend Tsukiko, a typical Japanese teenager whose crimes are the usual high school stuff: catty gossip, poaching boyfriends. Tomie carries a grudge, and to cite the movie's tagline *Tomie will not die*, so Tsukiko ends up on the receiving end of an eternal hatred married to otherworldly violence.

Speaking of grudges, Takashi Shimizu's ***Ju-On*** series represents the most coherent artistic vision of any of the J-Horror properties. Shimizu himself wrote and directed all of the ***Ju-On: The Grudge*** entries (five features and two short films already completed as of this writing, two more features in production), all of them haunted house chillers centered around a premise reminiscent of Nabou Nakagawa's 1959 classic. As in ***Ghost Story of Yotsuya***, a jealous hubby has slaughtered his wife and child, causing them to return as angry ghosts. The ***Ju-On*** stories are different, of course, but there is just enough similarity to the hallowed classic to beg comparison, and that comparison reveals a crucial distinction.

The husband in ***Yotsuya*** is a true villain, and his alleged cuckolding is a lie concocted to provide an alibi for his act of cold-blooded murder. His wife and son are innocent victims, who dole out their revenge in a targeted way on those who done them wrong. By contrast, the husband in ***Ju-On***, Takeo Saeki, has a genuine grievance against his wife Kayako. This is not to say that she deserves her fate or to excuse his insane response as justifiable, but merely to note that Kayako has made certain choices in her life that put her family at risk. In fact, her adultery is an act of unchecked romantic obsession similar to Tomie's immature crushes. Kayako's actions are especially irresponsible. Once she and her son Toshio are ghostified by Takeo's jealous rage, she proceeds to inflict her spectral vengeance arbitrarily. There is no rhyme or reason to which people end up her or Toshio's victims—aside from the blanket logic that anyone who enters her house is accursed for that alone. This isn't "revenge," because her victims did nothing wrong, aside from maybe making poorly informed real-estate decisions.

So who is the true villain in ***Ju-On***? The enraged cuckold, who opted for a hacksaw instead of couples' therapy, or the woman whose uninhibited passion initiated the horror and who returned from the grave to punish anyone who ever came near the home she ruined? If you're having a hard time answering that, you've arrived at the central theme of J-Horror: we just aren't sure if modernization is a good thing. Express that theme as you will—the clash between city folk and their country cousins in the equivalent of a Japanese backwoods, the conflict between towering metropoli of steel and technology against Mother Nature in all her aqueous glory, the ambivalence about the newly expanding role of women in society and the sexual freedom that accompanies that shift.

In Masato Harada's ***Inugami*** (2001), the heroine is a victim of forces outside her control. She is the offspring of an incestuous liaison that her isolated village has tried to conceal. Treated as an outcast for her wrongful birth, she is forced into a sort of servitude to a repressive and demanding family that denies her any independent existence. She falls in love with a schoolteacher (not knowing he is her brother, who had been sent away for adoption). Unknowingly, she is compounding the incest. The more she asserts her independent will and defies the oppression of the past, the more alive she becomes, but the more evil magic she unleashes on the lives of everyone she knows and loves. What's good for her is bad for everybody else.

The ghosts of Sadako, Tomie, Kayako and their various comrades are often the consequences of a youth marked by suffering. Many of the vengeful ghosts in these films are set on their path of destruction after a moment of betrayal by an object of love: a parent, a boyfriend, a subject of some irrational crush. Everyone has felt the burn of rejection—it is not a hard leap to imagine what havoc we might have wreaked had we been gifted with some awesome power at that moment of pain. The bad things that happen in life are not isolated or contained—when one of us is hurt, it affects us all. More importantly, when the family is threatened, the whole of society is endangered.

If the "girl" part of "Dead Wet Girls" relates to the vulnerability of childhood, then what of the "wet?" I have already suggested that the many bathtubs full of blood, dripping faucets, long wet hair, intense rainstorms, drownings and more drownings are the inevitable symbolism of a culture surrounded by and dependent on water. In Koji Suzuki's novel *Ring*, the evil girl was even fathered by an entity submerged in the sea. Suzuki's follow-up book, *Spiral*, warned "Life began in the sea, and it will end by the sea!" But the symbolism of water has additional connotations.

In Japan, the concept "wet" has a meaning not found in English; it also means "emotional." The Japanese say of themselves that theirs is a "wet" culture, as compared to dry Americans. By this they mean that Japanese culture places a higher priority on feelings and emotions, while Americans emphasize reason. If you see only the surface veneer of Japanese politeness and restraint, this may seem paradoxical, but it goes a long way towards explaining why American horror films spend so much time establishing logical rules while Japanese ones casually accept giant monsters, psychic powers, and paranormal experiences. Hollywood's horror movies may put the viewer on an immediate emotional roller-coaster ride, but once the movie is over and its thrills and scares are no longer present on the screen, the audience is likely to be left with little to take away with them. The Haunted School may give you little to scream about right away, but will send you home very, very sad.

Of the moniker "Dead Wet Girls," then, we have "Girls" and "Wet" accounted for, and the "Dead" part may seem obvious: you can't have ghosts without death. Before we move on to the movies, though, a few words about death, and ghosts. American horror movies tend to fixate on a fear of death itself, specifically a fear of that moment of transition when life ends. It is likely to be painful and violent (in scary movies, that is—I don't actually expect to be murdered by a maniac—do you?) and, let's be honest, it's not something we look forward to. Japanese movies, especially the works of the Haunted School, tend to localize their concept of death sometime *after* the precise moment at which life ends. They aren't movies about dying, but about the time afterwards.

This may be hard initially for Americans to grasp, because of cultural differences. Shinto, the indigenous religion of Japan, posits the existence of a vast spiritual world co-existent with our own but beyond our perception, a phantom world populated by gods and ghosts. Instinctively, Japanese people think of their daily lives as occurring in the shadow of those who went before. On one level, this helps explain why Japanese fantasy films take the existence of ghosts, psychic phenomena, and giant monsters so casually, where American films struggle to ground everything in scientific rationality. Beyond that, though, the difference in religious attitudes informs the basic conflicts at the heart of horror movies.

"When making horror films, the methods of describing the spiritual world and the expression of horror are totally different between Japan and the West," explains Hideo Nakata. "In a culture where the influence of monotheism such as Christianity is strong, the antimony, or confrontation between the devil and God, becomes the fundamental conflict. As in ***The Exorcist*** (1973), most Western horror movies are based on stories of people who have been possessed by demons. On the other hand, a typical example of the Japanese horror thriller is the classic ***Ghost Story of Tokaido Yotsuya***, a tale that has been performed as a kabuki play since the Edo period."

American horror movies rally around some singular monster—a Freddy, a Jason, a Michael Myers—on the theory that if we can find a way to stop or contain that one bad egg, then everything will be okay again. American horror movies also indulge in a Puritan morality, by which only the most virtuous heroine can triumph in the end. The Haunted School depicts supernatural horrors that propagate themselves, exponentially growing in power and reach with every new innocent victim. These are dark, unhappy tales of perpetual defeat and endless suffering, with no escape possible.

There is no correct response to the curse of the ***Ring***. The girl at the bottom of the well can never be made right again. Love her, help her, kill her, whatever, it doesn't matter, nothing changes. You'll just have to live in her world, you have to accept the future, whether you like it or not.

This is a powerful lesson for audiences in the grip of wrenching change. The 21st century is a scary place, with global unrest and technological advances changing the landscape in irreversible and often terrifying ways. Some people retreat into comfortable and reassuring dogmas, religious or political security blankets. J-Horror has spread across the globe in a time of anxiety and fear with another, less reassuring path, into the future: if you can't beat 'em, join 'em.

1. If we really wanted to complicate things, there are Spanish J-Horrors, but I have to draw the line somewhere.
2. I wish that I could give proper credit here to the person who coined the term "Dead Wet Girls," but I had not made a hardcopy of the discussion before mhvf.net's server crashed, destroying all old posts. If you coined it, I thank you.

CHAPTER 2

J-HORROR HAS TWO DADDIES

There was a time, not long before the 24-hour news cycle and the cult of meaningless celebrity became ubiquitous features of American culture, when a girl who was barely more than a baby became one of the most famous people in the United States. All of eighteen months old, this child obviously didn't achieve her status on the basis of any skill or ability of her own, yet she dominated the news above stories about a U.S. attack on an Iranian oil platform, Nancy Reagan's mastectomy, and the troubled Senate hearings for Supreme Court nominee Robert Bork. Instead, the perils and uncertain fate of poor little Jessica McClure held the nation in thrall.

Playing innocently in her own backyard, the girl happened to tumble twenty-two feet down a well where she remained trapped while crews worked for three days to rescue her. After 58 hours she was extracted, and went on to live a happy and normal life. During those anxious days there was ever the fear that she would die, alone and hungry and cold, while her parents and friends and the entire nation watched in helplessness. Of course this story captured the country's attention—it is undeniably horrible. At least Jessica had the benefit of loved ones who worked to reverse this unfortunate accident—in fact, even millions of strangers cared what happened to her. How much worse would it have been if she had been tossed down there intentionally? Left to die while the rest of world preferred to forget her entirely?

This is the horror at the heart of ***Ring***. An unwanted, unloved child, abandoned, forgotten, and rejected by everyone who should have been on her side. Left to die in a well, her very existence all but erased from history. Unlike Jessica McClure, this poor soul is no helpless baby but a young woman gifted with supernatural powers, who ends her life by bequeathing a terrifying curse on all of humanity, revenging herself on the entire world for letting such atrocities happen.

Her name is Sadako, this fictional girl in the well, Sadako Yamamura. She was an illegitimate child, and an aberrant mutation to boot. Part man, part woman, something not entirely human, she gave "birth" to an infectious curse whose "father" was the smallpox virus. Her victims are the latchkey kids, single parents, and disrupted families of modern-day Japan. The only defense from her evil spell is an act of selfishness—she has taken an alienating and isolated world and forced it to become ever more so.

And she was created, in our real-life world, by a loving father and parenting expert.

Writer Koji Suzuki was a stay-at-home dad, balancing a baby girl on his lap, who wrote a fictional parable about parenting gone wrong, in every possible way.

It began with an urban legend.

Suzuki was working as a "cram school teacher," helping students prepare for college entrance exams. For fun, he would tell them scary stories, made-up things from his own dark imagination. For that extra thrill of verisimilitude, he would pretend these stories were real events, from far-away places like New York. Time and again, he noticed how his students became genuinely scared by these tales, as if they believed the awful things were actually going to happen to themselves. Somehow that conceit, "this really happened to somebody else somewhere other than here," made all the difference. He filed that away in the back of his mind.

In 1989, his wife was the one teaching, while he stayed home to care for their two daughters. He was still a struggling writer, and he wanted to write something with a kick. Remembering his students' innocent fear, he wrote a horror novel about an urban legend that actually kills. The book was called *Ring*, and let's just say, it became popular.[1]

It tells the story of a single moment of pain and anger so intense that it turns death into life, that it spawns a whole new kind of life. A girl, drowned in a well, psychically projects her own fear up, out of the well, through time, to record her thoughts on videotape. Anyone who watches that videotape is marked for death. The girl's angry ghost will claim them in exactly a week's time. But, there's an out. Make a copy of the cursed video and show it to someone else, and be saved. It's like an evil game of "hot potato": *take this curse and pass it along*. Or, more apt, it is like a virus. The curse, and the memory of the girl's suffering, will spread throughout the population, expanding exponentially in a spiral of fear and horror destined to consume the world.

Koji Suzuki's novel was a masterpiece of suspense, brilliantly blending ancient Japanese folk myths with modern technology. It was so successful, in fact, that people actually came to believe that the urban legend of the cursed video was real—not that it was true, mind you, but that it had existed as a rumor before Suzuki's book.

In time, Suzuki became anointed the "Japanese Stephen King." No small feat for a man who has a low opinion of horror writing. Or, for that matter, Japanese literature.

"I don't believe in wispy things, like ghosts. I'm not interested in

Scenes from Nakata's Ring

Frames of the video

them," Suzuki admitted to journalist Tadayuki Naito in 2005. "I'm the complete opposite of a 'horror' sort of person. There's a pretty wide gap between me and the type you usually think of as a horror writer."

On the subject of Japanese fiction, Suzuki is even harsher: "It does not have an external logic," he told Japan Review in 2003. "Japanese novels, in my view, are very narrow. Japanese people read Japanese novels and they think it is interesting. People in other countries, I think, would not find it interesting in the least. Japanese literature does not have a global appeal nor does it meet global standards."

Despite these opinions—more likely, because of them—Suzuki would join that extremely exclusive club of Japanese authors published in the West. As the writer of *Ring*, *Spiral*, *Loop*, *Birthday*, and *Dark Water*, Suzuki's fancies formed the backbone of the nascent J-Horror genre.

For the moment, though, forget that Suzuki's writings helped change the direction of the Japanese film industry and helped crack open the American marketplace to Japanese popular culture. On a personal level, the *Ring* changed Suzuki's life. One day, Koji is changing diapers while his wife punches the clock at a high school. The next, Mrs. Suzuki is happily retired, the Suzukis are jetting around the globe, and Koji is indulging long-dormant dreams: such as motorcycling from Florida to California, or buying a yacht.

But it didn't happen all at once. *Ring* was published in Japan in 1991; the English translation not for another twelve years. In the first several years of publication, it sold about 500,000 copies; after the 1998 feature film version, that figure exploded to 1.5 million books and beyond. The film version was ever its destiny: Suzuki had attended a screenwriting class, using the group's feedback to hone and shape a cannily cinematic novel. Still it required an intermediary, a collaborator, a translator of words into pictures. J-Horror has two daddies. Without Hideo Nakata and his macabre imagination, who knows whether Suzuki would have ever bought that boat?

But we are not quite ready for Mr. Nakata to enter our story, not yet.

Come 1995 and Fuji TV knocks at the Suzukis' door asking for rights to turn *Ring* into a made-for-TV movie. Screenwriter Joji Iida and director Chisui Takigawa were assigned to the project, and they were studiously faithful to Suzuki's novel, down to certain details that would be abandoned in all future variants. If faithfulness alone were a marker of quality, then ***Ring: Kanzenban*** a.k.a. "Ring: The Complete Edition" would be excellent (and indeed Mr. Suzuki quite likes this version, perhaps for that very reason). By the modest expectations of a low-budget, shot-on-video TV drama, ***Ring: The Complete Edition*** was a remarkable success. So popular, in fact, that in 1996 it was even granted a limited theatrical release.

Not long thereafter, of course, this TV version would be eclipsed, made redundant and forgotten. To the extent that it is remembered at all today, it is for the near-constant nudity of pinup girl Ayane Miura as Sadako.

The essence of Suzuki's story is the reproductive impulse of the viral curse, its ability to inspire and compel its victims to propagate itself. In the trippy funhouse mirror of real-life, the story has the same effect on audiences. The book inspired the TV drama, and its popularity in turn motivated Asmik Ace Entertainment to license rights for a theatrical feature... oh, but we're getting ahead of ourselves again.

Around the time that ***The Complete Edition*** won its theatrical outing, another destined-for-video small-scale production was being put together by Bandai Visual Productions, the moviemaking arm of the toy giant. The Japanese title of this trim, efficient feature (a scant 75 minutes long) is ***Joyurei***, which has been alternately called in English "Ghost Actress" and "Don't Look Up." Since the only American release of ***Joyurei*** to date was a cablecast on the Sundance Channel under the title ***Don't Look Up*** and was mooted for a never-made American remake under that same title, we'll use that name for it here.

RINGU VS RING

If you go into an American video shop looking for Hideo Nakata's version of ***Ring***, expect to find it in a box bearing the title "Ringu," thanks to some unfortunate and idiotic misunderstandings. The folks at Dreamworks Pictures naturally decided that Nakata's ***Ring*** deserved a DVD release coincident with the US remake's, and understandably wished to distinguish the two in an obvious and straightforward way for potentially confused consumers. Since the Japanese title spells out "Ringu," that name was assumed to be the Japanese title. However, there is no Japanese word "Ringu." When Koji Suzuki went to name his book, he selected the English word "Ring" as his title, because it encompassed a variety of different meanings, all of which held relevance to the story he had written. No Japanese word worked as well as the English "Ring" in his opinion. But English words are hard to write in Japanese letters. Japanese consistently pairs consonant sounds with vowel sounds, making it impossible to end a word with a consonant sound. Japanese makes for great poetry, but English words end up transliterated into sometimes surreal parodies of the original word. The English "Ring" written in Japanese turns into "Ringu." But that doesn't mean the title was "Ringu," and so in this book I refuse to use that ridiculous title for Nakata's film.

This, then, is when Mr. Nakata joins us: his ***Don't Look Up*** is for all intents and purposes a prototype of ***Ring***. If you didn't know that by the time this thing was made in 1996 there had already been a book and one movie version of ***Ring***, it would be easy to assume that ***Don't Look Up*** was the true rough draft. Most of the elements are there: a mysterious motion picture artifact of uncertain (and possibly supernatural) origin; contact with that motion picture brings death; our hero is compelled to investigate the origins of the strange movie images and thereby uncovers a decades-old tragedy that is continuing to send ripples of pain and suffering into the present day. All that, and the ghost is a girl, dressed in white with long black hair combed down her face.

The similarities were lost on none of the relevant parties.

Fate had decreed that Hideo Nakata should oversee the theatrical adaptation of ***Ring***. This was the lightning strike, the moment of genius: the film he would make of Suzuki's book would become the most commercially successful horror film ever made in Japan, and one of Japan's biggest international hits of any genre. But who was this guy?

To answer that, we'll have to talk about porn. Back in the 1970s, one of Japan's major studios, Nikkatsu, settled into a comfortable and profitable rut making sex films. There are a variety of specialized subgenres within the universe of Japanese porn, and Nikkatsu's brand was "Roman Porno," or Romantic Pornography. But by the 1980s, the increasing availability of cheap video porn was driving the comparatively more expensive theatrical works under. This was around the time that Hideo Nakata, recently graduated from Tokyo University, joined Nikkatsu as an assistant director under Masaru Konuma.

Konuma had made his name crafting fairly elegant sex flicks back in the day, but by 1985 he was reduced to making a bargain-bin hardcore video called ***Woman in a Box: Virgin Sacrifice***. It was on this, and similar glories, that Nakata cut his eye teeth. Making full-length films in a week on a shoestring budget is perhaps the best training for an aspiring moviemaker, and Nakata learned his lessons well. Years later, once Nakata was an international superstar and on his way to being named by Time Magazine one of the Most Influential People of 2004, he would make the documentary ***Sadistic and Masochistic*** to honor his mentor Konuma.

Come 1991 (coincidentally the year that *Ring* was published), Nakata had noticed with a wary eye that his employer had drastically cut production, abandoning feature films altogether and basically limping along like a dying donkey. He wisely opted to leave the country, taking an artistic scholarship to London's National Film Archive to study the British Free Cinema movement. England's answer to the

French New Wave was a fairly short-lived movement, so studying it didn't take Nakata all that long. He found himself in Europe with time on his hands to travel and watch movies. Like Suzuki before him, Nakata found his greatest influences were to be Western rather than Japanese; like Suzuki he was destined to bring those Western influences back with him to help reinvigorate a moribund Japanese art form.

Nikkatsu collapsed in 1993. Still in Europe, Nakata realized he didn't have a job to go back to. So he decided to try his hand as an independent filmmaker. As a sign of his eclectic tastes and wide-ranging abilities, Nakata chose not to make a porno, like those of his past, nor a horror flick, like those of his future. Rather, he set out to make a documentary about legendary blacklisted director Jospeh Losey.

"When I came across the works of Joseph Losey, it turned out to be my most important experience in London," remembers Nakata. "It wasn't Losey's ideology that attracted me, but his craftsmanship as a director. He had all of these fascinating films from the 1950s that had never been screened in Japan. These were films that he shot on a shoestring budget with no real schedule. He even did a remake of Fritz Lang's ***M*** and it was amazing. I really became enamored with the artisanship of his work."

To finance work on his Losey biography, Nakata took what jobs he could. Such as directing another sex film, this time for Toei Studios. Or directing ***Don't Look Up*** for J-Movie Wars, a colorfully named subsidiary of a major Japanese satellite concern.

As far as ***Don't Look Up*** went, Nakata saw it as just another gig he had to take to make money for the Losey project. He had no special feeling for horror movies. In fact, just as Suzuki had contempt for the prevailing standards of horror fiction, Nakata dismissed the conventions of then-contemporary horror. "The least I can say is that I never liked splatter movies in the 80s, the Hollywood style ones. I never watched them."

Probably a good thing, too. His rejection of the established, tired style of horror paved a way towards something new and different. He'd already had a chance to start formulating that new approach, even before ***Don't Look Up*** came his way. Nakata's very first professional job as director was on the television horror anthology series ***Hontouni Atta Kowai Hanashi*** (1992) which translates as something along the lines of "Dreadful True Stories" and later garnered the official (if somewhat odd) English title ***Curse, Death and Spirit***. He had directed three twenty-minute episodes for this show, "Waterfall of the Evil Dead," "Cursed Doll," and "Ghost of the Inn," the latter of which features as its ghost a young lady with long black hair and a white nightgown—

imagery that Nakata would return to with ***Don't Look Up*** as he continued in the same restrained, less-is-more subtlety.

"A director once referred to film as a form of collective dreaming shared with strangers," says Nakata. "Using that analogy, horror films are nightmares. Nightmares shared with strangers. And when the film is over, everyone awakens from the nightmare together. With the lingering sensation of a cold night sweat, everyone files out of the theater together, still overflowing with shared emotion. Somewhere in the commotion and mood of that communal moment lies the real appeal of the medium of film."

In ***Don't Look Up***, a movie crew sits down to watch the dailies of their opening day's shoot on a WWII melodrama only to find that what they thought was a scrap of unused film from a previous production is apparently a scrap of undeveloped film from a previous production. Because of this small but critical difference, images from the older show are bleeding through and superimposing themselves on the new scenes. Puzzled by the mysterious footage, the director investigates the history of the older shoot, and discovers along the way a hidden tragedy, and the disquieting possibility that the film was exposed not by a camera but by a ghostly spirit.

Don't Look Up does not seem to follow any well-established horror film tradition from before it. If it owes to any pre-existing traditions, it belongs to that sub-category of movies about moviemaking. "One of my favorite films is ***Day For Night*** by Francois Truffaut," explains Nakata. Throughout ***Don't Look Up***, Nakata takes evident joy in toying with narrative ambiguity. There are multiple levels to his story, with present-day reality overlapping with past events, fragments of memory, and movies within movies. "The play's the thing," said Hamlet, hoping his Mousetrap will reflect true crimes well enough to uncover a secret tragedy; in ***Don't Look Up***, it is the even more recursively situated act of filming the film within the film that best reflects the secrets of the past.

The bulk of these scenes was shot by Nakata on the abandoned stages of the now-defunct Nikkatsu. Who better to find the ghosts in Nikkatsu's rafters than a man who watched the old Japanese film industry die?

Don't Look Up ran a mere six weeks on a limited release, during which time few people came—Nakata says only 800 viewers attended. Only later, in the wake of the ***Ring***, would a reissued ***Don't Look Up*** make back its money as a video release. Nakata was still a ways away from finishing ***Joseph Losey: The Man With Four Names*** (which would finally be released in 1998, once Nakata's own name finally meant something). Nonetheless, he had lit a match to the J-Horror fuse. ***Don't Look Up*** won the Best New Director award at the 1997 Michinoku International Mystery Film Festival. No, it doesn't sound like much of a prize, but for a youngster still making ends meet by shooting pornos and perfunctory crime thrillers, any recognition means a lot. Wheels were beginning to turn.

Takenori Sento of J-Movie Wars was the driving force behind ***Don't Look Up***, and he had recently joined forces with two other producers: Takashige Ichise and Shinya Kawai. Separately these three men already had illustrious resumes as solo producers and would continue to make important and popular films; together they would make history. They bought the rights to make a theatrical feature of *Ring*, and hired ***Don't Look Up***'s screenwriter Hiroshi Takahashi to adapt the material. It was just right to get the band back together, to reassemble the creative team that had worked so well on ***Don't Look Up*** and ***Curse, Death and Spirit*** (yup, Takahashi had been Nakata's scriptwriter on that thing, too).

At the time, Nakata was doing yet another horror anthology TV series, this time ***Gakkou no Kaidan F*** ("Haunted School F"—see next chapter for more on this franchise). Of the triptych that was ***Haunted School F***, Kiyoshi Kurosawa was directing one installment (see Chapter 5 for more on Kurosawa) while Nakata completed the other two. One of Nakata's episodes was called "Spirit Video," and dealt with the psychic projection of images onto film or videotape. As a struggling independent filmmaker, Nakata knew better than most how arduous it is to record images on film in the conventional way; in things like "Spirit Video" he began to visualize with some envy what it would be like to forge movies purely with the mind's eye. After working through the same notions in ***Don't Look Up***, he came to ***Ring*** ready to perfect his ideas.

"The ring video was a real challenge," recalls Nakata. "It caused me a fair amount of worry. I wanted people to come away with the sensation I don't know exactly what it was, but I just saw something very disturbing. And this was supposed to be *nensha* ("spirit photography"), so I didn't want anything that looked too explanatory."

Perhaps inspired by the central notion of ***Don't Look Up***, the Takahashi/Nakata version of ***Ring*** plays up the investigation of the videotape's curious imagery. By dealing with the supernatural story as a sort of film noir, a whodunnit mystery, Takahashi and Nakata avoid the odd pacing problems and awkward tone shifts that plagued the TV version.

To work out the solution to their predicament, ***Ring***'s two lead characters, Asakawa and Ryuji, have nothing but the tape to go on, and have to work backwards from it. Where was this filmed, how was it recorded, who were these people, what happened to them—in short, they are performing the tasks of a film historian. They deduce the meaning of images by researching how they were made.

In Suzuki's telling of the tale, Asakawa and Ryuji were both men. Asakawa is a family man, desperate to protect his wife and daughter from the curse he unwittingly inflicted on them. He turns to Ryuji to play Mulder to his Scully and help solve the riddle of Sadako's curse. Only together can they confront the horror, because only together are they a whole person. Suzuki based the two characters on his own psychology, splitting his more logical and his more creative selves into two fictional alter egos. Suzuki deliberately made both characters men to emphasize a point dear to him, as a stay-at-home father in a culture that overwhelmingly placed child-rearing duties on female shoulders. He wanted to show a strong, positive father figure, a man who takes his role as a father seriously.

Suzuki says, "My position is that there is no preexisting paternal instinct. Under the traditional patriarchal system, fathers never assumed any true responsibility for their families—they were basically just symbolic figures. So what I am trying to stress is the notion that fatherhood as a concept—this idea of paternal instinct—is something novel. Throughout Japanese literature, the men are forever telling their wives to take care of everything while they stumble out into the outside world, blindly accepting what they see as the natural family order... Japanese society is an overwhelmingly maternal society where men are indulged. But to the extent that they permit themselves to be indulged, men simply become a burden for women."

In adapting the material for the screen, Hiroshi Takahashi switched Asakawa to a single mother, and Ryuji became her ex-husband, estranged father of their son Yoichi.

Ask Suzuki and he chalks this change up to traditional Japanese patriarchy, a knee-jerk unwillingness to see a man as a true responsible father. Ask the average horror movie buff, and they might tell you that horror movies have long had traditions of heroines—just ask Jamie Lee Curtis. Ask Hideo Nakata, and he jokes, "I made Asakawa a woman because I like women!"

But let's not lose sight of the fact that Takahashi managed to enhance the very ideas Suzuki wanted to promote. The novel's Asakawa may have been motivated to protect his family, but he did a pretty poor job of it. His infantilization of his wife, treating her like a fragile glass doll instead of an equal, can hardly be said to be a positive image of Japanese manliness. The screen's Asakawa is a strong figure taking

PAPA-ISM

"Walking along a body of water, you sense ghosts being born," says Koji Suzuki. His watery obsessions are obvious: the ghostly girl Sadako at the center of his trilogy was drowned in a well. At one point the characters even develop a mathematical formula for hauntings: slow death + enclosed space + water = ghosts. *Dark Water* includes the line, "The sea itself was a mystery... a space where the world of the living and the world of the dead were commingled."

But Suzuki's feelings towards water run both directions. He is an expert sailor with a first-class yachting license. After the success of the *Ring* trilogy he felt entitled to abandon horror (for a while at least) to write seafaring novels.

As his primary literary influences he cites Hemingway, Sartre, Camus, and Mann. Not, you'll note, Edgar Allan Poe, or Stephen King. "I actually don't like all that supernatural stuff. I really dislike most horror writing." At Keio University he majored in French Literature...but it didn't come in handy in his early years as a writer.

Besides fiction, Suzuki has written about parenting. In books like *Papa-ism*, he attacks the prevailing tradition of Japanese salarymen—absent, negligent fathers in Suzuki's view. He cares about this issue, and has even spoken before the Japanese Diet on it.

"The theme of *Ring* is really about the love I have for my daughters... For me, the biggest fear is to lose my daughters or my wife. So in my novel, Asakawa, the protagonist, fought for the life of his wife and daughter... But that's not customary in Japan because the instinct to protect a daughter is considered more maternal, a mother's task... But I don't really think it's the way it has to be. I wanted to write a new type of novel because I was a new type of father in Japan—like the way I took care of my own daughters. And I think it was very important for a novelist to write about his own experiences."

charge of her life and fighting for her son's future.

To do so, she must ironically leave him alone for extended periods of time. At one point, Ryuji asks if little Yoichi is okay at home alone so often. Defensively, Asakawa replies, "He's used to it." We have already seen this to be true: the boy is mature beyond his years, a grown-up in a child's body.

If Sadako is a monster created by a deviation from traditional family structures, then the movies show how those non-traditional, disrupted families have themselves spread like a virus through society, seeding their own tiny horrors. These details, the single mother and her precocious latchkey child, would remain intact throughout the subsequent remakes—and echo through the other films of the Haunted School.

Suzuki localized a specific issue as his cause célèbre: the failing of Japanese men to fulfill their responsibilities as involved parents. Takahashi and Nakata enlarged this canvas and set the theme that would underlie J-Horror as a genre: that failed parenting, disrupted families, and ill-treated children create lasting social damage. One family's problem can really come to haunt us all. These social dilemmas can be ex-

GHOST GIRL

The image of Sadako, which would be slavishly mimicked by the J-Horror-meisters to come, had been percolating in Nakata's imagination for some time. A very similar ghostly girl haunts soundstage 8 in ***Don't Look Up***, and an earlier version of the specter had appeared in the "Ghost of the Inn" segment of ***Curse, Death and Spirit*** back in 1992. But this time, Nakata perfected it. "[To] Japanese people," Nakata told Ain't It Cool News, "long black hair of a woman has somehow a kind of supernatural power or emotion just by itself... There is a kind of subconscious fear for women's long black hair by itself. If they find on a bed an enormous amount of long black hair, that's scary by itself. That's somewhat different, maybe, from Western culture." Nakata had toyed with the ghostly image of a woman with long black hair in his early TV work and ***Don't Look Up***, but felt he had erred by showing too much of the phantom's face. "In my first feature film I revealed, at the end of the movie I revealed the ghost's face completely and that actually affected the...you know, some people didn't think it's scary enough.

"I've had people tell me, '***Don't Look Up*** wasn't exactly frightening, it was...' For me, of all the possible adjectives that could finish that phrase, the word I most long to hear is 'frightening.' That's the description I want to elicit."

"So with ***Ring***, I went in a completely different direction. OK, let's cover her face up completely."

In the Shinto belief system, Japanese people simply take for granted the existence of a spirit world overlaid on top of the physical one. Ghosts are not necessarily good or bad, anymore than living people are, they just are. One of the traditional Japanese ghost stories inspiring the imagery of ***Ring*** is Okiku, the maid killed in the story "Bancho Sarayasaiki." Her master kills her for breaking a valuable dish, and tosses her into a well, which she then haunts. "I myself when I lived in the countryside in Japan saw a well, about five meters deep, which is maybe not that deep, but for me as a child, it seemed like a bottomless hell. Because I thought once I got inside it I would never get out of it," Nakata told Donato Totaro in 2000.

Not all of Sadako's predecessors are traditional Japanese legends, however. For her terrifying exit from the world of the video (an idea added to the film by Takahashi and Nakata, and not part of the original story), Nakata admits to his primary influence being David Cronenberg's ***Videodrome*** (1983).

pressed as horror stories, represented by monsters.

The gut-kick of ***Ring*** is the sad realization that this monster Sadako is a monster now because she herself was a victim. The only way to escape her curse is to understand it, and the only way to do that is to develop some sympathy for the poor girl. Horror movies these days don't often ask their viewers to generate any sympathy for the devil, but ***Ring*** depends on it.

The new ***Ring*** they drafted became the default version. The subsequent iterations—various and sundry remakes and sequels—maintained the alterations made by Takahashi and Nakata.

In fact, in a weird development, the later remakes by Korea and Hollywood stubbornly retained a wide selection of seemingly trivial details created by Takahashi/Nakata—for example, a scene in which the Asakawa character steps onto a balcony of her apartment building while the Ryuji character watches the cursed video inside. It makes a certain sense that after the proven success of Nakata's rendition, his followers would want to mimeograph his version to every extent possible. But their cloning processes are imprecise, mutations occur: every version of the ***Ring*** yet made manages to disagree with every other version about exactly who the Sadako figure was and why she's in that well. Since the details of her unhappy life are the source point of her peculiar revenge, it would seem that her story would be the one common denominator of every ***Ring*** variant, not, for example, whether the reporter's niece was one of the first victims. But no—it appears that any number of different routes can lead to exactly the same narrative destination. Take that, chaos theory!

Sadako's backstory, according to the novels, derived at least in part from a few true-life cases of alleged Japanese psychics (see box on next page). Hiroshi Takahashi studied the same histories that inspired Suzuki and cleverly wove those Believe-It-Or-Not details throughout his script. Given this material to work with, Nakata found some profoundly disturbing ways to visualize spirit photography. The idea that Sadako's spell causes her victims to appear distorted or obscured in photographs is one such notion, original to the Takahashi/Nakata version, that Suzuki probably wished he'd laid claim to first.

None of this is intended to knock Suzuki. If you like ***Ring***, you have no excuse not to read the series of books by Suzuki, all of them nicely translated into English by Vertical, a New York publisher. But what makes great literature is not the same as what makes great cinema. Of all the various *Ring*-based movies, those that are closest to Suzuki's writings are the least effective as movies; those that are most successful as movies are those that stay closest to Nakata's vision; the

THE TRUE STORY BEHIND THE RING

And now for a forgotten moment of history: The year was 1910, and at the prestigious Tokyo University a certain Dr. Tomokichi Fukurai, Assistant Professor of Psychology in the Philosophy Department, staged a public demonstration of psychic abilities. For years, Dr. Fukurai had studied hypnotism and parapsychology. Recently he had become interested in the alleged clairvoyant powers of Chizuko Mifune. It was said this woman could read the contents of sealed envelopes or cause words to appear on blank sheets of paper. On September 15, 1910, he presented her to a skeptical audience. The reception was very chilly: she was derided as a fake, and Fukurai was seen as a fool. Devastated by the scandal, Chizuko took her own life the following year. Eventually, Dr. Fukurai would lose his position at the university for dabbling in pseudoscience, but not before trying again, this time with a young psychic named Sadako Takahashi. Sounds familiar? Koji Suzuki used this real-life case as part of his inspiration in creating the story of Shizuko and her daughter Sadako. In writing the 1998 adaptation, Hiroshi Takahashi returned to the story of Dr. Fukurai and his unhappy subjects. In his research, Takahashi discovered paranormal claims by some of Fukurai's subjects that they could manipulate photographic images without access to a camera. Although this ability was never attributed to Chizuko or Sadako, it intrigued Takahashi and he added it to the mix. The disturbing image of Sadako's doomed victims smudged in photos as an omen of their fate became so distinctive to ***Ring*** it recurred in all subsequent sequels and remakes, and the creepy visual possibilities of spirit photography were embellished in ***Ring 2*** and ***The Ring Two*** (don't be confused—check out the handy ***Ring*** family tree).

1998 ***Ring*** is the essential work of the franchise because it is the perfect balance of Suzuki + Nakata.

The '98 ***Ring*** does more than just balance the influences of its two creative fathers, it balances a variety of competing traditions and ideas. Classical Japanese horror films such as ***Kwaidan*** (1964), ***Onibaba*** (1964), and the works of Nobuo Nakagawa in the 1950s and 60s (see next chapter) present traditional ghost stories set in a distant past—much as Western gothic horrors of that era set their tales of vampires and werewolves in a preindustrial past. Modern horror in the post-***Scream*** mode, driven by Hollywood, focused on teenagers imperiled by urban legends. ***Ring*** cleverly mixed these two approaches into a single intoxicating cocktail.

Speaking of teenagers, horror films prior to ***Ring*** seemed to be set in a kind of ***Logan's Run***-style parallel universe where anyone over the age of thirty was euthanized, so as not to interfere with our narcissistic obsession with youth. ***Ring*** chills because it appears to take place in our real world: a place where multiple generations live interconnected lives, where cityscapes and countrysides coexist, where good and evil are relative concepts not easily determined. So much of popular culture these days limits itself to the New and the Now, while ***Ring*** solemnly reminds us that there was a past before us, and unresolved issues from the past may haunt us still. Just because some event is obscure or forgotten by today's generation does not mean it is unimportant.

In her own way, Sadako became a celebrity like little Jessica McClure. The 1998 film was made for about 1.3 million dollars. It earned about 15.5 million, returning a staggering 12 times on its investment.[2] Put simply, ***Ring*** was big business. Time for a sequel, the faster the better—even still, the producers of ***Ring*** have to set some kind of record. Its sequel, ***Rasen*** ("Spiral"), was released simultaneously! That's right: buy a ticket for ***Ring***, stay afterward for ***Spiral***. The double bill of these two movies established a tradition of double features that would characterize much of the distribution of J-Horrors to come.

The CYA logic behind the idea was pretty simple and straightforward. If ***Ring*** was a hit (which was certainly their aspiration) a sequel would be warranted, so why wait? And if you're going to give ***Ring*** to an up-and-coming boy genius whose past works covered similar territory, why not assign ***Spiral*** to a more conservative and conventional filmmaker who had already worked on a version of ***Ring***?

So it came to pass that ***Spiral*** was assigned to Joji "George" Iida. If you recognize the name, it means you were paying attention. You just read his name some pages ago, as the screenwriter of ***Ring: The Complete Edition***.

Curiously, Iida's career path was not dissimilar to Nakata's. He got his start in the film industry working as a screenwriter for Japanese porn, later becoming an assistant director. To break out of a career dead-end, he started screenwriting his own ideas with the hopes of getting backing to direct his own work. Like Nakata, he counted American filmmakers as his primary influences: Brian DePalma, John Carpenter, and the like.

Just as Nakata had "warmed up" for ***Ring*** by handling ghost stories in TV and low-budget films and had self-financed his own indie documentary while waiting for the industry to recognize his talent, Iida shot a 16mm amateur film about psychic powers before getting a job directing ***Battle Heater*** (1990), a sci-fi joke modeled on ***Attack of the Killer Tomatoes*** (1977). He wrote an extremely popular late-night drama series called ***Night Head***, which he later adapted into a feature film in 1994. Iida is a multitalented man, author of novels, director of both live-action and animated films, and a charming, self-effacing figure. Following his work on the ***Ring*** cycle, he directed an internationally well-received sci-fi/action opus called ***Another Heaven*** (2000).

It was back in 1995, when Iida was contracted to adapt ***Ring*** into a television script that he first met Koji Suzuki. Suzuki had just completed *Spiral* a few days earlier and was still giddy with excitement over the ways his story was evolving and spreading into new media. The two men formed a common bond over a desire to ground fantasy tales in logic and realism. When, a few years later, Iida had the opportunity to direct ***Spiral***, it was something of a dream come true.

"When I first read it, I was finishing up my work on the film version of ***Night Head***," explains Iida. "At that time, I was thinking that I wanted my next project to be an adaptation of a novel, so I was trying to read a lot of interesting books. And I'm not making this up, when I read *Spiral*, my first thought was that I'd love to make it into a film. While *Ring* was a story about a cursed video, *Spiral* was focused on uncovering a scientific explanation for the curse—it was very fresh material."

He preferred *Spiral* to *Ring* as a book and admired it as a work of science fiction rather than horror. "If Koji Suzuki wrote *Ring* as a horror, then *Spiral* is an idealized science fiction story," Iida told journalist Jasper Sharp. "*Spiral* shows realistically how to explain 'the unknown' in the physical world."

Iida recognized the awkward nature of his assignment: to make a sequel that would appear immediately after the first film, yet would be based on an entirely different template. "On the one hand," says Iida, " I wanted to make an independent work that would stand alone on its own merits, but of course there was the unavoidable link to the video, and the added complication of the film version of ***Ring*** introducing characters and material that differed from the original novel. Deciding how much to reference the other film was a real challenge. I had to decide how much continuity was required to keep viewers from getting lost."

Iida noted, "I had no intention of making a horror film out of ***Spiral***," and admitted that fans of ***Ring*** might find it disappointing. Unfortunately, he succeeded on both counts.

Film critics and other pointy-heads hold sequels in low regard as a general rule. This is because film critics and other pointy-heads want to reward artistry and vision instead of crass commercialism, and sequels wear their brazen mercenary nature so ostentatiously on their sleeves. That, and so many of them suck. But the fact of it is that unless you spend your time watching experimental 16mm installations at your local art museum, all of the movies you enjoy were born of the same commercial imperative.[3]

An institution elects to make a profoundly risky investment by funding the manufacture of an insanely expensive consumer good with the unlikely hope that enough people will want to pay to see it that the money will return with profits. Most movies fail in this mission, regardless of what viewers or critics may have thought of them. A handful succeed spectacularly enough to account for those that don't. This is the film industry.

Anything that can be done to reduce the risks of the investment, then, becomes mandatory. From our perspective as movie lovers, it's easy to say the obvious: we want good movies. Make them good and we'll pay to see them. It's just hard to write down "make it good" on a ledger sheet, so the pencil pushers who write the checks focus their attention instead on more quantifiable factors: is this movie star hot, is that movie star too pricey, does this director have a track record of staying on budget, did test audiences like that ending, will candy companies and toy manufacturers want to help pay for our marketing, and so on. Once a movie has leapt over that hurdle and become a success, copying it somehow (remake, sequel, extremely similar band-wagon-jumper) is so much easier for a movie executive to approve than creating something totally new and different—and risky.

The basic premise of a sequel is then to deliver more of the same. This sounds easier than it is, because while on paper it may seem simple to duplicate the success with a Part Two, actually figuring out which ingredients of the recipe were the key pieces that need to be retained... that's a tall order. If you serve chocolate cake to a happy family and want to follow it up with a sequel, what's the right sequel to chocolate cake? Chocolate pudding? Coconut cake?

Too often, sequels end up awkward and half-formed because of the knee-jerk attempt to carry over the main characters of a popular film into a new but strikingly similar situation. In the case of ***Ring***, there is a huge problem in making a sequel. You simply cannot maintain *both* the original characters and the original premise—and thus the sequel is compromised even before it starts.

Ring was a hit not because of its compelling characters. Even Koji Suzuki admitted his two protagonists were just halves of his own psyche. They were sketches, ciphers, stand-ins for real people. If you're a Type A person, driven, careerist, emotionally shut-off, then line up behind Asakawa. Type Bs, hippies, freethinkers, unreliable weirdos, you're with Ryuji. Now, here's your ghost story.

The real thrust of ***Ring*** was the mystery plot, which seemed to be solved by the end. Any sequel to ***Ring*** must then either change the rules of Sadako's curse so that the same characters have to solve a new, dif-

SPIRALS

When Koji Suzuki sold his book *Ring* to Kadokawa Shoten in 1990, he made less money up front than he might have otherwise but managed to retain film rights—a lucky draw that would benefit him untold times over in the years to come. Because the author would be involved in assenting to the various film adaptations, and profiting directly from them, he stayed close with the various producers.

Following the somewhat disappointing American sequel ***The Ring Two*** in 2005 (see Chapter 10), Kadokawa and Asmik Ace started talks for a new Japanese sequel, a ***Ring 4***. Suzuki asked if he could, this time around, write the screenplay himself. And so, Suzuki started writing—adapting the novel *Spiral*. In other words, he would finally get his wish for a proper version of ***Spiral***, as the story would spiral in, out, and back into the ***Ring*** franchise mythology. In the wake of this announcement, Hideo Nakata started talking about a follow-up film (***Ring 5***?) to adapt the final book in the cycle, *Loop*.

ferent problem, or place a new set of characters into the existing premise and have them face a mystery that the audience now already knows the answer to. Neither option sounds fantastic, so ***Spiral*** opts for c) all of the above.

In his follow-up novel to *Ring*, first published in Japan in 1995, Koji Suzuki essentially rejected everything to do with the original story: we are told that the original characters were wrong, possibly duplicitous, and dead; Sadako's curse was misunderstood; the whole situation is altogether different than we had first concluded. It's a brilliant strategy and a brilliant book, superior to *Ring*. Suzuki's distrust of supernatural horror pays off as he grounds the ghost story goings-on in the gritty realism of a Michael Crichton-style medical thriller, rich in character detail and grueling suspense. It expands the *Ring* scenario as it rewrites it, undermining your expectations while confidently refuting everything that held the first story together.

A good movie could be made from this riveting novel. Joji Iida did not make that movie.

"I'd love for them (the producers of the ***Ring*** series) to make a remake of ***Spiral***," opines Suzuki, which is a pretty damning review considering those same people already took one stab at it. Iida made a film that got rid of the original characters, changed the premise, and was made in a completely different style. Did you enjoy Sadako in Nakata's version, an inhuman wraith dressed in white, her hair combed in front of her face? Don't expect to see her here.

If the point of sequels is to offer more of the same, ***Spiral*** offers

THE FINAL CHAPTER

Investigating the mysterious circumstances surrounding the sudden death of his niece, Asakawa has retraced her steps to a resort cabin in Japan's countryside. There, in cabin B4, this poor girl and her three friends watched a videotape that somehow doomed them all. Now, Asakawa is going to see this tape for himself. What secrets will it hold?

Nervously, she places the cassette in the machine and presses "play." The TV screen flickers to life. What appears is...a music video by teen idol Nao Matsuzaki!

"This is ridiculous!" protests Asakawa in bafflement.

Welcome to the weird world of ***Ringu: Saishuu-shou*** ("Ring: The Final Chapter"). On January 7, 1999, almost exactly a year since Hideo Nakata's ***Ring*** hit movie screens for the first time and with a good seven months yet to go before Nakata's ***Ring 2***, the first episode of this 12-part television miniseries aired on the Fuji Television Network, the same one that had hosted ***Ring: The Complete Edition*** a few years earlier. While the ***Ring***'s previous appearance on TV had been a faithful adaptation of Koji Suzuki's novel, ***The Final Chapter*** takes liberties with the material and uses it as a springboard for a Perils-of-Pauline serialized thriller full of conspiracies, action, and smoldering sexual chemistry. The influence of ***The X-Files*** is palpable throughout.

Like ***Ring: The Complete Edition***, ***Ring: The Final Chapter*** exists on the margins of the ***Ring*** phenomenon yet boasts a pompous, self-aggrandizing title. It is a more accomplished, more ambitious, and better acted production than ***The Complete Edition***, and for all its idiosyncratic deviations from Suzuki's novel it has a distinctive creative vision. Much of the credit should go to screenwriter Koji Makita, who would later co-create the popular (and very similar) TV series ***Trick*** (see Chapter 7). Like Joji Iida and Hiroshi Takahashi before him, Makita chooses to copiously preserve certain minor details from Suzuki's story while rejiggering the major elements, mutating the main characters and their relationships into new and surprising forms.

When the music video appears at the cliffhanger climax of episode one, the viewer is primed by past experience with ***Ring*** to expect images of abstract menace. The impossibly innocuous pictures of the girly singer become exceedingly unsettling by their misplaced context. This sets the stage for Makita's approach throughout: to cut and paste familiar fragments into new material, creating a sort of ***Ring*** Extended Dance Remix (to keep with the pop music metaphor). So much is changed beyond recognition, while just enough is kept the same, to keep the audience constantly off-guard.

As with his later work on ***Trick***, Makita is knowledgeable about science and magic, and uses informed skepticism to debunk a lot of paranormal ideas. That rationalist backdrop then serves to emphasize those actual supernatural elements of his storytelling. Again, the ***X-Files*** dynamic can be seen in the shadows: Scully's skepticism giving Mulder's ideas more dramatic heft. Although the specifics of Makita's version vary wildly off the track Suzuki set, Makita is alone among the various screenwriters in capturing this aspect of Suzuki's writing. Throughout the *Ring* trilogy of books, Suzuki uses well-researched history, science, and understanding of human psychology to frame his ghost story in a logical, rational set of rules. Even Joji Iida's ***Spiral***, the most scientifically grounded of the films, seems uncomfortable with the realistic approach favored by Suzuki. But Makita knows that nothing deepens the shadows of the night than the light of day.

The twelve 50-minute installments were variously directed by Yoshito Fukumoto and Matsuda Hidetomo. The cast is almost uniformly strong, with two special standouts: Toshiro Yanagiba plays the male Asakawa with real complexity and sincerity, and ***Dark Water***-star Hitomi Kuroki plays cellular biologist Miyashita (a character from *Spiral*, retrofitted into this story).

Later in the year, a sequel series called ***Spiral*** picked up where ***The Final Chapter*** left off. Actresses Akiko Yada and Tae Kimura reprised their roles as Mai Takano and Sadako, respectively. ***Spiral*** ran in thirteen 50-minute episodes beginning in July 1999, just in time to coincide with the theatrical run of ***Ring 2***. Takao Kinoshita and Hiroshi Nishitani directed, from scripts by Kazuhiko Tanaka and Koji Takata. Unfortunately, the absence of Koji Makita was sorely felt, and the sequel was as misfired as the theatrical version.

none of the same.

Although Iida admired the medical realism of the book and saw it as a work of science fiction, he missed the opportunity to play up those strengths in his adaptation. What could have been lots of fun ***Andromeda Strain***-style scenes of our heroes figuring out how the video does its thing are here reduced to a few perfunctory moments of exposition. The onscreen revelation of the ring virus in all its glory certainly deserved more screen time than it gets. And as with the TV version of ***The Ring***, Iida indulges in sex and gore where Nakata exercised restraint.

The producers must have assumed they were getting a ***Ring 2*** with this. Certainly Iida defends his artistic choices compared to Nakata's as valid and true to Suzuki's intentions. The discrepancy between the gnawing horror and white-knuckle suspense of ***Ring*** with the cold and alienating effect of ***Spiral*** points to an ineffable difference between artists. It's hard to quantify talent. Like obscenity, you know it when you see it, and Hideo Nakata is simply more talented than Iida, and his film is better.

Spiral is not a bad movie. In the pantheon of J-Horrors, it's at best a lesser entry, but it is not without its own merits (among them, Iida has the distinction of offering the very first murky bathtub scene in all of J-Horror!). But those merits are obscured when seen in close proximity to ***Ring***. Issuing this thing on a double bill with Nakata's visionary work was the worst possible way to distribute it.

So producer Takashige Ichise did what anyone in his situation would do. He called a mulligan, and brought back Hideo Nakata to film a new sequel, a true ***Ring 2***, that would ignore the existence of ***Spiral*** and try to genuinely recapture what audiences liked about the original.

Hiroshi Takahashi's script touches on a few ideas similar to ***Spiral***, but expects the audience to forget the earlier film. Once again, actress Miki Nakatani takes center stage as Ryuji's "widowed" girlfriend Mai Takano. Together with Asakawa's reporter colleague Okazaki (***Don't Look Up***'s Yurei Yanagi, reprising his role from ***Ring***), they retread many of the same steps their opposite numbers did in the previous film, uncovering mysteries already well-known to the viewer.

Things pick up once Mai takes it upon herself to protect Yoichi Asakawa from Sadako, whose malefic influence is gradually turning him into a "bakemono." For you non-Japanese speakers, "bakemono" translates to something like "freak" or "monster." If you watch enough J-Horror it's one word of Japanese you're practically guaranteed to learn.

A FIELD GUIDE TO THE RING

Because ***Ring*** has spun off so many ancillary works in its spiral of inspirations, here is a handy guide to each subset:

Books by Koji Suzuki:
Ring (1991), *Spiral* (1995), *Loop* (1998), *Birthday* (1999)
Manga adaptations:
Koujirou Nagai's *Ring* (1996, adapted from the novel)
Misao Inagaki's *Ring* (1999, combining elements from novel, movie, and TV versions)
Meimu's *Ring 2* (1999, adapted from book and movie)
Mizuki Sakura's *Spiral* (1999, adapted from the book)
Meimu's *Birthday* (1999, adapted from the book)
Meimu's *Ring 0: Birthday* (2000, adapted from the movie)
Television adaptations:
Ring: The Complete Edition (1995, single 90-minute episode)
Ring: The Final Chapter (1999, 12 50-minute episodes)
Spiral (1999, 13 50-minute episodes)
Japanese movies:
Ring (1998), ***Spiral*** (1998), ***Ring 2*** (1999), ***Ring 0: Birthday*** (2000), *Ring 4: Spiral* (planning)
Korean movies:
The Ring Virus (1999)
American movies:
The Ring (2002), ***The Ring Two*** (2005)

Eventually, Mai and Yoichi submit to a bizarre experiment intended to dissipate Sadako's influence forever by projecting the psychic energy into a large body of fresh water—say, a swimming pool. Fresh water is called for because, we are told, seawater has the wrong chemical properties for this act of ghost-mosis.

As the story reaches its climax, Nakata gets the chance to indulge himself in even more water-based imagery, and an action-packed return to Sadako's well that Nakata would recycle later for his Hollywood version ***The Ring Two*** (2005). In fact, the American ***Ring*** sequel borrows a variety of ideas from this movie, such as the suggestion that protecting the child from the ring curse would look to an outsider much like child abuse (for more on ***The Ring Two***, see Chapter 10).

Where Iida rejected Nakata's presentation of Sadako as a monster and insisted on showing her as a "normal" woman, Nakata here goes even further in dehumanizing Sadako, devolving her into a reanimated clay maquette built on her skeletal remains!

Nakata keeps things moving, hopping nimbly from one showstopping scene to the next. Along the way, he pulls off some queasy creep-outs, some nightmare-inducing scares, and yet another yucky bathtub (fast becoming a de rigueur icon for J-Horror). But it never pulls together as a coherent whole. There's less at stake than before, no solid dramatic arc to the narrative. In screenwriter jargon, it lacks a "throughline."

If ***Spiral*** is a good story told without flair, ***Ring 2*** suffers from the exact opposite problem. As the saying goes, it's all sound and fury signifying nothing. Hideo Nakata succeeded in making a consistently disquieting movie, but it adds nothing to the mythology of Sadako and its best moments are designed to appeal only to ***Ring*** fans.

Whatever its flaws, ***Spiral*** can stand on its own as a film (and indeed works better when separated from memories of ***Ring***), while ***Ring 2*** never lets the viewer lose sight of its place as a sequel, a follower, a bonus round. Distributed on a double bill with another J-Horror, Shuinichi Nagasaki's ***Shikoku***, ***Ring 2*** did at least put money in the pockets of the producers at Asmik Ace Entertainment. Which is, after all, the one true mission of a sequel.

In the wake of ***Ring 2***'s marketing juggernaut came a book titled *Ring: Motto Kowai Yottsu no Hanashi*, or "Ring: Four Scarier Tales." This curious volume is the only significant piece of *Ring* literature not written by Koji Suzuki. In their efforts to make sure ***Ring 2*** would lead the franchise in the most profitable direction, unlike that damnably idiosyncratic ***Spiral***, Asmik Ace had solicited scripts from several fronts. Of the five submissions, they ended up giving the job to Hiroshi Takahashi (natch), but why waste the other four scripts? So, rather than junk the unfilmed ideas, they turned them into promotional fodder.

Meanwhile, Suzuki was cooking up a book of *Ring* leftovers of his own. The story had come to be conceived of as a trilogy, with *Loop* finishing the saga.[4] Since he was finishing the trilogy while ***Ring***-mania was ramping up, Suzuki recognized the financial value of taking another crack at Sadako's world. In 1999, he added a fourth installment to the trilogy: ***Birthday*** collects three short stories that filled in details in the margins of the established storyline.

Having successfully had seconds, Asmik Ace decided to go back for thirds. They hired Takahashi to adapt the middle section of ***Birthday***, a story called "Lemonheart" that chronicled a crucial tragic moment in the life of Sadako just before she was consigned to her fate in the well.

Taka Ichise offered the directorial duties to Nakata, who opted out to expand his blossoming reputation to other genres. He had only reluctantly accepted ***Ring 2*** anyway. "The producers told me, 'With ***Ring***, you showed people how frightening a Japanese film could be, but if you stop there, everyone will say it was just a fluke.' That was basically the pick-up line they used on me," explains Nakata.

Good riddance, said Hiroshi Takahashi, who felt that Nakata was not really cut out to be a good horror movie director. The franchise would be better served, thought Takahashi, by someone like Norio Tsuruta.

The bigwigs at Asmik Ace weren't sure. Nakata had made one of the biggest and most important Japanese movies of modern times, while Tsuruta had yet to direct a theatrical feature. But, Takahashi argued, Tsuruta's direct-to-video shockers are the things that inspired me to write the way I do. If it weren't for Tsuruta, there wouldn't have been a ***Ring***, this guy is the textbook example of a great horror director (for more about Tsuruta's inspirational J-Horror videos, see next chapter).

Since Takahashi was by this point one of the brightest lights in the J-Horror universe, there was no point arguing with him. And given what a fine movie Mr. Tsuruta made—as his debut feature no less—you have to give Takahashi credit for good instincts.

Tsuruta and Nakata could not have been less alike in attitude or background. "First and foremost," boasted Tsuruta to Fangoria's Norman England, "I am a horror director. It is all I want to do and all I have ever wanted to do."

He grew up at the movies—literally, in the theater owned and operated by his parents. This childhood experience created in him both attraction and repulsion to the world of filmmaking. On one hand, he was enraptured by the movies that formed his daily life. But on the other, the Tsuruta household was often visited by his parents' friends—filmmakers by trade, which meant they were itinerant, unemployed, living hand to mouth.

"The 1970s were a difficult time for the Japanese film industry. It went from being one of the largest in the world to just a fraction of its size in a little over ten years," recalls Tsuruta. Seeing the destitution of the men who made the movies overwhelmed whatever desire was inspired by watching their artwork; Tsuruta studied economics and became a businessman.

As it happened, Tsuruta ended up a salaryman at a video distribution company during the 1980s, the time of the great video boom. Overnight, the video business opened up new and vastly lucrative distribution channels for low budget films. Tsuruta worked in advertising, but he couldn't help but notice that opportunity was beginning to knock.

A notion was born: write a script for something that could be shot

HIDEOUS MACABRE

I made a misguided attempt to compose sections of this book using voice recognition software, only to watch as the dictated passages ended up as surreal nonsense, leaving me to type it up the old fashioned way. But one mistake amused me: Hideo Nakata's name, spoken aloud, was rendered as "Hideous Macabre" by the computer. Fans of Nakata's horror movies would appreciate that nickname, perhaps, but not likely Nakata himself. Although he acknowledges such movies as ***The Haunting*** (1963), ***The Exorcist*** (1973), ***The Omen*** (1976), and ***Suspiria*** (1977) as influences, he never aspired to make horror movies of his own. Having been so good at making horror movies, though, Nakata realized he was on his way to being typecast. "Honestly speaking, I don't like horror films, as a person or as an audience member. But critics and reporters look upon me as a horror film director, so it's almost inescapable for me now." After ***Ring 2***, Nakata elected to stay away from horror for a while to prove his mettle in other genres. ***The Sleeping Bride*** (2000) was a teen-oriented romantic fantasy riffing on the fairy tale of ***Sleeping Beauty***. Following that was the extraordinary suspense thriller ***Chaos*** (2000), which has been warmly received on video in the United States. While not a horror film, ***Chaos*** showcases Nakata's mastery of tension, in a fragmented ***Memento***-like puzzle of a plot. In 2002, Nakata directed ***Last Scene***, another making-of-a-movie drama like ***Don't Look Up*** (and shot on the same Nikkatsu soundstages) but without the supernatural trappings. Based on a story idea by ***Ring*** producer Taka Ichise, ***Last Scene*** afforded Nakata another chance to play with film-within-a-film juxtapositions. Although well received by international critics, Nakata's deviations from the horror genre were not commercial successes.

on the cheap and released straight to video. Tsuruta planned to simply skip all the unpleasant obstacles of a traditional film industry career: the long apprenticeships, the studio politics, the decay of Japan's film world. He wrote a horror script: it fit his inclinations and was a popular genre on video. Tsuruta pitched his idea to the companies for which he worked, adding that he wanted to direct it himself.

"The plan was approved," Tsuruta told Norman England, "and the movie became a hit." The movie in question was ***Honto ni atta kowai hanashi*** ("Scary True Stories," 1991), which may cause you some mild confusion. We've already run across something with an almost identical title, on which Hiroshi Takahashi and Hideo Nakata first collaborated. Tsuruta's was the first incarnation, a direct-to-video piece entirely written and directed by himself. It was successful enough to warrant a sequel (also 1991), which he again wrote and directed. It later inspired an unrelated TV rip-off co-produced by TV Asahi and Nikkatsu; this was the anthology that first brought Takahashi and Nakata together.

Throughout the 1990s, Tsuruta remained prolific and popular with his horror videos and TV shows. This consistent body of work won Tsuruta a consistent body of fans. Among them, Hiroshi Takahashi. Eventually, the two had a chance to work together, on the 1999 installment of the venerable ***Haunted School*** franchise (see next chapter). This TV special, ***Haunted School F***, featured a segment called "The Curse," written by Takahashi and directed by Tsuruta. Fast on its heels, Takahashi was back at Asmik Ace gearing up for the return of Sadako, and lobbying for Tsuruta to take the helm. By this point, Tsuruta already had thirteen well-received horror videos and television specials to his name (an auspicious number!) and was ready to explore the larger canvas offered by a well-budgeted theatrical feature.

Of all the sundry ***Ring*** sequels, Norio Tsuruta's ***Ring 0: Birthday*** is the most accomplished and effective. Unlike ***Spiral*** it doesn't alienate existing fans, nor does it cater exclusively to them as did ***Ring 2***. It adds substance to the ongoing storyline while suggesting new mysteries, and remains true to both the prior films and Suzuki's books without coming off as a mindless copy.

Hiroshi Takahashi's screenplay manages to follow the same contours as his script for ***Don't Look Up***, while exploring an aspect of Sadako's backstory he had previously omitted from his ***Ring*** scripts. Before becoming a terrifying wraith, Sadako Yamamura was an aspiring actress, an understudy for a theater troupe rehearsing a play that echoes the experiences of its players. The cast is uniformly haunted by a nightmare involving a well; they suspect the weird girl in their midst as being

WHO'S THAT GIRL

"Some of my friends teased me after seeing ***Ring***. They thought that Sadako, with her long black hair and small frame, looked like me," Yukie Nakama told Norman England during publicity for ***Ring 0: Birthday***. "I was often kidded and told I would be a natural for the part. Some time later, my agent called and said there was a casting call out for actresses to play Sadako. I thought it was a weird coincidence and so went to try out. Two weeks later, as if to prove my friends correct, I was cast... The other day I was walking down the street and some children ran up and shouted, 'It's Sadako!' I pointed a finger at them and yelled back, 'I put a curse on thee!'"

The psychic girl in the well may be the common pivot point of the many ***Ring*** stories, but each version has had its own unique take on her. In the television drama ***Ring: The Complete Edition***, softcore model Ayane Miura played the role of Sadako, mostly while undressed. Hideo Nakata cast Kabuki performer Rie Inou as his dehumanized Sadako in both ***Ring*** and ***Ring 2***, as her stilted staccato movements both emphasized the character's inhuman qualities and harkened back to the Kabuki traditions that inspired the story. Joji Iida brought in dancer Hinako Saeki to play a less monstrous Sadako in ***Spiral***. The most complex performance of the character came in ***Ring 0: Birthday***, in which Yukie Nakama played both a sympathetic Sadako and her dehumanized alter ego, all at once. Tae Kimura played Sadako in the two TV miniseries from 1999, ***Ring: The Final Chapter*** and ***Spiral***.

somehow responsible. Meanwhile, a reporter is following the unsolved deaths of everyone present at Shizuko Yamamura's botched ESP demonstration eleven years earlier; she too is closing in on poor little Sadako with her suspicions.

Like the ***Star Wars*** prequels, ***Ring 0*** expands the canvas of its story by following the tragic metamorphosis of a victim into a villain. To their credit, each of the parties involved in ***Ring 0***, from Takahashi to Tsuruta to star Yukie Nakama, recognize what makes the story tick and pitch the drama at just the right level. Throughout most of the film's one hundred minutes, the most monstrous behavior comes from the supposedly "normal" people, whose fear and hatred set the horror in motion. By the time the bill for all their cruelty comes due, the film has hit a degree of operatic emotional intensity so severe you half expect the characters to break into song.

The last reel lets loose all the psychic cruelty that had been piling up over the rest of the movie, but as the nightmare spins out of control there is no longer any room to think about who is a "good guy" or who is a "bad guy," or which characters deserve which fate. Instead, the scorched-earth finale punishes everyone unfairly. The climax leaves behind a legacy of victimization that will scar the future forever—as the subsequent ***Ring*** films have already shown.

"***Ring 0*** is a tragedy," explains Tsuruta. "Its core theme is about a young woman who is oppressed because she is different from everyone else. In Japan, there is great pressure not to stray too far from the norm."

This isn't just the theme of ***Ring 0***—it is a recurring motif throughout the genre. Women who attempt to break out of their proscribed roles provoke horrible consequences, J-horrible consequences.

The genre was born in iconoclasm. Koji Suzuki was a stay-at-home dad in a culture that devalued fathers, searching for novel ways to discuss the value of families. Hideo Nakata was a starving artist in a dying industry with a genius for visual storytelling but no special love of horror. Kicking against the pricks, these two men begat a new school of horror entertainment.

It's interesting that Suzuki and Nakata protest so much about horror. They saw horror as a tired set of conventions aimed at exploiting a specific demographic but lacking serious creative prospects. In making it their own, they made a form of horror designed for non-horror lovers, and thereby reinvigorated the genre and expanded its appeal to a wider audience. But they became trapped by their own success, increasingly frustrated at being pegged as Japan's answers to Stephen King and Alfred Hitchcock. For all their grousing about being pigeonholed as creators of horror—ugh! Horror!—neither Hideo Nakata nor Koji Suzuki really had much say in the matter. They had been involved with ***Ring***, and so they had left behind a life of struggling in obscurity for one that included money, fame, and influence. Suzuki could write his seafaring yarns, Nakata could make documentaries and romantic fantasies, but for most people they would always and ever remain the lords of the ***Ring***.

Not surprisingly, the forces of destiny made sure that Nakata and Suzuki would return to one another's orbit.

Back in 1996, between the publication of *Spiral* and *Loop*, Suzuki came out with a collection of short stories published under the banner *Honogurai mizu no soko kara* ("From the Murky Depths," better known as "Dark Water"). The stories ruminated on themes such as the human capacity for selfishness and cruelty, failed parenting, quirks of Japanese history, obscure facts about boating, and different ways in which people can drown. Oh, and Dead Wet Girls galore.

While Suzuki's publishers—Kodokawa Shoten in Japan, Vertical in the United States—trumpeted the "Japanese Stephen King" line for obvious marketing reasons, the better comparison is to Patricia Highsmith. Like Highsmith, Suzuki's prose style is distant and journalistic, observing his characters' failings and calamities with clinical detachment. In his scrupulous attention to little details, he gives even the most grotesque events the weight of reality.

Kodokawa Shoten, one of Japan's media giants, hired Hideo Nakata to adapt one of the tales from *Dark Water* into a film. This time, Nakata would not be teamed with Hiroshi Takahashi. Instead, it would be up to him and producer Takashige Ichise (one of many ***Ring***-holdovers in the production team) to adapt Suzuki's story into a screenplay. Unlike the narrative compression that was demanded when adapting the novel *Ring* into the cramped confines of a feature film, the adaptation of a short story allowed Nakata room for subtlety, nuance, and expansion.

Perhaps the Japanese, living as they do in the world's only true post-nuclear landscape, are more attuned to the metaphorical implications of the term "nuclear family." Like the bonds between subatomic particles, the bonds between parent and child are intensely powerful: crack those connections and you unleash vast, destructive energies. In the world of ***Dark Water***, breaking apart the nuclear family sets off the emotional equivalent of an atomic reaction, an H-bomb of psychic pain.

The trigger for ***Dark Water***'s psychological meltdown is Yoshimi Matsubara (played by Hitomi Kuroki from TV's ***Ring: The Final Chapter***). In her own unhappy childhood, she was abandoned by her mother; as a grownup woman she is unwillingly forcing her daughter through the same trauma in a bitter, take-no-prisoners custody dispute with her ex-husband. Yoshimi's situation is so sad, even her apartment building is weeping in sympathy. Torrents of water gush from her walls and ceiling—a curious phenomenon she fears may be connected to another family's tragedy in which a parent-child bond was severed in the most unutterably awful way. By bringing her own history of family disruptions to this of all places, Yoshimi has created the critical mass and begun the chain reaction.

Rippling under the surface of this Japanese Gothic tragedy is a soundtrack composed primarily of ominous noise. This backdrop of acoustic terror is the work of composer Kenji Kawai. Nakata hired him for all of his creepiest works: ***Ring***, ***Ring 2***, ***Chaos***, and ***Dark Water***. Kawai, who also created the soundtrack to the popular anime ***Ghost in the Shell***, punctuated Nakata's carefully crafted imagery with an aural collage of sound effects and dissonant music. "We've been working together for the whole series," Nakata said of Kawai during press tours promoting ***Ring 2***, "So it was a whole process of discussing everyday, even having disputes about the quality, the way to produce the sound effects... Your ear cannot separate the melody from the sound effects because they are so well integrated in the overall soundtrack." Nakata also knew when not to use sound. "I tend to stress long intervals in my tracks. Other people tend to use different sounds altogether to express horror, but I can increase the perception of it to the maximum by utilizing a very quiet sound. In Japanese culture we have the concept of 'aesthetics of subtraction.' Even an act of repression can be considered a form of beauty."

Good as it is—brilliant, heart-aching, and anguished as it is—by 2002 ***Dark Water*** was simply one of many. ***Ring*** changed the world. And in the world that it changed, it was no longer possible for one lone movie to stand out so distinctively. Sadako had successfully littered the world with numberless copies of herself.

Case in point: On Sunday, August 11, 2002, during the Japanese holiday O-Bon (The Festival of the Dead), a symbolic funeral for Sadako was held in Tokyo's Harajuku District. The site was the LaForet Museum, which just happened to be running a special exhibit called "From *Ring* to ***The Ring***," documenting the evolution of Suzuki's book through its movie adaptations. Suzuki himself was in attendance at the funeral, as was the president of his publishing company Kadokawa Shoten. A spokesperson from Asmik Ace explained the purpose of the PR stunt: the time had come to lay Sadako Yamamura to rest in order to clear the path for her reincarnation, across the sea, as Samara Morgan in the Hollywood remake of ***The Ring***.

But we'll save that story for later.

1. In Japanese, articles such as "a" and "the" are not used, only implied. So the English title could equally well be rendered as *Ring*, *The Ring*, or, if you wish, *A Ring*. Vertical, the novel's American publisher, has selected just plain *Ring* as the title of the English translation, and so that is how I shall render it here.
2. There is some fuzzy math at work here. Asmik Ace Entertainment has not released official numbers to the press, but it is commonly believed this figure represents the box office take of ***Ring*** and ***Spiral*** combined.
3. To those critics who casually dismissed Hideo Nakata's ***The Ring Two*** (2005) as a crass sequel, I would like to point out that Nakata considered his original ***Ring*** and its precursor ***Don't Look Up*** as gigs for hire; ***The Ring*** was already a remake right from Day One. It's hard to draw a valid distinction.
4. As with *Ring*, the Japanese title of this book is the English word "loop" rendered in Japanese letters. To date, no attempt has been made to film this story in any form.

Sources:

"Interview with Koji Suzuki," Kateigaho Winter 2005 issue, reprinted at int.kateigaho.com
England, Norman, "Celebrating Ring 0: Birthday," Fangoria issue 203, Starlog Group Publishing, New York, 2001.
England, Norman, "Sadako-Masochism," Fangoria issue 203, Starlog Group Publishing, New York, 2001.
Interview with George Iida by Kyoko Tomonaga, Ring/Spiral promotional booklet.
Interview with Hideo Nakata by "Quint": www.aintitcool.com, January 26, 2005.
Interview with Hideo Nakata by Kyoko Tomonaga, Ring/Spiral promotional booklet.
Interview with Hideo Nakata, Ring 2 promotional booklet.
Interview with Joji Ida by Jasper Sharp, The Spiral DVD edition, Artsmagic, UK.
Interview with Koji Suzuki by Shigeru Totsuka, Ring/Spiral promotional booklet.
Interview with Koji Suzuki translated by Kevin McGue, reprinted at www.theringworld.com
Kennedy, Randy, "Bringing Out the Horror of What he Knows Best," The New York Times, November 1, 2004.
Interview with Koji Suzuki, JapanReview.net, April 25, 2003.
Mes, Tom and Jasper Sharp, The Midnight Eye Guide to New Japanese Film, Stone Bridge Press, Berkeley, CA, 2005.
Nakata, Hideo, Foreword to The Midnight Eye Guide to New Japanese Film by Tom Mes and Jasper Sharp, Stone Bridge Press, Berkeley, CA, 2005.
Schilling, Mark, Contemporary Japanese Film, Weatherhill, Trumbull, CT, 1999.
Smith, Richard Harland, "The Ring Cycle," Video Watchdog No. 92, Februray 2003.
Suzuki, Koji, Dark Water, Vertical, New York, 2004.
Suzuki, Koji, Ring, English translation by Robert B. Rohmer and Glynne Walley, Vertical, New York, 2004.
Suzuki, Koji, Spiral, English translation by Glynne Walley, Vertical, New York, 2004.
Suzuki, Koji, The Ring—manga adaptation by Misao Inagaki, Dark Horse Manga, Milwaukie, Oregon, 1999.
Tateishi, Ramie, "The Japanese horror film series: Ring and Eko Eko Azarak," Fear Without Frontiers, FAB Press, England, 2003.

CHAPTER 3

THE HAUNTED SCHOOL

I saw ***The Ring***, in its American iteration, in a crowded multiplex on Thanksgiving weekend, 2002. The audience had sat enthralled throughout: the movie defied so many horror movie conventions that even the most jaded moviegoers amongst us could not anticipate what to expect. As it drew to a close, we heaved a collective sigh of relief. After such a nerve-jangling experience, it was comforting that the filmmakers were wrapping up the story with a satisfying, reassuring coda…and then it happened.

In deference to those of you who have not yet seen ***The Ring*** (how could that be?) I will avoid being too specific here—but those of you who have seen it know exactly what I am talking about. I have seen many horror movies in my day, and never have I heard an audience scream so loud.

Why is this moment so scary? Part of it, of course, is due to the expert cinematic execution: whether you watch the Japanese original, the Hollywood revamp, or the South Korean version, each one nails this scene with meticulous craftsmanship. And, after so many years of tortuous public debate about the possible detriments of watching too much violent entertainment, here is the metaphor brought to life: yes, watching scary movies can hurt you!

These things are true, but there is something else to this climactic shock that deserves notice. It cannot be said that the re-emergence of the dead wet girl is an unprecedented surprise. Far from it, horror movie cliché all but demands that the villain, thought defeated, return for a final scare. But even if we knew that "gotcha" scene was probably inevitable, her return profoundly violates our sense of order. She had not been "defeated," in the traditional horror movie sense, at all. The heroes of the movie followed a line of investigation and inquiry to discover who she was, what she wanted, why in the hell she was doing these cruel things. That process of deduction led them to the well, to answers that seemed to wrap the narrative up with a tidy bow. Her reappearance reveals those answers to have been false, incomplete, misleading. It is as if Sherlock Holmes has gathered his suspects in the drawing room to unveil his reconstruction of the crime and accuse the guilty party, only to discover he was stone wrong.

For human beings, thirsty for rationality, desperate for explanations for everything from why the sky is blue to why God lets bad things happen to good people, the repudiation of such hard-won solutions is bone-chilling.

Film critics around the world have settled on a pat answer to explain the ***Ring*** phenomenon and the J-Horror boom: Hideo Nakata's 1998 motion picture was an unqualified commercial and creative success that has inspired legions of lesser imitations. Next question.

If you have read this far, you already sense that such an "explanation" is wanting. Nakata's ***Ring*** did not appear from the dust in a moment of divine creation, it was preceded by a 1995 TV adaptation with all the same elements but the wrong style, and Nakata's own 1996 ***Don't Look Up*** which nailed the style but with a (slightly) different story. And perhaps you have already seen a few of the alleged "rip-offs," and found them at least as good. But even if such doubts nag at your mind, you must admit the official line is compelling. ***Ring*** is a story about a video that inspires others to copy it—how wonderfully apt to think that the movies reflected that pattern too.

But ***Ring***'s finale also cautions us against complacently thinking that just because the pieces seem to fit that we have put the puzzle together correctly. Sometimes the truth is more obscure, and contradicts what we thought we knew.

The year is 1965. The place, Cannes, France: one of the most beautiful regions in the world. A group of celebrities have gathered to perform a rather cushy task: serve as the jury for the planet's most prestigious film festivals. This year, such luminaries as director Alain Robbe-Grillet and actor Rex Harrisson have convened under the presidency of Olivia "Scarlett" de Havilland herself and author André Maurois. Among other prizes, they will award the Special Jury Prize to Masaki Kobayashi's ***Kwaidan***.[1]

A three-hour long anthology of traditional Japanese ghost stories filmed with voluptuous style and Nipponese grace, ***Kwaidan*** is inarguably a work of art. The first of four unrelated episodes, titled "The Black Hair," tells a tale reminiscent of Nobuo Nakagawa's classic ***Ghost Story of Yotsuya*** (see also Chapter 2). A poor samurai leaves his wife, remarries into wealth, and then regrets his selfish choice. He returns to his old home, to spend a lovely night of reconciliation with his first wife, unaware that she killed herself in despair a long time ago. He awakes to discover that the woman in his bed is but a corpse, with luxuriously long black hair that entangles him, dragging him into the well where he will join her forever.

Along with ***Ghost Story of Yotsuya***, certain icons, later to dominate J-Horror a generation later, are settling into place: the ghostly woman, the long black hair, drownings, a disrupted family as the source point of the hauntings. Also, these early classics of Japanese horror have a distinctive difference. In Western ghost stories, the presence of supernatural forces is signaled by deviations from the norm. A door closes without being touched, a sound comes from no obvious source, objects move of their own will—these are the harbingers of poltergeists. But in Japan, otherworldy spirits interact seamlessly with mortals.

Consider the second segment of ***Kwaidan***, "Woman of the Snow": another ghostly woman with long black hair and a propensity for halting, weird movements attacks a pair of unlucky travelers. One man survives the ordeal, and goes on to marry a beautiful girl and live a long and happy life. That is, until decades later, he discovers he's married the very same ghost that nearly killed him. Who knew?

In all of the stories one overriding theme resonates: ghosts are people, too. You can interact with them, even love them, and may not immediately recognize their inhuman nature.

Kwaidan was not a commercial success in Japan, but it was an enormous critical favorite at home and abroad. With its extraordinary visual abstractions, experimental use of sound, and elegiac tone it stood out as a distinctive Japanese achievement, unlike any other horror film.

Movies like ***Kwaidan*** and ***Ghost Story of Yotsuya*** have no true Western equivalent. They were not made within genre conventions established by foreign filmmakers, and although they were hailed on the arthouse circuit they did not inspire any Western mimics. These are uniquely Japanese creations, in which Japanese myths and traditions are adapted in a Japanese idiom for Japanese consumption: they are cultural products of a nation that had successfully isolated itself for so long it had become the cultural equivalent of the Galapagos Islands. But as Japanese culture started to mingle and intermix with that of the rest of the world, things would change.

Enter Terence Fisher, and England's Hammer Studios. Garishly colorful, irreverent, gleefully sadistic, and ripe with sexuality, Hammer's gothic horrors of the 1960s and 70s found an appreciative—and hungry—audience in Japan. The Japanese market for these things was so vital to their success, the producers were obliged to shoot additional material that catered to the Japanese taste for gore, crafting separate editions for Japanese distribution. It did not take long for Japanese filmmakers to try to follow suit and make Hammer-esque creations for themselves. Michio Yamamoto especially distinguished himself in this field with a series of vampire pictures that would have been unthinkable before British imports showed the way.

Yamamoto, though, found himself working in an industry in decline.

During the 1960s, Japanese cinema was a global powerhouse. Masaki Kobayashi, Kon Ichikawa, Keisuke Kinoshita, and of course Akira Kurosawa were all the rage at international film festivals and arthouse theaters around the world. Meanwhile, giant monster flicks from Toho and, yes, Akira Kurosawa's movies (again) proved to be commercial exports of great value. The Japanese film market, despite the country's size, was second only to the United States. Yet by the 1970s, it was all falling apart. The major studios were in decline, or outright bankruptcy. Filmmakers could no longer support their families with their peculiar trade. The world's theaters lost interest in Japanese movies, which increasingly catered only to Japanese audiences.

By the 1980s, even this wasn't working.

In Japan, domestic production holds on to about a third of the audience, with foreign imports (read: Hollywood) dominating the other two thirds. These numbers need context to really make sense. Remember, first, that Japan is the second-biggest film market, and then notice that Japan's one-third share is easily the best performance of a domestic film industry in the face of Hollywood competition anywhere in the developed world, and it might look like a pretty good situation. However, Japanese movies do not hold their own so well on merit alone. The Japanese film industry is vertically integrated, with studios owning their own distribution chains and theaters. They are permitted by law to set aside a certain percentage of screening times for their own films, shutting American imports out regardless of their popularity. It is not that Japanese audiences prefer Japanese films to foreign ones. In fact, without such protectionist policies, Hollywood imports would overtake the whole game. In the 1990s, polls showed Japanese audiences thought Japanese films were inferior, less entertaining, and more shoddily made compared to imports. By 1998, the number of films made in Japan had dropped to less than half the number made in 1960... But then, of course, in 1998 things took a different turn, thanks in large measure to ***Ring***.

One thing Japanese filmmakers could do to stay busy and pay the bills during such hard times was to work in television—and beginning with the video age in the 1980s, in the world of low-budget direct-to-video "v-cinema" movies. In the mid-1960s, even the legendary Nobuo Nakagawa took to TV with a series called ***Anata no shiranai sekai*** ("A World You Don't Know") dramatizing allegedly true encounters with ghosts. This launched a sub-genre of horror called "Shinrei Mono," or

"Spirit Stories." The formula was simple: urban legends and true-ghost tales, connecting the supernatural with the everyday. Over the years, Shinrei Mono entrenched itself as a durable specialty for TV and v-cinema use.

All it needed was a steady influx of fresh material, a constant supply of scary true stories.

In the mid-1980s, a schoolteacher started sharing ghost stories with his young students. And, no, I don't mean Koji Suzki—you can flip back to the previous chapter to read about his contributions. Instead, the man who helped trigger the Haunted School boom was middle school teacher Toru Tsunemitsu. At first his obsession with ghost stories led him around town, compiling urban legends from anyone willing to share them with him. But when he started to notice that an unusual percentage of these stories centered around schools, he narrowed his focus on those. He asked his students for school-based ghost legends, and to his amazement received over 160 tales in just two weeks.

For years, he collected these stories, and wrote them down in simple, easy language aimed at children. In 1990, the first volume of ***Gakkou no Kaidan*** (strictly translated: "School Ghost Stories") was published by Kodansha Publishing, and became an overnight best seller. In the years to come, he would release a total of nine volumes of this stuff to a hungry readership.

Kansai Television noted the blockbuster sales and snapped up TV rights. In 1994, Kansai broadcast a six episode miniseries of half hour long ghost stories, all set in schools. Over the course of the decade, there would be multiple one-off specials: ***Gakkou no Kaidan R*** (for Return), ***Gakkou no Kaidan F*** (for Final), ***Gakkou no Kaidan G*** (Great), ***Gakkou no Kaidan: Haru no Tatari***, ***Gakkou no Kaidan: Haru no noroi***, ***Gakkou no Kaidan: Haru no mononoke***... Meanwhile, Toho Studios launched a series of theatrical features, beginning in 1995. By the turn of the millenium, there had been four feature films, all of them commercial hits.

Don't worry if the titles blur together: the point is that the ***Haunted School*** (the official English title for the ***Gakkou no Kaidan*** brand) was an enormously successful and long-legged horror franchise, on which many of the filmmakers responsible for J-Horror would cut their teeth. On the ***Haunted School*** television programs alone, we find such J-Horror luminaries in their youth: Hideo Nakata, Takashi Shimizu, Hiroshi Takahashi, Norio Tsuruta, and Kiyoshi Kurosawa.

Kurosawa would soon become one of the leading standard-bearers for J-Horror. His 1997 film ***Cure*** would stand with ***Ring*** as one of the

GAKKOU NO KAIDAN: HAUNTED SCHOOL

Haunted School is packed with two scoops of wild, surrealistic visions, but no real sense of menace. A threadbare and uninteresting plot holds together 100-some minutes' worth of weird but mostly non-threatening spooks. However, this is a film aimed at youngsters—it was released in summertime to maximize vacationing kid audiences—and so the premise of the project was not to be too scary. This film is pitched at the right level for its intended viewers and was enormously successful with them.

When ***Haunted School*** raked in an impressive $14.5 million in Japanese ticket sales alone, its director Hideyuki Hirayama was quickly brought back for a sequel—which in turn made another $14 million. In the end, there would be four ***Haunted School*** films—three of them by Hirayama. ***Gakkou no Kaidan 3***, however, was directed by Shusuke Kaneko—the boy genius responsible for the 1990s ***Gamera*** trilogy and ***Godzilla, Mothra, King Ghidorah: Giant Monsters All Out Attack***.

Call it silly, call it slow-moving, but give ***Haunted School*** its props: it was a bona fide hit.

At the heart of the film is an urban legend, naturally enough. A story, whispered from student to student at Ichogaoka elementary school, about a ghostly little girl named Hanako who supposedly haunts the old, disused building on the grounds of the school. On the day before summer vacation, a group of students defy school rules to break into the old building in hopes of seeing the specter. Soon, they and their slapstick-prone teacher Shinichi are trapped in an alternate dimension, besieged by a slew of outlandish demons.

Fans of the old "Yokai Monsters" movies of the 1960s will be delighted with the bizarre designs of the apparitions, presented with uniformly high-quality special effects. If you've never seen the Yokai Monsters, then try imagining what would happen if Lucio Fulci's ***The Beyond*** was remade by the producers of ***H.R. Pufnstuf***. The point here is eye candy, not drama. The demons are more mischievous than frightening. The kiddie cast (a lackluster bunch) spend a lot of time screaming their fool heads off—but screamin' don't make it scary.

When we do catch a glimpse of the ghostly Hanako, it's just a flash of a girl in a red dress, her back to us and her black hair flowing in the breeze. A fleeting moment, but a potent seed of thrills to come, as Asian filmmakers found increasingly threatening variations of the image.

By 1998, Hanako's reign was quickly being supplanted by Sadako and her new breed of vengeful ghosts. No one enters the haunted house of ***Ju-On*** without being grievously cursed, but all the children escape Ichogaoka's old building not just fine and well but indeed better off for the experience.

Much of ***Haunted School***'s appeal to children lay in its uplifting, moralizing messages: listen to your elders, trust your friends, have faith in yourself, don't run in the hallway. Hideyuki Hirayama reassures us that you can be chased by giants, attacked by mannequins, and thrown into a void and still come home in time for dinner. The films that came in his wake had no such safety net.

commonly recognized inaugural points of the new genre, and he would earn the kind of arthouse critical acclaim last showered on Masaki Kobayashi a generation earlier. Before any of that came to pass, however, he took a job directing the first episode of the first TV edition of ***Haunted School***, in 1994. It was titled "Hanako-san," and it marked the first ever screen appearance of Hanako the Toilet Ghost.

What's that, you say? A toilet ghost?

In its simplest form, the legend goes like this: a schoolchild enters the girls' restroom, alone. She knows she is alone, but still she knocks on each stall door, in turn, calling out the name "Hanako." On the last door, her ritual knock is greeted with a distant, echoing reply: "Yes?"

Some tellings explained that Hanako had been the victim of bullying, driven into shame and despair from which she escaped only by killing herself, and that her angry ghost lingers in the stall where she was once taunted. Other versions omit any explanation of who she was and simply take for granted that she is.

The legend of Hanako, although it may sound fairly flimsy as scary stories go, was a pervasive and effective myth that spread like wildfire through elementary schools during the early 1990s. Teachers were suddenly confronted with a sort of mass hysteria, with children so terrified of the bathrooms they were wetting themselves in class, unwilling to enter the possibly haunted toilet.

To give the children credit, we're talking about some seriously spooky potties here. The school buildings had not been updated in decades, and the bathrooms in these decrepit facilities were in notoriously poor repair. Dark, dank, stinky, afflicted by unreliable flickering lights—what little kid in their right mind wouldn't conclude such places were haunted?

In the end, the school system was forced to upgrade their restrooms at a cost of $156,000 per school, just to dispel the myth of Hanako. By then, however, she found new digs: the variations on her story were collected in a book of her own, published in 1993.

Not to mention all the movies.

In addition to starring in Kiyoshi Kurosawa's premiere episode of ***Haunted School*** on TV, she also figures in the first ***Haunted School*** feature film in 1995. As if that were not enough, 1995 also saw the theatrical release of ***Toire no Hanako-san*** ("Phantom of the Toilet"). Two v-cinema features followed, and then Hanako returned to theaters in 1998 with ***Shinsei Toire no Hanako-san*** ("School Mystery"), a visually arresting J-Horror sucker punch with a gripping screenplay by ***Ring***-scenarist Hiroshi Takahashi.

Hanako was not the only name associated with haunted schools in the 1990s, however. In fact, for sheer commercial impact alone the top honor goes to Misa Kuroi, the Dark Angel herself. A trilogy of movies about her exploits began in 1995 with ***Eko Eko Azaraku***: the title is not Japanese and has no translation, it is the opening phrase of an ancient (and fictional) spell. Almost immediately, the trilogy was snapped up for distribution in the United States on home video, even before ***Ring*** signaled a new international audience for Japanese horror. In 1997, ***Eko Eko Azaraku*** made the inevitable spinoff to a TV incarnation, where up and coming director Higuchinsky started to make a name for himself (for more of his extraordinary concoctions, turn to Chapter 4).

The haunted school movies of the 1990s are the direct ancestors of a genre that would overshadow them creatively and commercially. With the notable exception of the ***Eko Eko Azaraku*** series, few of these pre-***Ring*** embryos have been released in the United States, and it is unlikely that more will follow: stylistically these films are in a different idiom from ***Ring***. If you like the serious, suspense-driven, atmospheric thrills of J-Horror, then you may not enjoy the wildly over-the-top, shock-driven, cheapjack stuff that preceded it—just as, if you are a jazz fan taken with the cool blue free-forming of Miles Davis or John Coltrane, you may not have an ear for the Dixieland swing of the nineteen-teens. There is a clear line of succession, one evolving to the other, yet they sound completely unalike.

By the mid-1990s, a coincidence of factors had come together to create the environment from which J-Horror as we now know it was born: 1) thanks to the longstanding decline of the Japanese film industry, talented young artists were forced to work in low-budget, direct-to-video horror productions; 2) those v-cinema programs thrived on supposedly true stories of supernatural encounters; 3) the much needed source material to fuel such Shinrei Mono arrived thanks to several high-profile books about haunted schools. So, it came to pass that Hideo Nakata, Hiroshi Takahashi, Kiyoshi Kurosawa, Joji Iida, Masayuki Ochiai, Higuchinsky, and Takashi Shimizu were all engaged throughout the decade in the making of low-budget horror movies about haunted schools and dead wet girls. Here they all are, all of the major players whose names dominate the rest of this book. In theaters, on television, and on video these men obsessively reworked the same raw elements, closing in on that combination of ideas that would define a genre.

And then, in 1998, along came ***Ring***, and the world gasped in astonishment at the accomplished end product of all this arduous preparation: wow, here is something new under the sun.

EKO EKO AZARAKU

Unlike Hanako, or Sadako, or the dead wet girls they inspired, little Miss Misa Kuroi is not dead, not a villain, nor in any way weak or retiring. This chick kicks ass. She is a teenage witch, charged with fighting the forces of darkness, and she has a disturbing past full of carnage. She transfers to a new school just in time to find it attacked by a cult angling to reincarnate Satan. Between the usual jealousies and social minefields of high school, Misa Kuroi will have to rally her limited resources to fight an ancient and overwhelming evil.

If this description sends images of ***Buffy the Vampire Slayer*** running through your head, you're not alone. But this is no knock-off. ***Eko Eko Azaraku*** hit screens two years before Joss Whedon's fabled hit premiered on Fox TV in the States. Whatever similarities it shares with ***Buffy*** (and they are plenty), ***Eko Eko Azaraku*** was adapted from a manga that had been popular in the 1970s: Misa Kuroi owes nothin' to nobody.

Not only is this particular franchise significant for its massive commercial appeal both in Japan and among Western audiences, but for this unique quality: *alone* among the movies covered in this book, it was made by a woman. For all the emphasis on sex roles and women's issues in the films of J-Horror, those movies are the works of an all-male filmmakers' club. ***Eko Eko Azaraku*** however comes from Shimako Sato, a young woman who learned her craft in London. She studied film in England first as a student, then on the job as the director of the low-budget vampire flick ***Tale of a Vampire*** (later rechristened ***Warlock: Tale of a Vampire*** to capitalize on its star Julian Sands' role in the unrelated cult hit ***Warlock***). She returned home to Japan with a desire to make a film about magic and witchcraft.

Having once harbored the dream of being a manga artist herself, she remembered the ***Misa Kuroi*** comics from her youth and set out to adapt them. The effects-heavy production was completed in two weeks, which may seem like a rush job by Western standards but was actually a rather luxurious indulgence for Sato, a notorious slowpoke perfectionist.

In addition to the high-octane ultraviolence of the thing, the first ***Eko Eko Azaraku*** also garnered attention for its lesbian subplot and especially steamy all-girl sex scenes. Pinup model Kimika Yoshino made her acting debut as Misa. She received her script the day before shooting started, barely met with her director beforehand, and mistakenly thought the whole project had been canceled—she had no choice but to play the role with an enigmatic, unfathomable distance which added to her character's allure. Costarring with Yoshino was the lovely young Miho Kanno, just a few years away from becoming the first screen Tomie (see Chapter 4).

Eko Eko Azaraku (also called ***Wizard of Darkness*** on American home video) hit it big. Sato was called back to helm Part 2 with some of the same cast, but was replaced on ***Eko Eko Azaraku 3: Misa the Dark Angel*** by director Katsuhito Ueno, promoted from his work alongside Higuchinsky on the TV version.

Well, almost everyone said that. When Norio Tsuruta saw ***Ring***, he barked, "This looks exactly like what I've been doing!"

We must now hit the rewind button and skip back in time to find the true genesis of the genre. You want an origin story? Well, guess what: J-Horror actually did emerge from the dust, fully formed. It just happened a long time before 1998.

Like so many of the other filmmakers profiled in this book, Norio Tsuruta spent his youth making amateur movies on 8mm, and dreaming of a future as a director. But in the late 1980s, the Japanese film business was a moribund beast that couldn't really support the careers of those directors already established. So the only viable jobs he found were in the mundane day-to-day tasks of handling distribution contracts, getting films subtitled for foreign release, putting together video box art, and so on.

Tsuruta took a position at Japan Home Video performing these kinds of services, when the direct-to-video market started to really take off. V-cinema proved to be especially popular for horror titles. American horror movies like ***Friday the 13th*** and ***A Nightmare on Elm Street*** flopped at Japanese theaters but thrived on video. Tsuruta could sense a door opening.

One day in 1990, Tsuruta was browsing in a bookstore when a manga caught his eye. The thing was called ***Honto ni atta kowai hanashi*** ("Scary True Stories"). A compilation of true-life encounters with ghosts, it was squarely in line with the established video genre of Shinrei Mono. It would not be hard or expensive to realize on video, either: the short vignettes would put few demands on actors, and special effects were limited. In all, a v-cinema adaptation would be a minor risk, and it was just the sort of thing Japan Home Video was looking to do.

Before pitching the idea to his bosses, though, Tsuruta wanted to have the cards in his favor. He had no directing experience and didn't want to give them an excuse to greenlight the idea but exclude him. So, the young man approached the manga's publisher and asked for the rights. They agreed, and didn't ask for any money. *Sure kid, you can have it, knock yourself out.*

Tsuruta worked up a complete plan, and presented his fully-formed idea to Japan Home Video. Happily, they agreed to take a chance. They gave him about $60,000 and a week; the untried kid cranked out a huge hit in return. As the cash started to roll in to JHV's coffers, they quickly assigned Tsuruta to helm a follow-up. It too did great business, and the team went back for thirds. Although ***Scary True Stories 3*** (or rather, ***All New Scary True Stories: Realm of the Specters***) also made a handsome profit, it would be the last of the series. By this point, the entire Asian economy was collapsing. The front office boys at Japan Home Video had blundered with their other productions, used up all their money, and decided to escape poverty by exclusively making pornography from then on out.

But in two short years, Norio Tsuruta had accomplished something simply extraordinary. Set aside that he proved himself a commercial director on his very first outing, set aside that he broke into his dream job when the avenues to doing so were closing all around him, and set aside that he had a unique experience with full creative autonomy (Japan Home Video let him assume total Orson Welles-style auteur responsibilities over every detail even down to approving his own video covers). What concerns us here is that Tsuruta invented from whole cloth a new horror movie aesthetic.

For years, Japanese horror movies were gore-drenched imitations of Western horrors. Tsuruta brought an unprecedented restraint. The three installments of ***Scary True Stories*** are marvels of quiet suspense, atmosphere, and cinematic storytelling. The initial 45-minute featurette collected a trio of unrelated short stories, adapted with a flair for the dramatic by screenwriter Chiaki Konaka (former ***Ultraman*** scribe, soon to write for ***Haunted School G***, Hideo Nakata, Kiyoshi Kurosawa, and Takashi Shimizu). It opens with an ominous narrator and menacing music playing over spooky photographic "evidence" of the spirit world, before launching into a tale of a veritable Dead Wet Girl.

By volume two, made later the same year, Tsuruta had already matured as a director, and started to refine his formula. This second tape is more acutely focused, more suspenseful. Come1992's ***All New Scary True Stories: Realm of the Specters***, Tsuruta has installed a confident narrative control that keeps the audience off-guard, refusing to spoon-feed the viewer. By this third program, Tsuruta has also abandoned the spooky photos and stentorian voice introducing the show, and just jumps in, daring the audience to keep up. If the first anthology was horror movie gold, then Tsuruta topped himself, and then went and topped himself again.

Over the course of the ten shorts making up the three volume series, Tsuruta manages to run through every major archetype that J-Horror would use over the coming decades. Here's a haunted house, here's a haunted hospital, here's the fragmented narrative discontinuity Takashi Shimizu would make his own, here's a ghostly encounter that Kiyoshi Kurosawa would practically mimeograph into ***Pulse***... Of the many movies profiled in this book, there is little to see that does not appear in condensed, concentrated form somewhere in ***Scary True Stories***.

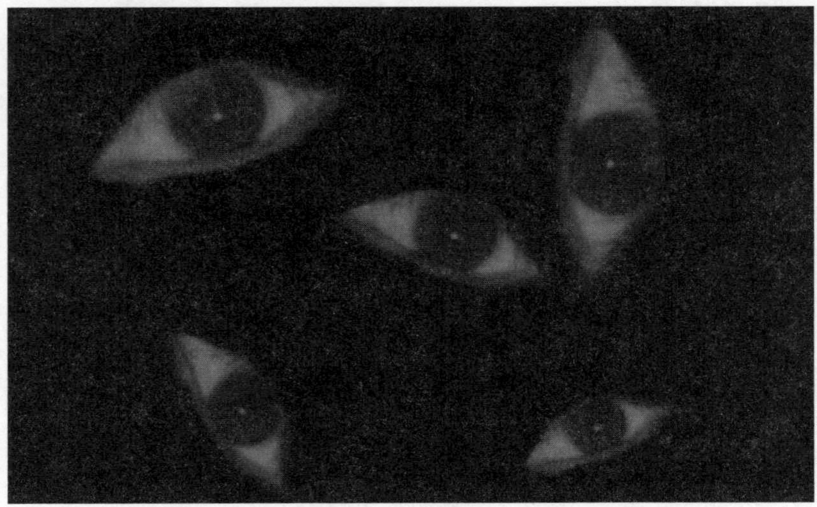

Scary True Stories

There is a saying: necessity is the mother of invention. To an extent, the genius of Tsuruta's style was a product of a specific hurdle. In the summer of 1988, Tsutomu Miyazaki began a grisly murder spree. For nearly a year, this monster raped and killed young girls, eluded a police manhunt, and terrorized the nation. When he was finally caught, the police discovered his apartment was filled with child pornography and gruesome horror movies like the notorious ***Guinea Pig*** series—the kind of bloody entertainment that defined Japanese horror movies at the time. Suddenly, the question of whether violent videos led to real-world violence had a terrifying new urgency.

Japan Home Video was one of several video companies caught in the crossfire. On the one hand, horror movies were good business. On the other, anguished citizens scandalized those companies that trafficked in gory videos. In the middle of this maelstrom, Tsuruta proposed to make a horror movie without gore or violence, something that got its chills the old-fashioned way.

And this new suspense-driven elegance had an unexpected side-effect: without gore, the videos would be shelved in stores next to mainstream, non-genre movies. Historically, horror movies had been sold to a predominantly male audience. ***Scary True Stories***, pioneer that it was, sold overwhelmingly to young women. For the first time, horror had found a female audience—and this would remain true for the J-Horrors to come.

The year that Tsuruta released the third and final edition of ***Scary True Stories*** was the same year that Hideo Nakata and Hiroshi Takahashi first met. Nakata and Takahashi, you may recall from Chapter 2, collaborated on a TV series called ***Hontouni atta kowai hanashi*** ("True Fear Stories", now on DVD as ***Cursed Death Spirit***). If it sounds suspiciously like ***Honto ni atta kowai hanashi*** (Tsuruta's baby), well, that's the whole point. If it sounds so much alike you can't tell the difference, well, that's why I'm using English titles in the book. The TV show was an unrelated project designed to appeal to the same audience, but with poorer results (think back to when ***Battlestar Galactica*** tried to piggy back on ***Star Wars***' success in 1978).

It was not until 1994 that Hiroshi Takahashi finally got to meet Norio Tsuruta in person, and tell him this: Takahashi hadn't just been hired to rip off Tsuruta's style, he was doing it out of love. Takahashi considered Tsuruta his greatest inspiration, and wanted nothing more than to make Tsuruta's style the dominant one. This he did on his very next gig, ***Don't Look Up*** in 1996 (see Chapter 2). And when the offer came to write the script for the theatrical version of ***Ring***, Takahashi implored the producers to tap Tsuruta for it. They demurred, saying

Tsuruta was just a video director—and opted instead for Hideo Nakata, who had proven his theatrical-feature-making skills already.

Meanwhile, Tsuruta kept busy in the low-end world of horror v-cinemas. One such assignment came in 1996. While his biggest fan, Hiroshi Takahashi, was off giving ***Don't Look Up*** that "Norio Tsuruta feeling," Tsuruta himself was hired by Daiei to replicate ***Haunted School***. And thus, ***Bourei Gakkyu*** ("Phantom Class," released on video as, ahem, ***A Haunted School***). It was his biggest budgeted creation yet, and from there he got to work on the actual ***Haunted School*** franchise for one of its TV specials in 1999.

Eventually, Tsuruta got his break into real theatrical features with ***Ring 0: Birthday*** (thanks to Takahashi's continued lobbying). By now, Tsuruta was in the odd position of giving his inflections to ideas and images that had originally been fashioned in an attempt to reproduce his techniques. Imagine asking Paul McCartney to sing lead vocals in your Beatles cover band.

The movies discussed in the rest of this book resemble one another not (just) because they follow in the footsteps of ***Ring***—they were created by the same people, over and over, who formed their aesthetic principles together, at the same time, under shared circumstances.

What we are talking about here is a school of art. And how better to designate that school than with the most obvious name: the Haunted School. During this fertile period of experimentation throughout the decade, these talented young filmmakers had the opportunity to churn through endless variations on the same basic raw material, honing the aesthetic principles based on what "worked." Things that clicked with the audience, as measured in yen, would be retained.

By the end of the decade, the principles of J-Horror were well in place. Gone was the emphasis on special effects that had once compelled Kiyoshi Kurosawa to hire Dick Smith (see Chapter 5), or had Toho Studios scrambling to fill the halls of the ***Haunted School*** with as many outlandish monsters as their SPFX guys could conceive. Instead, horror would be a quiet dread emerging from family tragedies, in which the weakest and most vulnerable members (children and women) would avenge their victimization by visiting supernatural pain on the world. Urban legends abound—ancient visions of horror mix and mingle with the details of modern life.

Before we conclude our chapter of the origins of J-Horror, one last piece of the puzzle remains to fit. From ***Ring*** onwards, this new breed of horror movie would often posit a threat that multiplies itself exponentially—growing and spreading with each victim. In many cases, the viral analogy is made explicit—but even when it is not, the sense of

POTTY GHOST

Ask the average Western filmgoer about a potty ghost, and ***Harry Potter***'s Moaning Myrtle is likely the only answer you'll get. As none of Hanako's films or videos have yet been released in the West, this may stay the case for some time, so you will be denied the pleasure of ***School Mystery***, and spared the boredom of ***Phantom of the Toilet***.

Phantom of the Toilet is a slow-paced film about an elementary school allegedly haunted by Hanako, the ghost that lives in the last stall of the sixth grade girl's bathroom. A new student transfers in, but her odd behavior makes her fellow classmates believe her to be Hanako's physical manifestation. There's a lesson to be learned here: acting like a freakazoid isn't the best way to win friends and influence people. As it happens, children are indeed going missing, but what the kids chalk up to Hanako's supernatural mischief is actually the work of a real, living serial killer/pedophile.

Many of the familiar tropes of J-Horror are to be found here, including the genre's emphasis on fractured families and absent parents. But the film is a clumsy affair, with director Joji Matsuoka equating loud music with scares. It performed poorly at the box office, but Hanako was not down for the count.

Toshiaki Nakazawa had produced the film for Shochiku Studios, and after its limp returns he tried again on the small screen with a pair of videos in 1997. These two videos were co-produced by Nakazawa and Hirofumi Ogoshi. In 1998, Ogoshi took the Hanako franchise back to the big screen at Toei with a feature written by the redoubtable Hiroshi Takahashi, hot off ***Ring***, and directed by Yukihito Tsutsumi, a talented maverick who would make a considerable name for himself over the next few years with such hits as ***Trick*** and ***2LDK*** (see Chapter 7).

These two men turned ***School Mystery*** into a stunningly creepy and adult thriller full of suspense, mystery, and cerebral horror. Just a few years separate ***School Mystery*** from ***Phantom of the Toilet***, but the creative gulf between them is vast. It remains as of this writing the last great J-Horror not yet awarded an American DVD release.

TIMELINE

1990: Publication of ***Gakkou no Kaidan***

1991: ***Honto ni atta kowai hanashi*** (***Scary True Stories***) by Norio Tsuruta and Chiaki Konaka

1992: ***Hontouni atta kowai hanashi*** (***Curse, Death and Spirit***) by Hideo Nakata and Hiroshi Takahashi

1993: book on Hanako the Toilet Ghost published

1994: ***Gakkou no Kaidan*** TV series with Hanako segment directed by Kiyoshi Kurosawa

1995: Sarin gas attack in Tokyo subway
Eko Eko Azaraku by Shimako Sato

Toire no Hanako-san (***Phantom of the Toilet***)
Gakkou no kaidan (***Haunted School***)
Ring: The Complete Edition (TV version) by George Iida

1996: ***Eko Eko Azaraku 2*** by Shimako Sato
Bourei Gakkyuu (***A Haunted School***) by Norio Tsuruta
Don't Look Up by Hideo Nakata and Hiroshi Takahashi
Gakkou no Kaidan 2

1997: ***Cure*** by Kiyoshi Kurosawa
Parasite Eve by Masayuki Ochiai
Gakkou no Kaidan F (TV special) by Hideo Nakata and Kiyoshi Kurosawa
Toire no Hanako-san videos
Eko Eko Azaraku (TV series) by Higuchinsky

1998: ***Shinsei Toire no Hanako-san*** (***School Mystery***)
Gakkou no Kaidan G by Takashi Shimizu and Kiyoshi Kurosawa
Eko Eko Azaraku 3: Misa the Dark Angel
Ring/Spiral double feature by Hideo Nakata and Joji Iida
Tomie by Ataru Oikawa
Gakkou no Kaidan 3 feature film

hauntings as a plague remain a defining feature of the genre. If spiraling horror is one of the key characteristics of J-Horror, it is the only one conspicuously missing from Norio Tsuruta's manifesto, ***Scary True Stories***. To explain the heritage of this one last factor, we need not look back at a generation worth of Japanese film history nor even a decade worth of busy experimentation, but simply at a single day of unutterable tragedy.

The critical moment of transition is 1995. In that one year, the major Haunted School franchises all saw their theatrical debut: ***Haunted School***, ***Phantom of the Toilet***, ***Eko Eko Azaraku***, as well as the first adaptation of Koji Suzuki's ***Ring***. By 1998 all of these franchises had mutated into new forms. By the end of the decade, movies based on similar source material and including similar elements were treated with a different style compared to earlier incarnations. Compare the 1995 TV ***Ring*** to its 1998 version, or 1995's ***Phantom of the Toilet*** to its vastly more disturbing counterpart ***School Mystery*** in 1998, and it is easy to see that something critical had been changed in the formula.

1995, you see, was the year of Japan's 9-11.

On March 20, 1995, a religious cult called Aum Shinrikyo (Aum Supreme Truth) chose to celebrate their faith by murdering innocent people. Cultists released lethal sarin nerve gas in the Tokyo subways, immediately killing a dozen souls and leaving hundreds more wounded, brain damaged, or otherwise traumatized.

This was bad enough, but there was more. Police eventually

learned that Aum had previously gassed the city of Matsumoto in June the previous year, and had tried—unsuccessfully, thank the heavens—to unleash additional horrors on Tokyo in the form of biological plagues: botulism and anthrax. For a people already prone to wearing breathing masks and gloves in daily life, even the suggestion of such man-made pandemics cut chillingly close to the bone.

This is not to say that J-Horror emerged as a response to the tragedy, for this is obviously untrue. Much of the aesthetics of the movement predated the "Aum Affair," as did the writing of Koji Suzuki's novel *Ring*. And as we shall see later in this book (especially Chapters 8, 9, and 10), the principles of the genre took root in other cultures that had not experienced this trauma. However, what the events of March 20, 1995 did contribute to film history is easily understandable: audiences, already terrorized by real-world evil, found extra resonance in the works of J-Horror. Films like ***Ring*** spoke very loudly indeed to the Japanese nation in the years after the incident.

Horror movies of the past were built on a logical cause-and-effect sequence: if you do something risky, then bad things occur. Go into a haunted house, for example, and you get what you deserve. In J-Horror, that cycle is broken. In its place, ghosts are free to attack anybody at any time for no real reason. You can be minding your own business and find yourself targeted by some spectral grudge. You can be riding the subway and find yourself gassed by a maniac. Things can go wrong at any moment, without warning. Live with that.

"After the Sarin episode, the Japanese people knew that sudden unreasonable death could be a part of everyday life," Norio Tsuruta admits. "Even young people realized death could be imminent. Without this change in consciousness, I think J-Horror would not have caught on."

1. The word "kwaidan" is the same one that appears everywhere else in this book as "kaidan," and means "ghost story" or "ghost stories" (Japanese relies on context, not spelling, to indicate plurality). The standards by which Japanese words are converted into English transliterations changed over the years, such that the "w" is no longer used in such cases. This is the official English title for this movie, however, so we're stuck with the discrepancy.

Sources:

"Chilling Summer: In Japan, Summer is the Time for Ghosts," Trends in Japan, www.web-japan.org, October 15, 1999.

"School Ghost Stories," What's Cool in Japan, www.web-japan.org, July-September 1999.

Bickers, Amy, "Japan Reflects on 1995 Sarin Gas Terror Attack," Middle East News On line, November 4, 2001.
Hammond, Billy, "The School Restroom Ghost: Hanako-san," http://tanutech.com/japan/hanako.html, May, 2002.
Hiroaki, Hamasaki, "Prior to the Ring: The History of Shinrei-Mono," www.fjmovie.com/horror.
Kim, Mi-Hee, "Japanese Horror Flicks to Invade Korean Local Theaters," www.asiandb.com, February 21, 2001.
Schilling, Mark, "Contemporary Japanese Film," Weatherhill Inc., Trumbull, CT, 1999.
Tsuruta, Norio: personal correspondence 2005-2006.
Whipple, Charles T., "The Silencing of the Lambs," www.charlest.whipple.net/miyazaki.html, January 27, 1999.
www.sarudama.com.
Zahlten, Alex and Kimihiko Kata, "Interview with Norio Tsuruta," www.midnighteye.com, January 2006.

CHAPTER 4

JUNJI ITO WILL NOT DIE

My daughter is at that age when she's just about getting old enough to be immersed in all the "tween"-oriented programming and advertising that saturate our wildly oversexed culture, but still enough of an innocent child to not fully understand any of it. So, she talks about boyfriends and dates and relationships—all of the time—but as abstract concepts devoid of meaning. Eventually the time will come when she is old enough to get it, and when that adolescent day comes she'll be fully equipped with a ready vocabulary to handle it.

When that happens to girls, they already look like little women. Boys at that age are just ugly, distorted children. When boys start to abandon the "girls are gross" attitudes of childhood, they don't even quite look like the same species as girls of the same age—and they lack the half-decade or so that girls have spent in relationship prep. No wonder boys get intimidated by girls.

When he was a teenager, Junji Ito was scared of girls. Terrified. This was nothing unusual. The only thing unusual was Junji Ito himself.

One day, tragedy struck the school. A classmate—a girl—was killed in a car accident. Word spread, the class grieved. And it was at this moment, amidst all the sorrow, that Ito found himself wondering what would happen if the girl were to suddenly walk into the room. Here's everybody trying to process her death, and what if at that moment she came back as if nothing had happened? Wouldn't that be freaky?

As a teenager, Junji Ito was enthralled by the horror comics of the legendary Umezu Kazuo, and he dreamed of someday creating his own. But making a living drawing pictures of demons and ghosts is what you might call a long shot, so he went to dentistry school and got a good, stable, boring job as a dental technician.

Then, one day (one day in 1986, that is) a prize was offered for horror comics, and this prize was named in honor of Umezu. Ito entered this contest, and he won. Not just won, mind you, but one of the judges awarding him the top prize was none other than Umezu himself. It was not yet clear, but a torch had been passed.

His comic was published, first in a magazine and later as a freestanding book. After a few years, Ito was so successful as a published manga artist he was able to quit his day job and be the man he always dreamed of being. Which is just one of the many uplifting and inspirational stories about the good things that come to those who draw pictures of monsters.

The manga that launched Mr. Ito's storied career was a dark and tragic fable of young love gone very, very wrong. He had taken as his inspiration that awful day when his classmate had been killed, and told a story about what would have happened if indeed the dead girl had returned from the grave as if nothing had happened. This visual launching point allowed Ito to then focus on another painful memory of adolescence as his thematic base: his overwhelming terror of girls, embodied in the person of Miss Tomie Kawakami.

Eternally beautiful, utterly self-absorbed, Tomie is a man-eating bitch. You can recognize her by the distinctive mole beside her left eye, her bewitching sexual allure, and her curious ability to return unharmed from the grave, and if necessary regrow missing body parts. She has a voracious appetite to be loved and desired by others, but gives no love in return. She is everything Junji Ito feared about the opposite sex: selfish and self-centered; desirable yet unapproachable and cold; catty and jealous; needy and demanding. Tomie is an exaggeration of a teenage boy's misogyny: she's a sex object singularly obsessed with relationships who rejects desperate boys. Add to that the fact that she is a deathless monster with psychic powers and you've got serious bad news.

In her schoolgirl uniform, as an unavailable object of lust, she is like a Japanese model in "cosplay" porn. It's all a cocktease come-on, an act designed to sexually manipulate the men around her. Her beauty is all she has, and so she uses it ruthlessly to get what she wants: legions of horny men at her beck and call.

Such behavior is sure to provoke an extreme reaction, and because she taunts immature boys or sexually frustrated old men, that reaction is aggressively negative. This, too, is part of her plan. Her ultimate purpose is to get herself killed—in the most brutal way possible.

The Tomie of the manga is rapidly multiplying, since every body part can regenerate—even her blood has the power to reconstitute itself—so her habit of provoking people into killing her, and mutilating her corpse, can be seen as a (totally whack) reproductive strategy. One Tomie + one angry boy with an axe = 10 or more Tomies.

In the original comic, schoolgirl Tomie Kawakami inspires such profound jealousy and desire in the boys of her class, that they are driven mad. In sexual frustration and jealous anger, they hack her to pieces in a possessed rage. This is a group act: a crowd of kids collec-

THE MANY FACES OF TOMIE

There have been six actresses to date to have starred as Junji Ito's fabled teenage black widow (seven if you count the Tomie-esque performance by Mi-Jo Yun in the South Korean ***Secret Tears***, covered in Chapter 9). You can take for granted that all of these young ladies are "idols," whose primary line or work is selling sexy pinups and singing fluffy J-pop tunes. The most accomplished actress of the bunch is Miho Kanno, Junji Ito's handpicked choice for the 1998 maiden installment. Her career took off in 1995 with a turn in the first ***Eko Eko Azaraku*** film by Shimako Sato (see also Chapter 3). Following her work on ***Tomie***, Kanno starred in Masayuki Ochiai's ***The Hypnotist*** (see Chapter 7) and Takeshi Kitano's ***Dolls***. For ***Tomie: Replay***, Kanno was replaced by ***Suicide Club***'s Mai Hosho, née "Mai Kitamura." Takashi Shimizu recast the role with Miki Sakai in ***Tomie: Re-Birth***. Sakai is a very busy actress with a resume full of various TV and movie work, but prior to playing Tomie she had never done horror. She had, however, released three albums of her songs and two picture books worth of cheesecake shots, earning her own fan club "Mickey's Club." ***Forbidden Fruit*** showcased Nozomi Ando, star of the ***Last Alive*** TV series. For the two-header ***Tomie: Beginning***, Ataru Oikawa tapped Rio Matsumoto. Also sometimes credited as "Megumi," Matsumoto is a singer, pop idol, and anime voice artist who is in many ways a Japanese counterpart to Hilary Duff. For my money, though, the best Tomie was in the forgotten TV special, ***Tomie: Another Face***. Runa Nagai would go on to fame as the head of the Miniskirt Police on late night Japanese TV, and she uses that jailbait sex kitten act to great effect as Tomie. Nagai's Tomie is credibly a teenager, a world-weary woman, and an impish spirit of selfish evil, all at once.

tively murdering one of their own, scattering her body parts to conceal the crime. Tomie's misused friend and rival Tsukiko Iszumisawa witnesses the killing, and is next in line for the hacksaw treatment herself, only to experience something even more traumatic: Tomie regenerates from her severed body parts and starts the ugly cycle all over again.

Writer-director Ataru Oikawa admired the comic as a "fairy tale in bad taste" and aspired to make a moody, atmosphere-driven horror movie. Instead of the shock effects and gore that typified horror movies, Oikawa wanted to focus on recognizably human fears of growing up, the loss of innocence. A teenager is not just afraid of the opposite sex, but of the realization of mortality and the transition from a life of dependence to one of individual responsibility. "Even if there aren't monsters or ghosts, the worries and agonies are the great elements of horror," says Oikawa. "It shouldn't be the type of movie where people scream with fear. I didn't imagine that kind of horror movie. I wanted this to be more like a drama for youth."

It was a noble thought, and in the post-***Ring*** environment, as filmmakers rushed to make similarly themed and similarly restrained suspense thrillers, it was a savvy thought. Problem was, Ito's comic was a blood-drenched tale of repeated violence, severed heads, and barbarism. Oikawa decided that even though the comic could be seen as a sort of de facto storyboard, he preferred to work from a clean slate. Although he would seek Ito's input and approval, he would not feel beholden to the manga.

One of the principal questions to be answered in adapting the comic to the screen was the choice of actress to play Tomie. Junji Ito suggested (or demanded, take your pick) the lovely Miho Kanno, based on the evocative nature of her distinctive eyes. Ito provided a sketch of Tomie, and from it Kanno drew a mole onto her own face to match the drawing.

Despite the attention paid to selecting the right screen Tomie, Kanno does not show her face directly to the audience until nearly an hour into the 95-minute long movie. Oikawa, a protégé of Kiyoshi Kurosawa, adheres to Kurosawa's less-is-more aesthetic and keeps the audience at arm's length as long as possible. Oikawa lets suggestion and doubt carry the film forward in place of actual narrative development. It is a slow-burn kind of film, and not all audiences will have the patience to wait for the pay-off. Oikawa's ***Tomie*** is simply ponderous—a problem that would dog the series as a whole.

The screenplay borrows characters and situations from the stories "Photograph" and "Kiss" from Junji Ito's original manga, but not as a straightforward adaptation. Instead, the movie ***Tomie*** operates more or less as a sequel to the comic, picking up after the events of those two tales. Some reviewers have speculated that the filmmakers assumed the audience would already be familiar with the comic and approached their adaptation with that in mind. I doubt it: for one thing, even after the recent boom of Ito-adaptations, his books remain hard to find even in Japan. His fan base may be loyal in their intensity, but they are a vocal minority. The film is clearly aimed at a larger audience. The variations made to plot points or character details would only baffle viewers who were trying to understand the film solely as a follow-up to a pre-established storyline. In fact, viewers are destined to be baffled anyway, since the events of the film do not make sense without the context provided by the comic's story. Yet, over twenty minutes elapses before Oikawa gets around to explaining all that critical backstory. Instead, the movie ***Tomie*** reworks Ito's source material into a new form with a different intended effect.

Oikawa opens the picture with a startling and memorable image.

A young man with a bandaged face (Kenzi Mizuhashi) makes his way down a busy street, carrying a large plastic bag. A passerby bumps into him, tearing the bag. From the gap in the plastic stares a woman's eye!

This unhinged fellow rents a room directly below aspiring photographer Tsukiko Iszumsawa (Mami Nakamura), and nurses the severed head as it regrows a body... Tsukiko doesn't know any of this, but she's already having nightmares.

For three years, Tsukiko has suffered amnesia and insomnia following what she believes was a traffic accident. Hypnotherapist Dr. Hosono (J-Horror fave Yoriko Douguchi) tries to help Tsukiko recover those lost memories, but after a troubling visit from police detective Harada (Tomorowo Tamaguchi) she rethinks this strategy. Harada explains that Tsukiko was never in a car wreck at all: she was a witness to some horrifying crime so extreme she has suppressed all memory of it.

Seems that three years back, a schoolmate of Tsukiko's named Tomie Kawakami was brutally murdered, and in the aftermath of the killing her school ripped itself apart. Some of the students committed suicide, some were admitted to mental institutions, others disappeared without a trace. Harada is having a hard time with the case, because Tomie's body was never found, and he's desperate for a lead.

But wait, there's more! Harada has hit upon a number of identical past cases: dating back to the turn of the century, with the same basic facts over and over, *and in every instance the victim was a teenage girl named Tomie Kawakami*. Her destiny is to get herself hacked to bits, and then come back to get killed all over again. Harada has stumbled across a reverse serial killer scenario. Instead of a single killer using the same methods on various victims, here is a single victim repeatedly murdered in the exact same way by different killers. A serial killee, I guess you'd call it.

What will happen when Tsukiko's emotional defenses wear down and she finally remembers the dead, wet girl at the heart of the tale? How will she react when she learns Tomie is living right underneath her, already provoking Tsukiko's friends into acts of murder and self-destruction?

Compared to ***Ring***, ***Tomie*** is a more conventional horror film with a harder edge. It has nudity, gore, and sadism—not much, mind you, but some, and enough to undo Oikawa's ambition of grounding the horror exclusively in spooky atmospherics. More damning, the effects work behind such shocks as severed heads and boiled-up eyeballs are cheaply done and amateurish. The various Ito-inspired movies all struggle with the issue of gore: what might look disconcerting as a black-

and-white line drawing looks vastly more grisly when rendered with realistic-looking flesh and blood.

To his credit, Oikawa has paid attention to detail: keeping with the theme of dismemberment and beheading, cinematographers Akira Sakoh and Kazuhiro Suzuki frame many of the shots in such a way as to cut off the heads of the actors. And the theme song by the Japanese pop act World Famous is one of the most disturbing pieces of music in horror movie history. Most of the cast is excellent, with Kanno and Tamaguchi as particularly notable standouts, but Yoriko Douguchi's flat, distant performance pushes the viewer away. As hypnotherapist Dr. Hosono, she seems bored by the movie (and it is sometimes hard to blame her).

Tomie is an imperfect movie, with a variety of flaws, but it deserves respect as a pioneer of the Haunted School. Later J-Horror movies had the benefit of an established template, a genre complete with a proven commercial track record and a full set of visual and narrative ideas. But somebody had to go first. ***Ring*** and ***Tomie*** launched successful movie franchises almost from scratch and created the foundations for all that would come later. ***Tomie*** plays with many of the same ideas as ***Ring***: scary girls with flowing black hair, parenting gone wrong, a viral menace reproducing itself through its victims. But it hails from source material that predates Koji Suzuki's *Ring* novel, and treats these shared elements in substantially different ways. By doing so, ***Tomie*** helped reinforce these as crucial ingredients of the J-Horror formula.

As with ***Ring***, ***Tomie*** presents its monster as an expression of a social problem; since that social problem remains unaddressed the monster cannot be stopped. In this film, in the comics, and in all of the ***Tomie*** movies to come, parents hardly figure in the story at all. For the most part, the teenagers of the story exist in a separate all-teen universe of their own. What adults we do see are distant, ineffectual, and single, divorced, widowed, what have you. You will not find a single example of a complete, stable nuclear family in any of these movies.

The importance of this fact may be lost on most American viewers, who are increasingly accustomed to a society riven by divorce and unmarried parents. However, these phenomena are rare in Japan. The fractured, incomplete and ineffective families on display in the ***Tomie*** movies are a flashing red light to alert the attentive viewer of the real issues at the heart of this story.

The cultural pressure on mothers in Japan is intense. The school system for the entire country is run by a national ministry of education that establishes very high expectations of its students, and a rigorous system of tests to maintain it; in order to succeed in this high-pressure environment, children must be pushed to their very limits, and it is the mothers who fulfill this role. There is a term in Japan, a not entirely positive one: "kyoiku moms," or "education moms." These women micromanage their kids' lives—everything from arranging special tutors and consulting with teachers to sharpening their pencils for them and pouring them tea while they study. In order to lavish all the necessary time and attention on their children, kyoiku moms must quit their full-time jobs...but in order to pay for the expensive tutors and special classes, they must take on part-time jobs.

It is an enormous sacrifice. And it doesn't ease the psychological pressure for women to realize that they are charged with shuttling their children—especially their sons—into a job market that is largely closed to them personally. If their children falter or struggle at school, it is the mothers who take the blame, and may be socially ostracized. Don't look to the dads to help out—Japanese society expects nothing more from fathers than a steady paycheck (Koji Suzuki notwithstanding—see Chapter 2).

In olden times, the burden of parenting was something mothers could share with an extended family and a virtual family of friends and neighbors. But the old "it takes a village" idea works in a village but not so well in crowded cities where reliable neighbors are few and extended family is missing. In the 1960s, the Japanese coined the term "kagikko" to describe a situation Americans in the 1980s would call the "latchkey kid."

However, here's where it goes wrong: while it may be unfair and sexist to dump all the responsibility on mothers and expect them to carry it alone, it cannot even be done when mothers cannot as a practical matter be there to do it. The whole system of absent salaryman fathers and obsessive education moms is premised on solid, stable, well-paying jobs for the men. As the 20th century drew to a close, the job market started to shrivel and die. Fewer and fewer young men are finding the kind of jobs on which their fathers depended.

The Japanese government in 2005 studied its population trends and discovered to its horror that the average amount of money needed to raise a child was almost out of the reach of single-earner families. The only way a couple could afford to have a child was to have both parents working full time, at which point they no longer had time to give to their children. Add to that the dearth of affordable day care and an urban lifestyle that leaves parents to fend on their own.

Since Japan has a low divorce rate and frowns on out-of-wedlock births, the response to this situation has been simple: women are not getting married at all, or when they do they don't have kids. Thus, the

Japanese birth rate is too low to sustain its current population. Japan is shrinking.

We've strayed from ghosts and monsters, and I don't want to lose you, so let's sum up all this sociology in one easy-to-swallow sentence: Japanese women are tasked with maintaining the future of the Japanese race and continuing the historically high standards of achievement of its children, so once women refuse to surrender their own lives to that end you have a serious crisis on your hands.

It is a crisis few in Japan speak of openly. Occasionally there is an article or an op-ed piece decrying "radical feminism" for corrupting Japan's women, or denouncing the sexism of Japanese society for restricting women's roles unfairly, but few solutions are proposed, and nothing changes.

This brings us to manga. In the 1990s, manga constituted 40 percent of all Japanese publications; anthropologist Anne Allison called it "the national language of mass culture." She also noted that much of those graphic novels were misogynistic and sexually graphic. Even in children's cartoons it was common to find sexually suggestive material that in the United States might be reserved only for pornography. Throughout manga, she found consistent images of women being degraded, attacked, victimized, humiliated, and demonized. Despite the widespread popularity—the ubiquity—of manga, it is still not accepted as "normal" literature. As Junji Ito points out, "Although I believe it is not as bad as it is in America, when bizarre youth crimes occur in Japan, the blame always seems to fall on horror manga and video games... Horror manga aren't considered 'healthy.'"

In her study, "Permitted and Prohibited Desires," Anne Allison theorizes such anti-woman material was a safety valve: "[I]t helps to dissipate what might explode into hostility, rage, and frustration. In a society where there is so much expectation and pressure, this is where you turn for a momentary escape. But it's also understood that this is how it is bracketed. So in a sense, the way it operates is really quite conservative. To us, it seems radical and perverse and wild, but it is so conventionalized and relegated to these particular media that it hasn't really triggered radical acts. The question, of course, is what will happen as Japanese society changes. What will happen as more women enter the work force and occupy a traditionally male-dominated domain?"

Since horror manga and their cinematic cousins are ruminating on "women's issues" (even if not always in a good way), these formerly male-oriented forms of entertainment have found an unprecedented new popularity with girls. Indeed, the primary audience for J-Horror in Japan is teenage girls. Akiko Funatsu, the marketing genius behind some of J-Horror's biggest hits, marvels, "When we released ***Ring*** and ***Spiral*** in Japan, most of the audience were high school girls. For most horror movies, the audience is young males.

"I think we did a good promotion for ***Ring***," Funatsu continues. "That's how we reached our teenage-girl audience. We ran a lot of TV commercials and worked together with publishing companies. We ran several advertisements in women's and girls' magazines. I'll admit it's unusual that a horror movie can gain a majority female audience, but the main reason why this movie became so successful was because we were able to tap that audience."

Junji Ito elaborates, "The main readers of horror manga are teenage girls... I think that the 'desire to see something scary' is a kind of instinct to increase your power to resist the dangers or fears of things that might actually happen to you in the future. I think that people who have a high sense of anxiety and have a survival instinct like to read horror."

This is the mission of J-Horror. It is no accident that the filmmakers of the Haunted School return time and again to issues of parenting, and of evil schoolgirls, licentious women, and the like. Japanese society is at a moment of crisis where longstanding traditions of male-female roles are at odds with the modern economy. There is a growing quorum of voices criticizing those customs as chauvinistic, and increasingly the statistics prove them as flatly untenable. But few are talking openly or honestly about these wrenching, fundamental transitions. It is too painful. Modern Japanese women are making utterly legitimate choices that challenge the very future of what is considered Japanese culture. There's no way to talk about that kind of thing without raising emotions to a fever point.

So, instead of talking about it openly, these issues have been coded into a new context. Japanese pop culture has taken such concerns and used them as the understructure of seemingly escapist fantasy entertainment. J-Horror is most notable in this regard, and in ***Tomie*** some of the biggest fears of Japan can be safely confronted, hidden behind a false front of a scary girl who uses sex not to create babies but to advance her own selfish agenda.

Junji Ito was delighted with the film, and even appeared in a brief cameo. He had good reason to be happy—the enormous success of the movie (and its many sequels) gave him a prominence and a fame that a dozen years of hard work as an artist had never earned. In just over a year, he would enjoy an unprecedented surge in popularity, with two theatrical features and five made-for-TV movies based on his art appearing almost simultaneously.

"In the beginning it was like a dream that my comic was turned into a movie," says Ito. "Although I have been drawing comics, originally I was a movie buff." In addition to Ito's widely cited admiration for manga pioneer Kazuo Umezo, he also cites a healthy list of Western horror movies as inspirations. William Friedkin's ***The Exorcist***, Stanley Kubrick's ***The Shining***, the Gothic horrors of Hammer Studios' Terence Fisher, and Sam Raimi's ***Evil Dead*** trilogy all have claims on Ito's demented imagination.

"Tomie will not die," goes the tagline to the first flick, and what a fine promise for a movie franchise. In the years since Junji Ito first created the 1987 graphic novel, he invented enough continuing adventures for her to fill four complete free-standing books. At a press conference to promote the first movie, the filmmakers joked that they had launched a franchise that was sure to generate multiple sequels: "*Tomie 2, Tomie 3, Tomie 5, Tomie vs. Jason, Tomie vs. Freddy…*" All joking aside, they weren't far off in their estimates of how many sequels would come: six theatrical follow-ups and one made-for-TV edition to date.

After the first few chapters of the first ***Tomie*** manga, Ito abandoned all thoughts of a continuing storyline with recurring characters and instead opted for an episodic series of tales placing different manifestations of the deathless girl in wildly different settings and contexts. A wise strategy, it bequeathed to the ongoing movie cycle a freedom to reinvent itself with each movie, with no need to feel beholden to any particular cast members or story notions. While the makers of the ***Ring*** sequels struggled to think of logical extensions of the established story, the ***Tomie*** movies could enjoy total creative anarchy. If you are interested in ***Tomie***, you need not work your way through all seven in sequence: if you want, you could just grab ***Tomie: Replay*** and ***Tomie: Forbidden Fruit*** and be done with it.

In August of 1999, around the time that various efforts were being made to continue ***Ring*** (on TV, in theaters, and in South Korea), the first ***Tomie*** sequel made its appearance, not on movie screens but on video. Toei Studios and Kansai Television collaborated on ***Tomie: Another Face***, a direct-to-video quickie. Short on money, and with a trim 72-minute running time, this modest little production managed to upstage some of the more ambitious ***Tomie*** theatrical movies. The greatest flaw of the ***Tomie*** series is its leaden pace, which ***Another Face*** deftly avoids by taking its already short running time and chopping it up into three shorter vignettes.

The theatrical ***Tomie*** features make the mistake of taking Ito's short-n-sweet manga chapters and stretching them across a larger cinematic canvas. With the exception of ***Tomie: Forbidden Fruit***, they never succeed in embellishing the skimpy material enough to justify the running time. Instead they scatter a few good ideas across vast expanses of screen time, like a farmer planting just a handful of seeds in otherwise empty fields. The makers of ***Tomie: Another Face*** stayed true to Ito's spirit by eschewing any grand narrative for punchy little macabre treats, loosely linked.

Meanwhile, Daiei Studios was busy making ***Tomie: Replay***, the next theatrical film in the cycle. This sequel strayed far from Ito's storyline but stayed closer to his artwork, resulting in a more satisfying motion picture, released in 2000 as the bottom half of a double bill with another Junji Ito-inspired film, the superlative **Uzumaki**.

As the title ***Tomie: Replay*** implies, this is not so much ***Tomie 2*** as ***Tomie Take 2***, ***Tomie: Mulligan***, ***Tomie: Do-Over***. This is not a sequel in the commonly understood sense of the term: it does not in any way expect (or, for that matter, reward) previous knowledge of the character. You do not have to have seen the first film, or read the comic, since it is fully self-contained. Screenwriter Satoru Tamaki and director Fujiro Mitsuishi are primarily concerned with re-vamping ***Tomie*** from a fresh perspective. What the first film got wrong, they corrected—and while they were at it, they also made sure to fix what wasn't broke.

Whereas Oikawa had openly professed a desire to make a film that was disquieting rather than scream-out-loud-scary, Mitsuishi opts for the screams and loses the haunting aspects in the process. The result is zippier, faster paced, with one ooky creep-out after another in rapid succession, but lacking the human dimension that gave the first film its grounding. That is, unless you happen to be one of those people whose biggest problem in high school was being driven to psychotic obsession by an immortal beauty queen who can regrow body parts like a fungus. If that describes your greatest fear, this movie will speak deeply to you.

This is a more energetic and intense film than its predecessor. As it embraces its illogic and runs crazily on towards ever greater extremes, ***Tomie: Replay*** gets better and better. Since there are no answers to be had, why waste time looking for them?

Tomie: Replay has suggested gore aplenty—bodies hacked to pieces just out of view, a headless corpse walking around, a man beating his head to a bloody pulp against a stone wall—but overall the effect is more restrained than in the first film. In fact, the overall cinematic style is more conventional and direct: cinematographer Hideo Yamamoto does not "cut off" anyone's head with the camera, nor does the soundtrack worm its way into your nightmares the way ***Tomie***'s did.

By way of comparison, Oikawa's ***Tomie*** plays for about twenty confusing minutes before a character shows up to explain in a single wordy speech the premise of the story. Mitsuishi's version *shows* us that premise over the course of its first twenty minutes, with compelling images and little dialogue.

Tomie: Replay, like the first film, opens with a bang. A six-year-old girl is rushed into the ER with severe abdominal distress. Her swollen belly is pressing on her insides, but the doctors have never seen anything like it before. An ultrasound scan shows the presence of a second heartbeat coming from her stomach. The child can't be pregnant, can she? In fear, the surgeons slit open the bulge, only to be horrified by a grown woman's face staring cruelly out from behind the incision!

The surgeons keep the living disembodied head in a tank, where it regenerates a body and decides the time has come to be movin' on. The naked Tomie (played this time by Mai Hosho) latches onto a hospital intern named Takeshi (Masatoshi Matsuo), immediately setting to seducing and rejecting him.

Meanwhile, Takeshi's friend Fumihito (Yosuke Kubozuka) worries about his buddy's abrupt disappearance. He finds common cause with Yumi Morita (Sayaka Yamaguchi), whose father, the director of the hospital, has mysteriously vanished following that fateful night in the ER. Seems just about everyone on duty the night that girl was brought in has either quit or outright disappeared.

Yumi discovers her father's diary, which describes what happened *after* they extracted the disembodied yet living head of Tomie Kawakami... As she reads the journal, though, the increasingly frantic writing reveals the deteriorating psyche of the doctor as he discovers that some of Tomie's blood has gotten into his own bloodstream and taken control of his body.

Screenwriter Satoru Tamaki loves that journal trick, and recycled the idea almost note for note when he scripted ***Kakashi*** (another Junji Ito adaptation). Notably, the journal scene also appears in much the same form in the ***Ju-On*** films, just one of numerous moments in which ***Tomie: Replay*** channels Shimizu's films, which had themselves already been studiously pirating ideas off the ***Tomie*** mangas (see also Chapter 6).

One example of the ***Ju-On/Tomie*** connection concerns an aspect of the character that was glossed over by the first film: her ability to not just regenerate but multiply. Mitsuishi indulges the Fangoria set with a wild scene of one Tomie taunting and insulting a second, bodyless, Tomie head. In the comic, an army of Tomies descend on a town—the movies never go this far, but the video ***Ju-On 2*** cribbed the scene for its own purposes.

It should not surprise you then to learn that ***Ju-On*** wunderkind

Takashi Shimizu got his theatrical feature break at the helm of ***Tomie: Re-Birth*** in 2001. However, it is somewhat surprising, and sad, to note what a disappointment ***Tomie: Re-Birth*** is. Having proven himself the master of splintered, jigsaw-puzzle stories, he probably should have taken the cue from ***Tomie: Another Face*** and designed his entry as a collage of short stories. Instead, Shimizu is held back by a wooden screenplay by Yoshinobu Fujioka that makes even the leaden ***Tomie*** seem fast-paced.

Fujioka's story follows the established pattern in which no complete nuclear family is shown, just distant single mothers and teenagers raising themselves. The film begins with a familiar moment: an angry young man (Sho Oshinari, of ***Battle Royale 2***) killing his bitchy girlfriend Tomie Kawakami (Miki Sakai). His buddies arrive in time to help him bury the body in the woods, but they are gobsmacked when she later shows up, *ta daa!* at a party they're holding to help them forget their crime.

Something of a cat and mouse game ensues, as Tomie works her way through the men, one at a time, picking them off, while they in turn kill her repeatedly. Tomie has an edge in the game, since Hideo was dumb enough to mix some of her corpse's blood with the paint he used for her portrait: allowing her to regenerate a new body from the painting. She manages to kill Hideo, and enthrall his friend Shun (Masaya Kikawada, another ***Battle Royale 2*** veteran). When it comes to Takumi (Satoshi Tsumabuki, star of ***Sabu***), though, Tomie chooses a different tactic: she worms her way into his mousy girlfriend Hitomi (Kumiko Endo) and starts to possess the girl's body and mind.

In the finale, which borrows ideas from Ito's story "The Basin of the Waterfall," Hitomi/Tomie starts to divide into two bodies in a startling special effect that showcases a brand new method of reproduction for the character.

Throughout the film, Shimizu balances two competing aesthetics. As with the ***Ju-On*** films, he is keenly attentive to small details and imbues every little nuance with subtle menace. But opposing that minimalist sense of style, Shimizu also gleefully indulges in pushing certain ideas to their risible extremes, risking losing the audience to giggles. There are several shock scenes in ***Tomie: Re-Birth*** that seem more likely to induce laughter than screams.

For some time, Shimizu had been telling interviewers he wanted to make a comedy but felt typecast with horror. When he met his young actors and discovered they not only had not done horror movies before but were a little scared of the idea, he reassured them. "I told them it would be a dark comedy." Since both Shimizu and Junji Ito have expressed admiration for Sam Raimi's ***Evil Dead*** horror comedies, it seemed—on the face of it at least—a sensible idea.

This notion took hold deeply in the cast. In promotion for the film, the stars all repeated the mantra that ***Tomie: Re-Birth*** was a dark comedy. Miki Sakai, Tomie herself, said, "There are also some funny parts. I laughed at some parts." Kumiko Endo added, "Our director told us that horror movies are a mixture of funny parts and scary parts." Which would have been fine, if Yoshinobu Fujioka had provided such a mixture in the writing. Instead, Shimizu awkwardly pokes fun at his own scares and never quite hits the delicate balance he claimed for the film.

THE LONG HAIR OF DEATH

In one especially striking and successful moment, Tomie's hair comes to life by itself as a seething web of black fibers, pulsing and stretching. We have seen in many J-Horrors a recurring symbolism of long black hair as a portend of evil. Junji Ito often returned to such imagery in his manga, and this sequence in ***Tomie: Re-Birth*** pilfers directly from Ito's "Long Hair in the Attic," reprinted in the 2000 collection ***Flesh Colored Horror***.

Shimizu also felt he needed to change how Tomie was presented to the audience. The previous movies had emphasized her monstrousness. In order to distinguish his take on the character, he asked Miki Sakai to play her more human. Tomie would appear in more scenes, she would have more "normal" dialogue, and would at least appear more ordinary on the surface, with her supernatural side lurking underneath. To hint at that hidden monstrousness, Miki Sakai made a point of not blinking on camera. When asked about what made Tomie a monster, Shimizu responded, "She is a little masculine."

By that, I assume Shimizu was referring to Tomie's aggression and manipulation of others rather than her sexual leanings, but the next ***Tomie*** flick explored that suggestion more fully. ***Tomie: Saisuusho*** translates literally as ***Tomie: The Final Chapter***, but that is a misnomer since Ataru Oikawa later added two more sequels to the franchise. Instead, the official English title is ***Tomie: Forbidden Fruit***—a far more apt moniker for something that adds lesbianism and child sex to the formula.

This time around, returning screenwriter Yoshinobu Fujioka actually delivers the dark comedy that Takashi Shimizu promised. Unfortunately for us, director Shun Nakahara has not returned to the J-Horror genre for a follow-up, but his ***Tomie: Forbidden Fruit*** is so good it practically redeems the entire franchise in one fell swoop.

It begins with what seems for all the world like a recap of the finale from a previous movie, marking this as the most "sequelish" of the many sequels. In this flashback, we see a young man named Tajima hack Tomie to bits and then hang himself: a particularly unpleasant lovers' pact. His friend Kazu Hashimoto finds the bodies and is distraught because in one awful moment he has lost both his best friend and his one true love.

Leaping forward twenty-five years, we meet Kazu Hashimoto's nerdy, bookwormish daughter Tomie (named after his long dead object of love, and played by Aoi Miyazaki). She is perpetually bullied by a trio of haughty pretty girls, Japanese Heathers as it were. When Tomie Hashimoto makes friends with a mysterious new girl in town, Tomie Kawakami, it is a shock to Kazu (***Ichi the Killer***'s Jun Kunimura), who can't help but recognize the girl he saw killed a quarter of a century ago. Tomie K. nurtures a lesbian attraction for Tomie H. while separately trying to arouse the girl's father.

Her effect on the Hashimotos is palpable. Tomie H. blossoms into an unselfconscious young woman, her best qualities and inner strength brought out by Tomie K.'s influence. However, Kazu is all but ruined. He destroys his dead wife's shrine, rejects and almost kills his own daughter, and actively lusts after the teenage girl who taunts him with distant memories of his own bygone youth. He is driven to various crimes, including a profoundly violent attack on the three mean girls. His violent temper and frustrated sexual impulses lead him to carve up Tomie K. and dump her body in the river—where Tomie H. retrieves the severed head and starts to nurture it back to health while it regrows a body from its bloody stump.

This is where things start to get wacky. The final third veers dizzily into absurdist satire as Tomie H. carries the disembodied head of Tomie K. around in a duffel bag, as the two girls go on the town in search of cheap thrills and expensive caviar. In the end, it is in this wildly ridiculous sequence that the human dimension of ***Tomie: Forbidden Fruit*** comes through most clearly. Although Tomie K. maltreats Tomie H.—exploiting her as a sex toy, emotional punching bag, and gopher—there is a real friendship too. Tomie K. genuinely helps Tomie H. become a strong, stable young woman. For her part, Tomie H. is never thrown by finding her pal's living head and is happy to help nurse it back to health. That's all fine by her, maybe a bit weird, but nothing she can't accept in the name of friendship. What tears it is when Tomie K. treats her cruelly. Only then does Tomie H. call her a "bakemono" (monster). For Tomie K. there is no greater insult than being called a bakemono, and the only reason Tomie H. did so was not because the other girl has demonic powers but because her personality is so ugly.

Tomie K. is a bakemono because she's so utterly selfish.

All of this leads towards a finale that is one of the most touching in all J-Horror. In the span of a few short minutes, the film manages to cycle through practically every emotion a movie can elicit, one after another. Just as you start to get your breath back, it finishes off by hitting you with a moment of parental love and unselfish personal sacrifice that rejects all the cynicism and narcissism Tomie K. has been peddling throughout the movie. Not to give too much away, the climax recalls some of Hideo Nakata's works, such as ***Dark Water*** or his American ***The Ring Two***. But where Nakata saw such love as a maternal force, here the self-sacrifice comes from a single father, who (belatedly, and with great difficulty) lives up to his parental responsibility in a way that just might point the way out of Japan's looming crisis...

Tomie: Forbidden Fruit was a brilliant swan song to a hit-and-miss series, wrapping up the themes of Junji Ito's creation in a way that earned the alternate title "The Final Chapter." However, you can't keep a good monster down, so Tomie returned a few years later, as did Ataru Oikawa. By 2005, J-Horror was a booming industry with an international audience. If it has a spooky chick with long black hair in it, there was all but a guarantee it would find a DVD release in the United States—maybe not the same kind of profits as a big-budget Hollywood remake like ***The Ring*** or ***The Grudge***, but still a solid enough business model to justify cranking out as many J-Horrors as possible. So, Oikawa was brought back to revive the franchise he'd inaugurated, with an unusual near-double feature notion. On April 9, 2005, the Theater Ikebukuro in Tokyo would premiere ***Tomie: Beginning***, where it would run for a week; then, on April 16, it would be replaced by ***Tomie: Revenge*** for its week-long booking. The two films would be unrelated, with Rio Matsumoto and Anri Ban respectively assuming the title role.

Writing for the online magazine KFC Cinema, Alexis Glass speculated that the primary impulse behind having the Tomie cycle keep on keepin' on was to provide a platform for the ritual display of hot young Japanese actresses. Each new iteration gave the press an excuse to gush over the latest babe playing Tomie. "That is, after all, probably the biggest reason why ***Tomie*** movies keep on getting released," he laments, "while otherwise more desirable Junji Ito comics like ***Uzumaki*** only got one movie, and many of his other great stories get none."

This is not entirely true. The ***Tomie*** craze did open a market for Ito-adaptations that exploded in 2000. Ten years worth of his manga back-catalog were reissued as the 16-volume ***The Junji Ito Horror Manga Collection***, and just counting the year 2000 alone there were five made-for-television adaptations and two feature films of Ito's work.

BEGINNINGS AND ENDINGS

Six years out from the first ***Tomie*** and the casual observer could be forgiven for thinking the series had petered out. That last one had been called "The Final Chapter," hadn't it? Well, yes, but a name is but a name, and the world of Japanese horror franchises are replete with examples of producers giddily unconcerned with shoving a "Final Chapter" designation into ongoing cycles. The ***Tomie*** brand was a stolid enterprise: Ito had already published seemingly countless short stories in manga form, ripe for the taking, and all one needs to crank out a new ***Tomie*** flick is a ravishing young starlet willing to stick a mole on her eyelid.

The return of Ataru Oikawa in 2005 with a brace of pictures that serve as bookends to the series, harkening to its roots in Ito's manga, promised to reestablish the director as the creative force of the film versions.

Tomie: Beginning is just what the title says it is—a prequel, adapted faithfully from the original manga and concluding where the 1998 film begins. It is as if Oikawa listened to his critics and heeded their advice: if the 1998 film is awkwardly positioned as a sequel to a story the audience was unfamiliar with, well, here's the backstory; and if the 1998 film is a leaden-paced slog-fest, well, this one zips along at a trim 75 minutes. This much is true, yet Oikawa stumbles over what should be the gimme: without a reliable cast to give emotional weight to Ito's bizarre visions, ***Tomie: Beginning*** seems cheap, even amateurish, at times. Oikawa has assembled a nicely photogenic gaggle of fresh young faces but their inexperience shows at the wrong moments.

Oikawa's follow-up, ***Tomie: Revenge***, is superior, even if it too suffers from awkward performances at times. Adapted with less fidelity from Ito's manga of the same name, the story is sufficiently complicated to sustain the 75-minute running time with a genuine sense of mystery, even for longtime ***Tomie*** know-it-alls. ***Revenge*** has the most atmospheric style of any of Oikawa's entries, as well as real suspense, dry wit, and an odd post-9/11 awareness (there is a Japanese Department of Homeland Security with a special task squad attending to "Tomie Incidents" which they fear as a supernatural form of terrorism).

Whereas ***Beginning*** presents the gorgeous Rio Matsumoto as the original teenage seductress, ***Revenge*** brings in Anri Ban to take over the role. Between the two films, Oikawa spends a fair bit of time bringing rationality and science to bear on the question of understanding Tomie and how she does what she does. Where the previous films simply presented her as a fait accompli, a ready-made bakemono, here she is compared to both a virus and a planaria worm, by way of "explaining" why so many different actresses have played the same character over the years.

It is Oikawa's assertion that in the end, everyone becomes Tomie—her powers of possession and regeneration are mutations destined to triumph in a survival of the species. A harrowing thought indeed, and one that connects the ***Tomie*** series ever closer to the world of Sadako and her similar ambition.

Most of the direct-to-video entries were low-budget junk destined for obscurity: Zenboku Sato's ***Oshikiri***, Kenji Nakanishi's ***The Face Burglar*** and ***Gravemarker Town***, Kazuyuki Shibuya's ***Lovesick Dead***, even the anthology collection ***The Hanging Balloons*** with one episode by Takashi Shimizu.

Ito himself expressed gratitude and pride that his comics were being rendered into movies and openly acknowledged the debt he owed to Hideo Nakata for the opportunity. "The ***Ring*** movies, including the novels they were adapted from, are a major factor in the current horror boom. The movie adaptations of my manga also take after ***Ring***."

Yet for all the Junji Ito-mania of the millennium year, most are deservedly obscure. Only one of the direct-to-video Ito flicks from 2000 is worthy of being remembered, ***Nagai Yume*** ("Long Dream"). It was made by a singular weirdo named Higuchinsky. The fellow has a real name, Akihiro Higuchi, but he never uses it so just get used to seeing Higuchinsky all by itself on the title credits. And I do mean get used to seeing it, because this guy is a talent to reckon with.

Higuchinsky mounted ***Long Dream*** as an hour-long TV special, shot on video with a miserly budget, and gave it all the cinematic style of a lavish feature film. At times it plays like a long-lost color episode of ***The Outer Limits***, and at other times it feels like your own most vivid nightmares have been teased out of your subconscious and broadcast to the world.

The plot concerns a desperate man named Mukoda (Shuuji Kashiwabara) who checks himself into a hospital with a singular complaint: he suffers from "long dreams." He means this literally. The few hours while he sleeps feels to him like months, years, decades, centuries. "From my point of view, yesterday happened last year," he tells Dr. Kuroda (Masami Horiuchi). The good doc does some tests and discovers poor Mukoda is telling the truth. Each night's sleep is "longer" than the last, and it is taking a physical toll. Mukoda even starts mutating, his body transforming to keep pace with the eventual evolution of mankind, millenia in the future.

Down the hall, another patient (Tsugumi) starts fearing sleep because she believes she's being hunted by Death. When her doctors finally persuade her to sleep, she too starts to experience increasingly long dreams. Which means Mukoda's illness is contagious...or does it signal something even worse?

For something so modest in scope, ***Long Dream*** is a miracle of cinematic power and would be an impressive calling card for Higuchinsky if he hadn't upstaged it himself earlier that same year. The Ukrainian-born Akihiro Higuchi had gotten his start in music videos, his star rapidly rising through the early 1990s. In 1997 he was directing episodes of the TV series ***Misa the Dark Angel*** (see Chapter 3). Finally, in 2000, he got his feature film break, collaborating with Junji Ito on a theatrical rendition of ***Uzumaki***. Based on Ito's manga of the same name, it played as the top half of the double bill with ***Tomie: Replay***, released in February.

This bizarro concoction is a whack-ass masterpiece that is unique even by the already loony standards of Japanese pulp cinema. ***Uzumaki*** is without argument a superlative motion picture and one of the most astonishing accomplishments among all of the movies covered in this book. If you're reading this looking for recommendations of what to see next, drop this book immediately and run as fast as possible to the nearest video store and get yourself a copy. Every second you delay is a second of your life you've wasted. Having said that, I must admit ***Uzumaki*** is one of the strangest things you will ever see.

"I really wanted to make something like ***Star Wars***, but realized that because I'm Japanese, I should do something different," explains Higuchinsky. "This film is that product. It's as fantastic as ***Star Wars***, but it's very Japanese in everything from style to story to images."

The English title is ***The Spiral***, which is a poor translation of the word uzumaki, which is probably better rendered as "whirlpool" or "vortex." In any event, there is already a J-Horror called ***Spiral*** (see Chapter 2) and since ***Uzumaki*** is marketed on video in the United States under its Japanese name, I'll stick with that title here. The spiral of that title, though, is the "monster" of the piece. We're not talking about a literal monster, though, no ghosts or anything tangible. ***Uzumaki*** chronicles a small Japanese village that is besieged by a geometric concept.

I told you you've never seen anything like this.

Eriko Hatsune, one of several ***Long Dream*** cast members pulling double duty under Higuchinsky, stars as Kirie Goshima, a very ordinary teenage girl with ordinary teenage problems: the overwhelming academic pressures of Japan's high schools for one, and the awkward budding of adolescent sexuality for another. She and her childhood chum Yuichi (Fhi Fan) are finding their decade-long innocent friendship evolving into a more adult romance. But these workaday issues take a backseat to a completely unusual problem, unique to their backwater village of Kurouzu.

Shuichi's dad is first to succumb to the esoteric curse. He is gripped by an obsession with the spiral uzumaki pattern. Lucky for him, the uzumaki is everwhere: anything that can possibly kink itself into curlicues does so, even some things that probably can't.

Uzumaki: The Spiral

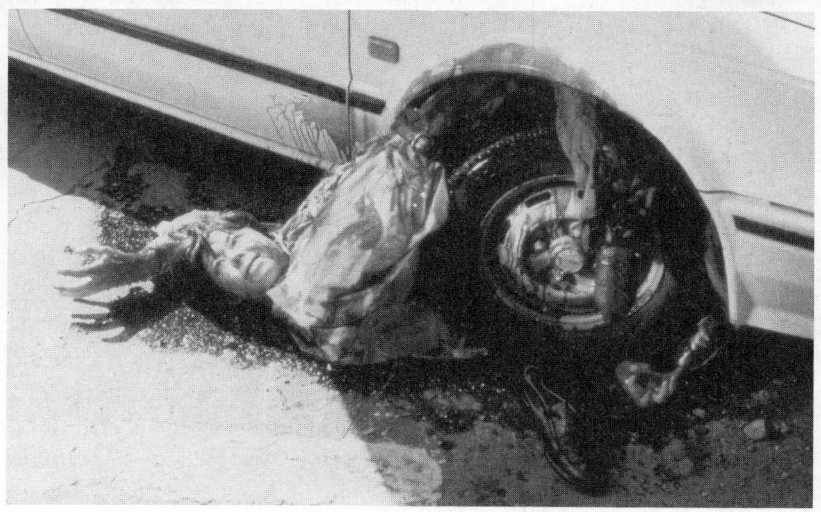

Kirie's papa is a pottery maker whose handcrafted art exhibits uzumakian whorls as a matter of course, and he is happy to accept a commission for spiral-themed dishes and bowls. It's worth noting that this fellow is two recurrent Ito-symbols in one: as a widower he is yet another single parent in Ito's pantheon, and he is also an artist. Throughout Ito's work we find artists of all media: photographers, painters, puppeteers, pottery makers... Like his focus on obsession, the repetition of artist characters was an aspect of his manga of which he was not consciously aware until a journalist asked him why he kept coming back to the same themes.

Obsession in Itopia is an extremely dangerous and self-destructive force. Shuichi's father cannot stop himself. It is not enough to collect helical knicknacks or steal coiling signs from local businesses, or even to eat curly food. He wants to become a spiral! And, with the help of a running washing machine and a death wish, this he finally accomplishes.

And if there is one thing spirals do well, it's spiral. The uzumaki obsession spreads. Shuichi's now-widowed mother becomes so afraid of twisty shapes she slices off the tips of her fingers to remove the offending spiral fingerprints. Once she learns that the inner ear is shaped like a corkscrew, she grabs the nearest poker and stabs it into her own head.

But spirals don't just grow inside the human body, but start to, well, spiral out of it as well, in grotesque inhuman growths extruding from the inhabitants of Kurouzu, a town spinning, slowly but inexorably, into a vortex of doom.

Ito has said that he always starts with a visual image and then builds a story around that picture, but when asked about ***Uzumaki*** he admitted the work came from a different kind of inspiration: "I was really just interested in making a story about people who lived in a traditional Japanese row-house and seeing what happened. I lived in a crowded row-house myself a long time ago, you know. If you live there, it can be hard to get along with your neighbors, so I started by wanting to draw a bunch of people living in that sort of place." As he started drawing the row-houses, he found himself drawing a long, long, long house that, in order to be as ridiculously long as possible yet still fit on the page, coiled in on itself into a spiral shape. And thus was ***Uzumaki*** born.

Higuchinsky gets everything right, in this the definitive Junji Ito movie. It is a visually exhausting and hypnotic experience. This isn't eye candy, it's eye heroin. And for all its darkness and morbidity, the film is also riven through with an acerbic wit. Higuchinsky has assembled an extraordinary cast of Japanocult performers. In addition to ***Long***

Dream double-dippers, he's cast Eun-Kyung Shin (star of ***The Ring Virus***, playing a reporter here as a clever in-joke) and Hinako Saeki (from that other ***Spiral*** movie back in 1998, as well as ***Godzilla, Mothra, King Ghidorah*** and ***Misa the Dark Angel***); Denden, Taro Suwa, and Asumi Miwa of Takashi Shimizu's original ***Ju-On*** videos join the venerable Ren Osugi, whose CV covers the bulk of Kiyoshi Kurosawa's and Takashi Miike's output, along with Hideo Nakata's ***Don't Look Up***. By cast alone, ***Uzumaki*** is all but a J-Horror family reunion.

The production was backed by Toyoyuki Yokohama's powerful Omega Project, a company that married Japanese and foreign monies to make J-Horrors for an international market. This was the same company behind Takashi Miike's globally popular hits ***Audition*** and ***Ichi the Killer***. With Omega Project behind it, ***Uzumaki*** won a limited run in San Francisco concurrent with its Japanese distribution.

"We wanted to create some buzz for the movie by simultaneously opening in the States. We were into the idea of opening in San Francisco, because of all the internet activity there," explains Omega's vice president Akiko Funatsu. "We showed ***Uzumaki*** in a very good theater, the Four Star. It turned out well. A writer from Variety saw the film there and he wrote about it for Variety, which is unusual for a very small Asian film which hasn't been presented at any international film festivals."

Unfortunately, despite this sudden multimedia celebration of all things Ito in 2000, as the 21st century proper got underway only the ***Tomie*** series continued. There was no ***Uzumaki*** sequel, and few efforts to get Ito's comics onto the big screen. Instead, the Ito craze returned to the unprestigious marginalia of low-budget direct-to-video releases, such as ***Marronnier*** (2002).

In 2001, Norio Tsuruta followed up his work on ***Ring 0: Birthday*** with the Ito adaptation ***Kakashi*** (which translates as "The Scarecrow," but the film is marketed in English speaking countries under the name ***Kakashi***). This haunting drama shares with ***Tomie: Replay*** the same screenwriter, and at times the same script. There are a great many critics—among them, virtually all of the J-Horror avatars whose research and advocacy informs this book—who find ***Kakashi*** irredeemably slow and boring. I respectfully disagree, and consider this elegiac tragedy one of the strongest and most accomplished movies in J-Horror, even if Tsuruta's approach represents the polar opposite of Higuchinsky's everything-plus-the-kitchen-sink excess.

Throughout his many comic books, Ito returned time and again to a handful of driving themes. Chief among them was the idea of a bizarre

MARRONNIER: THE DOLL-HORROR

In 2002, Junji Ito joined forces with multimedia artist Hideyuki Kobayashi for a self-financed amateur video adapting Ito's *Marronnier* to feature-length. The story concerns a mad puppeteer who kills women and waxifies their corpses so he can turn them into lifelike marionettes. Kobayashi wrote, directed, videotaped, and edited the thing, largely as a venue to showcase his own prodigious doll-making skills. Kobayashi built all the puppets for the movie, working from Ito's designs. Oh, and he also appears in the movie and did the music too. Although it doesn't specify in the credits, one imagines Kobayashi also cooked all the food for the cast and crew and maybe drove everybody home at night. Ito, who gets "Supervising Producer" credit and above-the-title identification, also got into the DIY spirit of things and appears, sort of as himself, in one clever cameo. The high point of the movie is a puppet show featuring an ***Uzumaki***-inspired Junji Ito doll with spirals for eyes. Unfortunately, that high point lasts for a few brief seconds, and the rest of the 80+ minutes are an exercise in sadistic misogyny. Kobayashi tosses a few J-Horror symbols at the viewer—a murky bathtub here, a cell phone there—but this is no J-Horror. It is a throwback to the crueler kind of horror movie dominant in Japan prior to ***Cure*** and ***Ring***. The plot samples from ***House of Wax*** and Edgar G. Ulmer's ***Bluebeard*** by way of ***Audition***, with gory effects and stage blood taking precedence over characterization or story. The whole thing is frenetic, frantic, and sloppy. If you have enjoyed the Junji Ito movies covered in the rest of this chapter and see this on your video store's shelf, be advised it is strong stuff that appeals to a completely different audience.

love triangle in which a supernatural being tries to wedge itself between a preexisting couple. That couple might be a pair of young lovers but could also be a parent-child relationship or a set of siblings. In those cases where the evil force interferes with a family relationship, the resulting jealousies and passions almost inevitably take on a whiff of incest. In ***Kakashi***, the lurking undercurrents of incest fuel the already incendiary love triangle.

Maho Nonami stars as Kaoru Yoshikawa, whose brother Tsuyoshi (Shunsuke Matsuoka) has suddenly and inexplicably gone missing. Her one clue as to her brother's fate is a curious love letter from one Izumi Miyamori (***Battle Royale***'s Kou Shibaski). There are two things wrong with this letter: for one, Kaoru didn't realize that Tsuyoshi had such strong feelings for Izumi, and for another, Izumi is dead. Hoping to clear things up, Kaoru travels to Izumi's remote rural village, Kozukata, in search of her brother. What she finds is a village full of suspicious weirdos warning her off, urging her to get out now or she won't be able to. No, scratch that: get out now, or she won't want to…

WELCOME TO KOZUKATA

The name Kozukata translates as something along the lines of "Whence Never to Return." The name comes from an old legend of Iwate where, the story goes, demons were exorcised and told "never to return." The Kakashi Festival happens annually in Yamagata between September 8 and 16. To my knowledge, though, the festival does not actually revive the dead.

It turns out, the little hamlet of Kozukata has a peculiar geographic feature: it coexists with the land of the dead. So, if you've lost someone close to you, it's just a simple matter of making a kakashi scarecrow and letting his or her deceased spirit reinhabit the body of straw and cloth. If that doesn't strike you as the best idea in the world, there's no place for you in Kozukata. There are only two types of people here: the reanimated scarecrow zombies, and the folks who love them. This town is packed with people who can't move on past their grief, who've chosen to remain forever frozen in their pasts, enthralled and perhaps enslaved by the memories of the lost.

Complicating matters, Izumi is one of those dead wet girls, who died angry and plans to return angrier. She killed herself in a suicidal rage, determined to return kakashi-style to wreak vengeance on the person she blames for her failed love life: Kaoru. What Kaoro can't bring herself to admit is, the ghost has a point. Kaoru did try to keep brother Tsuyoshi to herself, so much so that everybody mistakes the siblings for a couple. "We don't have parents, I am his only family," says Kaoru in an acknowledgement of yet another broken family in Itoville, but it seems Kaoru has done more for her brother than just replace his missing mother.

The film recalls ***The Wicker Man*** meets ***Deliverance*** meets ***Solaris***, but for all the wild ideas implicit in the plot, Tsuruta maintains a determinedly realist focus. Atmosphere is everything (and for this, Tsuruta owes a debt of thanks to cinematographer Wataru Kikuchi and composer Shinichiro Ogata). Tsuruta works his way through the story with careful deliberation, every frame of film exposed with absolute precision. Even the autumn leaves on the trees seem to have been directed, as if Tsuruta ordered the trees to change colors on cue.

Color matters, in ways Western viewers might miss. Early in the film, Kaoru comes across preparations for the annual kakashi festival, bedecked with bright crimson banners and pinwheels. She shudders. Red, in Japan, is the color of evil. Izumi committed suicide in a blazing red dress, which adorns her kakashi as well—the color was a statement of purpose. She wanted to call upon the evil gods to help her return as an angry ghost, a curse upon Kaoru (with her hair combed in front her face, too). Thanks to the vivid color of her garments, it's easy to spot her as she flits through the half-seen backgrounds of various shots, a bright red shadow of an increasingly dark world.

Ultimately, Izumi's plans for violent retribution get short-circuited by Tsuyoshi. The boy has become equally smitten by obsessive love, and with the aid of a little fire sees to it that he joins her in the afterlife (scarecrows do burn so well, what with all that dry straw). Here, Tsuruta ends his ominous tale on a final note of gloom: having found but again lost her brother, Kaoru realizes she too no longer wishes to move on with her life and opts to join the ranks of the walking-dead/dead-walking of Kozukata. She need never say goodbye to Tsuyoshi this way. The final image is seemingly upbeat and sunny, but can this possibly be a happy ending?

Ito said that his aim was to expose the horror hidden in the ordinary. Life may seem "normal" on the surface, but everyone has anecdotes of personal encounters with the strange or disturbing. The eerie and the ordinary go hand in hand.

"I just come up with ideas from my daily life," he has told interviewer Akiko Iwane. "An idea could come from something I hear on the radio. It's interesting to take things and look at them from a backwards perspective. I don't specifically try to depict horror, or to come up with ideas that will be horrific, specifically. If I think of something interesting, I'll go with it and maybe add the horror part in later. So, in my case, I don't really know what's considered scary."

Ito also says that his warped perspective on things is something he shares with his family.

"When I was a kid, my granddad had some experiences like that and he often told me about them," Ito remembers. "Nothing paranormal, but stories about collecting bodies that had been hit by trains and that sort of thing... Also stories about taking down the corpses of people who had hanged themselves. With slightly decayed bodies, when they'd try to pull them down sometimes there'd be this sliding sound and the insides would come out...just leaving the surface behind."

Ito also recalled a peculiar practical joke his mother once played. "During the war, when my mother worked at a factory, all the women slept together in a giant room. One night, my mother and two of her friends apparently walked around the room quietly and brushed the cheeks of the sleeping women, telling them later it was the work of a ghost. They never told anyone about it, so those women might be telling the ghost story to this day."

It would be apt if Ito's mother indeed had such an effect. Certainly her son has given millions of people around the world cause to feel the shiver of goosebumps, the chill of the night, the adumbrations of an ominous other world whose ghosts and bakemonos haunt us even in the most ordinary of places.

Sources:

"A Child-Rearing Environment," The Japan Times, September 5, 2005.
"Ghost Story Roundtable: An Interview with Junji Ito," Da Vinci Magazine, July 2003 (Vol. 10, no. 7, pp. 184-185).
"Ghost Story Roundtable: An Interview with Junji Ito," Da Vinci Magazine, July 2003 (Vol. 10, no. 7, pp. 184-185).
Booher, Bridget, "Discerning Cultural Questions: Journey Into Japan," www.dukemagazine.duke.edu.
Collingridge, Mandi Apple: "Tomie: Replay Review," www.mandiapple.com/snowblood, 2004.
Eaton, "Japan Research: Findings and Conclusions," www.ucf.k12.pa.us/~jeaton/JapanResearch.html.
Foutz, Scott David, "Kakashi Review," www.foutz.net, 2005.
Give a citation to the Marronnier DVD extras here.
Give citation to Tomie: Rebirth DVD extra from Toei Hotline here.
Glass, Alexis: "The Expanding Horror Influence of Junji Ito," www.kfccinema.com, January 6, 2002.
Glass, Alexis: "The Expanding Horror Influence of Junji Ito," www.kfccinema.com, January 6, 2002.
Interview with Junji Ito, www.j-popcinema.com/uzumaki
Interview with the Omega Project, www.j-popcinema.com/uzumaki
Ito, Junji: Tomie, Comics One, April 1, 2001.
Kim, Mi-hee, "Japanese Horror Flicks to Invade Korean Local Theaters," www.asiandb.com, February 21, 2001.
Sharp, Jasper: "Tomie Review," www.midnighteye.com, April 24, 2001.
Sharp, Jasper: "Tomie Review," www.midnighteye.com, April 24, 2001.
Tanaka, Yuko, "The Tenement Way of Life—Reflections on the Value of Person to Person Connection," Haikumania, www.cddc.vt.edu.
www.omega.co.jp
www.twitchfilm.net

CHAPTER 5

YOU ARE THE DISEASE AND KIYOSHI KUROSAWA IS THE CURE

One day, Japanese pulp cinema auteur Kiyoshi Kurosawa was watching TV. There as here, what bleeds leads, and the nightly news was a parade of horrors about the arrest of a murderer. The reporters shoved their mics in front of the perp's neighbors and asked all the familiar questions: What was he like? Did he act unusual? Did you ever suspect you were living next door to a monster? And there as here, the answers are always frustrating: he was just a nice, quiet man who never aroused any suspicions. He must have been a monster disguised as a man.

People around the world want to be able to explain away crime as something aberrant. The press tries to meet this need, to package the reporting of crime in ways that pit us versus them. But Kurosawa, an intelligent and cynical man who studied sociology before becoming a moviemaker, recognized these impulses as delusional. The murderer, his neighbors, his victims, the detectives who caught him, and the reporters who covered the tale are all made of the same stuff. Kurosawa saw the disquieting truth: anyone can be a monster. Even you.

This was in the mid 1990s, a period when the world's cinemas were clogged with serial killer dramas all hoping to be the next ***Silence of the Lambs***, or ***Se7en***. Or at least hitch a short ride on their coattails. Most remained just that—wanna bes, never weres, nots. This is the story of the film that did become the Next Big Thing, and along with Hideo Nakata's 1998 ***Ring***, invented J-Horror.

Kurosawa had spent most of the preceding fifteen years toiling in Japan's B-movie industry. The rules of the game were simple, if brutal. To make a living making movies in Japan, you had to make lots of movies, make them fast, and make them cheap. The theaters were dominated by American imports (if not for protectionist policies by Japan's exhibitors, there would be no room at all for domestic productions), so movies had to have a viable life on video. Certain genres became entrenched as the prevailing mode of commercial filmmaking: pornos, yakuza shoot 'em ups, and horror movies.

Kiyoshi Kurosawa was capable of playing this game very well. Low budgets didn't discourage him at all, and indeed he considered them something of an advantage: "I think when you very quickly churn out a screenplay and film it over the course of a few weeks and just complete the film very quickly, it may be a little slip-shod in technique, but I think you are able to retain a primitive strength of that uninhibited creative impulse," he told the website DVD Talk in 2005. When he was hired to direct ***Bright Future*** in 2003, the first thing he told producer Takashi Asai was, "I'll come in on time and on budget." Asai was a little taken aback by this promise: "A director who before saying I'll make a great film or a compelling film says, 'I'll come in on budget and schedule,' a director who announces this to the producer is either really great, or I don't know... I don't know really know what to make of it."

Furthermore, Kurosawa eagerly embraced genre limitations. "I am a genre director," he proudly announced to interviewer Tom Mes. In the documentary ***Ambiguous Future***, Kurosawa elaborated, "80 percent of my films are genre films. It's much easier for me to make a film within the context of genre, and to the extent that I'm an original thinker, my writing talents are better expressed through genre."

Kurosawa's first forays into cinema, back in his university days, were amateur 8mm movies. There were no rules, just imagination. His experiments ranged in length from ten minutes to an hour. But the more he studied filmmaking, the more he came to recognize the cold facts of professional reality: the things are made to be sold, and the industry expects them to be a certain predetermined length. "Whether a film portrays a single day of events or an epic story, it's the same length basically," he told Tablet Newspaper in 2003. "It's the genre approach to filmmaking that dictates that length... If you're going to somehow tell a story within 90 to 120 minutes, I think that the conventions of genre can be very helpful to you. Also, in the different ways that you tell a story, through the conventions of genre you can abbreviate unnecessary passages or emphasize others."

In short, Kurosawa was an almost ideal B-movie hack. He appreciated his boundaries and was willing, even enthusiastic, to work within them. Like American low-budget pioneers Edgar Ulmer or Roger Corman, he was prepared to use the seeming limitations of his circumstances to create personal works of art that could be profitably marketed.

But, that's not the whole story.

He embraced genre conventions in order to toy with them, to recombine them in new forms and at times undermine audience expectations. He specializes in highly commercial genres but does so with a distinctive aesthetic. His movies are arthouse cool, yet emotionally cold, cinematically precise (the camera moves as if controlled by factory robots), and are riven through with a martini-dry wit.

He had studied film theory under the legendary Shigehiko Hasumi, who believes strongly in the larger cultural importance of cinema beyond mere escapism—and as a trained sociologist, Kurosawa was in a position to wield his films as a tool of social commentary. Perhaps more importantly, Kurosawa was a serious movie buff whose extensive exploration of Western genre pictures not only gave him mastery of their filmic language, but an ability to cut and paste their techniques and ideas into his own work.

It's not really possible for me to describe Kurosawa's cinema with mere words. I can try—I will—but nevertheless I am at a loss to recreate for you the singular experience of his unique vision. You need to see it for yourself, and I hope that after reading this chapter you will be compelled to do just that.

By way of describing the indescribable, I can say this: Kurosawa's

THE USUAL SUSPECTS

Because Kiyoshi Kurosawa places such high demands on his actors yet is prepared to offer them little in the way of direction, he necessarily has come to rely on a select few performers who return, film after film, as his dependable stock company players. One of these stalwarts is the versatile Ms. Yuriko Douguchi. This remarkable actress began her collaboration with Kurosawa in 1985 on ***The Excitement of the Do-Re-Mi-Fa Girl***, appearing in a nightie while brandishing an AK-47. She acted alongside Kurosawa in his only onscreen dramatic role to date, the bizarre 1991 fantasy thriller ***Mikadroid***. Douguchi has since appeared in several Kurosawa movies, such as the ***Suit Yourself or Shoot Yourself*** series, ***License to Live***, ***Cure***, and ***Charisma***. Look for her also in the 1998 ***Tomie*** (see Chapter 4) and the original ***Ju-On*** video (see Chapter 6).

Another recurring face in Kurosawa-land is the extraordinary Ren Osugi, who also pops up in a huge number of the movies covered in this book. A favorite of both Kurosawa and Takashi Miike, Osugi's amazing list of credits includes ***Audition***, ***Non-Stop***, ***Shall We Dance?***, ***Don't Look Up***, ***Shikoku***, ***Uzumaki***, ***Crazy Lips***, ***MPD Psycho***, ***Dead or Alive***, ***Cure***, ***Séance***, ***Charisma***, and many, many more. If you watch a lot of J-Horror and don't learn to recognize his face, you aren't paying much attention.

Kurosawa has a conscientious dedication to bringing out the best from his actors. He tailors roles for specific stars during the writing, casts actors in roles that alternately rely on their established personas or allow them to stretch outside the boundaries of type-casting, and always begins his shoots with relatively minor scenes so that he can afford to experiment with their performances by offering strange, ambiguous, or arbitrary directions intended to provoke their own creativity.

peculiar gifts have been granted to others before him. There was a time, back in the late 1950s and 1960s in France, when a similar set of cultural influences and commercial restrictions produced a similar kind of filmmaking. Claude Chabrol, Jean-Luc Godard, François Truffaut and others of the French New Wave grew up gorged on American B-movies, rankled against the decaying and insular French film industry, and set about regurgitating those pop inspirations as personal—and often political—arthouse concoctions. It is as if the French New Wave skipped a few generations and leapt across Eurasia; Kiyoshi Kurosawa would have felt right at home alongside Godard and Chabrol.

This talent would ultimately serve him, and Japan's entire film world, in good stead. But first he would have to learn to control it, and for many years his greatest gifts would be a liability.

In 1980, still in college, he made a parody of gangster films called ***Shiragami Gakuen*** ("Vertigo College"), his first full-length 8mm production. It won a prize from the most prestigious forum for young independent filmmakers, the PIA Film Festival. This became his entry into the professional film world, and he took his now irrelevant sociology degree with him to become an assistant director. Within three years, his apprenticeship served, Kiyoshi Kurosawa was ready for the big leagues: directing ***Kandagawa Inran Senso*** ("Kandagawa Wars") for Nikkatsu Studios.

Which is pretty much the same thing as saying it was a porn film.

Nikkatsu existed primarily on the basis of a genre they perfected, affectionately called "Roman Porno," or Romantic Pornography. If you've read Chapter 2, you've already seen the role this genre played in the early career of Hideo Nakata. You can be sure it'll crop up again later in this book, too. Now, the whole point of pornography is the on-screen depiction of sex acts. In their book ***The Midnight Eye Guide to New Japanese Film***, Tom Mes and Jasper Sharp described some of the reasons Nikkatsu's producers were less than happy with ***Kandagawa Wars***: "[Kurosawa] frequently interrupted the all-important sex scenes with such images as the tribulations involved in crossing the river, the sudden appearance of a choir on the roof of one of the buildings, and the frequent quoting of film titles."

Neither party learned their lesson. Nikkatsu hired this temperamental artist to do another sex flick, ***Joshi Daisei: Hazukashii Seminar*** ("College Girl: Shameful Seminar"), and Kurosawa took the opportunity to continue challenging his limits. The studio brass refused to distribute the result.

"I thought I had fulfilled the porn aspect of the film," explained Kurosawa in his interview with DVD Talk, "but according to them what I didn't fulfill was the romance aspect of the film. I didn't have a love story storyline, which I completely ignored. Instead I chose to portray a university that was beset with various factions who were infighting amongst themselves. The studio decided that my film didn't qualify as romance porno and decided that they weren't going to release it. I said, in that case, let me buy it and release it myself."

Happy to get some cash instead of write off the whole thing, and still certain the movie was unmarketable, Nikkatsu agreed. Of course, the director didn't have enough money on his own to do this, and he turned to a consortium of established directors (the same ones he had apprenticed under) to invest in the idea. He then reshot portions of it and went back to the cutting room to make it even more of his own personal vision. Under the new title ***Doremifa Musume no Chi wa Sawagu*** ("The Excitement of the Do-Re-Mi-Fa Girl"), his revised version hit theaters in 1985, where it won over audiences with its bizarre imagery and irreverent attitude.

Kurosawa's resulting good press only stoked Nikkatsu's anger. How dare these upstart directors second-guess corporate decisions? How dare they challenge our authority over what movies should be made or shown?

Of course, if the studio didn't want to be shown up in this way, they could have avoided the dust-up by releasing the picture themselves, or less charitably, by simply not selling it back to Kurosawa in the first place. But there's no point arguing. Forget it, Kiyoshi, it's Nikkatsu-town.

Kurosawa was now effectively blacklisted in the Japanese film industry, and it would be several years before he would get another chance to direct. Eventually, the enormously powerful Juzo Itami asked Kurosawa to join him on a haunted house project called ***Sweet Home*** (the first example in Kurosawa's CV of a trend: using English titles instead of Japanese ones). Itami was a prominent actor and filmmaker, and he had a mind to produce a spooky chiller in the tradition of ***The Haunting*** or ***Poltergeist***. Since he intended to be onscreen in the thing, along with his wife Nobuko Miyamoto, he needed someone to direct. And, since Itami had been in the cast of ***The Excitement of the Do-Re-Mi-Fa Girl*** and had come to like and respect Kurosawa on that delirious project, he knew whom to call. In turn, Kurosawa called in Hollywood make-up god Dick Smith to handle the extensive special effects work.

Unlike Kurosawa's later J-Horror work, his earlier stuff like ***Sweet Home*** is obscure, hard to obtain even in Japan. If you do, someday, get a chance to see this, be prepared for a shock. Compared to the aloof, highly stylized abstraction of his more recent films, ***Sweet Home*** is a conventional, traditionalist work with its eye keenly on mimicking the dominant Hollywood style of horror.

It concerns a TV documentary crew that visits the abandoned mansion of famous painter Ichiro Mamiya, in hopes of discovering and restoring the vast mural he created there entitled "Home Sweet Home." The fact that the title of the movie omits one of the "homes" from the mural's name is a tip-off: this home isn't all there. It was the site of a family tragedy as Mamiya's child died in a horrible accident. Mrs. Mamiya, in her grief, went mad—and the spirit of a woman wronged is more powerful even than death. The lady Mamiya may be dead in body, but her angry ghost (face obscured, you guessed it, by her flowing black hair!) continues to haunt the premises.

Although the family tragedy, the dead child, and the ghostly woman all prefigure the trappings of J-Horror, this 1988 production has virtually no recognizable relationship to Kurosawa's later work. Think Lucio Fulci's ***House By The Cemetery*** with a Japanese cast and you're halfway there. During the film is a telling argument between the characters as to which of them holds final decision-making responsibility for the TV program they have come to make: the director, the producer, or the star. Meanwhile, behind the scenes, the very same argument was brewing between Kurosawa and his star.

Part of the disconnect between the tone of ***Sweet Home*** and, say, ***Pulse*** lies in the fact that ***Sweet Home*** is not a full-blooded Kurosawa picture. Itami considered Kurosawa a gun for hire, and after the director finished his work he was helpless to prevent his producer/star from reshooting and reediting the end result.

Helpless, that is, but not resigned. He chose the impolitic route of suing Itami—that is, suing the man who had been willing to break Nikkatsu's blacklisting efforts and give an undisciplined young man a second chance.

Kurosawa now went looking for a third chance.

He found it in the form of the bustling underworld of low, low-budget horror movies. Some of these things were TV productions (such as the ***Haunted School*** series, which is discussed at greater length in Chapter 3), some were direct-to-video (a.k.a. "v-cinema"), but all were fast, cheap, and out of control. It was in this world that Kurosawa thrived. He was surrounded by other misfits, outcasts, and nonconformists. And, more importantly, his whack-a-mole style suited horror filmmaking well. The formal experimentation that undermined the erotic quotient of his pink films served to enhance the tension and creepiness of his horror movies. Here, at last, was a venue within which to explore and tinker and innovate, while having a steady income and a constant supply of subjects. Over the next seven years, he would crank out seventeen B-movies: from slasher flicks like ***Door 3*** and ***The Guard From the Underground*** to yakuza actioners like the ***Suit Yourself or Shoot Yourself*** cycle.

"It's been very valuable for me to have the experience of making program pictures," offers Kurosawa. "Generally in that type of production environment, the subject and story are already fixed. Also you recreate the same type of film several times with only a slight difference. When the studio system existed, many directors went through that experience. Today, there is only v-cinema that can give you a similar experience."

That period of experimentation led to an apogee in 1997. Daiei Studios, once one of Japan's leading film companies, now struggling to reestablish itself after bankruptcy, contracted Kurosawa to handle a theatrical feature. It was still a shoestring sort of affair, but a bigger chunk of money than the director was used to in the v-cinema ghetto. Furthermore, it was a chance to write his own screenplay—something he had been largely denied in the past.

What he wrote, inspired by watching the television coverage of a killer being caught, fusing his familiar genre territories of crime and horror, was ***Cure***. Kurosawa says that with the likes of ***Se7en*** and ***The X-Files*** consciously on his mind, he felt a serial killer drama had obvious commercial prospects. There was also a stroke of genius at work; this would be no mere knock-off. Yes, he was starting with a tried and true formula, but in this case his habit of undercutting genre expectations would carry an added punch.

The premise is this: Tokyo is gripped by a wave of brutal killings. The victims are slaughtered in a ritualistic way, a huge X slashed through their necks. However, it is *not* the work of a serial killer, not in the traditional sense. Each murder is its own separate crime, each one committed by a different killer. The killers are just ordinary people, normal unassuming joes, who for no evident reason are suddenly seized by the impulse to kill whoever happens to be handy, and to do so with meticulous adherence to a grisly template that they can have no knowledge of. Each killer is caught, easily. Each killer confesses. But there is no connection between them, nor any connection between their victims. So what is the hidden link that explains the recurring pattern? Has crime become a disease, with murder itself spreading like a contagion?

It is this viral notion that gives ***Cure*** its distinctive slant. Like ***Ring***, which appeared in theaters almost exactly a year later, ***Cure*** reverberated powerfully in Japan, a crowded society increasingly threatened by pandemics both manmade and natural. In the aftermath of ***Cure***'s release, other Japanese directors would explore similar themes; the viral idea would become practically de rigueur for the genre. Masayuki Ochiai would all but remake ***Cure*** in his own idiom as ***The Hypnotist*** (see Chapter 7).

The title, rendered as the English word "Cure" without so much as a katakana transliteration, has a number of possible readings. An inveterate fan of American pulp movies with a penchant for quoting Western films, Kurosawa is almost certainly making a sly reference to Sylvester Stallone's famous quip from ***Cobra***: "You're the disease and I am the cure." But don't jump to any conclusions about who or what that cure might be, or the nature of the "disease," for that matter. As the bleak finale suggests, Kurosawa does not believe in tidy resolutions.

This is the common denominator of Kurosawa's films: he believes in questions, not answers. Between arch social satire and clinical observations of human misbehavior, his films posit that we can never fully know one another—but if you had to take a guess, chances are your fellow man is either already or about to be a murderer.

"Ideally speaking, a person should have an identity, but does anyone really have an established identity?" says Kurosawa. "Could a person say that he is this one single being and nothing will alter that no matter what? That's why the people we see in ***Cure***, including the main character, display different personalities as situations emerge. They're unlike the characters usually seen in films. They don't have clear-cut identities. They don't have easily discernable personalities. But from my point of view that's more natural as a human being."

Capturing that sense of human realism, even within the confines of an implausible or bizarre plotline, is one of Kurosawa's overriding objectives. "Well, it's about what I consider 'ordinary,'" he opines in the ***Ambiguous Future*** documentary. "I'm not sure if the word 'real' is what I'm getting at. In the simplest terms, it is what I think of as 'the real.' But the thing is, most people live their lives very ambiguously. You don't find Hollywood movie characters anywhere in real life."

The protagonist of ***Cure*** is Detective Takabe, played by Koji Yakusho. Yakusho is one of Japan's greatest living actors (see box) and this performance marked his first collaboration with Kurosawa. It earned him a Best Actor Award from the Japan Academy (an honor he has monopolized for nearly ten years running). Takabe struggles with his incomprehensible case by day, and goes to home to a mad wife by night. She is undergoing psychiatric treatment, but is deteriorating, and his selfless care for her is taking a severe toll on his own psyche. Something is going to crack.

The catalyst for Takabe's ruin is the enigmatic Kunihiko Mamiya (played to demented perfection by Masato Hagiwara, also seen in Hideo

MAN OF A THOUSAND HANDSOME FACES

"Generally, I am a director who does not do much directing," says Kurosawa, "but I do even less with Koji, because he knows very well what he should do."

In the seven years spanning ***Cure*** and ***Doppelganger***, Kiyoshi Kurosawa and Koji Yakusho worked together an amazing six times. "First of all, I think he is a great actor," Kurosawa told Midnight Eye's Tom Mes. "He can play any type of character. He can be a regular guy, but he can also become a monster, a person of whom you don't know what he's thinking. Secondly, he is the same age as me. So our points of view are alike. We're on the same level as human beings."

When pressed, Kurosawa admits to using Yakusho as something of an onscreen alter ego. For his part, the actor is mum on this point.

Born Koji Hashimoto, he was given his stage name by his acting teacher, Tatsuya Nakadai. He did not develop an interest in acting until relatively late, originally training in civil engineering. He has said that at the time he thought actors were "sissies." But when a colleague gave him tickets to a Maxim Gorky play, he found himself so overwhelmed by the performance that he radically changed gears in his life.

After years of stage plays and TV soap operas, Yakusho gradually built up a loyal fan base and a solid background of experience. In 1996 he played the lead in ***Shall We Dance?*** (Richard Gere took his role for the American remake) and won international stardom and his first Best Actor award from the Japan Academy. For the next decade he would dominate the awards shows and work with Japan's top directors. In addition to his body of work with Kurosawa, Yakusho also starred in Masato Harada's ***Bounce Ko Gals*** in 1997, appeared nude in Shohei Imamura's ***Warm Water Under a Red Bridge*** in 2002, and helped dub Steven Spielberg and Tom Hanks' ***Band of Brothers*** for Japanese audiences.

In 2004 he starred in ***University of Laughs***, an extraordinary comedy set in pre-WWII Japan with Yakusho playing a government censor whose attempts to suppress controversial material in a cut-rate farce causes him to morph into an increasingly politicized comedy writer himself. While it is commendable that the J-Horror boom has opened up opportunities for Japanese films to reach American audiences, it is a little sad that while anything remotely ghost-related gets a DVD release, a masterpiece like ***University of Laughs*** is unlikely to find American distribution.

Nevertheless, Yakusho is grateful that so many of his performances have reached audiences beyond Japan's shores. "When I come to think that those films in which I have appeared are now being shown in distant foreign countries, I feel very happy," says Yakusho. "One of the pleasures of appearing in films is that after the filming sessions are over, the films start 'walking by themselves' in various countries."

Nakata's ***Chaos***). Mamiya is an amnesiac lunatic wandering Tokyo in a daze, pestering everyone he meets with the same persistent question: "Who are you?" He remembers nothing of his self or his past and is never satisfied with the perfunctory answers he gets to his question. Everyone he meets identifies themselves by job title—I'm a doctor, I'm a cop—instead of indulging the soul-searching he seems to crave. There is also this: if Mr. Mamiya asks you who you are, then the next you know you'll be compelled to slash an X into somebody's chest. Somehow, he's part of this contagion. But is he its cause, or just one of its symptoms?

As an inveterate fan of Fritz Lang, Kurosawa surely knew of Lang's most enduring creation, the sinister Doctor Mabuse. In a cycle of noirish gothic thrillers, Fritz Lang's megalomaniacal fiend proved his hypnotic power and homicidal ideology could survive, and infect others, even after Mabuse's death. Mamiya seems to have picked up where Dr. Mabuse left off, a Johnny Murderseed who leaves a trail of death and suffering guaranteed to outlast the man who planted them.

"I really try to leave things as undefined as possible," boasts Kurosawa. And that lack of closure makes ***Cure*** one of the most disturbing movies you will ever see.

Although it was not a major commercial hit in Japan, it was something much more valuable: an international critical hit.

It is perhaps too easy to discount what that meant. In 1997, the Japanese film industry was in the process of renewal. It had been years since Japan had been a major player in the global film world. Back in the 1960s, Japan generated both mass-market commercial products and rarefied arthouse faves. Japanese cinema could be alternately cool, or chic, or slummy good fun. But the once proud studios fell into decline, the once fabled directors died or retired, and the industry collapsed in on itself. Through the 1980s and 90s, Japanese filmmakers had a hard enough time getting Japanese audiences to care about their films, much less the world.

Kiyoshi Kurosawa got the Western press, once again, interested in Japanese cinema. Almost for the first time since that other Kurosawa, Akira (no relation), got the foreign press all excited, the name Kurosawa was once again the big story. And then, a year later, Hideo Nakata bequeathed to his homeland the biggest global hit anyone had seen in a very long time.

Kurosawa was a little miffed that he hadn't been given the chance to make ***Ring*** himself. Its screenwriter, Hiroshi Takahashi, was an old friend of his. Takahashi and Kurosawa had been roommates back in college at the University of Rikkyo. That was back when Kiyoshi was tinkering with 8mm films, and together the two made a short film in that vein. They started cooking up a feature film idea, but fate took them in separate directions before anything came of it. Years later, Kurosawa and Takahashi were reunited on the various ***Haunted School*** TV specials, and it was here that Kurosawa also met and befriended Hideo Nakata. The year was 1997, and Kurosawa was on the cusp of his breakthrough hit ***Cure*** when he and Takahashi and Nakata were making ***Haunted School F***. This was an anthology project, comprising a collection of short horror movies. Kurosawa made one chapter, while Takahashi and Nakata made the other two—a critical pre-***Ring*** proving ground for the ideas they would soon perfect.

"In the end, Hideo Nakata inherited [***Ring***]. And had a lot of success," Kurosawa admits. "I am very happy for my friends, but I do feel some regret since I always wanted to make the film."

He did get his hand in, in a small but meaningful way. During the final act of ***Cure***, the detectives uncover a craggy old videotape copy of a scratchy old film record of a psychic experiment from the distant past, which they fear may relate somehow to their present difficulties. A similar scene, you may recall, figures prominently in ***Ring***. Nakata asked Kurosawa's advice on how to recreate the same profoundly unsettling effect.

When ***Ring*** started to rake in the cash for its makers, the rest of the industry scrambled to join the party. Kansai TV called Kurosawa to ask him to make a ghost-themed television movie, based on the book ***Séance on a Wet Afternoon***. Back in 1964, British filmmakers Bryan Forbes and Richard Attenborough had made a highly regarded adaptation. Kurosawa's would not be a remake in the normal sense; he was unaware of the earlier film and did not feel bound to be too faithful to the original story. In the spirit of collaboration, Hiroshi Takahashi gave permission to Kurosawa to poach some dialogue out of the original ***Ring*** screenplay, lines Takahashi cut from his script that his old pal wanted to borrow.

Séance, or as it is known in Japan, ***Kourei: Ushirowo Miruna*** ("Spiritualism: Don't Look Behind You"), takes the opposite creative path from ***Cure***. Whereas ***Cure*** started with the genre of detectives-versus-serial killers and gradually transformed it into a supernatural thriller, ***Séance*** sets up an unambiguously supernatural premise and twists itself into a suspenseful film noir that could easily have been penned by the likes of Patricia Highsmith or Cornell Woolrich.

"What interested me about the narrative story in the book," Kurosawa explains, "was that it featured a ghost, in other words a dead human being, as well as an average couple who had been living very normal lives who, in fact, became criminals."

Meet Mrs. Sato (Jun Fubuki), a medium. Yup, she sees dead people. Her gift is an intrusive, disruptive force that has all but denied her a normal existence. Life is dreadful, and she desperately craves either to be free of her power, or to see it bring her—just once—something other than pain. Her husband (the ubiquitous Koji Yakusho) is a professional sound effects man for a TV production company, and a mild-mannered, henpecked, unassuming man.

When a young child is kidnapped, the desperate cops turn to a psychic. Guess who.

Mrs. Sato does indeed know where the child is, but not because of any magical ability. Her husband had been out in the woods recording sounds one day when the child attempted to flee her captor and hid inside his trunk of equipment. Oblivious to her, he packed the box up and left it sealed in his garage, where the poor kid is now barely alive. Mrs. Sato discovers the girl, but instead of doing the right thing (i.e., call an ambulance, tell the police, return the child to her grieving family), she cooks up a cockamamie plan to keep the girl hidden until she can stage-manage "finding" her with her second sight and thereby become a rich and famous hero.

Unsurprisingly, the plan goes wrong fast. The Satos find themselves, not heroes, but unwitting murderers now obliged to sneak the child's body into the dark of night and bury it during a torrential rainstorm—a textbook Dead Wet Girl. What was that thing novelist Koji Suzuki once wrote about death + enclosed space + water = angry ghost? If there's one thing people inclined to visions of the dead should avoid, it's making angry ghosts.

Compared to the extremely male-dominated movies of his career, ***Séance*** is a J-Horror chick flick. Koji Yakusho's character is so passive as to be almost more of a ghost than the one that haunts him. Jun Fubuki takes the lead as the spiritualist, and her nuanced performance manages to upstage one of Japan's most accomplished and decorated thespians.

"I'm very interested in the position of men and women in Japanese society, especially concerning work and family," says Kurosawa, articulating the same themes that permeate the works of his J-Horror peers. "Men tend to be fortunate in the working world, while women are generally more bonded with their families. But things are changing and many women are reluctant to adopt these traditions and wind up alone and neglected."

When asked why Japanese ghosts are almost exclusively depicted as women or young girls, Kurosawa suggested, "It's a very male-dominated world, so the reason why ghosts tend to be female is that they are oppressed in life, they are more powerful in death, so they are able to avenge themselves once they are dead."

Compared to his earlier work with ghosts in ***Sweet Home***, ***Séance*** is a mature, self-confident movie that takes from past films only what it needs but stands firmly and idiosyncratically on its own. In a few years, Kurosawa had truly come into his own as a filmmaker. Even Kurosawa himself realized that ***Cure*** marked a point of bifurcation in his career. In fact, he now rejects his entire pre-***Cure*** back catalog as inferior, embryonic experiments. The past was just prologue.

Kurosawa was not the only one eager to forget the past. Nikkatsu, his erstwhile nemesis, suddenly came begging, asking one of Japan's now-hottest directors to make a TV movie for them. What a difference success makes. Kurosawa reached into his cupboard, pulled out a dusty script called ***Charisma***, and headed off into the woods with Koji Yakusho to make one of the strangest, most unclassifiable movies of all time. It is, to a certain extent, an unofficial sequel to ***Cure***, although one written nearly a decade previously.

In the late 1980s, during a time of intense public debate about environmental issues in Japan and during the early days of his fertile v-cinema period, Kiyoshi Kurosawa penned a screenplay for an allegorical horror/action/comedy absurdist thriller that twists Steven Spielberg's ***Raiders of the Lost Ark*** into an oblique drama about a killer tree. Got all that? When Kurosawa took his idea to the Sundance Institute's Screenwriters' Workshop, his fellow writers were equally puzzled.

He was at the time but the second Japanese filmmaker ever invited to the workshop. "It was a very precious and special time for me," he remembers. "It was my first exposure to the international film community." That exposure taught him an important lesson: the expectations of American audiences, and by extension the expectations of the film industry that caters to them, are very rigid.

"My understanding of American cinema is that the protagonist must be taking actions toward a clearly defined goal. In [***Charisma***], there are many moments where my protagonist has no goal. He is just existing. Many of the Americans there kept bothering me, kept saying 'What's going on with this character now? What's his intent? What's his motive?' And I would have to say, 'He doesn't have any intent. He's just being.'"

Kurosawa left Utah with a stronger, punchier script (which he continued to improve over the next seven years), but the other writers insisted what he had wasn't, you know, a movie.

The experience of developing the project with an international—

Western—group of collaborators persuaded Kiyoshi that, perhaps, he could work in Hollywood after all. But he also realized ***Charisma*** could not be made there, at least not the way he wanted to make it. Only in Japan would he find sufficient creative freedom to ignore, or contravene, audience expectations. When Nikkatsu finally gave him the chance to make the thing, he knew the time was right—even if he would have to compromise some of his vision to conform to the tight budget. It had been written with an eye to being made in Italy, or some other foreign landscape, but the money only permitted him to travel to the outskirts of Tokyo—places like Yamanashi and Shizuoka. Familiar ground, but the movie he made there would be anything but.

Yakusho again plays a detective, a burn-out who could easily be a reprise of his role from ***Cure***. This guy has a new name (Goro Yabuike) and an off-screen family (or so the dialogue tells us, they seem to have no real value to his character), while his deteriorated psychology connects powerfully with his earlier performance. He is sent to negotiate a hostage situation but screws it up because he sympathizes equally with both victim and villain. He vainly hopes to save each of them, but saves neither, and leaves the force in disgrace.

Seeking solitude in the deep forest, Yabuike finds his old problems reflected back at him in the form of a rare tree called "Charisma." Nobody's quite sure about the actual botanical name for the thing, since it may be a unique breed or some kind of mutant, but the moniker Charisma fits it well. This is one compelling, seductive tree. It is also, as far as the plant world goes, a stone cold killer. This tree sucks the life from all other plants to nourish itself.

Yabuike realizes that the plant world and human society follow the same ruthless rules. Survival is just another word for murder; every living thing thrives at the expense of some other living thing. But ***Charisma*** demonstrates the danger when that awful balance of survival tips too far in one individual's direction. "If you had to choose between one special tree or the whole forest, which would you choose?" he anguishes.

The weird thing about his dilemma is that it isn't even his. Yabuike is supposed to be on "vacation." The fate of Charisma is being fought by other forces: a lady ecologist who figures the only way to save the ecosystem is to kill the tree, a corrupt Environmental Protection agent who wants to sell the rare organism for a fortune, and an escaped mental patient determined to save his beloved tree at all costs.

Mi obsession es su obession, in Kurosawa's world. Just by getting to know people with especially pronounced fixations you will start to share their passion and carry on their mission after their death. In ***Cure***,

Mamiya's peculiar homicide-by-proxy obsession could infect other people who simply had the bad luck to try to carry on a conversation with him; in ***Charisma***, the insane passion of young Kiriyama (played by Hiroyuki Ikeuchi) is equally catching.

Charisma the tree survives because of its human defenders, the Renfields to its Dracula (I did say Kiriyama was a mental patient, didn't I?), each one inexplicably picking up the torch from the last in return for no obvious reward. And Yabuike is next in line to be the tree's Renfield.

In his long brown duster coat and reticent manner, Koji Yakusho channels the spirit of Clint Eastwood, from his spaghetti western days, as the wild card in this epic struggle, with everyone waiting to see when he will make his move, and on whose side he will ultimately stand.

When Yabuike finally decides whose side he's on—everybody's!—he makes the same fatal mistake as before. In a conflict between the selfish individual and the good of society at large, trying to help both is the same thing as helping the selfish individual. Charisma represents a kill-or-be-killed, every-tree-for-himself philosophy that threatens the world. In his search for that magical third path where everybody lives, Yabuike dooms us all.

If Kiriyama is Renfield, and the scrawny more-dead-than-alive tree is Dracula, then the Van Helsing of the woods is Dr. Jinbo (played by Yoriko Douguchi, another of Kurosawa's stock players). Her determination to euthanize the forest in order to remove Charisma's poisonous influence is endangered by the actions of corrupt forest ranger Nakasone (played by the venerable Ren Osugi, see box "Bright Future").

In the end, however, this breakdown of the various characters' conflicts with one another is but guesswork on my part. Kurosawa's aesthetic rejects the idea that we can ever really know one another. He can show us what his characters do, but it is up to the viewer to deduce why. He shoots his movies from a distance, both emotional and visual. Close-ups are rare, and characters are often seen from the back, or in shadow.

"It is my opinion that directors these days use way too many close-ups of human faces. It is true that close-ups of the face are extremely effective in revealing the psychology of the character, what he's feeling," says Kurosawa. But for a man who doesn't have much patience for trying to reveal his characters' psychologies, this is a useless approach. So he turns instead to long shots that reveal the action as a whole, each scene rendered as if it were on a stage and we were in a theater audience.

He maintains this aloof stance even for action scenes. In watching him work on the set, one is struck by how much time and attention is

BRIGHT FUTURE

Kiyoshi Kurosawa's films often ruminate on the ambiguities and fungibilities of individual identity: which is just a highfalutin way of saying that in a crowded, conformist, communal society such as Japan, a unique individual identity is a rare and precious commodity. You may think you have a unique set of experiences, desires, and fears, but any day somebody else could just co-opt them and live your life for you, or at least a part of it. In films like ***Cure*** and ***Doppelganger***, he expresses such notions through crime thrillers in which the murderous instinct and the actual murderous act might happen to reside in two separate bodies. Kurosawa continues to play with this theme in ***Bright Future*** but with some interesting variations. Using a technique familiar from ***Doppelganger***, Kurosawa fragments the frame into sections, imposing gaps into the cinematic space between characters that serves to visually highlight the arbitrary distinction between one character and another.

In an interview with Tom Mes of the website Midnight Eye, Kurosawa admitted he thought of ***Bright Future*** as a "monster movie." But this is not a genre piece in the traditional sense, and it marks a step away from the J-Horror movies that have been the mainstay of his recent career; it's also a leap from Kurosawa's comfort zone in that it notably lacks Koji Yakusho, the superb actor who has been Jimmy Stewart to Kurosawa's Hitchcock.

Instead, Tadanobu Asano and Jo Odagiri star as a pair of listless twenty-something slackers adrift in a world they care nothing about. One day, for no good reason, Nimura (Odagiri) decides to mercilessly slaughter his boss' family, but arrives at the house to find his roommate Mamoru (Asano) has already done it. So while Mamoru heads off to death row in Nimura's place, Nimura takes Mamoru's place, adopted by Mamoru's bereaved father, and determined to carry out his friend's mission in his stead: acclimating a poisonous jellyfish to fresh water and then releasing it into Tokyo Bay (more of Kurosawa's familiar treatment of personality as a germ that can be passed between characters).

While the various characters swap identities, family roles, and crimes as casually as they might borrow one another's clothing, other themes begin to emerge in the margins of the story. If Kurosawa's remark about monster movies means anything, it is that we should be primed as viewers to see the symbolism of the story, to see its hidden layers. It is a cautionary fable about trying to take a misfit organism into an inhospitable environment, and what chaos can result from letting the creature loose before it is ready to function in its alien home. And I'm not talking about the jellyfish here.

Bright Future is an understated drama, full of the director's characteristic quirky black humor and some carefully crafted visuals. Like his other films, the direction is quiet and spartan, allowing the camera to sit unmoving at a distance from the actors as if each scene is a little filmed play.

It is a technique that defies conventional wisdom about what audiences expect from movies these days and demands a great deal from the actors themselves. It says a lot about Kurosawa's skill as a director that he can pull such warm performances from young actors whose roles have been written so abstractly.

During pre-production, Kurosawa found himself working with a team of producers who were unfamiliar with his working methods and eager to push him into new ground. Typically, Kurosawa refuses to spend much time working with his actors before a shoot because he fears that they will ask him pesky questions about their characters' motivations. "I hate that," he says. Oftentimes, even Kurosawa, the writer-director of his films, doesn't know why the characters he invented do the things he thought of them to do—and while he can fob off actors' queries on the set with vague "I dunno" answers, he knows he can't get away with that kind of trick if he's asked months ahead of time, "Why does my character do this?" To his dismay, his producers Takashi Asai and Harumi Noshita didn't let him off the hook, and insisted on a rehearsal period. To his relief, his cast—Tadanobu Asano, Jo Odagiri, and Tatsuya Fuji—were content with his screenplay and never asked for more.

When all was said and done, even the cast and crew admitted they were not 100% sure what the movie was about. Harumi Noshita conceded that her star director was an enigma, and "emotionally reticent." When even Japanese people start calling you distant, that's saying something.

As with his past films, ***Bright Future*** had its own bright future at international film festivals, but the programmers at Cannes balked at its original 114-minute running time. So, Kurosawa returned to the editing room to craft a shorter version for international sales. He managed to shear a full twenty minutes off and decided that the Cannes cut was his own preferred edition. It was a rare instance when the "Director's Cut" was shorter than the theatrical edition, but Kurosawa especially liked how the tighter cut was punchier, and it must be said, substantially more oblique and harder to understand.

paid to special effects artists and stuntmen for movies that, in their final form onscreen, do not feel graphic or violent at all. Charisma is packed with brutality and aggression, but even as we watch the slaughter unfold we are left, as always, to conjure up our emotional reactions on our own.

"My approach as a filmmaker is that whether it's a scene of violence or a conversation or a meal, I want to shoot it the same way. In that sense, I don't employ special techniques for introducing violence. I have no interest in portraying violence as being a different or separate part of any other scene that's been on."

Running underneath the violence, the allegorical discussions of moral principles and ecological concerns, and the abstract invocations of Hollywood thrillers, is a razor-sharp comic timing that makes some of the most cruel moments funny and horrifying all at once.

Although his Sundance experience cautioned him against getting hopes up too high, after the success of ***Cure*** Kurosawa wanted to keep all doors open. Nikkatsu was paying for a TV movie, but he shot ***Charisma*** on film in a widescreen format so that, in case any film festivals were interested, he would have something classy to show them. The strategy paid off.

As Kurosawa's star rose higher and his prominence as a leading figure in Japanese cinema grew, ***Charisma*** joined ***Cure*** in finding fascinated audiences around the world. Interviewed for the American DVD release, the famously self-deprecating Kurosawa offered such anti-promotional sentiments as "If you ask me what's good about this film I can't say."

In the final scene of ***Charisma***, Yakusho's character Yabuike realizes that the world as he knew it has succumbed to some unutterable apocalypse—possibly the run-amok consequences of Charisma's me-first agenda. In his next film, a true theatrical feature and a prestige production with twice the budget of ***Cure***, he lets us see that apocalyptic horror up close.

A rarity in Kurosawa's recent work, ***Kairo*** has no onscreen English title. Some J-Horror fans took to calling it "Circuit" before it appeared on U.S. shores, but in the last days of 2005 it finally showed up in American theaters (in advance of its impending Hollywood revamp) as ***Pulse***.

Before I go any further, let me say that ***Pulse*** is one of the most unsettling and haunting movies I have ever seen. See it just once and you'll never be able to look at an ordinary grease stain again without having nightmares. If you're reading this book, then ***Pulse*** is your kind of movie.

The plot is almost too simple to be worth synopsizing. I could boil it down to a high-concept pitch for you: *ghosts on the internet!* However, that might give the wrong idea. Most of the times Western filmmakers have tried to make computers seem scary the results have been risible. Think ***The Net***, or ***Fear.com***, or ***Cry Wolf***. Kurosawa's ***Pulse*** steers wide of the silly, offering a sober and ominous vision of a world enough like our own to be very, very scary.

After a tantalizing vision of Koji Yakusho in the opening sequence (he barely appears in the film, and probably consummated his involvement in the picture over a lunch break from some other job), the focus of the film shifts to a trio of teenagers, each one a stranger to the others, but whose fates will soon intertwine. Michi (Kumiko Aso) grieves the sudden and unexpected suicide of her friend, baffled at what unknown anguish could have driven him so far into despair. Elsewhere in the city, a young man named Kawashima (Haruhiko Kato) makes his first foray into cyberspace. Where most newbies are confronted by pop-ups, viruses, email scams, and buggy software, Kawashima's biggest headache is a pesky web site offering/threatening an opportunity to meet real ghosts. It would be easy to shrug the thing off as a hoax, except that a) the webcam views of ghosts it presents sure seem convincing and b) the computer has started acting possessed. Looking for answers, he turns to the school's computer lab run by Harue (Aso Koyuki). She has a goth's fixation on death, a geek's love of technology, and a spiritualist's urge to use the one to explore the other.

As the unexplained mysteries start to pile up, we in the audience start to realize what the heroes do not yet want to accept: they are each confronting the same phenomenon from a different perspective. What haunts one, haunts them all—and so the doom of any one of them will set the dominoes crashing to doom everyone.

The key to the riddle lies in a place forebodingly called "The Forbidden Room." In an abandoned building, a place rejected by the rest of society, is a room walled off with red electrical tape. Well, the place is "forbidden" for a reason.

Abandoned buildings figure prominently in Kurosawa's films. If you spend a lot of time watching J-Horror generally, you're likely to come away with the impression that Japan consists almost exclusively of schools and hospitals. But if you narrow your attention to the works of Kurosawa, you'll conclude Japan is blanketed by disused hotels, rundown factories, decrepit shacks, and other cast-off architecture. For a man whose cinema is replete with misfits, losers, outcasts, and weirdos it is only natural that his landscapes would reflect the same sense of outsiderdom.

The urban wasteland of junked buildings also highlights the sense that Tokyo's famously crowded confines are a conundrum: a place where people are packed together but also kept apart. Kurosawa is concerned with the space between, the wasted space as a symbol of disconnection. "One of the major themes of my films is individual life in the metropolis called Tokyo. I'm not sure how this plays out in the U.S., but what we have in Tokyo is individual human beings living completely cut off from traditional, regional communities that had supported them in the past. The theme is that of a human being, isolated amidst a huge aggregation of people and information systems, but the individual remains entirely alone within this metropolis."

In Harue's lab, a grad student has set up a graphic representation of this very idea. Tiny dots roam across the computer screen, simultaneously attracted and repulsed by one another. Blips on a screen, held in an orbit that keeps each one single—and in this she sees her own life, desperately lonely.

Where Western stabs at similar concepts involve evil, menacing technology, the computers in ***Pulse*** are not malevolent. They are simply tools, just like in real life, through which people can connect with one another virtually while remaining physically apart. Like Harue's dots, the World Wide Web is a network of people whose act of connection also keeps them separate, and it is this very separation that threatens them as the world of the dead starts to intrude into this one.

Pulse is arguably Kurosawa's most approachable, conventional recent work. From a straightforward "horror"-themed musical score by Takefumi Haketo to gritty, chiaroscuro cinematography by Junichiro Hayashi (who previously photographed ***Charisma*** for Kurosawa, not to mention both the 1998 ***Ring*** and 2000's ***Dark Water***), ***Pulse*** announces its genre without equivocation. In one of its most astonishing scenes, we witness a suicide in what appears to be a single take as a woman walks up a ledge and throws her body to the street below. In fact, a little professional stunt work, safety nets, and CGI tinkering enabled such a shot to be done without actually requiring the actress to kill herself, but even if you know the trick the scene is jaw-dropping. The special-effects heavy climax leads up to a final coda that references classic old-school Japanese end-of-the-world movies such as ***The Last War*** (1961) and Kinji Fukasaku's ***Virus*** (1980). Like ***Invasion of the Body Snatchers***, ***Pulse*** finds its heroes picked off one by one, as everyone succumbs to the horror, leaving just one survivor—but how long can she hope to hold out? Ever since the menacing clouds of the final shot of ***Ring***, J-Horror movies have felt it incumbent upon them to conclude with some kind of scorched-earth, everybody's-doomed punch line, but ***Pulse***'s finale manages to one-up them all.

When DVD Talk's James Shapiro told Kurosawa that ***Pulse*** was "one of the scariest movies I have ever seen," the director was pleasantly surprised. "It makes me very happy to hear someone from the United States say that they find my film very scary, but at the same time it feels a little strange because the ghost in ***Pulse*** does almost nothing. It's basically an inactive ghost. To me, I find a ghost who does nothing to be terrifying, but my understanding of many American scary films such as ***Alien*** or films about pathological killers is that what is considered scary in the States is something that attacks us. The ghost in ***Pulse*** doesn't really do that."

Nevertheless, as ***Pulse*** made its way through international film festivals, it did scare American viewers—among them, Wes Craven.

Kairo (*“Pulse”*) *poster*

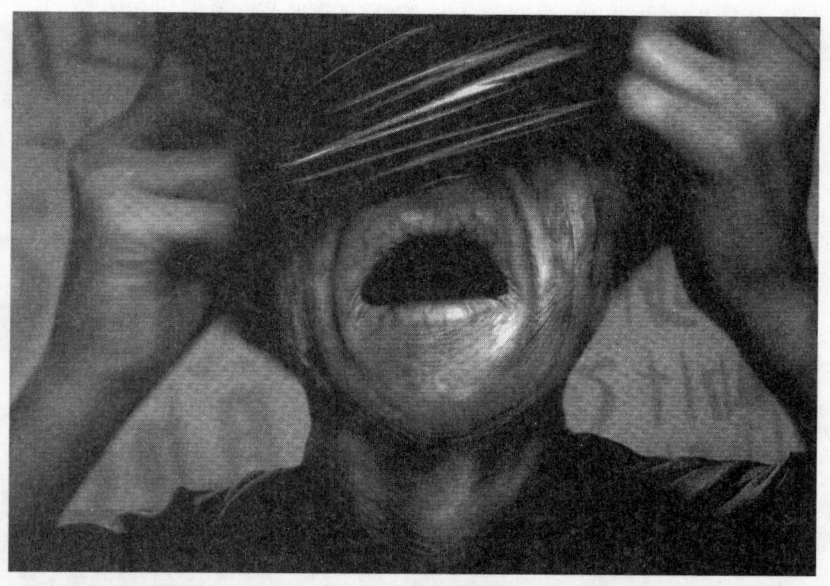

From the film

The man behind Freddie Kruger and the ***Scream*** cycle immediately asked for remake rights. Miramax bought the property for him, and Kurosawa found himself in Hollywood, at long last, to help usher the ***Pulse*** remake through the development process. This was 2001, before Dreamworks' cover version of ***The Ring***, so the appeal of J-Horror in the States was still untested. Craven and Miramax's Weinstein brothers loved ***Pulse***'s easily expressed "ghosts on the internet" hook, though.

Kurosawa was already obliged to be in America to help promote the U.S. release of ***Cure*** and to appear at various arthouse retrospectives of his recent hits. For a while, Miramax considered allowing Kurosawa to direct the American rendition, but then Wes Craven started making noise about wanting it for himself, and Kurosawa was shoved aside. Craven eventually let go, but by this time Kurosawa had returned to Japan, frustrated. He had spent almost all of 2001 in America, having made neither a film in Hollywood nor in Japan. Only after a wave of Americanized J-Horror interpretations became box office hits would ***Pulse*** come off the back burner (turn to Chapter 10 for more).

In 2003, Kurosawa returned with a vengeance, with two extraordinary productions appearing almost simultaneously. With the nightmare visions of ***Pulse***, Kurosawa had perhaps gone as far as one possibly could into darkness and cynicism; the one-two punch of ***Doppelganger*** and ***Bright Future*** took his art in new, more hopeful directions.

In the case of ***Bright Future***, a pair of producers who had never before worked with Kurosawa wanted to hire him for a project explicitly intended to push his boundaries and explore new territory. The result, an odd drama about a man who raises a killer jellyfish, found appreciative audiences at Cannes and gave the filmmaker a chance to emerge from the bleakness of ***Pulse***. "Even though there are many negative elements in the film, in the end it becomes positive, just like the jellyfish that emerge from dark water. The audience wonders how they can find positivity amidst all this darkness, which is exactly what I wanted them to feel… This is the difference with the other films, and so my message at the end is 'Let's live in society and head for the future without giving up hope.'"

Doppelganger (like ***Cure***, the original print doesn't even bother with a Japanese transliteration) reunites the director with Koji Yakusho for another supernatural story. In ***Séance***, the notion of a doppelganger had been first introduced as a ghostly apparition of one's self that foretells death. In the opening sequence of ***Doppelganger***, this is exactly what happens to a young man: he appears twice over, with the ghost self consuming his real one. The doppelganger effect is apparently a viral phenomenon in which if you encounter someone else's duplicate, it is likely to trigger the appearance of your own. The doubles tend to be mischievous, selfish manifestations of their originals' personalities. We've already seen, especially in ***Cure*** and ***Charisma***, how selfishness is itself a contagion. The arrogance of the doppelgangers spreads egotism like a plague...to an extent.

You see, ***Doppelganger*** is unlike ***Cure*** in that it is wickedly funny. Razor-sharp comic timing and a palpable sense of the absurd have always been hallmarks of Kurosawa's movies—even ***Pulse*** has its comic moments. ***Doppelganger*** merely pushes that comic element out front.

The main joke of the film is that we can't actually tell Koji Yakusho's "real" self from his double. This time, Yakusho plays a brilliant inventor whose past successes have now run up against the scientific equivalent of writer's block. The R&D company that writes his paychecks expects him to design an artificial body for paralyzed people (a sort of Dalek-wheelchair thing that is, in every possible way, ridiculous). Unable to find that spark of genius on which his future depends, the man's psyche splits in two: one, a meek, mousy, "good" self, and the other an aggressive, selfish, sexualized "id." But both are him, and the differences between these two personalities are so slight that it is all but impossible to tell them apart.

This inevitably leads some critics to think Kurosawa is using his inscrutable characters to create specific social commentary.

"Probably not because I studied sociology at university," the director cautions, "but because I watched so many films and those are the elements from the films that I have seen... [E]ssentially most of the knowledge that I have comes from films and then I take that and combine them with what I have seen and observed through the years, things that I have been thinking about. And in fact making a film is my chance, my outlet for a lot of those thoughts to be expressed."

For Kurosawa, it is essential that these expressions take place within film because of its unique role as a communal cultural experience. What makes cinema special as an art form is its theatrical exhibition, where audiences from all ages and walks of life gather in the dark to experience something together. "Films are that place where we have no choice but to acknowledge our own identities in a social context. That's what I call film," he explains. "If you only watch at home, you only know your own reactions."

In the films of Kiyoshi Kurosawa, identity is a mutable, fungible, tradable commodity that slips from one person to another as easily and unintentionally as when one person's yawning triggers a wave of yawns in his fellows. What you are, I could be, whether I mean to or not. And in the dark, in the theater, the crowds sit and watch his movies. Crowds of Japanese people, Americans, French, movie critics and academic theorists, genre buffs, you name it—and all of us, whatever differences we may think we see between us, are enthralled alike.

"Do you belong, or are you alone? Film is the place you discover that."

Sources:

"Ambiguous Future," DVD extra on "Bright Future," DVD edition from Palm Pictures.

Estigarribia, Diana: "Reeling: J-Horror," Entertainment Geekly, www.entertainment-geekly.com, June 7, 2002.

Interview with Kiyoshi Kurosawa, "Charisma," DVD edition from Home Vision.

Interview with Kiyoshi Kurosawa, "Cure," DVD edition from Home Vision.

Interview with Kiyoshi Kurosawa, www.filmforce.ign.com.

Interview with Kiyoshi Kurosawa, www.midnighteye.com/interviews/kiyoshi_kurosawa.shtml

Interview with Koji Yakusho, "My 40s" Magazine, April 2003, www.pymmik.com.

Mes, Tom and Jasper Sharp: "The Midnight Eye Guide to New Japanese Film," Stone Bridge Press, Berkeley, California, 2005.

Schilling, Mark: "Contemporary Japanese Film," Weatherhill, New York, 1999.

Sperling, Seana, "Interview with Kiyoshi Kurosawa," Acid Logic, October 16, 2003.

www.projecta.net/kurosawa.html

CHAPTER 6

A GHOST IS BORN

There is a moment towards the end of Takashi Shimizu's 2000 direct-to-video quickie ***Ju-On*** that is, quite simply, one of the scariest things ever filmed. The scene itself liberally borrows imagery from William Friedkin's ***The Excorcist***, and if you really wanted to quibble you could say little of what happens in the film makes much sense. But it's awfully hard to complain when you're screaming your fool head off. This scene is, it must also be said, the capper to a long series of astonishing scares, one of them literally jaw-droppingly shocking.

Ju-On snuck out on video during a fallow period for J-Horror. The Japanese film industry was resigning itself to the conclusion that the post-***Ring*** boom had played itself out. ***Ju-On*** was shot on digital video by an essentially novice writer-director, marketed directly to true believers. It was to be a quick cash-in and nothing more.

Except…it was extraordinarily good.

Like ***Ring*** before it, ***Ju-On*** was passed from fan to fan. Word of mouth spread: "You gotta see this."

Eventually one of the tapes was handed to Sam Raimi, of ***Spider-Man*** fame. He was so overwhelmed, he decided to produce an American remake. Because he respected the original as a unique horror masterpiece showcasing the visionary mind of a genuine cinematic talent, he opted not to tamper with the winning formula. Instead, Raimi hired Shimizu to remake his own film. Shimizu was allowed to shoot in Japan, with American movie stars joining Japanese actors in a film that is substantially in Japanese, with subtitles. The biggest difference between the Japanese ***Ju-On*** and the "American" ***The Grudge*** is that the one produced by Sam Raimi cost more.

But by that point, Shimizu had already directed a total of four Japanese ***Ju-On*** installments, graduating the series from the shot-on-video ghetto to serious theatrical feature. It had reversed the fortunes of the J-Horror genre, joining ***Ring*** as one of the biggest J-Horror series. The American ***The Grudge*** and the American remake of ***Ring*** are the two most successful horror remakes in Hollywood history. As I write this, Shimizu has contributed films to two other major J-Horror franchises and directed stunning free-standing thrillers; he has two more ***Grudge*** entries in the works.

In short, it is virtually impossible to overstate the importance of

GHOST DESCENDING A STAIRCASE

As the first ***Ju-On*** video spirals towards its conclusion, the ghostly Kayako comes crawling down the stairs to menace poor schoolteacher Kobayashi, and the viewer can't help but react (between terrified screams), "Somebody's been watching ***The Exorcist***." There is no denying that Kayako's spider-crawl down the stairs (repeated in 2003's ***Ju-On: The Grudge*** and 2004's ***The Grudge***) looks very much like Linda Blair's unusual method of locomotion in the revamped reissue of William Friedkin's ***The Exorcist*** (1973). Between 1998 and 2000, the recut version of ***The Exorcist*** toured Europe and the U.S. Although it did not appear in Japanese theaters until well after the first two ***Ju-On*** videos were finished, it's not hard to imagine that jet-setting Hiroshi Takahashi and Kiyoshi Kurosawa caught one of the screenings of the new edition of Friedkin's classic and brought back some inspiration for Shimizu. With its subliminal, barely perceived flashes of horrific visions and its fear of evil children, ***The Exorcist*** shares much with the ***Ju-On*** series. It is also worth pointing out, however, that Kayako's descent also echoes the emergence of Sadako from the TV at the climax of the 1998 ***Ring***—an image Hiroshi Takahashi was directly involved in creating. For his part, Shimizu credits the scene to his own childhood fear of stairs!

Takashi Shimizu in the establishment of J-Horror as an internationally profitable genre and a serious art movement within Japanese cinema. And if the movies themselves warn against the potential tragedies of being in the wrong place at the wrong time, Shimizu's personal career trajectory speaks to the advantages of being in the right place at the right time.

Shimizu started out as so many young people do, dreaming impossible dreams of making his mark as a celebrity director. He had been studying drama and art but dropped out of school to work at a movie theater, writing screenplays in his spare time for projects he hoped one day to make. By 1998, he had a day job as assistant director for film and video productions. At night, he studied film production at the Film School of Tokyo. As luck would have it, his teachers included Kiyoshi Kurosawa and Hiroshi Takahashi. In case you've turned directly to this chapter without reading the previous chapters, here's what you need to know: Kurosawa was a critic's darling whose arthouse horrors such as ***Cure*** (1997) had won international acclaim and established much of the artistic foundation of the Haunted School; Takahashi was the screenwriter behind ***Don't Look Up*** (1996), ***Ring*** (1998), ***Ring 2*** (1999), and ***Ring 0*** (2000).

One of Kurosawa's assignments for his film class was to write and direct an original, three-minute short. Shimizu made his scary, which in other circumstances might have marginalized his efforts. But Kurosawa and Takahashi were serious about horror and eager to see it taken seriously by others. Shimizu's student film caught their eye.

This is what is called "a good career move." Having the patronage of powerful figures in the industry can only help.

Sure enough, Kurosawa recommended Shimizu to the folks at Kansai TV, where Takahashi was working on a TV-movie called ***Gakkou no Kaidan G***, or "School Ghost Story G." Yup, this was the television spin-off of ***Gakkou no Kaidan*** a.k.a. ***The Haunted School*** (see Chapter 3). Shimizu explains, "The G is supposed to mean 'Great,'" and shrugs, "Maybe the producer came up with the title to compete with ***Dragon Ball Z***."

The project was an anthology of ghost stories, and Shimizu scripted several thirty-minute segments. Despite Kurosawa's recommendation, the producers had little confidence in a young, inexperienced, untested newbie. They ditched Shimizu's suggestions and asked instead if he would make two three-minute pieces. "I wondered, how can I scare the audience in so short a time?" recalls Shimizu.

He needn't have worried.

The first of the two segments, "4444444444," finds a high school student discovering an abandoned cell phone, ringing. The caller ID displays the unlikely number 4444444444. In Japan, the number 4 is like the number 13 here, a superstitious omen. The number 4, spoken in Japanese, is a homonym for "death," you see. As if this weren't creepy enough, when the kid answers the phone, all he hears on the other end of the line is a cat meowing. He thinks it must be a prank, but every time he hangs up the phone rings again, just to meow at him.

"Are you watching me?" he demands, and is surprised to hear a human voice answer, "Yes." He

THE BLACK CAT

You can always tell when little Toshio Saeki is nearby, from the curious meowing of his ghostly familiar, a black cat. From Toshio's very first appearance in ***Haunted School G***, the boy's spirit associates with a ghostly black cat. He meows, and seems at times to transform into the shape of a cat. Yet the symbolism of black cats as harbingers of supernatural terror is Western, not something familiar to Japanese. The color black has ominous connotations, as the color of death, but the black cat of the ***Ju-On*** movies is not a reference to Western superstitions. Instead, it is a reference to Shimizu's own love of cats. "I personally love black cats," explains the filmmaker, "but I'm a single guy and I'm always working so I can't have one now. So I have a lot of black cat figurines and things that I collect."

turns to see, beside him, a child. Naked, his skin pale from decay, black blood oozing from his mouth...

In the second clip, "In a Corner," two high school girls are caring for the class pet, a rabbit. One girl leaves for a moment, and returns to find her friend and the animal brutally slaughtered. From the woods comes the attacker. It is a woman, but not human. She is dressed in a nightgown, her hair flowing in front of her face. she crawls like an animal. The remaining girl braces herself for the inevitable...

These two episodes of ***Haunted School G*** are, for all intents and purposes, the starting point of ***Ju-On***. Although not yet identified by name, these two ghosts are Kayako and Toshio Saeki, the mother-son team who haunt the ***Ju-On*** series. In fact, it is actress Takako Fuji as Kayako, the mama ghost, making her first appearance in a role she has played in every version of ***Ju-On*** yet made (Takashi Shimizu was obliged to recast Toshio from time to time as the various child actors grew too old for the part).

The characters of Kayako and Toshio are dissociated from context in these two short films. While it would be easy to cut these scenes

CURSES AND GRUDGES

When Takashi Shimizu set out to expand his two short films into the first video feature, he initially planned to call it ***4444444444***, the same title as the first short. As the project evolved, he cooked up a better title: ***Ju On Rei***, which fused the kanji ideograms for "curse," "grudge," and "ghost." Eventually he decided that amounted to overkill, and discarded the "Rei" part; the producers of the ***Ju-Rei*** series cribbed the abandoned title along with Shimizu's other leavings for their exercise in plagiarism, as discussed elsewhere in this chapter. The term "Ju-On" is a made-up word meaning "Cursed Grudge." When the 2003 theatrical feature of ***Ju-On*** was distributed overseas, the first in the series to get international attention, the producers translated the title as ***Ju-On: The Grudge***. Later, as Western fans discovered the existence of the earlier video versions, some started to identify them as ***Ju-On: The Curse*** as an easy way to distinguish them from the otherwise identically titled theatrical follow-ups. While I admire the effort to bring clarity to confusion, I do not use the titles ***Ju-On: The Curse*** or ***Ju-On 2: The Curse*** in this book because they are merely arbitrary conventions initiated by fans. They are no more authoritative than a similar attempt to rechristen the films by calling the 2003 ***Ju-On: The Grudge*** "Ju-On 3" (sorry, that's a different movie altogether) or "Ju-On: Final" (nope, nothing final about it at all). Instead I use the same naming as that employed by the producers. I'll refer to the Japanese theatrical versions as ***Ju-On: The Grudge*** but drop the English subtitle for the v-cinema versions.

into their proper places within the later ***Ju-On*** movies, they appear in ***Haunted School G*** as non-sequiturs of fear. Menace without meaning, they are deeply unsettling because they defy explanation.

Hiroshi Takahashi so liked the segments, he helped Shimizu connect with ***Ring***-series producer Takashige Ichise. Under Takahashi's supervision, Shimizu would flesh the idea out to full length (give or take) as a direct-to-video release produced by Ichise and financed by Kansai TV. Running a trim 70 minutes, the video was christened ***Ju-On***.

Shimizu's job was to expand what he had established in the short films, to fill in that missing context. Ever since Shimizu had been a kid, he had been fascinated by ghosts. In an interview promoting the American version of ***The Grudge***, Shimizu explained, "In my opinion, to American people real things like serial killers or murderous neighbors, that sort of notion is more scary. But in Japan, and in Japanese culture, the ghosts—particularly people who died with a grudge can turn into a ghost. That is the most scary thing in Japan."

He followed this line of thinking to its logical conclusion. If dying in the grip of anger and fear can turn someone into a ghost, then that ghost's victims would themselves turn into ghosts, and on and on. If you visit a haunted house, you could end up taking evil spirits back to your own house. Victim by victim, such a haunting would spread like an infection.

The viral aspect of hauntings was already an established underpinning of J-Horror, running all the way back to ***Ring*** and Kiyoshi Kurosawa's ***Cure*** (see Chapter 5), and Shimizu's restrained approach to suspense was also in keeping with the aesthetics of the Haunted School. However, Shimizu brought some significant innovations to the table. First, his screenplay was a patchwork of short vignettes, assembled in an episodic and fragmentary collage. Rather than tie the story chunks together in an overarching linear storyline, Shimizu leaves huge gaps between the pieces and presents them in a non-chronological sequence, covering an ambiguous period of time. There are links between the story shards, but Shimizu leaves it to the viewer to reassemble the puzzle in their own heads as they watch.

It is a canny strategy. Like ***Ring***, the movie is a mystery—but the process of discovery is for us, not the characters. The jumbled jigsaw puzzle of a story forces the viewer to become actively engaged in (re)telling the story; you are pulled into the drama and obliged to pay attention to the smallest details. In one scene you may hear one side of a phone conversation, and later in the movie discover the other end of the call, creating a thrill of recognition as you put the chronology back into order.

Secondly, Shimizu directs his works in what amounts to an anti-horror style. Choice after choice, he opts to do the exact opposite of what horror-movie tradition demands. His movies take place in sunny daylight, in familiar locations. Men are in danger as much as women. The characters have access to cell phones and call the police for help. Gore is used sparingly. The pacing is slow and deliberate. Scares are created through careful composition, deviant editing, and disturbing sound effects.

Despite the choppy, episodic nature of the story itself, the telling is careful and measured. In an age where horror audiences are accustomed to the accelerated pace of MTV, video games, and rapid-fire advertising, it is daring indeed for Shimizu to adopt such a damnedly deliberate approach. There is a fine line between minimalism and boring, between slow-burn atmospherics and stultifying airlessness. ***Ju-On*** stays on the right side of that narrow gap, thumbing its nose at nearly every genre convention.

Yet he knew he was participating in an existing genre with established aesthetic conventions. Shimizu was greatly inspired by Kiyoshi Kurosawa and Norio Tsuruta (see Chapters 2 and 3 for more on Tsuruta) and admired their approach to subtlety and suspense. Although he would deviate from the J-Horror mold by showcasing his ghosts where other directors hid them, he knew his work would be judged in the context of what had gone before.

Takashi Shimizu has, arguably, perfected the "less-is-more" aesthetic. While this earliest iteration of ***Ju-On*** has the least—in terms of budget, running time, plot, what have you—it also has the most in terms of effect. Few filmmakers have done so much with so little, a promising start for a young director's career and for a landmark horror franchise. Shimizu's subsequent revisions enhance or embellish without substantially improving on the formula.

Shot on video with a shoestring budget—Shimizu miraculously managed to shoot both ***Ju-On*** and its sequel in a mere nine days—this is a true marvel. There are plenty of films covered in this book with bigger budgets and broader ambitions that do not even have a fraction of ***Ju-On***'s sucker punch power.

Key to the project's success was Shimizu's inspired casting. Where other direct-to-video works most often fail is in the inexperience of the performers. Not so here. Shimizu assembled a fantastic line-up of Japanese cult movie stars whose convincing portrayals take place against a realist backdrop that makes the supernatural story seem like a cruel documentary. The cast includes Yurei Yanagi (***Don't Look Up***, ***Ring***, ***Ring 2***), Asumi Miwa (***Uzumaki***), Yoriko Douguchi (***Cure***, ***Tomie***), Taro

Suwa (***Cure***, ***Ring 2***, ***Uzumaki***, ***Tomie: Rebirth***), Denden (***Cure***, ***Uzumaki***, ***Godzilla 2000***), Chiaki Kuriyama (***Kill Bill Vol. 1***, ***Battle Royale***), and Yuuko Daike and Makoto Ashikawa (who also appeared together in ***Zatoichi***).

But the real star of ***Ju-On*** and all the other works in the series is a seemingly ordinary suburban house in Japan. This house, sad to say for the folks who live there, is a real house in Saitama prefecture, and Shimizu chose it because he thought there was something fundamentally spooky about the place.

In the context of the movies, that "something spooky" has to do with the past: a harrowing crime that took place there. Takeo Saeki (Takashi Matsuyami, who plays this role in all subsequent sequels and remakes as well) discovers his wife Kayako (Takako Fuji, who also plays the same character in all other versions) has been unfaithful to him. He finds her diary, revealing an unhealthy, girlish crush on her son's teacher, Kobayashi (Yurei Yanagi).[1] In a jealous rage, Takeo avenges his wounded pride on his wife and son, and then punishes Kobayashi's family as well, leaving behind enough grudges to populate the world with angry ghosts. Everyone who comes in contact with his accursed home, or the places his victims touched, is gripped by the curse.

Like his mentors Hiroshi Takahashi and Kiyoshi Kurosawa, Takashi Shimizu created a monster that spread like a virus. That this notion of viral curses keeps recurring in J-Horror is more than mere plagiarism. Certainly each successive filmmaker looks back at the winning formulas that preceded and carries over proven ideas; yet the viral metaphor gets at something deeper. It is almost too abstract a concept to allow for easy mimicry. Something else is at work here.

To understand why this concept resonates so effectively throughout the Haunted School, it helps to look at conditions in Japan around the end of the twentieth century and the launch of the twenty-first. Like other Asian nations, Japan is a densely populated society dominated by communal values and strong notions of honor and family. This simple fact informs J-Horror in two fundamental ways. First, it is hard in such a crowded society to draw meaningful distinctions between what happens to one person versus what happens to many people; your problem cannot help but be everybody's problem. Real-life plagues such as SARS or the Avian Flu devastated Asian countries first, before spreading globally, because containment is so difficult. Manmade biological disasters such as the Sarin gas attack by Japanese terrorists in Tokyo's subways in 1995 only enhanced such fears. Many Japanese people regularly wear face masks and gloves to protect themselves from more quotidian germs. To live in Japan is to live under the threat of viruses, real and imagined.

Secondly, because these crowded conditions cause everybody to share in one another's common welfare, it has been the role of Japanese social traditions to provide comfort and protection to the weakest members of that society: children, women, the elderly. Family is important because the family unit is a miniature society, wherein each person has a defined role designed for mutual benefit. In Japanese, the family name comes first, and the given name second: one small token of how one's family is prioritized and prized. But these traditions are also at odds with modernity.

Some in Japanese politics, such as the so-called "Japanese Joan of Arc" Hiroko Mizushima, have added their voices to those of social critics like Koji Suzuki who argue against the current gendering of responsibilities. As things stand now, too many men feel increasing pressures to be the financial bedrock of their families. This pressure can lead to death, either from suicide (as Japanese suicide rates soar) or from a unique Japanese phenomenon called "karoshi" (literally working oneself to death). Meanwhile too many women feel forced into narrow constricting roles as care-givers and mommies. Women who choose to work outside the home, for whatever reason, are criticized, their children given the short end. Women who stay home are burdened with the care of an elderly population that every year lives longer, and accumulates more health problems. The pressures of work and family need to be better distributed between men and women, but the conformist pressures of Japanese society resist modernizing the traditional sex roles.

Without deep changes to the society, these problems remain insoluble. It is unfair to expect women to sacrifice their own freedoms and lives to care for the rest of the family, but unless men step forward to share those responsibilities, women who seek modern lives do so by abandoning their children and their aging parents.

These issues lie at the heart of ***Ju-On***. The opening sequence of the 2000 ***Ju-On*** introduces a helpless, suffering child seemingly abandoned by his family in a chaotic household left to ruin, while the opening of the 2003 ***Ju-On: The Grudge*** features an aging, Alzheimer's-afflicted woman seemingly discarded by her family in the same decrepit house. Throughout the series, the ghosts of Kayako and Toshio strike at those people who symbolize familial dysfunction. Kayako attacks schoolgirls thinking about sex, a loveless couple, a motherless boy, a fragile old woman and the son who did not take care of her himself, a single father and his motherless daughter. Meanwhile Toshio haunts childless career women. At no point does the series depict a stable, traditional nuclear family, multigenerational and loving; and at no point in the series does anyone escape the ghosts.

The ***Ju-On*** movies are scary not simply because they have spooky monsters in them, but because those fears emerge from real-world problems the Japanese people struggle with daily: the horror touches very close to home.

As in so many of the movies discussed in this book, the source point of the drama is a woman who defies her traditional role. A small family tragedy then spirals outward to consume others, as one person's tragedy is shared like a germ. Kayako's infidelity—or her perceived infidelity—provokes murderous jealousy in her husband. He is the one truly at fault, no doubt, for his extreme reaction. His violent response to her is not uncommon in an honor-driven culture like Japan, but the movie does not condone his actions at all. The premise recalls some of the classics like ***Ghost Story of Yotsuya***, with a killer justifying his crime by citing his wife's unfaithfulness. But there is an important difference.

Whereas the cruel samurai in ***Ghost Story of Yotsuya*** kills his wife and his child and is then punished by her avenging ghost, when Takeo Saeki kills his wife and son, he unleashes their avenging phantoms on *everybody*.

The various books and movies of the ***Ring*** cycle posited different possibilities for bringing closure to Sadako's curse. While not all of these charms worked, it was always assumed that *something* could be done to neutralize her threat. Kayako and Toshio do not seem to want anything anymore, and the havoc they cause is uncontainable. Kayako is victim and villain in one package. In risking her family in order to pursue a selfish sexual urge, what she did was wrong. But what was done to her was also wrong. And the wrongs accumulate, multiply, and spread.

Whether by accident or design, Takashi Shimizu managed to hit franchise gold. Taka Ichise and Hiroshi Takahashi had struggled to continue the ***Ring*** series in the face of basic narrative hurdles—how to expand a story that had come to a fairly conclusive end. But with ***Ju-On***, there is no narrative endpoint. Furthermore, the non-chronological narrative structure meant the story could expand outward in a variety of non-linear directions, all the while maintaining compelling mystery even for those fans who already knew what the grudge was and how it functioned. The ***Ju-On*** premise could be reused almost indefinitely, for any number of sequels, and remain effective as long as Shimizu could keep cooking up disturbing images to fuel his vignettes.

A second direct-to-video ***Ju-On*** movie was made simultaneously

Kayako

with the first, and released fast on its heels. If you were in a particularly cynical frame of mind, it would be possible to dismiss ***Ju-On 2*** as a rather crass piece of marketing. A better name for it would be ***Ju-On 1.5***. It clocks in at a scant 75 minutes and the first half hour is just the end of the previous video, cut-and-pasted intact.

Paying full price for just 45 minutes' worth of new footage would be annoying but forgivable if this were a theatrical feature following some time after the first installment, hence requiring a recap of previous events. But remember that this is a direct-to-video release, or "v-cinema" as such things are sometimes called, hitting stores barely over a month later.[2] The only likely audience for the thing would be fans of the first one, who could be safely assumed to already *have* the previous episode.

When the recycled sequence ends and new footage starts, we meet Nobuyuki Suzuki (Tomohiro Kaku), the son of a real estate agent we met in the first installment. Strange things are happening at the Suzuki place. Nobu is watching a horror flick on TV (yes?) when the girl on the screen seems to look right at him... Then, she comes right out of the screen to touch him. We have finally started to get some new material here in ***Ju-On 2***, and it's a straight lift from ***Ring***!

Despite such quibbles, ***Ju-On 2*** escapes any harsh judgments because Shimizu's masterly command of the frame is undeniable. The duplicated footage from the first video is extraordinarily gripping and dramatic, and it directly sets up the events to come in the rest of part two, whereby the canvas of the story is significantly expanded. Splice the two videos together into one movie, running about 100 minutes, and you'd have one of the scariest and most inventive horror movies ever made. Even at its most derivative, ***Ju-On 2*** is working magic.

Whereas the first video centers on the haunted house where the Saeki family murders set the grudge in motion, in ***Ju-On 2***, the curse also extends out of the house. Not all of the victims in part one died on the premises, and part two reveals that the survivors carried the haunting out with them.

The apparitions plaguing poor Nobuyuki are the first sign that the grudge is a bigger threat than the first film implied. Why is he being attacked? He never went to the haunted Saeki house, so did his father somehow bring the demons home with him after trying to sell the place? That theory is unsettling enough, but it turns out the Suzukis have a worse problem. Their new apartment was, thanks to an unhappy coincidence, the former home of schoolteacher Kobayashi—the object of Kayako Saeki's desire. When Takeo went nuts and killed his own family, he also went to Kobayashi's place to exact revenge on him. The hideous murders that happened in Kobayashi's home left their own grudge behind. The Suzukis are doubly cursed, having been touched by two separate but related ju-ons. Takeo Saeki, by being such a busy madman, seeded ghostly menaces in diverse locations. Their victims spread their own curses, and as time goes on, the grudge is covering exponentially more ground.

The audience discovers this, along with the characters, through a clever chronological trick played by writer-director Takashi Shimizu. In the first ***Ju-On***, he had jumbled the story into a patchwork of discontinuous vignettes with only a few scattershot clues left for the audience to try and reassemble the actual linear narrative for themselves. Things get weirder in ***Ju-On 2*** as characters actually cross over these fractured timelines to experience, psychically, events of the past. In certain circumstances, characters encountering ghosts relive some of those spirits' final moments. Nobu Suzuki and his aunt Kyoko actually witness Takeo's attack on Kobayashi's pregnant wife, even though this crime took place years in the past.

This is why so much of the first video has been sampled back into this one. The events detailed in the climax of part one are the direct triggers for much of what happens in part two, and the entire story is about how the past is coming back to get revenge on the future. There is no escape from the ju-on, no magic charm.

Fans of the series have invested a great deal of effort into unraveling the complicated chronology of the storyline. This is harder than it sounds because there are so few definitive clues as to the proper sequence of events. Moments from the far future are entangled with fragments of the distant past, because time has no fixed meaning. Time is flattened out, and events of the future are already linked to events of the past. Each character's sad fate is already written, already incorporated into the next cycle of the curse. Everyone is doomed.

Where part one focused mostly on Toshio, the little boy spook, part two lets Kayako go to town—quite literally. In one show-stopping sequence, Kayako's specter multiplies itself hundreds of times over, and an army of ghastly blue women in white nighties descends on some terrified schoolkids. In shooting this sequence, Shimizu simply called in a bunch of extras who had no idea what they were in for. He combed their hair in front of their eyes, taught them to stagger around George Romero-zombie-style, and let them loose.

The resulting image is, coincidentally, very much like one from Junji Ito's original ***Tomie*** manga. Ito conceived of his villainess Tomie as being able to essentially clone herself through her spectral mischief, but the makers of the Tomie films had never really pursued that concept. Kayako and Tomie are similar characters in some respects. Both women are driven by obsessions that they mistake for love, and their passions survive their physical deaths to wreak havoc in the afterlife.

Hardly surprising, then, that Shimizu got his first true theatrical feature gig at the helm of the ***Tomie*** franchise's latest episode, ***Tomie: Re-Birth*** (2001). For more on this subject, flip back to Chapter 4, but for now merely savor what young Mr. Shimizu must have been feeling at that point in his life. His head was spinning.

His meteoric rise from film school student to professional director tagged him as a horror creator, but he harbored thoughts of making a comedy next. That project would have to wait—his producers had decided it was time to take ***Ju-On*** to the next level.

Taka Ichise is a savvy businessman. During a time when Japan's film industry was increasingly moribund, he managed to produce a prodigious slate of internationally popular hits. Not only is he the producer behind the ***Ring*** cycle, the ***Grudge*** series, the ***J-Horror Theater*** "hexalogy" and ***Dark Water***, but also such non-J-Horrors as ***Last Scene***, ***Princess Blade***, ***Crazy Lips***, ***Crying Freeman***, ***The Mystery of Edogawa Rampo***, and ***Necronomicon***. This resume alone stands testament to his moviemaking acumen. Having said that, though, even he could not have predicted the success of the two ***Ju-On*** videos.

The various ***Ring*** sequels varied in quality but none came close to the broad commercial appeal of the 1998 release. The ***Tomie*** films had not yet reached far beyond Japan's shores. Major J-Horror works by important directors, such as Masato Harada's ***Inugami***, were opening to disappointing box office returns (see Chapter 7). The pervasive understanding within the industry held that J-Horror had reached its peak and was diminishing. Instead of big-budgeted theatrical features aimed at broad audiences, the genre was shrinking back to play-it-safe formulas: low-budget direct-to-video quickies aimed at the core horror market. Ichise fully expected to make a profit from the ***Ju-On*** videos or he wouldn't have greenlighted them. But they resonated with audiences in a way unseen since 1998, and Ichise did the smart thing: he asked Shimizu to make a bona fide ***Ju-On*** movie.

"Since I still had a lot of ideas that I wasn't able to explore in the video, I agreed," Shimizu says.

Some things would stay the same. The same house would be used, and cast members Takako Fuji and Takashi Matsuyama would reprise their roles as Kayako and Takeo Saeki. The familiar fragmentary, episodic approach would also return. Shimizu realized that the trick was essential for keeping the plot from feeling repetitive.

This was an important consideration, because Shimizu was openly

THE LADY IN WHITE

While Takashi Shimizu may have needed persuading to cast a woman as his protagonist, he never wavered in his conviction that the ghosts should be a woman and her child. "I think that men physically are very strong and women are weak, but inside, like a mother's instinct, women are really strong inside. Psychologically and mentally, women are a lot stronger than men, so when it's a serial-killer-type violent movie it may make the audience more scared [to have a male villain], but with a woman as a ghost it's scarier, because she looks like us physically but inside she has lots of strength, and that's what makes it really scary subconsciously." As for the creepy little kid Toshio, Shimizu avers, "Sometimes [children] can be scary and even inhuman. Everyone was once a child, but once you get older it gets harder and harder to see the world through their eyes."

courting existing ***Ju-On*** fans to come to, not a remake, but a sequel. Although the 2003 theatrical feature would share the same title as the 2000 v-cinema version (and be later identified as ***Ju-On: The Grudge*** for foreign sales), it would add to the established storyline rather than simply retread old ground.

The script does borrow the structure of the original video: a social worker of some type visits the house to check on a vulnerable charge and discovers an unkempt household. The movie jumps around in time to show various other people falling afoul of the curse before looping back to the social worker, who finally discovers the truth of the situation and faces his or her ultimate fate. In the theatrical version, the social worker role is played by actress Megumi Okina, and her role is substantially larger than that played by Yurei Yanagi in the video.

"The main difference between the video and the film is that the video ***Ju-On*** didn't really have a main character," Shimizu later explained to interviewer Patrick Macias. "You could say that the main character was the cursed house itself. For the movie, it was agreed that we need someone to be the protagonist, either a hero or a heroine... I wanted the film to have a male protagonist, a working-class middle-aged guy, but producer Takashige Ichise said, 'Who wants to see some old guy?' So that's how we ended up with such an attractive female cast!"

Once again Shimizu collected an outstanding team. Megumi Okina was joined by several returning cast members such as Misaki Ito and Misa Uehara, as well as the prolific character actor Kanji Tsuda (whom Asian cinema expert Bey Logan likens to a Japanese Steve Buscemi). Child actor Yuya Ozeki was cast as Toshio this time around after impressing the filmmakers by misbehaving during auditions.

The accomplished cinematographer Tokusho Kikumura added ***Ju-On: The Grudge*** to a resume that already included Kiyoshi Kurosawa's ***Cure*** and Hideo Nakata's ***Chaos***. Noboyuki Takahashi, editor of Nakata's ***Ring 2*** and ***Dark Water***, handled the cutting. Hajime Matsumoto took over special effects duties, having proven his mettle on the 1998 ***Ring/Spiral*** pair, Shusuke Kaneko's 1995 ***Gamera*** revival, and 2001's ambitious ***Godzilla, Mothra, King Ghidorah: Giant Monsters All Out Attack***. Rounding out the mix, Shimizu brought back Shiro Sato as the resident ***Ju-On*** musical composer.

The bigger budget meant he could shoot on film instead of video and give the whole endeavor a more sophisticated production gloss, but Shimizu sticks close to his minimalist roots. He knows simplest is best, and scariest. A boy in blue makeup, a shadow, and a quick discreet cut away is all you need to raise the hairs on a viewer's neck.

"Timing is very important," says Shimizu. "Doubt and fear will pile up little by little, and that makes for suspense. You have to calculate this, along with the timing, to perfectly control the audience. Also, I think horror is the art of misdirection. You think something is over

NO MONSTERS UNDER THE BED

Some of ***Ju-On***'s curious inversion of traditional horror movie imagery comes from essential differences between American and Japanese culture. The monster under the bed, the dark places in a spooky cellar—these are not part of ***Ju-On***'s world. "In America and Europe, an attic can be a room where someone lives," notes Takashi Shimizu, "but in Japan it is always dark and abandoned. Even the closets in Japan are different, with sliding doors instead of doors that fold open. I think non-Japanese people are afraid of what is under the bed, but in Japan people sleep on the floor." Instead of creeping up from below, Shimizu's ghosts come down from above, from the attic and through the ceiling to strike their victims from overhead.

In one startling moment from ***Ju-On: The Grudge*** (recreated in the American remake and revisited in a new way in the sequel ***Ju-On 2***), Kayako's ghost appears lurking on the ceiling, like a spider. This is another example of Shimizu's clever appropriation of ideas from other sources: Kayako's crawl across the ceiling mimics a similar scene in ***Tomie: Replay*** from 2001. Shimizu had borrowed from the ***Tomie*** movies before and would do so again—and repay the favor by directing the third in that series, ***Tomie: Re-Birth***—but this is one of those cases where the idea fits better into ***Ju-On*** than it did in its original place. There is an actual narrative reason for Kayako to emerge from above, since her mutilated body was wrapped in plastic and left to rot in the attic while her husband went out to continue his killing spree. She inhabits that attic more than any other place, and her curse descends down from those haunted rafters.

there, then you realize that someone is behind you and maybe it is not even human."

Lucky as ever, Shimizu once again reaped the bounty of being in the right place at the right time. His theatrical ***Ju-On: The Grudge*** came out in the immediate aftermath of the global release of Gore Verbinksi's remake of ***The Ring*** (see Chapter 10). Where J-Horror had once been seen as on the downward slide, the one-two punch of ***The Ring*** and ***Ju-On: The Grudge*** proved it was still ascendant.

Hiroshi Takahashi was initially dismissive of the project and chided his friend Shimizu that the audience had already grown tired of the ***Ju-On*** format. When he saw the final film, however, he ate those words. "I think you made it fresh again, so that makes me think that it could become a continuing series," said Takahashi.

Sure enough, a fourth ***Ju-On*** was put into production (called, ahem, ***Ju-On 2: The Grudge***). In fact, ***Ju-On: The Grudge*** had not yet even opened in theaters when Taka Ichise approved plans for a sequel.

In the final minutes of ***Ju-On: The Grudge***, with all of the characters consumed by the curse, Shimizu let his camera float out across an eerie desolate Tokyo. One of the world's busiest, most bustling cities—it should never appear so empty. The audience was left to file out of the theater with the uneasy thought that the grudge would eventually destroy everybody. This set the stage for the sequel, in which we see how rapidly the curse spreads outside its boundaries. Like the video, ***Ju-On 2*** leaves the haunted house behind to follow the ghosts as they multiply across the land, seeking new schoolgirls and unwed mothers to victimize.

Taking the lead in the sequel, Noriko Sakai plays Kyoko Harase, a popular horror movie star who is invited to appear on a TV program about the haunted Saeki house. Kyoko joins TV host Tomoka Miura (played by Chiharu Niyama, of ***Godzilla, Mothra, King Ghidorah: Giant Monsters All Out Attack***) at the seemingly innocuous house where, one by one, everyone who has ever set foot inside has died or disappeared.

This is the sort of thing superstitious people call "tempting fate."

Sure enough, within a day almost everyone involved in the shoot has been claimed by the curse. All except Kyoko, who was almost killed in a car accident, which almost caused her to miscarry her unborn baby. That's a lot of "almosts," and it suggests she has escaped the worst of it for some specific reason.

Fans of the ***Ring*** and ***Tomie*** series might be able to advise Kyoko that her pregnancy has been hijacked by an evil force hoping to reincarnate itself. Nevertheless, she goes ahead and gives birth, with tragic consequences for everybody not yet attacked by the ghosts of Kayako and Toshio Saeki. For all its focus on dysfunctional family dynamics, the ***Ju-On*** movies had yet to deal directly with pregnancy and human reproduction. As Shimizu himself noted, "The theme of ***Ju-On 2*** is motherhood."

Ju-On 2 reunited nearly the entire production team of the previous film but gave them just $2.3 million—roughly half of the $4 million budget from the first go-round. Ever the one to spin gold from dross, Shimizu let the reduced budget work to his advantage. ***Ju-On 2*** manages to look vastly more polished and cinematic than its predecessor. Between its superb production values, excellent special effects, and more coherent storyline, ***Ju-On 2*** is arguably the most satisfying entry in the series.

One of Shimizu's greatest strengths is his ability to wear his inspirations plainly on his sleeve without it feeling unduly derivative or plagiaristic. ***Ju-On 2*** is full of familiar J-Horror tropes: creepy cell phone calls, people attacked by hair, things captured on video that cannot be seen with human eyes. Towards the climax he copies show-stopping set pieces from Hideo Nakata's ***Ring*** and Fujiro Mitsuishi's ***Tomie: Replay*** without a scrap of shame. One can always tell what movies Shimizu has been watching, but when he borrows ideas from other filmmakers he makes them his own. It's a gift he shares with Hollywood's Sam Raimi. In films like his ***Evil Dead*** trilogy, Raimi mixed George Romero-style gory shocks with Three Stooges-style slapstick for an end product that was distinctive and personal, regardless of its heritage.

In fact, Shimizu admired Sam Raimi and considered him an influence. As a teenager, Raimi's ***Evil Dead*** films were the only horror movies Shimizu could bring himself to watch. So when Sam Raimi contacted him to ask if Shimizu would like to come to America to remake ***Ju-On***, the puzzled Japanese filmmaker could only answer, "What the hell are you talking about?"

Raimi had seen ***Ju-On: The Grudge***, reacting with nothing short of awe. "This is the most frightening film I've ever seen," he said as he set to acquiring remake rights. In the aftermath of his success with ***Spider-Man***, Raimi and his friend Scott Spiegel had formed a company to produce and distribute moderately budgeted motion pictures aimed at an international audience. ***Ju-On: The Grudge*** had already proven itself an international hit, and its success was not due to specifics of dialogue or characterization that would be hard to translate across cultural boundaries. Its strength was in the directing. So much so that Raimi marveled, "Oh my God, I'm being schooled now in horror!"

Although Raimi felt there was room to Americanize the production by adding familiar English-speaking movie stars and simplifying the abstract plot a little, there was no need to replace Shimizu. Shimizu was the reason ***Ju-On: The Grudge*** worked in the first place.

"Clearly I was concerned at the language barrier but actually it wasn't that bad," recalled Shimizu. "For me, the biggest challenge and difference was working within the Hollywood studio system, so it was important that I was able to at least utilize a predominantly Japanese crew so I could have a similar situation as when working in Japan."

Raimi and Spiegel did him one better. The Hollywood ***Grudge*** would be shot mostly in Japan, with American stars such as Sarah Michelle Gellar, Bill Pullman, and Kadee Strickland joining Japanese actors in Tokyo. The Americanized script by Stephen Susco (who grumbled disappointedly that he had wanted to direct the remake) left many sections in Japanese, to be subtitled in the stateside release.

The whole thing was nearly unprecedented. In the past, foreign directors had at times been called to Hollywood to Americanize their overseas hits. On the rare occasions this has happened, though, it has been for European directors, and nobody considers Ole Bornedal's ***Nightwatch*** or George Sluzier's ***The Vanishing*** superior to their own original versions. For all the praise heaped on Hideo Nakata for ***Ring***, it had not occurred to Dreamworks to fly him over from Japan to helm the remake. Shimizu had won a prize that had never been proffered before.

In later interviews, Shimizu noted that the process of Americanizing ***Ju-On*** was not too terribly involved: "It's a remake, so there are no surprises, but being a Hollywood film, it's perhaps a little tidier in keeping with modern Hollywood expectations. When I did the original Japanese version, I had no idea that it would be released in America, so I only concentrated on what a Japanese audience gets scared of. For the American remake, I had to adjust my ideas for what is scary to American people. At the same time, the American producers saw the original version, and they said it's really scary and then decided to do the remake, so I believe that the Japanese scares are going to be reinterpreted for America. If the American producers didn't think the original version was scary then they wouldn't have wanted to do the remake. I trust that the Japanese or Asian horror is going to be interpreted into the American [sensibility] well enough, but at the same time it's crucial to adjust some parts for an American audience so that they will feel like the remake is really scary also."

As Stephen Susco polished his screenplay and plans for the new ***Grudge*** were finalized, Shimizu found himself with some time to spare, so he went and made another movie.

It is somewhat amazing that Shimizu managed to complete ***Marebito*** ("The Stranger From Afar") in a scant eight days—an accomplishment diminished by the fact that a few years earlier he'd made two v-cinema movies in just nine days. The project was conceived as part of a collaboration between Shimizu's alma mater, the Film School of Tokyo, and the Eurospace Cinema of Tokyo's Shibya district. Various filmmakers would be tapped to make a grand total of eleven low-budget movies shot on digital video in one of three genres: horror, comedy, and eroticism. Hiroshi Takahashi oversaw the horror productions and found time also to make his own directorial debut with ***Sodom no Ichi*** ("Town of Sodom"), a horror comedy inspired by Fritz Lang's Dr. Mabuse thrillers.

For his contribution to the undertaking, Shimizu was reunited with writer Chiaki Konaka, who had supervised the ***Haunted School G*** program all those years ago. Konaka had a novel of his he wanted to adapt; it riffed on the works of H.P. Lovecraft to combine weird supernatural imagery with a scathing critique of modern Japanese society.

Starring in the film was Shinya Tsukamoto, himself the warped filmmaker behind a demented piece of Japanese fantasy cinema called ***Testuo: The Iron Man***. Tsukamoto plays Masuoka, a freelance videographer obsessed with capturing pure fear on tape. One day he stumbles upon a suicide in the Tokyo subway system and gains fifteen minutes of fame as the cameraman of a real-life snuff film. Reviewing the footage, Masuoka becomes convinced that the look of abject terror on the man's face is not the result of his impending death, but the cause of it: he must have seen something down there that he could no longer live with.

In his search for the source of this fear, Masuoka penetrates the earth's surface to find another world inside, inhabited by ghosts, demons, and "detrimental robots." There he finds a feral girl, naked and chained, a human leading a subhuman existence. He brings her back into his world with tragic consequences.

Marebito is a raw, disturbing movie different in many ways from the ***Grudge*** movies with which Shimizu made his name. Shimizu focuses the film tightly on the performances of Tsukamoto and Tomomi Miyashita as the wild girl he names simply "F." Where the ***Ju-On*** movies invite the viewer to work through the mysteries, ***Marebito*** proceeds in more linear fashion towards a final-act plot twist that casts the preceding events in a new light.

On May 22, 2004 ***Marebito*** made its world premiere at the Seattle International Film Festival. Over the next few months the film toured festivals around the world, earning the Golden Raven Award at the

JU-REI THE UNCANNY

For American fans of J-Horror, the planets aligned in a unique conjunction in the autumn of 2004. At least in those urban areas large enough to have arthouse movie theaters, it was possible to see Takashi Shimizu's Japanese version of ***Ju-On***, then cross the street to the multiplex and see the remake with Sarah Michelle Gellar all on the same afternoon. Anyone not totally Grudged-out by that point could then go to a well-appointed video store and find something on the new release shelf called ***Ju-Rei: The Uncanny***.

Along with the declaration "The Most Horrifying Film From Japan" on the video box was a picture of a spooky kid who looks for all the world like ***Ju-On*'s** Toshio. ***Ju-Rei***'s title even echoes ***Ju-On***. It is shot on video, and follows a chronologically fragmented collection of interconnected vignettes about a haunting that reproduces itself like a viral infection… In every respect save those that count, ***Ju-Rei*** positions itself as more-of-the-same for ***Grudge*** fans who can't get enough but who also have fairly low standards. If the five installments of ***Ju-On*** were an elegant five-course meal cooked up by a master chef, ***Ju-Rei*** is the Hostess Ho-Ho served as dessert.

My contention in this book is that J-Horror is often best understood not as a conventional genre but as an art movement. Most movie genres follow a pattern of mimicry and rip-offs trying to replicate commercial success without creative innovation. By contrast, the films of the Haunted School present remarkably similar ideas with remarkably similar visualizations but yet remain discrete and distinct. The Haunted School is a bit like winemaking—sample sixty different bottles of wine from different vineyards and you'll have sixty different experiences, despite the common ingredients.

Ju-Rei punches a big honkin' hole in my theory. This is exploitationist filmmaking at its crassest. This *is* a derivative movie, with virtually nothing to recommend it. Where Takashi Shimizu exceeded his budgetary limitations with his early ***Ju-On*** videos, director Koji Shiraishi's cheap production values here never seem like anything more than amateurish.

It is too easy, however, to dismiss ***Ju-Rei*** as a shoddy knock-off. There is more behind it than just that. The most uncanny thing about ***Ju-Rei: The Uncanny***, you see, is that it is the fifth installment in the ***Ju-Rei*** franchise!

To chart the curious history of ***Ju-Rei***, we need to set our Way Back Machine for the year 2000. At this point in time, the J-Horror bubble seemed to have burst and was devolving into direct-to-video productions aimed at the already well-established horror audience. This was the impulse behind Shimizu's ***Ju-On***; and over at Broadway Productions (now there's a Japanese name for you!) it led to director Akiyama Yutaka's shot-on-video quickie ***Ju-Lei: Spiritual Mystery File*** (2000).

That's no typo: the romaji characters on the video box clearly spell out ***Ju-Lei***. Japanese makes no distinction between the L and R sounds (which is why monster movie fans argue pointlessly whether Godzilla's "real" name is Gojira). Spelled either way, the word Ju-rei/Ju-lei means "cursed spirits" and is strikingly close to the original title for Shimizu's series.

Like ***The Twilight Zone*** or ***The Outer Limits***, the title ***Ju-Lei*** functions as a brand name for a franchise of videos that share a general spookiness but do not share any characters or continuing plots. The first one, ***Spiritual Mystery File***, is an episodic jumble of unrelated short stories linked by profoundly ineffective narration (Rod Serling turns over in his grave). The evidence suggests this video was profitable since a second one, ***Ju-Lei 2: Satsujin Genba no Noroi*** was rushed into stores later the same year, from director Kenji Murakami. Tonshu Takeshima's ***Ju-Lei 3: Noroi no Ekusosisto*** ("Ju-Lei: The Haunted Exorcist") followed in 2001.

By 2003, there was no doubt that the J-Horror boom was far from over, and the wise stewards of Broadway Productions decided it was time for the ***Ju-Lei*** series to transition from direct-to-video releases to genuine theatrical runs, with Kenji Murakami brought back to helm his second installment in the cycle. In the same way that ***Ju-On*** rebooted its theatrical feature to be the start of a new cycle rather than be called ***Ju-On 3***, ***Ju-Lei***'s fourth installment started the clock over again, and switched the romaji spelling from L to R to further emphasize the change.

Ju-Rei: The Movie (2003) is yet another grab bag anthology of unconnected ghost stories with a slightly better budget and mildly higher ambitions. The following year, Broadway tapped a different director, Koji Shiraishi, for the second theatrically-destined feature (though still shot on video) ***Ju-Rei 2: Kuro Ju-Rei***. This would then be retitled ***Ju-Rei: The Uncanny*** for unwary Americans and distributed in the U.S. timed to piggyback on the marketing for ***The Grudge*** (2004).

Ju-Rei: The Uncanny is the first in its series not to be built on the anthology format. This time out, the vignettes are part of a single story, broken into ten chapters, which are played in reverse order, so we watch the movie backwards. The elements are familiar: a disrupted family, crumbling under a divorce, sets in motion a tragedy that snowballs through its victims; an urban legend of a dark figure; schoolgirls getting cell phone calls from ghosts... In open acknowledgement of the film's inspirations, at one point some of the characters go to a movie theater to see something called ***Cursed Video: The Movie***. Oh, but wait—you think that's a sly jab at ***Ring***? No, it's just cross-promotion by Broadway, a little plug for their execrable ***Rensa: Noroi no Bideo*** ("The Connection: Cursed Videotape") from 2000.

Shiraishi's movie is not without its merits—or its defenders—and if you have watched everything else discussed in this book and desperately hunger for more, then it cannot hurt to give ***Ju-Rei*** a try. But for everyone else, there is so much more deserving and more rewarding J-Horror out there worth seeking out—***Kakashi***, ***Inugami***, ***Uzukami***, to name just a few. It is a shame that in the wake of the U.S. release of ***The Grudge***, it was not Shimizu's terrific 2000 video original that showed up on rental shop shelves but its pale shadow.

Brussels International Festival of Fantasy Films, before arriving at its intended home in the Eurospace Cinema in Tokyo on October 23, 2004.

Just one day previously, Shimizu's American version of ***The Grudge*** opened in the U.S. During the Halloween season, the Americanized ***Grudge*** raked in a staggering $39 million, making it one of only a few genuine hits in a year that saw many intended blockbusters tank. By the end of its run, ***The Grudge*** had earned over $115 million worldwide, the 21st best-grossing movie of the entire year. Based largely on their backing of this film, Premiere Magazine called Sony Executives Amy Pascal and Michael Lynton the fifth most powerful movers in Hollywood (for more on ***The Grudge***, see Chapter 10).

Shimizu chalked up the fuss to the simple superiority of the Haunted School. "Japanese horror is genuinely scarier than their American counterparts," he says. "There's sophistication in Japanese scariness, of which there are two types. Japanese horror is intended to give audiences more mental scares, while in Hollywood it's more simple surprising scares. I think audiences want to be more scared than in traditional Hollywood films, and Japanese films provide those."

Sony's management promptly authorized a sequel, ***The Grudge 2***, for Shimizu to prepare for a 2006 release. Meanwhile, he felt compelled to return to Japan for a different installment in the series, ***Ju-On 3***. "It has always been my intention to finish the ***Ju-On*** series in Japan. So I am writing the third one just now—and it is to be made there. I see ***Ju-On*** as being three movies—a trilogy." Between the rapidly accumulating ***Ju-On*** sequels, Shimizu was also tapped to direct the third installment in Taka Ichise's latest J-Horror franchise, ***The J-Horror Theater*** (clever name, eh?).

There is something to be said for the benefits of being in the right place at the right time, every single time.

1. Diaries and journals are J-Horror's Number One way to represent mental illness, with the same basic scene appearing in ***Tomie: Replay*** (2001) and ***Kakashi*** (2001).
2. Beginning on March 25, 2000, ***Ju-On 2*** did play theatrically, for one week only, on a single screen in a single movie theater (the Box Higashi-Nakano) but this hardly counts.

Sources:

Boustany, Nora: "Japan's Joan of Arc Advocates New Way of Life," Washington Post, July 15 2005.
Collingridge, Mandi Apple: "Ju-On Review," www.mandiapple.com/snowblood, 2003.
Wilson, Staci Layne, "Takashi Shimizu: Director of The Grudge," www.horror.com, October 5, 2004.
Macias, Patrick: "The Scariest Horror Ever? Ju-On Director Takashi Shimizu Interview," www.jap-attack.com.
Sharp, Jasper: "Ju-On Review," www.midnighteye.com, December 23, 2002.
Jonas, Mike: "The Attic Crawlspace," http://p209.ezboard/bjuonthegrudge.
Raimi, Sam and Scott Spiegel: Audio Commentary to Ju-On: The Grudge, Lions Gate Home Entertainment DVD, 2005.
Interview with Takashi Shimizu, Ju-On: The Grudge, Lions Gate Home Entertainment DVD, 2005.
Logan, Bey: Audio Commentary to Ju-On: The Grudge, Premier Asia DVD, 2004.
Shimizu, Takashi: Audio Commentary to Ju-On, Toei Video DVD, 2002.
Shimizu, Takashi: Audio Commentary to Ju-On 2, Toei Video DVD, 2002.
Shimizu, Takashi, Taka Ichise, and Takako Fuji: Audio Commentary to The Grudge: Unrated Extended Director's Cut, Sony Pictures Entertainment DVD, 2005.
DuFoe, Terry and Tiffany: "Kadee Strickland on Killer Snakes and Nasty Grudges," Phantom of the Movies' Videoscope #53, Winter 2005.
Sharp, Jasper: "Stranger From Afar Review," www.midnighteye.com, June 15, 2005.
Atherton, Mike: "London Raindance Film Festival," www.cinemaminima.com, October 7, 2004.
Burns, Larry D: "Ju-On 2 Review," www.mandiapple.com, 2004.
www.filmhorizon.com
Gilchrist, Todd: "Takashi Shimizu Interview," www.scifi.com
Fischer, Paul: "Takashi Shimizu Interview," www.darkhorizons.com, September 24, 2004.
www.subwaycinema.com
www.moviesonline.ca

CHAPTER 7
THE UNQUIET DEAD

Taka Ichise knew the score: Make more J-Horrors! "As a producer I know it's good business so I have to keep making it," he told Japan Times correspondent Mark Schilling.

He also knew the danger: allowing the cycle to deteriorate into a pale shadow of former glories. "The quality [of films like the ***Nightmare on Elm Street*** series] declines, but they can still sell the videos on the title alone. That doesn't interest me—I'm not doing this just because I want money. What's fun for me is making interesting movies that also happen to become hits. I don't want to churn them out until they become crap—what's the fun in that?"

So it came to pass that a year after the double feature of ***Ring*** and ***Spiral***, he packaged a follow-up double feature: ***Ring 2*** and ***Shikoku***. ***Ring 2*** you already know (skip back to Chapter 2 for a refresher if you need it). ***Shikoku*** was based on a novel by Masako Bando. Adapted by Kunimi Manda and Takenori Sento (you remember his name, don't you? The J-Movie Wars mogul behind both ***Don't Look Up*** and ***Ring***), the story has more than a little overlap with ***Ring***, as we shall see. Producing for Asmik Ace was genre stalwart Masato Hara, one of the hands behind ***Ring***.

Along with that J-Horror pedigree, the movie itself is serious, distinguished horror filmmaking of a most old-school stripe. Had Nobuo Nakagawa survived into 1999 to be making movies, ***Shikoku*** is probably the kind of thing he'd have been doing.

Yui Natsukawa stars as Hinako, a young woman drawn back to the small rural village in Shikoku where she lived as a child. There, she discovers seething discontent. Not long after she left, her best friend Sayori committed suicide, and the girl's bereaved parents have come apart.

Turns out a simple spelling change can turn *Shikoku* (the four lands) into *Shikoku* (land of the dead). To actually pull off such a trick in real life, as opposed to calligraphy, takes a mote more effort. And in J-Horror, of course, the dead are never really taken far from us, especially if the deceased happens to be a girl with extraordinary psychic powers who died by drowning. Cue the long black hair, and action!

Chiaki Kuriyama plays the undead Sayori, in what ought to have been an inspired bit of casting. Kuriyama's genre credits are prodigious:

School Mystery, ***Persona***, the original ***Ju-On*** video, ***MPD Psycho***, ***Battle Royale***, and Quentin Tarantino's ***Kill Bill*** cycle. With her crazed bug eyes and twitchy body language, she channels Peter Lorre's ability to play eerie by simple birthright. She doesn't seem to have been given sufficient time to prepare, however. Despite her amply demonstrated talents elsewhere, here she seems ill-at-ease and amateurish.[1]

The root of the horror lies in a family tragedy, natch: a teenaged girl whose self-destruction left behind a family unable to move on with their lives. However, that tragedy itself had its roots in the girl's dissatisfaction with her life. Anyone in such a stifling small town could be forgiven for wanting out—which is precisely what Hinako did, moving off to a more satisfying existence in the big city. Sayori hated her friend for leaving because it only rubbed in her own inability to escape; she was destined by birth to be the next priestess of the Hiura family. Forced against her will as a child to perform psychic stunts, poor little Sayori even had to fight her mother for permission to go to school. Her desire for independence sets off a chain of supernatural circumstances that endanger everyone.

You can easily tick off a catalogue of familiar elements: the city girl who visits her country cousins whose rural lives are ruled by ancient superstition; the tentative alliance between a boy and girl whose former passion has faded but who must rely on each other to investigate and face down a supernatural menace; obsessive graphophilia and ripped up photographs; and of course the dead wet girl revived in a pool of murky water. If you're in the market for a slow-burn creep-out about a backwards village rent asunder by one girl's transgression against tradition—well, you should probably start with ***Inugami***, ***Kakashi***, or ***Trick*** before this relatively tepid entry in that languid sub-genre.

However, before damning ***Shikoku*** with faint praise (the only way, honestly, by which to damn it), an important point must be made. The J-Horrors made prior to the American ***Ring*** allowed for a greater variegation of style and tone; after 2003 the forces of commercialism enforced greater uniformity. Early J-Horror productions like this one manage to incorporate a set of common ingredients without producing the same end results, while the most recent films cannot help but feel increasingly formulaic. Yet the impulse to criticize that commercial imperative and the conformity it enforces on creativity is misguided. Early pioneers pave a path that their subsequent followers often improve upon. If we wish to shrug off the bandwagon jumpers and mimics to favor those who went first, we'd have to hail ***Don't Look Up*** over ***Ring***, and ***Shikoku*** over ***Inugami***, ***Kakashi***, and ***Trick***. It would be foolish to do so, as the later films are superior, yet the latter triad also undeniably copy a pattern first laid down by ***Shikoku***. As I have tried to argue in this book throughout, we need to approach J-Horror without the preconceived notions that drive so much of film criticism: to look not for innovation but for refinement.

The time has come to finally put a fine point, then, on just what J-Horror is.

The year is 1776. While on one side of the world, rebels and political theorists are crafting a new kind of government, in Japan, a man with a colorful past is collating Japanese and Chinese folktales into a work he will call *Ugetsu Monogatari* (Tales of Moonlight and Rain). Much as Shakespeare took established traditional stories and made them his own, Akinari Ueda rewrote myths in his own poetic style. Hundreds of years later, his masterpiece would still be hailed as a national treasure.

In 1953, filmmaker Kenji Mizoguchi set his mind to adapting *Ugetsu Monogatari* for the screen. And why not? Japanese culture has been suffused with ghost stories ever since Ueda put his calligraphic brush to paper. More importantly, the postwar American Occupation was no longer in a position to stop him.

Japanese film had from the silent era onwards indulged in horror movies, as had the cinemas of every country and culture that made motion pictures. But Japanese horror films up until WWII had adapted traditional folk legends, set in the Tokugawa period. General MacArthur feared that references to the feudal past would stir up troubling feelings of nationalism, the very thing he was keen to suppress. The Occupation maintained strict censorship of Japanese media and art despite the new constitution's guarantee of freedom of expression. In 1951, a peace treaty formally ended the American military control of Japan, and a new age of Japanese cinema began to flourish.

Mizoguchi's screen version of ***Ugetsu*** is a true movie classic of peerless quality. In its wake came Nobuo Nakagawa with ***Ghost Story of Yotsuya*** and Masayuki Kobayashi with ***Kwaidan*** (see Chapter 3).[2]

It is in these gothic classics of Japanese cinema that crucial J-Horror symbols are established: lady ghosts with long black hair, family tragedies and dead children, conflicts between husbands and wives resolved by drownings, ghosts so human you could know and love them without realizing their spectral nature.

In turn, these symbols arose from long-established Japanese cultural traditions. The themes derived from the morals and meanings of stories written in the eighteenth and nineteenth centuries, while the images derived from a school of printmaking in the 1800s called ukiyo-e prints. These startlingly graphic depictions of gory violence and monstrous figures have been cited as one of the principal roots of manga, and indeed many ukiyo-e pictures were illustrations of familiar scenes from traditional ghost stories.

Meet Hokusai, Japan's most fabled artist. He lived from 1760 to 1849, during which time he created some 30,000 artworks. Hokusai is a pseudonym—the man changed his name as often as his laundry, and "Hokusai" is merely the handle by which he is known today. At one point, he collected a cycle of his woodblock prints together in a bound volume—and voilà, the world's first manga was born.

In 1830 (give or take), Hokusai illustrated the *Hyaku Monogatari* (The Hundred Stories), another short story compilation full of ghosts and demons. One of his most indelible images from this collection is the Laughing Hannya, a grotesque demon woman with flowing black hair, snacking on a baby's head. Here it is, folks—the origin of Sadako.

When Norio Tsuruta, Hideo Nakata, Kiyoshi Kurosawa, and others began to revamp these ancient traditions in the 1990s, they pulled off a trick that Mizoguchi, Nakagawa, and Kobayashi had never contemplated: take the classical images and ideas out of the old texts and woodcuts and drop them, intact, into a modern world of cell phones, computers, and VCRs.

The presence of spirits is, for Japanese people, a real-world fact. Psychics exist, your dead relatives live in the family's butsudan altar, a world of phantoms commingles with this one and can—under the right circumstances—be glimpsed. Having ghosts and demons rampage around feudal Japan, with samurai wives and Tokugawa-era mores, makes those scares distant, unreal, harmless. But what if the Laughing Hannya was hanging around the school gym, or waiting at the bus stop? J-Horror used ancient tricks to hit the audience where they lived.

By way of example, producer Masato Hara followed up ***Shikoku*** with a film that self-consciously yanked elements of *Ugetsu Monogatari* into the new millennium. Clips of Mizugochi's 1953 masterwork even appear in ***Isola***, another Dead Wet Girl opus from Asmik Ace, written and directed by Toshiyuki Mizutani and based on a novel by Yusuke Kishi. ***Isola*** is a punchy little film about a crippled scientist, a psychic, a schoolgirl with thirteen personalities (all of 'em bad), a suicide-riddled post-disaster community, and a ruined lab in a crumbling building.

In the aftermath of the 1995 Kobe earthquake, Yukari Kamo (played by Yoshino Kimura) volunteers to help the survivors in the postapocalyptic ruins of the once-proud city. Her power brings her into the orbit of a troubled young girl named Chiharu Moritani (Yuu Kurosawa). This poor child is beset by tragedy. Victim of incest from her uncle-cum-adoptive father, subject of intrusive experimentation by cold-hearted scientists, she is also surrounded by death. Her mere presence is enough to trigger others into acts of suicide and/or homicide. And did I mention that she suffers from multiple personality disorder?

One of Chiharu's alter egos calls herself Isola: this is the persona suspected of causing so much death and destruction. Believing the name to be a reference to *Ugetsu Monogatari*, Yukari watches the 1953 film as a sort of cinematic Cliff's Notes. She speculates that poor Chiharu, sexually mistreated by her uncle, has generated Isola as a form of self-protection and revenge rolled into one. However, this theory requires revision once Yukari learns of the secret experiments of Dr. Yayoi Takano (Makiko Watanabe). Seems Yayoi was in the habit of stripping nude and settling herself into the murky water of a sensory deprivation tank, in an attempt to sever the link between her spirit and her physical body. When the earthquake came along and killed her body, you had the explosive combination of a dead wet girl, an angry ghost, and a schoolgirl with more than enough psychological fragmentation to provide at least temporary shelter. Add psychic Yukari to the mix and things are certain to get hairy (forgive the pun).

Isola giddily juggles familiar J-Horror constituents, yet it feels fresh and vibrant—more fun to watch than the dour, slow-paced ***Shikoku***, but more schlocky as well.

Stepping down another rung into cheap-grade B-movie production was Masato Hara's next J-Horror for Asmik Ace, ***Otogiriso*** (or ***St. John's Wort***, on American DVD). Takenori Sento returned as writer, adapting a book by Shukei Nagasaka, but billed on DVD as being based on a Playstation Video Game. Director Ten Shimoyama cluttered the movie with plenty of sound and fury, and the shot-on-video cinematography by Kazuhiko Ogura pulls every MTV-style trick in the book: slow-motion, sped-up motion, freeze frames, jump cuts, crash zooms, solarized images... The viewer at home is inclined to reach for the joystick to control the action onscreen.

Ju-On's Megumi Okina stars as Nami, a graphic designer haunted by her unsettled and half-forgotten past. She was put up for adoption as a child, and forever since harbored the feeling her family had abandoned her. When she inherits her father's mansion-like home in the country, it offers her a chance to revisit that lost heritage and seek answers about why her family rejected her. Meanwhile, ex-boyfriend and coworker Kohei (Yoichiro Saito) tags along to document her journey on his camcorder, so that the place can be digitally rendered as a location in the video game they are creating.

A flimsy plot device strands the two of them in the house overnight during a torrential rainstorm, but they never lose contact with their buddies back at the office, who are able to watch along in real-time to a live feed from Kohei's camera.

The walls of the place are covered with disturbing paintings by Nami's father, a crazed reclusive artist whose vivid depictions of pain were inspired by actual visions of genuine terror conjured up in his own home (see also Kiyoshi Kurosawa's ***Sweet Home***, Chapter 5). The house also contains the mummified remains of children, kidnapped and tortured to provide inspiration for these nightmare portraits. When Nami discovers a photograph revealing she had a twin, she begins to fear what horrible fate befell the child unlucky enough not to have been "abandoned" by such a father…

Amazingly, this low-budget v-cinema manages to wring considerable atmosphere and suspense out of what comes down to little more than watching two characters bumble through an old dark house. Few other characters appear in the film at all, few other sets are used, but this bare-bones reductionism is awkwardly mated to the over-the-top excesses of Ten Shimoyama's style. The movie itself is like one of the paintings in it: simple visions of fear rendered with overly florid Brueghelesque indulgence.

The same day that ***St. John's Wort*** hit video shelves, ***Inugami*** reached Japanese theaters, a brooding drama that right from frame one blurs the dividing line between the distant past and the everyday present.

During the opening credits of ***Inugami***, Miki Bonomiya (Yuki Amami) is seen at her craft: making paper by hand, following ancient traditions passed down through the generations of the Bonomiya family.

When a motorcycle speeds past, it initially appears to be an anachronistic intrusion into feudal Japan, when it is actually the other way around. The village of Omine is the anachronism, stubbornly committed to a simple rural lifestyle.

Omine is the ancestral home of the Bonomiya clan, who are preparing for the 900th anniversary of their Ancestor Rites. This is a ritual celebration so complex and involved it takes months to organize and obliges the villagers to dress in period costume. The Bonomiyas are like Japanese Amish. They reject modern technology, and although clan leader Takanao has made a concession to the times by getting a computer (and permitting the use of electricity to run it), little else about the village has been touched by the passage of time.

Since ancient times, the Bonomiya women have been charged

with tending the dangerous Inugami, evil gods whose jealousy and malice can only be contained by constant vigilance. Miki now holds this duty, and there's suspicion that she has fallen down on the job. *Everyone* (except Miki herself) is plagued with sleepless nights and traumatic nightmares, and inexplicable tragedies strike the villagers. Superstitious rumors start. The villagers talk of exorcism.

Enter Akira Nutahara, a handsome young teacher who quickly falls for Miki. Their sexually graphic affair, full of couplings in dank caves surrounded by furious rainstorms or pressed up next to Miki's paper-making vat, has a curiously rejuvenating effect on Miki. She seems to age backwards, growing younger and more beautiful every day. Soon it is hard to imagine she is actually old enough to be his mother…

Spinster she may be now, but long ago, she bore a child under circumstances so secret, no one dares speak of them. She and Takanao made love and conceived a child. Neither knew at the time that they were brother and sister, but when Miki's mother learned of the union she vowed to get rid of the offending offspring.

Miki has lived with the guilt of this tryst her whole life, blamed by everyone for her wanton ways (when Takanao bore at least equal responsibility for their unwitting crime). She believed that the child of this act of incest was stillborn, but in fact he has grown up to be a handsome young man—named Akira Nutahara! Miki has not only slept with her brother, but has managed—unwittingly—to commit double-down incest. Now that Miki is pregnant with her own grandchild, it seems the ancient evil of the Inugami is gathering to doom the village forever…

Is Miki a fundamentally evil person, accursed, whose inner corruption projects the power of the Inugami outward through those around her? Is she a victim of those same Inugami, consumed by a curse handed down over generations? Or, equally possible, is she a victim of social forces—nothing supernatural at all—by which she is punished for the crimes of the Bonomiya men? Is the legend of the Inugami simply a handy excuse to blame her for Takanao's crime?

Her whole life has been spent atoning for one moment of consensual sex with a man who paid no price himself. Now, as adults, Takanao is prepared to give away everything Miki holds dear, simply for his own selfish needs. Miki dares want a life of her own, a life defined by her choices and not by the dictates of her family or the suffocating confines of Omine. But her attempts to reject tradition set in motion a chain of circumstances that brings ruin to all.

Incest, abortion, birth defects, and lots of dark, murky water form the backdrop for a story about a woman who desires a life beyond her village's backwards, restricting traditions. She is right to want what she wants, and the audience is on her side, even as her choices spell doom for herself, her loved ones, her entire way of life, and countless innocents.

Japan at the millennium is undergoing a cultural transformation similar to that experienced by the United States in the 1970s. In ever growing numbers, women are joining the workforce and choosing non-traditional lifestyles, a fact that discomfits the patriarchial society and has yet to be fully absorbed. Horror films by their very nature are designed to deal with taboos and transitional moments, so it is no surprise that the films of the Haunted School are preoccupied with Japan's feminist revolution. Over and over we see the oppositions of urban vs. rural, tradition vs. modernity, and male vs. female underlying the supernatural goings-on. Over and over, deviations from traditional family structures—such as divorce, abortion, or homosexuality—figure somewhere in the plot of these ghost stories.

Masato Hara especially fixed his attention on those stories most steeped in "female troubles." ***Shikoku***, ***Isola***, ***St. John's Wort***, and finally ***Inugami***—four J-Horrors in a row all for Asmik Ace, all by producer Masato Hara, all dealing with incest and child abuse. One wonders if Hara's friends started feeling leery of spending time with the guy.

These are also themes that speak to Masato Harada. Please note that this is not a misspelling. For now, we are no longer concerned with producer Masato Hara, but rather, a very different man with a coincidentally similar name. Writer/director Masato Harada knows what it is like to yearn for something more than what is offered by life, to rankle against the ignorance and bigotry of others, to sire children who are shunned because of their difference.

Harada was a chubby kid, teased and tormented for his weight. As a teenager, his dreams of becoming a filmmaker chafed against the limited opportunities in the Japanese film industry of the late 1960s, so he left the country.

In 1972, Harada was studying English in London when he saw a revival screening of Howard Hawks' 1939 classic ***Only Angels Have Wings***. It was an epiphany, and Harada set his sights on meeting Hawks to talk directly with the director he most admired. It took some time of shuttling from film festival to film festival across Europe, but eventually Harada made contact, and a bond was formed. Hawks became Harada's mentor, a surrogate father, teaching the young man lessons

DOG BLESS YOU

In Japanese folklore, the Inugami are "monstrous dog spirits." Legends vary with the telling, but the Inugami are most commonly associated with righteous vengeance. The magician who captures, summons, and uses the power of the Inugami does so to punish a wrongdoer. The attack of an Inugami spirit is supposed to be so awful that the magician would likely regret it or might even be destroyed by the spirit's backlash. Using an Inugami for revenge, then, is an essentially suicidal act.

In 1976, the legendary Japanese director Kon Ichikawa directed ***Inugami-ke no Ichizoku*** ("The Inugami Family") from a novel by Seishi Yokomizo. It was the first of five Yokomizo adaptations from the team of Ichikawa and star Koji Ishizaka and broke box office records in its day. ***The Inugami Family*** is a mystery thriller and was produced by Haruki Kadokawa—the man who founded Kadokawa Shoten, the publishing and media giant behind the J-Horror boom.

In 2006, Taka Ichise approached Ichikawa with an enticing offer: why not head up a modern remake of this classic of Japanese cinema? Ichikawa itched to bring new technologies like CGI to bear on the story, and in turn asked Koji Ishikaza to return as well, to reprise his own role.

Ichise was delighted. The project was the perfect marriage for him of art and commerce: "It's not that I hate foreign film festivals—I enjoy them—but the prizes hold no appeal for me," he explained to Mark Schilling. "At the same time, I don't think a movie is good just because a lot of people like it. A movie may be great even if only a minority likes it."

he learned in the trenches of Hollywood.

Harada lived for years in America as a film journalist, immersing himself in American film culture. Eventually his contacts in the American movie biz got him gigs handling the Japanese subtitling and dubbing of such hits as ***Star Wars*** (1977) and ***Full Metal Jacket*** (1987). He started a family, collaborated with Irvin Kershner on ***The Ninja*** (1981), and more or less made Los Angeles home.

Los Angeles was not home, though, not for real. Harada moved his family back to Japan, intending to start a new life as an auteurist director in the Howard Hawks mold, making socially conscious pictures aimed at Western audiences. To an extent, this happened. Films like ***Bounce Ko Gals*** (1997), about teenage prostitution, earned him a reputation as one of Japan's leading social critics and international critical acclaim. But he was seen as an outsider in his native Japan. His American-born children were ostracized as not-true Japanese. And even films like ***Painted Desert***, shot in Nevada with a cast of Hollywood movie stars, failed to crack the elusive American market.

Harada started to feel like a man without a home, rejected by both Japan and the United States. He began to nurture an inner life of pain and resentment.

Then, in the wake of the J-Horror boom after 1998's ***Ring***, he was handed the book *Inugami* by Masako Bando. One of Bando's other novels had already yielded ***Shikoku*** the previous year, and the project seemed ideal for Harada's unique sensibilities.

The legend of the Inugami appealed to Harada on multiple levels. As a sci-fi buff, he liked the ghost story aspects. But he also knew that the Inugami had been part of a certain kind of class discrimination.

"It actually happened," says Harada, "and there are still some local villagers in the western part of Japan and in the island of Shikoku who remember this kind of Inugami prejudice. It's a term that the first settlers used for the second generation of settlers. People would say of new settlers, 'They're rich because they're possessed by Inugami. If you cross them, they'll release the Inugami at you, attack you, and you'll get killed.'"

Implicit in the story, then, was a chance to indulge his penchant for wild visual imagery, critique retrograde Japanese prejudice, and confront the basic opposition between old and new that has been an important part of Japanese society throughout the ages.

"There are so many taboos associated with the dark side of Japanese traditions, so this movie deals with two different types of Japanese traditions," explains Harada. "One is positive and one is negative. For example, Miki has this legacy of papermaking, which is a positive side of Japanese traditions... Another thing is she is the inheritor of this prejudicial tradition. And that's where the spiritual story takes place in the movie."

Harada continues, "What we need in Japan right now, in every sense, is taboo breakers. And Miki becomes a taboo breaker by accident, by committing incest, which is a taboo for every society. And therefore she becomes capable of breaking heavier, bigger social taboos."

Harada saw Miki's character as a Hitchcockian sort of heroine, a beautiful but cold woman whose sexuality awakens as terrible things happen around her. The role also called for an actress who could convincingly cover a range of ages, from a fortysomething spinster to a hottie in her twenties. He immediately thought of actress Yuki Amami, one of Japan's brightest stars at the time. Harada credits much of the film's effectiveness to Amami's sensitive, moving performance.

On all levels, ***Inugami*** was an extraordinary artistic achievement. From the cast to the photography to the haunting musical score to the careful, precise editing, Harada led a team that was working at the height of their respective disciplines.

For all that, though, the picture was a hard sell. Since it dealt with incest, the Japanese ratings board gave the film an R-15 rating. This was actually a concession negotiated by the producers, since under normal circumstances the subject matter would have warranted an automatic X rating. The R-15 classification kept away the family audience that had given so much commercial boost to others in the Haunted School. The likes of ***Ring*** benefited from being free of graphic violence and gore, but ***Inugami***—free of violence, and not even particularly scary—was handicapped for its treatment of an Oedipal theme.

Harada steeled himself with the hope that foreign audiences would embrace his haunting vision. European festivals greeted ***Inugami*** with bafflement, however. It was a respectful bafflement, reflected in various award nominations, but ***Inugami*** was not destined for theatrical release in the U.S., was not snapped up by Roy Lee for remake rights, and would ultimately show up on video shelves with little fanfare.

Disappointed by the tepid response, Harada figured that the J-Horror bubble had burst.

We know now that this was far from the case. J-Horror was still on an upswing. Yet to come were the likes of ***Pulse***, ***Dark Water***, ***Suicide Club***, and ***Ju-On: The Grudge***. Not bad for a popped bubble.

Inugami was a well-made thriller replete with intriguing ideas. It just wasn't what audiences wanted.

In the heady days after ***Ring*** hit it big, J-Horror-makers were drunk with possibility. For a few years, the Haunted School hammered out a wildly diverse selection of movies. Books, manga, and real-world legends all served as inspirations, and a common set of visual symbols marked them as part of a thematic grouping, but there was room enough under the J-Horror tent for divergent aesthetics and quirky approaches. Some would be more popular than others.

Few of these experiments came anywhere close to the popular appeal of ***Ring***, and so, over time, the Darwinian pressures of the marketplace coerced film producers to conform closer and closer to those formulas that made for the biggest hits. J-Horror would live on, but filmmakers were on notice that experimentation was risky.

Take for example ***Ikisudame***. The title actually translates as "Doppelganger," but to avoid confusion with the Kiyoshi Kurosawa flick of the same name, it has been marketed in English as ***Shadow of the Wraith***. This was the work of director Toshiharu Ikeda, best known for the ***Evil Dead Trap*** series of gore flicks, persuaded in 2001 to jump on the J-Horror bandwagon.

Keenly aware that the target audience for J-Horror is teenage girls,

Ikeda's film features two brothers who blow off the pressure of high school in a band called Martial Law: the roles are played by the real-life brothers Koji and Yuichi Matsuo of the J-Pop band Doggy Bag (yes, Martial Law is a way cooler name).

The movie is split down the middle into two separate stories. The first showcases Koji Matsuo as high school hunk Ryoji, object of an obsessive crush by weird girl Asaji (played by Hitomi Miwa, from the original ***Ju-On*** video and ***Misa the Dark Angel***). Like Asaji's spiritual twin Tomie, the girl has got her eyes on the prize. She will score Ryoji one way or another. If necessary, she'll visit him in his dreams to deliver some succubal treats, or murder anyone who stands in her way. She won't even let being killed stop her. Extra points if you guessed she lets her long black hair hang in front of her face.

In the second hour, the story shifts to Ryoji's brother Kazuhiko (Yuichi Matsuo) and his sweetie Naoko (Asumi Miwa—who, like her real-life sister Hitomi, has an impressive CV full of Japanocult titles such as ***Uzumaki***, ***Gamera 3***, and the v-cinema ***Ju-On***). Naoko is evidently the target of a curious progressive curse, which is methodically zeroing in while eliminating everyone around her one by one. Together, Naoko and Kazuhiko find themselves trapped in a reductionist mishmash of ***Dark Water*** blended with ***Ju-On***.

Although Ikeda's career has mostly focused on gore, violence, and porn, he brought confidence and skill to this restrained, atmospheric material. The extravagant use of color symbolism calls to mind Mario Bava. But this is a case of leftovers served with love. It does what it does very well, but ***Shadow of the Wraith*** is merely a shadow of greater hits: it is a formula film, self-consciously cashing in, and as such a sign of things to come.

The haunted school still had original ideas, though, and one of the most strikingly idiosyncratic films to come out of this genre has to be ***Trick***. Its originality has won it a legion of ardent fans: to date ***Trick*** has spawned two TV series, two theatrical features, and a manga adaptation. Often cited as the Japanese answer to ***The X-Files*** (for its premise of a boy and girl investigating bizarre mysteries), the more apt reference is ***The Avengers*** (for its premise of a boy and girl confronting bizarre mysteries with absurdist humor). ***Trick***, you see, is a comedy.

It started in 2000 with a television miniseries commissioned by Asahi TV from writer Koji Makita and director Yukihiko Tsutsumi. The eagle-eyed readers among you may remember we first met Mr. Makita in Chapter 2 as the screenwriter of ***Ring: The Final Chapter***, a looney TV adaptation of Koji Suzuki's novel that freely added all manner of digressions, embellishments, and innovations. The best of these ideas Makita returned to, and improved, in ***Trick*** (the onscreen title uses the English word, with the letter K reversed). In 2002, Toho Studios asked Tsustumi and Makita to bring the popular television series to the big screen, which they did with gusto. Like the best J-Horrors before it, ***Trick*** makes magic with paltry resources. This is not a big event picture.

Chief among Makita's concerns is the role of skepticism in supernatural horror. This fact alone makes him unique. The bulk of Japanese horror, traditional or modern, simply assumes the existence of ghosts and monsters and runs with it. In both ***Ring: The Final Chapter*** and ***Trick***, Makita stops the story cold to debunk various paranormal assumptions. ***Trick: the Movie*** opens with a brief, historically accurate, recounting of the story of Robert Houdin, the father of modern magic. Houdin was a French magician in the nineteenth century whose fame on stage brought him to the attention of the authorities. The French government had a favor to ask of the illusionist. A rebellion was brewing in the French colony of Algiers, and the locals there were highly superstitious. Houdin's job as official ambassador of the French government was to go flummox the unruly Algerians with a show of magic designed to convince them that France was unbeatable. The spirit of Houdin hangs over ***Trick*** throughout, the dominant theme being that if you believe in magic, it's only because you're a weak-minded person who hasn't put enough effort into figuring out the trick.

Inspired by the story of Houdin, emissaries from the rural backwater Itofushi seek out aspiring magician Naoko Yamade (played by the delightful Yukie Nakama). Their village labors under a myth that every 300 years a terrible catastrophe threatens their survival and can only be averted by the intervention of a god. They want Naoko to pretend to be a god, do a few magic tricks to demonstrate her miracles, and pacify the terrified villagers back into their normal routines.

Unfortunately, Naoko has a few problems to overcome. First among them, she is no Houdin—she is a clumsy, inexperienced magician with a limited repertoire of fairly unimpressive tricks. More problematic, she is not the only magician hired to play god. And to top it all off, the villagers have decided to pit the various "gods" against one another in miracle show-downs. Anyone who doesn't pass the test is exposed as a fraud, and summarily executed!

Luckily, Naoko is not alone—also in Itofushi is the famous skeptic Jiro Ueda (Hiroshi Abe). Between them is a push-me-pull-you romantic tension and professional rivalry that keeps sparks flying, but they make a good pair. Together they hope to use logic and mathematics to expose their competitors as tricksters and discover the secret truth behind Itofushi's troubles.

Yukihiko Tsutsumi honed his directorial talents with years of toil in the Japanese TV drama business. Tsustumi has been awarded the prize for Best Director six times by the Japanese Television Academy—once for ***Trick***. He has also started to branch successfully into theatrical features, with the strongest screen version of Hanako the Toilet Ghost in 1998's ***School Mystery*** (see Chpater 3), the ***Trick*** franchise and the riotous action comedy ***2LDK***. It's a tough assignment he handed himself, to blend slapstick with suspense. Most horror comedies don't even try for both and settle instead for netting laughs at the expense of spoofing the horror elements. Occasionally, a ***Shaun of the Dead*** happens along to treat its humor and its horror with equal sincerity; ***Trick*** proudly stands in that rarefied company.

Tsutsumi carefully builds ***Trick*** towards a dark, apocalyptic ending not evident during the lighter first half. Out of the laughs, a deeper horror is slowly revealing itself, and like the more austere films by producer Masato Hara, it is a horror derived from the taboo of incest. Somehow, this funky funny movie managed to tackle this taboo in a widely distributed and popular film, while the likes of ***Inugami*** found only censorship and audience resistance. Perhaps what Masato Harada chalked up to the death of J-Horror as a genre was really just sour grapes; the audience didn't much care for his beautiful yet dispassionate tragedy. ***Trick*** handles the same red-hot subject matter with a pulpy sense of fun, razor-sharp wit, and total artistic self-confidence. ***Trick*** comes out swinging, with a playful and witty script designed for puzzle lovers, with room enough for potty humor and ***Ultraman*** jokes.

If ***Trick*** alone were not proof enough that the genre could happily accommodate movies whose debt to ***Ring*** and ***Ju-On*** was never obvious, wunderkind Shion Sono inaugurated 2002 with a movie so discomfiting and unsettling it stands as a pure cinematic nightmare.

A multitalented prodigy, Shion Sono's extraordinary accomplishments lie mostly outside the scope of this book. Whereas so many of the filmmakers we celebrate here made their names and fortunes within the confines of the J-Horror genre, Sono is a poet, a performance artist, and a pornographer as much as he is an arthouse filmmaker. His 2002 thriller ***Jisatsu Sakuru*** ("Suicide Club," also known as ***Suicide Circle***) marks his biggest commercial success in a career that has rarely even tried for such a goal.

Suicide Club centers around schools and hospitals—the two primary institutional fixtures of J-Horror—and is a police procedural about the evident viral contagion of self-destruction. The detectives know that something is wrong, but struggle with how to investigate what is not, on the surface at least, a crime. What drives these people to kill themselves? Is it some kind of hypnosis, a biological plague, or just another sign of a decadent society collapsing under its own corruption? What connects the victims?

Following this line of inquiry, a staggering discovery is made: a spool of human flesh, wound like a reel of movie film, composed of strips of skin peeled from the victims—get this—*before* they killed themselves. If the spiral shape of the skin-spool has you thinking of ***Spiral*** or ***Uzumaki***, you may also be interested to note that there is a web site keeping a careful accounting of the suicides. The dead are tallied up as dots on a computer screen, in an image freely borrowed from Kiyoshi Kurosawa's ***Pulse***. Like the spiral of skin, this web site is premonitory: the dots accumulate, accurately, before each mass suicide takes place. Somehow, someone knows of these suicides before they happen...

Sono is accumulating a tally of his own, collecting tidbits from other J-Horrors the way his Suicide Club collects souvenir strips of flesh. Along with references to ***Spiral***, ***Uzumaki***, and ***Pulse***, there is a potentially life-threatening music video (see ***Ring: The Final Chapter*** in Chapter 2), an emailed chain letter that may offer protection from the rash of suicides (an urban legend that suggests ***Ring***'s methodology of self-preservation), and an overall plot structure echoing Kurosawa's ***Cure***.

To delineate these references is not in any way to denigrate Sono's independent artistic achievement, which swept awards at international film festivals. Fans around the world thrilled to its brazenly shocking opening sequence: fifty-four schoolgirls linking hands and joyfully leaping as one in front of a subway train at Shinjuku station, splattering blood everywhere. This scene, a caption tells us, takes place on May 26 (no year given).

The audience takes a collective gasp.

For a story about the terrorist use of mind control, spreading like a virus, to begin its horror in the subway system inevitably invites the viewer to remember the shattering tragedy of March 20, 1995. As you will recall (from Chapter 3), that was the date that Aum Shinrikyo released Sarin nerve gas in the Tokyo subways—the worst attack on Japanese soil since the end of the Second World War. But Shion Sono's reference is even more specific than that, and more subversive.

Shinjuku Station had a particular significance in the events of that day. There were five cult members who boarded five different trains, each intending to release the gas by puncturing a hole in the plastic bag containing the poison. The perpetrator who boarded at the Shinjuku Station that morning poked too small a hole in his to cause any deaths. Although two hundred people were injured by inhaling the gas, authorities managed to search the train and dispose of the toxin before any fatalities occurred. So, to correct their oversight, Aum hit that train line a second time, on May 5. This time they used a different tactic: separate containers of sodium cyanide and sulfuric acid. Combining these two chemicals would produce deadly hydrogen cyanide and potentially slaughter as many as 20,000 commuters in a single whiff. Again, though, the attack was botched, and the police successfully destroyed the chemicals without a casualty. A third attack on Shinjuku Station took place later in the summer, using the same approach as the May 5 one, and with identically harmless results.

As for May 26, that was the day that, in 1998, the leader of Aum, Ikuo Hayashi, was up for sentencing. He escaped the death penalty, sentenced instead to life imprisonment.

In the opening frames of ***Suicide Club***, Shion Sono not only invokes memories of the terrorist incident, but targets specifically the most divergent, ambiguous moments of that story. It would be like an American filmmaker referencing not the horror of 9-11 itself but just Zaccharias Moussaui and Richard Reed. With a poet's understanding of the power of symbolism, Sono fixes our attention on the points in Aum's cruel history where things went unexpectedly. As ***Suicide Club*** unfolds, then, we are on notice not to jump to conclusions: things are not what they seem.

Without giving away too much of the film's surprises, Sono roots his horror not in the supernatural but in the ways in which adults fail children. Other movies discussed in this chapter, such as ***Isola*** and ***Trick***, indict individual families for victimizing their most vulnerable members. ***Suicide Club*** accuses an entire generation on behalf of an entire society.

These movies began to appear in theaters at the same time that Japan began to confront a problem they had convinced themselves did not, and could not, exist. "In pediatric circles we thought there wasn't much child abuse," explains Dr. Seiji Sakai of the Center for Child Abuse Prevention, "and that we were different from the United States because our culture was different." As Sakai told The New York Times in the summer of 1999, "The single biggest problem was [Japan] realizing that there is child abuse."

Statistics show a steadily rising trend of child abuse in Japan, a twenty-fold increase over the last ten years. However, there is some debate as to whether these shocking numbers reflect an increase in the actual occurrences of abuse or an increasing willingness to report and document it. In 1993, the prefectural government of Osaka published a manual for dealing with cases of child abuse and neglect but found their local efforts hampered by an archaic system on the federal level where ancient traditions and dusty laws helped obscure the problem.

The Japanese had long considered their culture safe from such horrors since their families were stronger. But the traditional Japanese family unit, as we have seen throughout this book, is under new pressures. Even if it was once true that Japanese values held such horrors at bay (a dubious proposition), a brave new world of economic uncertainty, record unemployment, rising divorce rates and increasing tension between traditional gender roles may have irrevocably changed all that.

"Child abuse is on the rise in Japan," says Machiko Ayukyo, a lawyer with the Center for Child Abuse Prevention. However, Jun Saimura, speaking for the Child and Family Research Institute, argues, "Awareness of child abuse is growing, but there are still many more cases out there that go unreported. We just do not know what the real figure is." It was not until 1999 that the Ministry of Health and Welfare even tried to collect official statistics on the problem and start offering counseling for abused children. Masaaki Noda, a professor at Kansei Gakuin University, fears that as long as the Japanese resist society's "interference" in families' private lives, the full scope of the problem will remain outside the culture's control. "Society itself is abusing children," he says.

Within its almost slavish adherence to the formula and aesthetics established by ***Ring***, ***Chakushin ari*** ("One Missed Call") dramatizes how child abuse sends ripples of horror through entire societies, on into the future, in an unending spiral of victimization. Despite being adapted from a novel by Yasushi Akimoto, the premise seems calculated to echo past hits: people receive mysterious cell phone calls, apparently from their own phones but from the future. The voice mail messages foretell the callers' deaths, which then occur exactly as predicted. The curse spreads in a viral fashion, using the call logs of each victim's phone to jump to the next target. The cops are at first puzzled by what appear to be psychically compelled suicides; as ever, the authorities are useless in the face of new and unfamiliar threats.

Kou Shibasaki, last seen in Norio Tsuruta's ***Kakashi***, stars as Yumi, an abuse survivor desperately trying to unravel the mystery behind all the carnage that surrounds her. She traces the psychic phone calls back to a poor little girl, Mimiko Mizunuma, the child of a rape, disowned and abused by her family. Can it be a coincidence that Yumi's past is pockmarked by the same betrayal and pain that ruined

Mimiko's? Is Yumi's dark secret the one thing that will enable her to connect with the dead wet girl and end the horror, or will she only make things unutterably worse?

At its best, ***One Missed Call*** recalls fond memories of ***Ring***, but at its worst it collapses under the weight of its own illogic. Whereas Koji Suzuki paid scrupulous attention to detail, ensuring that there was a solid and logical explanation for how and why his ghost used a cursed videotape to wreak her revenge, ***One Missed Call*** sets up an oddball idea and blithely refuses to explain it.

Nevertheless, ***One Missed Call*** was a hit in Japan, and as such demanded a sequel. For round two, the filmmakers recognized that they had an obligation to explain why cell phones had anything whatsoever to do with this particular spook; having patiently answered that question, they then proceed to insert all manner of new irrationality into the storyline, much like citrus producers extract water from orange juice only to put it back in later.

Much of the first reel is simply given over to restating what happened in the previous film, to catch up those viewers who maybe forgot (which, given the original's blandness, was only to be expected). Like the ***Ring*** sequels, it is obliged to recreate the same menace from the original film but provide a new explanation for its mysteries, which it does reasonably well. This time we get more child abuse for our money: Takako (Asaka Seto) is an abuse survivor whose twin sister was murdered as a child. She joins forces with Kyoko (played by the model Mimula), a social worker who helps abused children. Together, they hope to reveal whether the killer cell phone calls originate with Mimiko's ghost, or another badly mistreated child who had her mouth sewn shut and was left to die in a mineshaft. Li Li, the ghost of the mine, is a standard-issue bakemono, with wild long hair and a white nightgown (do all Japanese ghosts shop at the same store?), but fans of the first film may have already guessed that it is no coincidence that one of the heroines experienced abuse first-hand.

In 2005, TV Asahi sanctioned a television miniseries based on the popular films, directed by Manabu Iso. The following summer, Iso brought his efforts to the big screen for the third installment, ***One Missed Call: The Final Chapter***. Of course, had it been as big a hit as the first two, there would have been wiggle-room to continue past that "Final" designation. And even if the series had fizzled to a halt in Japan, there was life left in the premise.

Not long after ***One Missed Call 2*** opened in Japan to record-breaking box office returns, the announcement came down that Kadokawa had allied with Warner Brothers to fashion an American remake of the first film. French director Eric Vallete was slated to begin shooting in the summer of 2006 from a screenplay adaptation by writer Andrew Klavan. One doubts that the American remake is likely to differ much from the originals. The two Japanese films hailed from two different filmmakers, yet the anonymous style employed would never signal that to the viewer. As an early work by a television director, ***One Missed Call 2*** by Renpei Tsukamoto manages to look exactly like the first one—which was directed by none other than Takashi Miike. Although ***One Missed Call*** bears Miike's name, it does not have his stamp. Say what you will about Miike, he is a singular talent.

Let's talk about Takashi Miike. The auteur behind such extremist entertainment as ***Audition*** and ***Ichi the Killer*** has got himself quite a cult following in the U.S., not to mention some serious critical attention from mainstream reviewers not generally inclined towards genre product. Like Kiyoshi Kurosawa, he is a prolific filmmaker whose output mixes personal concerns with genre traditions. Where Kurosawa works magic with restraint and suggestion, Miike's strength is outrage and excess.

Much of Miike's output is beyond the scope of this book, but he intersects our story with the television miniseries ***MPD Psycho***. Backed by the media powerhouses Omega Project and Kadokawa, this lavishly appointed television epic adapts the manga by Shou Tajima and Eiji Otsuka. Published in 1997, the comic followed the bizarre exploits of a police profiler afflicted with multiple personality disorder. Inside the poor man's fractured psyche lived his original identity, Yosuke Kobayashi, as well as that of an evil serial killer with a sick sense of humor, Shinji Nishizono. Unable to reconcile his good and wicked selves, he generated a third, more stable personality, Kazuhiko Amamiya, and literally exorcised Nishizono. However, Nishizono did not go gentle into that good night but instead survived as a free-floating phantom, ready to hop at will into other bodies.

Each of the six episodes of the 2000 TV adaptation is a more-or-less separate story. But while each episode poses a new investigation with its own weirdo case, the answer to the whodunit is always the same, Nishizono. In the spirit of the old Dr. Mabuse thrillers, this is a less than helpful solution: it remains a question who Nishizono is this week, what he's up to, and how (if at all) he can be stopped. Miike has a peculiar gift for dramatizing psychopaths, and as the title implies, here he is given the opportunity to do so multiple times.

Like the mythology episodes of ***The X-Files***, the individual stories do not completely resolve themselves but gradually accumulate details on a larger, highly complex, over-arching intrigue. As Amamiya works with detective Sasayama to hunt down and defeat the ghost of Nishizono, we learn tidbits of a larger story involving, among other things, a 60s era radical named Lucy Monostone who combined trippy rock music with urban terrorism, a cult of mutants mysteriously branded with bar codes on their eyeballs, a plot to negate the idea of motherhood by stealing babies from pregnant girls' wombs, the fate of Amamiya's missing wife, and the secret agenda of Amamiya's enigmatic associate, Machi Isono. True to the manga, the series does not tie all of its plot threads neatly, leaving more questions than answers.

Miike surrenders plot mechanics to visual dynamism, and if the result is barely coherent it is never less than thrilling. This is perhaps, next to Higuchinsky's ***Uzumaki***, one of the most cinematic translations of a manga yet. Miike practically redefines the phrase "over the top" with a voracious aesthetic that confidently veers from absurdist humor à la Samuel Beckett to grisly violence to cartoon animation. At one point, Sasayama gives his case briefing to his police superiors as a vaudeville routine, complete with singing and staged jokes! The pleasure here is in the delirious journey, not the narrative destination. You keep watching not to have your questions answered but to see just what surrealistic vision is coming next: human flower pots with pretty blossoms blooming from their exposed brains, a limbless body delivered by mail in a Styrofoam cooler, dead women with cell phones where their wombs used to be, a crime scene diorama made using Barbie dolls, a dismembered body

THE LOCKER

In an especially uncomfortable moment in Takashi Miike's ***MPD Pyscho***, a woman opens a coin-operated rental locker, places a newborn baby inside, closes the metal door and walks away. American audiences may see this shuddering image as yet another example of the wild surrealism pervading the show, never having seen or heard of anything like it before. However, the "coin-operated locker baby" is a peculiar form of infanticide, mostly perpetrated by unwed mothers, that shook Japan in the late 1970s. The most publicized recent incident occurred in May of 1999 when a couple interred their five-month old baby in a locker so as to eat undisturbed at a nearby restaurant.

In other words, yes, this actually happens, and doesn't that make it even scarier?

Miike has plans to direct a film called ***Coin Locker Babies*** from the novel of the same name by Ryu Murakami. This project is more of a futurist drama than a horror story, though, and as such has had difficulty finding funding, despite the fact that Miike's previous Murakami adaptation, ***Audition***, was his biggest international hit.

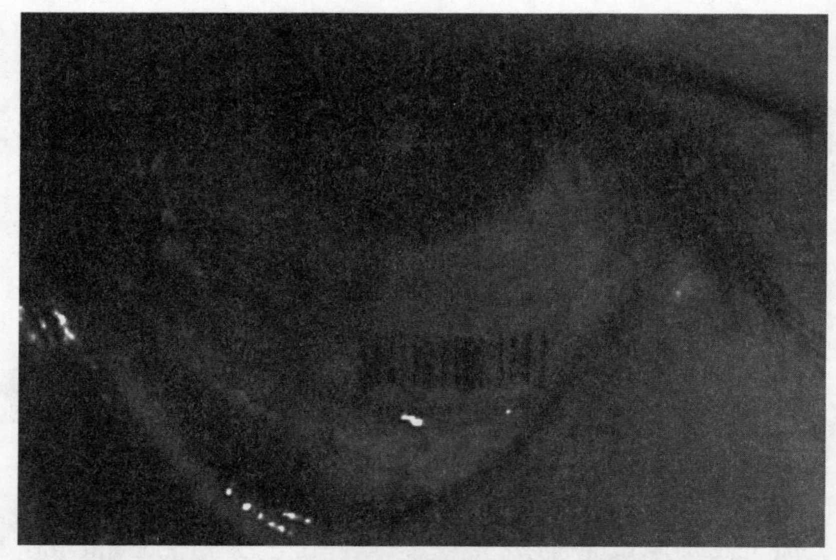

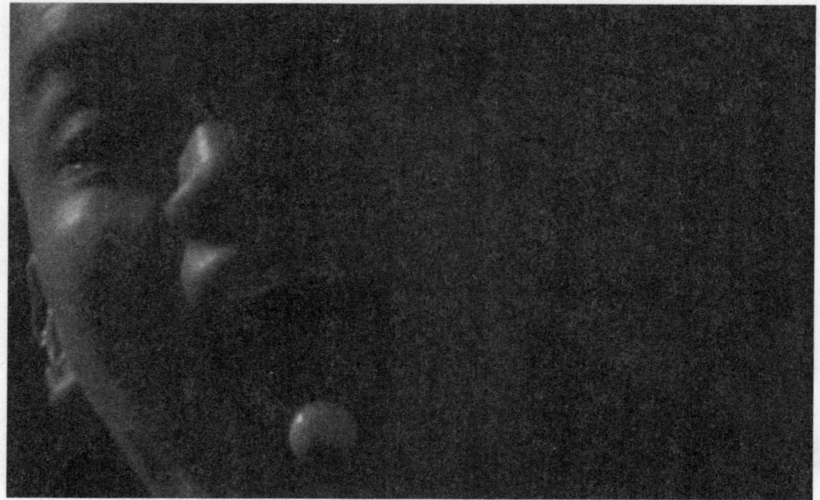

Takashi Miike's

MPD Psycho

tattooed with numbers for use in a demented game of Bingo, a gang boss with a human eyeball affixed to his tongue like a piece of jewelry... Somewhere in Heaven, Salvatore Dali's heart surges with pride.

Around the time that ***MPD Psycho*** appeared on DVD in the United States, Norio Tsuruta and Masayuki Ochiai happened to be passing through. They were flabbergasted to discover the stateside reputation of a director considered "mediocre" back home. Seems Miike is not big in Japan. Call it the Stella Artois Effect: some things are just better appreciated on foreign soil as exotic imports.

Tsuruta and Ochiai were on a press tour to promote the first two installments of Taka Ichise's latest J-Horror franchise, called, well, ***The J-Horror Theater***. But we get ahead of ourselves. Before we get into what Ochiai was making in 2004, we need to see what he was doing in 1997. Ochiai is one of the true pioneers of the movement, a figure as important and seminal as Tsuruta or Nakata or Kurosawa. And his story begins, and ends, in a haunted hospital with a sentient contagion.

In the operating room of the hospital, talented surgeons remove the kidney from braindead accident victim Kiyomi Nagashima and transplant it into the teenage body of Mariko Anzai. In an ideal world, such an operation would save the girl from the ordeal of dialysis and allow her to return to a normal life.

Then again, in an ideal world, the whole thing wouldn't have been masterminded by an ancient parasite as part of a vast inhuman conspiracy. Long dormant bacteria inside Kiyomi's very cells escapes, reproduces, and evolves into a shapeshifting monster. In the guise of Kiyomi, it seduces her grieving husband. With a fertilized parasite-human egg inside it, the thing kidnaps poor Mariko, with the gruesome idea of implanting it in her womb. It is an appalling plan, and it threatens the future of all human life.

This is *Parasite Eve*.[3] Before *Ring* had even enjoyed its first screen adaptation, Hideaki Sena's novel was a bestseller and a cultural phenomenon bar none. Much like Koji Suzuki's *Spiral* (also published in 1995 by the same company, Kadokawa Shoten), *Parasite Eve* was an exhaustively researched science-fiction thriller about a supernatural menace who manipulates the lives of others to allow her entry into our world, and to redirect the course of evolution. Even more so than *Spiral*, though, Sena's novel had its outsize horror premise grounded in hard science and factual data.

Sena was at the time a 26 year-old graduate student in pharmacology. Although he admired American horror fiction, especially that of Dean Koontz, Sena had never written such material himself. But when he explained his day job to a friend one day ("I go to the lab at night and conduct experiments on animals by injecting them with syringes filled with drugs"), he realized that his actual life was as creepy as any story.

Eons ago, when life on Earth consisted of single-celled organisms, times were tough. Those fragile early life forms were vulnerable to chemicals like oxygen and dependent on sheer dumb luck for food supplies to more or less fall into their laps. Along came bacteria, parasitic life forms with the ability to convert oxygen into energy. These bacteria attacked the primitive cells, and latched on to them in symbiosis. If you don't recall the word symbiosis from high school biology, think codependency. The bacteria found a stable home, and the cells gained the ability to generate vast amounts of energy—and thereby the ability to move, to seek out food, to adapt, to evolve.

The multicellular animals of today carry around inside their cells the remnants of those ancient parasites: mitochondria. They have their own DNA, separate from ours, but no longer a separate existence.

Sena's day job involved testing various drugs on mitochondria to enhance their ability to convert fatty acids into energy. A television documentary on mitochondrial symbiosis got him thinking: *What if these things had a will of their own, what if they didn't feel like keeping up their end of the symbiotic relationship?*

Using his scholarly background, Sena rooted his horror story in meticulously researched and often jargon-heavy science. Sena's focus on scientific accuracy (within an admittedly far-fetched premise) was rare and brought the book wide attention. It was the first book awarded the Japan Horror Novel Award and was an immediate sensation.

In the years that followed, Dr. Sena continued to write fiction but also co-wrote a serious scholarly work, *Living with Mitochondria*, to bring the subject to a broader, less-specialized audience. "I feel that science, science fiction, and horror are linked," he told interviewer Daniel Robert Epstein. "For many people who aren't interested in science, *Parasite Eve* was an entryway for them. Vice versa, scientists who don't usually read novels might read that co-written book about mitochondria and say, 'Hey, this guy seems to have written a novel about it too. Why don't I read that one?' So I hope this will be a bridge going both ways."

In 1997, Kodokawa Shoten decided to use its film production arm to put out a movie version of the bestseller. To handle the task, they brought in brash young filmmaker Masayuki Ochiai, who may be entering this book rather late but should not be considered any the lesser for it. In the earlier part of the decade he had directed the television series ***Night Head*** for Fuji TV, Kadokawa's production partner in ***Parasite***

Eve. And to complete the circle, ***Night Head*** was the brain child of Joji Iida, who would soon be hired to direct the film version of Koji Suzuki's ***Spiral*** (see also Chapter 2).

"Masayuki Ochiai seems to be pretty obsessed with hospital horror," chuckles Sena in a profound understatement. Ochiai's entire contribution to the world of J-Horror explores the spooky aspects of modern medicine—something he attributes to a traumatic childhood memory. "When I was three years old my aunt died of acute appendicitis," he explained to Daniel Robert Epstein. "Then at the hospital everyone went to watch her operation but me, so I was abandoned in the hallway for hours. I was really terrified. That was my first impression of a hospital as a lonely area."

In a passage from the book, Sena describes the ubiquitous green surgical gown and its use during the kidney transplant operation: "the green color dampened the visual impact of blood." Ochiai took that passage to heart, and his films consistently invoke green-red color symbolism. In fact, the overall visual palette is often reduced, so as to emphasize the bold greens and red when they occur. (In his later film

MY MITOCHONDRIA'S TRYING TO KILL ME

In 1987, *Nature* published a paper in which the heritage of mitochondrial DNA was traced back through the ages to its source. In turn, this resulted in what the BBC would call "the most poorly understood scientific idea of the 20th century."

During sexual reproduction, both the mother and father pass along portions of their own genes, but only the mother passes along her mitochondria. Exactly why this is remains the subject of speculation, but since it is true it enables scientists to work backwards matrilineally to find a common ancestor. Some 200,000 years ago, there lived a woman in Africa who is the common ancestor of all living humans today. *Nature* named her "Mitochondrial Eve."

The name "Eve" has such heady mythological connotations that a lot of people misunderstood the paper to mean that this woman was in fact the *first* human woman, the original mother of us all. This in turn led to questions about how one person could all by herself populate a planet, which is of course ridiculous. Mitochondrial Eve was not the first woman nor did she live alone—it is simply the case that her descendants survived while the descendants of her contemporaries did not.

Although parts of ***Parasite Eve*** are indeed based on fact, there's no call for fearing a rebellion from within your own cells. Mitochondria are the descendants of once-independent bacteria, and while they retain genetic differences from the host cells, roughly 99% of the original bacteria's DNA has been lost or absorbed by the host.

Infection, the greens and red take over, leaving no other color left.) Thanks to Ochiai's aggressive use of color, the majority of Japanese respondents to a recent poll answered that mitochondria are green—not so, but popular movies can have an enormous effect on how people see the world.

Between the massive popularity of Sena's novel and Ochiai's film version, ***Parasite Eve*** began to infect other media. In 1998, it became a Playstation game, which Sena happily approved. "I am actually impressed by how well the game makers translated the novel," he gushed. A follow-up game arrived in 1999, around the same time as a manga adaptation of the book. Rumors of a Hollywood remake of the film abound, but nothing official has yet been announced. Sena has revealed his hope that the American version, were one coming, be written by William Goldman—Sena's favorite American screenwriter. Ochiai put his two cents in for the chance to handle a remake himself. "I was not really happy with the circumstances I was under when I had to create [the original film]," Ochiai confessed to Daniel Robert Epstein. "First of all I was forced by the producers to make it a love story. There were so many compromises I had to make that it couldn't be a true horror movie."

In adapting Sena's book into a workable screenplay for Ochiai to film, writer Ryoichi Kimizuka faced several challenges. Straightening out the non-chronological nature of Sena's narrative into a linear progression was one of them, but the bigger issue lay in Sena's meticulous research. This is a book so detailed it has a glossary and frequent asides to the reader to catch them up on the latest mitochondrial discoveries. Short of issuing study guides at the theater entrance, the film had to simplify things into something more accessible to the average Joe. For example, the opening sequence finds our scientist hero Dr. Toshiaki Nagashima giving a lecture on biology so basic that any real college student would probably have been insulted—but the students seen onscreen actually argue with Nagashima about the value of even studying mitochondria at all, by way of giving the film a chance to explain things to the viewer. Hiroshi Mikami plays Nagashima like a sadsack Japanese Frankenstein: a man so obsessed with his work he fails to realize he's creating a monster. As with so many J-Horrors, the madness of the characters comes out via scribbled rants in a diary.

The biggest challenge faced by the filmmakers was how to adapt the ending. Sena whips his novel up to a wild finale that sets a new standard for "extreme." Suffering Mariko is forced to give birth to the monstrous mitochondrial creature, but the thing has a confused gender identity. Flipping between male and female, unable to resolve its sexuality, it melts away in a pool of hatred and pain. The book adds a variety of asides and epilogues to patiently explain to the reader why this happened, to ground the conclusion in the same scientific convictions that underlie the rest of the story. Anxious to concoct a cinematic ending that would rely less on gore and nudity while remaining comprehensible to non-Ph.D.'s, Kimizuka and Ochiai substitute a simpler ending in which Nagashima sacrifices himself to stop the parasite's plan even before she/it gets around to raping and impregnating a helpless teenager.

It was an auspicious ending. While Sena rightly complained that the film deviated significantly from his text, the screen version was influential in the development of subsequent J-Horrors. "Compromised" or not, its notion of parental self-sacrifice would be echoed by such films as ***Dark Water***, ***Tomie: Forbidden Fruit***, ***Premonition*** and more.

When ***Parasite Eve*** arrived in the United States on DVD many years later, some critics took one look at the ghostly girl with long black hair and white dress and summed it all up as a ***Ring***-ette, but in fact ***Parasite Eve*** predates Hideo Nakata's blockbuster hit.

As the J-Horror boom exploded after Nakata's ***Ring*** made its international splash, Ochiai followed up with a punchy piece of pulp fiction, ***Saimin*** ("The Hypnotist"). Made in 1999, it clearly draws direct inspiration from 1997's ***Cure*** and provides direct inspiration in turn to 2002's ***Suicide Club***. But rather than see Ochia and Sono as ripping off Kurosawa's ***Cure***, a closer look at ***The Hypnotist*** may reveal an alternate hypothesis.

Decades before J-Horror-makers started reprocessing recent traumas as pulp myths, a group of German artists watched in impotent horror as the Nazis started to take over Germany. It was the rough years after World War I, and the economic and social decay of Germany inspired many an angry young artist to express his fear in Dadaism, Surrealism, Expressionism... Together, a journalist named Norbert Jacques and a movie director named Fritz Lang turned this seething social corruption into a roiling fantasy drama about an evil criminal mastermind and a secret conspiracy. All of the real-life symptoms that were so hard to understand were converted on screen into components of Dr. Mabuse's masterplan. ***Dr. Mabuse the Gambler*** became one of the most influential films of the silent era, and the character of Mabuse became the signature creation of Lang's storied career.

Claude Chabrol, one of the pioneers of the French New Wave, cited Lang's Mabuse films as the reason he became a filmmaker. For years, he dreamed of making his own contribution to the story of Mabuse. Finally, in 1989, the opportunity presented itself, and Chabrol's ***Dr. M*** (also known as ***Club Extinction***) revived Mabuse for a generation nearing the millennium.

Whatever ***The Hypnotist*** shares with ***Cure*** pales next to how closely ***The Hypnotist*** follows ***Dr. M***—unintentionally. ***The Hypnotist*** is billed as an adaptation of a novel by Keisuke Matsuoka, but fans of the Dr. Mabuse thrillers will be surprised at how closely this film models Chabrol's ***Dr. M***. Both Ochiai and Chabrol open their pictures with a triptych of outrageously staged suicides which occur simultaneously but without evident connection. As a wave of suicides spread through Tokyo like a virus, the police debate whether this is even a crime. The only link between the victims, aside from the troubling fact that every single one of them wanted to live while indisputably taking their own lives, is that each one, moments before death, spoke cryptically of a "green monkey." With this clue, the detectives join forces with a hypnotism specialist who reminds them—ahem—that hypnotism cannot be used to induce someone to do anything they do not want to do.

Along the way, Ochiai and Chabrol share much of the same imagery such as the use of music as a post-hypnotic trigger and the placement of subliminal imagery in billboard ads. Although the final reel veers away from Chabrol and Mabuse into more typically ***Ring***-like territory (even down to a ghostly girl in a white dress with flowing black locks!), the conclusion stays true to the Mabusian precept that evil is not any one person, be it a criminal mastermind or a psychic villainess, but an ugly coruscation inside us all.

Ochiai has never mentioned Mabuse in connection with his work, and ***Dr. M*** did not receive wide attention in Japan (or much of anywhere else for that matter). Yet, ***The Hypnotist*** operates as a virtual remake. The similarities stand as exhibit A for the argument that when movies share elements in common, the cause may not be plagiarism so much as common inspiration.

Cure, ***The Hypnotist***, ***Suicide Club***—and even ***MPD Pyscho***—are brothers, reflecting their makers' collective concerns. Cults like Aum Shinrikyo were prepared to commit acts of atrocity in the name of making the world a better place and unleashed a destructive power that was as invisible as it was lethal. The world that beat Aum back is one of mass-marketing and social conformity where individuality is already a scarce, degraded commodity. The victims of Aum were anonymous, chosen at random, interchangeable, and the survivors were too.

Inspired by the horrors of the Aum Shinrikyo attack, author Keisuke Matsuoka launched a series of novels chronicling the fictional Green Monkey cult and their Mabusian use of mind control and hypnosis, with ***The Hypnotist*** but one of the set. Matsuoka himself scripted the screen adaptation of ***Senrigan*** ("Clairvoyance") as the sequel. Not so much a horror film as a tawdry action thriller, ***Clairvoyance*** provided the big-screen debut for director Manabu Asou, who had served as Yukihito Tsutsumi's assistant director back on ***School Mystery***. Asou provides plenty of flash and noise, but Matsuoka's screenplay lacks the dramatic punch and queasy menace of ***The Hypnotist***. ***Clairvoyance***'s strongest element is star Miki Mizuno, graddaughter of the legendary Kumi Mizuno from Toho's great monster epics of the 1960s. While ***Clairvoyance*** failed to make much impact at the box office, the creative forces behind the television serials of ***Ring: The Final Chapter*** and ***Spiral*** pulled the same trick with ***The Hypnotist***.

Of all these digressive variants, Masayuki Ochiai's ***The Hypnotist*** stands out among the pack of J-Horrors in part for his vigorous directorial style and for his refreshing focus on men. As Saga, the idealist student of hypnotism, Ochiai cast Goro Inagaki, a very talented young actor (who later returned as Saga in the ***Hypnotist*** TV series). A few years later, Inagaki would costar with the legendary Koji Yakusho in the absurdist masterpiece ***University of Laughs*** (there are precious few actors capable of holding their own next to Yakusho in what is essentially a two-person performance). Ochiai also dug into the world of Japanese superheroes when he cast Ken Utsui as Detective Sakurai. Utsui hadn't had much work lately but had been quite busy back in the 1950s and 60s as Super Giant (a.k.a. Starman) in a series of giant monster flicks. To play opposite such strong male leads, Ochiai tapped Miho Kanno, fresh from creating the role of Tomie in Ataru Oikawa's 1998 hit, to play the mistreated psychic girl with multiple personality syndrome (a surprisingly common affliction in Japan, if these movies are accurate).

Meanwhile, Ochiai himself might have been feeling a twinge of multiple personality syndrome, given how he was spending his time. From 1998 through 2001, Ochiai was writing and directing an anthology horror program for Fuji TV. ***Yo nimo kimyou na monogatari*** (or in English, "Tales of the Unusual") was similar to Norio Tsuruta's ***Scary True Stories*** template in that it collected ghostly short stories under an umbrella banner, but Ochiai's ***Twilight Zone***-inflected series made no pretense to being true. This was just Ochiai's fervid imagination run amok.

Tales of the Unusual was a popular program, and Ochiai dug deep into his nightmares to keep it fueled. In 2000, to celebrate the tenth anniversary of the show, he directed a feature film version, still in anthology format. Another year's worth of episodes, though, and he was spent. The show went off the air.

However, the anthology format had proven a popular one for J-

Horror producers as a cheap way to keep the form alive, and it kept directors employed between low-paying features. Taka Ichise's Oz Company joined with TBS (the Japanese television company TBS, that is, nothing to do with Ted Turner) to create a one-off anthology special called ***Suiyo puremia: sekai saikyou J hora SP Nihon no kowai yoru*** (Wednesday Premiere: World Best J-Horror Special: The Scary Nights of Japan). That mouthful of a title turned into ***J-Horror Television: Dark Tales of Japan*** when released on video in America. It was the first step in a larger strategy of Ichise's: to embrace the J-Horror name and genre officially and to collate all the top names in the field under that brand name.

J-Horror Television finds Ochiai joining Norio Tsuruta, Takashi Shimizu, Koji Shiraishi (of the abominable Ju-Rei, discussed in Chapter 6), and Yoshihiro Nakamura (from the same low-rent v-cinema shallows as Koji Shiraishi). Norio Tsuruta's "Crevices" would make a fine short subject introduction to Kiyoshi Kurosawa's ***Pulse***, and surprisingly one of the strongest shorts is "The Spiderwoman," by one of the lesser lights of this all-star team, Yoshihiro Nakamura. Evidently, Takashi Shimizu made his while in Hollywood for the remake of ***The Grudge***, and his is the only one shot on film as opposed to video, with an American crew and distinctively American locations. Ever the jokester, Shimizu peppers his short "Blonde Kwaidan" with ironic touches. The lead character, played by Tetta Sugimoto, complains that Hollywood is no longer interesting, since all it does now is remake Japanese horror films. Sugimoto is then haunted by a standard-issue J-Horror ghost—except for the fact that, since this is LA, he has to contend with long *blonde* hair instead of long black hair!

Ochiai's contribution to the show, "Presentiment," concludes the U.S. DVD release but was shown first on its original broadcast. Like Shimizu, Ochiai winks at the audience: the final scene has the character of Death informing the viewer that his next task will be to attend a stricken hospital where an unknown infection is about to claim the lives of many doctors and nurses. Sure enough, that's where Ochiai himself was off to—for his 2004 thriller ***Kansen*** ("Infection").

This was the inaugural installment of Taka Ichise's newest franchise, the ***J-Horror Theater***. The brightest stars of the J-Horror universe were to be brought into Ichise's employ to make six free-standing films. The roster comprised Masayuki Ochiai, Norio Tsuruta, Takashi Shimizu, Kiyoshi Kurosawa, Hideo Nakata, and Hiroshi Takahashi.

Ichise followed this bold announcement with another bombshell. On May 14, 2004, he helped form Entertainment FARM, to be headed by Yasushi Kotani as CEO. Entertainment FARM is the first Japanese company dedicated to providing financial backing for motion pictures. Naturally, there had been movie studios before, which pooled their own resources to manufacture and distribute their own films, but Entertainment FARM would operate like an investment firm, focusing exclusively on film investments. And Ichise's acumen paid off handsomely right off the bat. Entertainment FARM's initial investment was the backing of the ***J-Horror Theater*** line, which in turn had only just begun production on Ochiai's ***Infection***. Ichise happily announced he'd already sold the foreign rights to the entire six-film series—none of which had even yet been made—to Lions Gate, one of the largest independent movie distributors in America. At a time when it was a rarity for Japanese movies to get foreign distribution at all, and rarer still to pre-sell those rights, Ichise had done it six times in one day.

This is why they pay him the big bucks.

It is also testament to the importance of adhering to formula. Lions Gate bought into ***J-Horror Theater***, rewarding the investors of Entertainment FARM and making Japanese financial history, on the basis of the high concept: proven directors in a proven genre, with the brand name promising familiar ***Ring***-like thrills. The express mission of ***J-Horror Theater*** was not to stray far from the ranch.

Ichise turned to Ochiai and Tsuruta to set the tone for the new series—that is to say, familiar. As a further tip of the hat to the tradition of the genre, their films would be presented as a double feature, like the ***Ring*** and ***Spiral*** pair that set it all in motion. On October 2, 2004, Ochiai's ***Infection*** and its companion, Tsuruta's ***Yogen*** ("Premonition") enjoyed their joint premiere.

Infection returns Ochiai to his favorite stomping ground: a haunted hospital. In fact, Ochiai wrote the screenplay, adapting one of his earlier scripts for a segment on ***Tales of the Unusual***.

A claustrophobic chamber piece of a movie, with a small cast confined to one cramped setting, ***Infection*** is an overwhelming sensory experience that employs every cinematic trick in Ochiai's repertoire to establish a tone of intense dread.

The setup recalls ***ER*** back in the days when it was good: an overworked urban hospital whose dedicated, idealistic staff struggles to do right by their patients while fighting institutional problems and their own inner demons.

For the staff of ***Infection***'s "Central Hospital," the challenges are only compounded by a system in total breakdown. The hospital is out of money, the directors may have even skipped town, most of the nursing staff have quit, supplies are running low, and nobody's been paid in a while. Under extreme stress, a patient's care is fatally botched. The doctors and nurses face an awful choice: whether to fess up to the mistake and risk their careers, or cover up the actual cause of death.

Their fragile conspiracy is tested further by the untimely arrival of an emergency patient suffering from an unidentified contagion. With shades of Toho's 1957 ***The H-Man*** peeking into the scenario, the infection causes the victim's body to dissolve into green slime (Green! Of course!). Along with the horrifying biological threat of this bizarre disease is a curious psychological component. Infected people are haunted by visions of their worst fears and are compelled to acts of self-destruction. Indeed, the killer germ seems to be transmitted not by the usual viral vectors *but by guilt*.

It all builds towards a third-act plot twist that has been cropping up a lot lately. In fact, this particular twist is fast on its way to becoming this generation's equivalent of the old "it was all a dream" gag, an overused plot convenience that shrugs off all plot holes. However, while I loathe this plot device in nine out of ten instances, this may be that rare one out of ten that gets it right. Credit is due to writer-director Ochiai who cleverly seeds the first half of the movie with subtle clues that only pay off in the furious finale.

Interestingly, most of the lead actors in ***Infection*** are veterans of Toho's recent giant monster pictures. Shiro Sano, as Dr. Akai, hails from both ***Godzilla 2000*** and ***Godzilla, Mothra, King Ghidorah: Giant Monsters All-Out Attack*** (Christopher Walken is rumored to be destined for this part in the planned American remake). Also from ***Giant Monsters All-Out Attack*** is Kaho Minami, here playing the harpy-like head nurse. Masanobu Takashima, from both ***Godzilla vs. Biollante*** and ***Godzilla Final Wars***, stars as Dr. Uozumi. Rounding out the main cast is Koichi Sato as Dr. Akiba, more or less the "hero" of the film, who never faced Godzilla but did play Ando in Taka Ichise's first, misfired, ***Ring*** sequel, namely ***Spiral***.

Speaking of ***Ring*** descendants, Tsuruta's ***Premonition*** seems coldly calculated to play as a virtual remake of ***Ring***, even down to opening the film with a recounting of the case of Chizuko Mifune, the real-life case on which ***Ring*** was based. One can easily imagine how Tsuruta must have longed to establish his own claim to ***Ring*** and the J-Horror boom that it triggered. But the poor man has a problem: as the pioneer of the J-Horror aesthetic later popularized by Hideo Nakata's version, the more the fellow works in his own idiom the more he risks unfavorable criticism as a mimic of the very genre he launched. In the world of movie lovers, "derivative" is a bad word, while one is unlikely to go to an exhibit of Picasso and Braque and grumble with disappointment, "Gee, these losers are just copying each other!"

Tsuruta burst onto the scene as a fully-formed talent whose debut effort obliged all who came after to follow its lead. But whereas ***Scary True Stories*** was forged in an environment of total creative autonomy, he has since struggled for his position in the industry, his rare theatrical features often compromised by interfering producers.

If Tsuruta is the Orson Welles of J-Horror, then Taka Ichise is its David O. Selznick. He is at once a producer of extraordinary commercial power as well as a creative force in the movies he oversees. Together, he and Tsuruta made Tsuruta's to-date best theatrical feature, ***Ring 0: Birthday***. With ***Premonition***, they set out to recapture that magic.

Communiqués from the spirit world foretelling doom, spirit photos, ghostly phone calls, videotaped warnings from the dead, viral curses, ill-fated teenagers in their school uniforms. Even the promotional tag line reads "If You See It, You Will Die" (compare with ***The Ring***'s "Before you die, you see the ring").

Parasite Eve's Hiroshi Mikami again plays a workaholic who only appreciates family when it is cruelly wrenched from him by a car wreck. Here he stars as a schoolteacher who loses his five-year-old daughter in an awful accident, the sort of thing that leaves permanent, irreversible psychological damage and costs him his marriage. Years later, both he and his ex-wife (***Ju-On 2***'s Noriko Sakai) have become obsessed with an odd phenomenon straight out of ***The Twilight Zone*** (see "Nick of Time" and "A Most Unusual Camera" among others). It seems some people (Mikami especially) are bedeviled by psychic visions of newspaper accounts of future catastrophes. Mind you, they are not seeing clairvoyant images of the actual events, but of newspaper headlines describing them. Mikami tries to use his foreknowledge to save some of the yet-to-be-victims but is punished with a bizarre infection that leaves his life measured in mere days. Fate doesn't like to be defied.

Ostensibly, the storyline is adapted from Jiro Tsunoda's manga *The Newspaper of Terror*. According to Ichise, he lifted the basic concept and dreamed up a new plot for the film himself. Over the span of two years, Ichise, Tsuruta, and a writer named Noboru Takagi rewrote and revised the thing until Ichise was ready to put it into production as Volume 2 of ***J-Horror Theater***. Tsunoda disliked the script and was worried the film would not represent his manga well, but reportedly softened his view once he saw Tsuruta's finished product.

When ***Premonition*** works best, it shrugs off the ghosts of past horror flicks and settles into its own groove. The final reel is a standout. Mikami's character undergoes a total deconstruction of identity and starts to re-experience the worst moments of his life from literally every possible perspective. This disorienting sequence is worth the price of admission alone. Here, in the movie's closing moments, Tsuruta states the underlying principles of J-Horror in clear terms: these ghost stories aren't about scares for scares' sake, but are modern day parables about family values. Mikami was too withdrawn from his wife and child to even share in a car-trip sing-a-long, and all of the horrifying nightmares that ensue are his fault. The wretch had been destroying his family all by himself, long before the crash. His punishment is to come to grips with that, with a little help from some supernatural forces and their otherworldly printing press.

On October 27, 2005 the third entry in the ***J-Horror Theater*** debuted at the 18th Tokyo International Film Festival, and opened officially in Japan on January 7, 2006. ***Rinne*** ("Reincarnation") stars models Yuka and Karina as well as Tetta Sugimoto, who worked with Shimizu on the "Blonde Kwaidan" story in ***Dark Tales of Japan***. A fourth entry, to be directed by Kiyoshi Kurosawa, is in the works.

Where ***J-Horror Theater*** positions itself as a best-of highlights reel—the superstars of J-Horror play all their favorites for you!—Yoshiro Hoshino's 2004 ***Cursed*** jeers at what has gone before. The original Japanese title, ***Cho kowai hanashi A: yami no karasu*** translates to "The Most Horrible Story A: Crows of Darkness" and is the first theatrical feature under the ***Cho kowai hanashi*** brand name. These had started as a popular line of books, and after this feature also spawned an anthology movie, also in 2005. However, literal translations miss the point: "cho" is trendy Japanese slang, and a better English reading would be "Like, Really Scary Stories." This is a spoof, the J-Horror equivalent of ***Scream***.[4]

Unlike, say, ***Scary Movie 4***, where scenes from ***The Grudge*** are reenacted with fart jokes, and which might as well have a blinking sign reading "PARODY" superimposed over the frame, ***Cursed*** rarely goes for a laugh, and when it does, the laughter is a nervous response to something played a little too intensely, much the way Takashi Shimizu imagined ***Tomie: Rebirth*** to be a comedy (see Chapter 4). However, despite the fact that the cast and crew all maintained straight faces through their press tour promoting ***Cursed*** as the Next Scary Thing, there's no easy way to accept it as a straight horror film.

Busty model Hiroko Sato makes her movie debut starring as a part-time clerk at a haunted 7-11. That's basically the plot. The OK Mart is host to any number of troubling phenomena, and Sato has her work cut out for her surviving the experience. Like the haunted house in ***Ju-On***, this really quite miserable little store is a bad place, and people who go there for cut-price noodles or collectible action figures are just as likely to get a free ghost following them home.

In fact, there's a lot about ***Cursed*** that apes ***Ju-On***. The structure of the film is a jumble of disconnected set pieces, each a separate scare. In one such segment, a ghostly woman comes crawling out of the fridge under the evident misapprehension that she's on the set of one of the ***Grudge*** flicks. Later, a young man washes his hair and is horrified when he finds strands of long black hair coming off in his hands—a direct quote of the famous shower scene from ***Ju-On: The Grudge***.

The spidery hairs in his hands are a familiar touch, long black hair as a portent of ghosts. But the symbol has become shopworn and ***Cursed*** seems to revel in its meaninglessness. Much the way some people look at abstract modern art and say dismissively to themselves, "Hey, I could do that," the makers of ***Cursed*** have a disrespect for the Haunted School and casually throw together familiar ideas on the assumption that doing so is in and of itself sufficient to make a scary movie.

A bouncing white ball, a bathtub, long black hair, distorted photographs—the overall effect is like J-Horror refrigerator magnet poetry. The symbols are not in service of any underlying theme, they connect to one another not at all, and are assembled more or less at random.

If ***Cursed*** is a comedy, the joke seems to be on the audience: *You think a bunch of unrelated scares and empty atmospherics are spooky? Well take this!*

Ju-On's house was haunted because of a family tragedy so awful it burned its anger into the very fibers of the wood; OK Mart is a nasty place to shop because to save money the construction firm used ground-up graves as building material. Novice writer-director Yoshiro Hoshino (promoted to features from the world of industrial videos and promotional shorts) gets the individual symbols right but misses the connective tissue that gave those symbols their meaning. Had ***Cursed*** been made in 1989, before ***Scary True Stories***, it would have been nonsensical. By 2004, J-Horror had established those symbols so thoroughly that even though ***Cursed*** disregards building a solid foundation for its house of cards, the movie manages to stay standing—even work a scare or two along the way, almost despite itself.

Those symbols, such as the black hairs in our hapless boy's shampooed hand, were originally rooted in specific moments of Japanese culture, history, and tradition. If they can function now, divorced from their origins, in something like ***Cursed***, then does it follow that these symbols can continue to hold their power when completely removed from Japan?

Turn the page, and find out.

1. I am reminded of Yuriko Douguchi in ***Tomie***, a similar situation in which a very talented actress fumbles a role that should have been a gimme. And in both cases, the stultifying pace of the film may be at fault.
2. ***Ugetsu***'s producer, Masaichi Nagata, went on to launch the ***Gamera*** and ***Daimajin*** movie franchises—further proof, were any needed, that tony art-house class and funkier commercial moviemaking are not so far apart as snobby critics would like you to believe.
3. Like *Ring*, the book's title is English wording rendered in Japanese letters; the movie's onscreen title simply uses English.
4. The pedant in me is compelled to note that ***Scream*** was not the first American slasher film to surrender to irony and self-parody, merely the most prominent and popular.

Sources:

"Inugami Review," www.filmfestivals.com

Buruma, Ian, Inventing Japan: 1853-1964, Modern Library (Random House), New York, 2003.

Epstein, Daniel Robert, "Infection Director Masayuki Ochiai Interview," www.suicidegirls.com.

Epstein, Daniel Robert, "Parasite Eve Author Hideaki Sena Interview," www.suicidegirls.com.

Gatto, Robin: "Interview with Masato Harada," www.midnighteye.com, August 15, 2001.

Gatto, Robin: "Inugami review," www.midnighteye.com, August 15, 2001.

Interview with Norio Tsuruta and Masayuki Ochiai, www.horrorview.com, May 2005.

McCurry, Justin, "Japan rocked by soaring child abuse," The Observer, August 8, 2004.

Mes, Tom, "Suicide Club Review," www.midnighteye.com, April 22, 2002.

Otsuka, Eiji and Shou Tajima, "Multiple Personality Detective Psycho," Kodokawa Shoten, 1997.

Personal correspondence with Norio Tsuruta, December 2005-January 2006.

Rucka, Nicholas, "The Death of J-Horror?," www.midnighteye.com, December 22, 2005.

Schilling, Mark, "Producer Takashige Ichise: Make it spooky, and they will come," The Japan Times, October 6, 2004.

Takahashi, Rika, "Multiple Personality Detective Psycho," www.ex.org.

WuDunn, Sheryl, "Child Abuse Has Japan Rethinking Family Autonomy," The New York Times, August 15, 1999.

www.andreas.com/hokusai.html

www.snowbloodapple.com

www.sonosion.com

Zahlten, Alex and Kimihiko Kimata, "Interview with Norio Tsuruta," www.midnighteye.com, December 22, 2005.

CHAPTER 8

WHISPERING CORRIDORS

Stop me if you've heard this one before.

There's this really scary movie, about a cursed videotape. Anyone who watches this seemingly abstract collage of surreal images dies exactly one week later. A reporter—a single workaholic mom—researches the origins of the tape in a desperate bid to save not only her own life but her child's. The trail leads back in time, to a sad young woman, drowned in a well some thirty years ago.

The movie adaptation of this tale is an unexpected blockbuster hit, helping to rescue a moribund film industry and reinvigorating a discredited genre. It is followed by a slew of like-minded productions united by a common set of themes and symbolic imagery.

We are talking, of course, about Dong-bin Kim's ***The Ring Virus***, made in South Korea in 1999.

Kadokawa fronted half of the production funds for the remake, with the South Korean company AFDF providing the other half. It was a groundbreaking co-production deal between the two countries, and AFDF immediately followed it up by partnering with the Omega Project to finance Takashi Miike's ***Audition*** later the same year.

By and large, ***The Ring Virus*** duplicates the minimalist atmospherics of Hideo Nakata's 1998 film. Many of the ideas that had been original to the Nakata/Takahashi screen version are faithfully ported over to the Korean edition: the lead character is still a single mother, the tape's victims appear as distorted swirls when photographed, even the final image of an ominous cloud rolling in as the tape's curse begins its pandemic spread (an image now twice borrowed, since Nakata took it from James Cameron). At the same time, Dong-bin Kim's screenplay cannily returns to Koji Suzuki's novel to restore many ideas left out of the Nakata/Takahashi version. Of all the major theatrical adaptations of *Ring*, the Korean one is the most faithful to the book.

Despite this, Suzuki was taken aback—he wasn't aware of having authorized the Korean adaptation. Nakata was equally flabbergasted at how closely Kim cloned his style, down to identical shots at key moments.

Ring fans, too, took up sides. In one camp were those who found ***The Ring Virus*** to be the scariest and most effective movie version; on the opposing team were those who found the Korean take to be a pale shadow. Few fell between these polar extremes. Odd that, since the movie is so similar to the Japanese version. If heated emotions were going to get stirred up, it would seem more likely to be regarding the real odd men out, ***Ring: The Complete Edition*** and ***Ring: The Final Chapter***. Dong-bin Kim may have said, "The Japanese version focuses on horror, but I wanted to emphasize a mood of mystery," but this is just puffery. His version differs little in terms of style.

Where the Korean version steers away from Nakata's is in those story details rescued from Suzuki's text. ***The Ring Virus*** is alone among the major theatrical adaptations to present Sadako (or Eun-suh Park, as she is named here) as a hermaphroditic actress, incestually raped, and killed because of her sexual deformity. Hideo Nakata's adaptation, and its subsequent American remake, confidently discarded this key point, but its reinstatement in the Korean version is significant. As we have seen, the bulk of Japanese J-Horrors concern themselves with women's issues, but they pale compared to the degree that Korean J-Horror singularly obsesses over female deviancy.

Korean J-Horrors, you ask?

South Korea has been turning out a substantial number of atmospheric supernatural thrillers that in all meaningful senses of the word are J-Horrors. It would be a futile academic exercise to cook up a new term for these Korean horrors ("K-Horror" takes everything wrong about the term "J-Horror" and makes it worse). They are simply J-Horrors made in Korea. In them we will find all the familiar elements: grudges, psychic schoolgirls, ghosts with long black locks and white negligees, contemporary family problems and sociology turned into horror movie metaphors, haunted schools, urban legends, cursed cell phones, supernaturally-inflected videotapes and otherworldly web sites, murky water and half-glimpsed shadows of underworld revenants.

However, while we find the same imagery at work in Korea's J-Horrors, enough so as to call them by the same name, the Korean-manufactured strain of J-Horror cannot be said to be derived from the Japanese form. It may be tempting to say so—to chalk it up to a Korean cash-in on the ***Ring***-craze, bandwagon jumping from a neighboring country—but this is quite simply, and demonstrably, untrue.

Korean filmmakers minted their own horror traditions, paralleling J-Horror as they did so, before having seen Japanese horror movies. Because, until quite recently, Japanese movies were *banned in Korea*, Korean filmmakers could not be copying J-Horror—they'd never even seen it.

Korea comes by its anti-Japanese attitudes honestly. In 1910, Im-

GONE TOMORROW, HAIR TODAY

A ghostly girl with long black hair crawls out of a camcorder's viewfinder in ***Nightmare***, through a window in ***Wishing Stairs***, from between the floorboards in ***A Tale of Two Sisters***, out of a pool of blood in ***Red Eye***. In fact, ***Red Eye*** (also by Dong-bin Kim) considers long black hair to be all by itself a sufficient symbol of ghosts. The heroine finds herself attacked by disembodied hair, only to discover it is just a wig. Whew! But that wig later strangles someone! And speaking of wigs, ***The Wig*** posits a ghost that lives in the titular hairpiece, possessing those foolish enough to wear it. In ***The Phone***, a dead girl's corpse is walled up inside a summer home, but behind the drywall her hair has continued to grow, even in death, until her spidery locks have actually replaced the electrical wiring of the house. By 2004's ***Face***, the equation of hair and haunts had become so ubiquitous that it became a joke, and the hero tells the ghost, "Do something about your hair, it's distracting."

OK, so we know that Korea's ghosts all have flowing dark locks. But why?

Ki-hyung Park, director of many key Korean horrors, says that the use of long-haired ghosts in his landmark ***Whispering Corridors*** reflected the strict conformism enforced by the rigid school system: "These girls have two choices in how they wear their hair: cut it really short or long in a ponytail to keep it neat. It is the only freedom they have!"

In other words, a girl who defies the rules and wears her hair long and untied is a true iconoclast, a disorderly force. Korean ghosts are girls and women who break the rules.

perial Japan annexed the Korean peninsula as a colony and subjected its people to brutal oppression until the end of World War II brought the whole shameful affair to an end. During those thirty-five years of colonization, Japan suppressed Korean culture, forbade the Korean language, and prohibited the use of Korean family names. Men were sent off to forced labor camps; women were enlisted as sexual slaves.

The ostensible purpose of it all was to make the Koreans Japanese. It was a fool's game. For all the propaganda insisting that Koreans were actually, after all, the same race as the Japanese, Koreans were never treated as anything better than second-class citizens. In 1916, liberal reformist Sakuzo Yoshino wrote that to be Korean was by definition to be anti-Japanese, and as historian Ian Buruma notes, this is pretty much still true today!

The yoke of Japanese oppression was lifted at the end of World War II, but Korean life didn't turn into all sweetness and light. The northern half of the country, occupied by Soviet forces, turned around and imposed on themselves a homegrown form of tyranny much like the one just removed. North Korea then more or less disappeared into the Dark Ages. Down south, the region under American occupation fared better only by comparison: the next forty-odd years would be marked by one military dictatorship after another, each transition accomplished only by violent coups and assassinations.

Eventually, some university students decided they'd had enough of the "new boss, same as the old boss" routine (it's always students who radicalize first). The youngsters who took to the streets at Chonnam National University in May of 1980 ostensibly hoped to pressure the authorities to release a political prisoner, but really their wide-ranging grievances spanned pervasive governmental corruption, stifling censorship, and the overall suckiness of life. In one of the lowlights of his presidency, Ronald Reagan publicly backed Doo-hwan Chun's use of force to quell the unrest, and by "use of force" I mean paramilitary troops opening fire indiscriminately into crowds of unarmed civilians.

The bloodbath of the Kwangju Massacre (as it came to be known) totaled some 200 murdered souls if you believe the official government figures. Independent sources tallied the body count at 2,000.

Chun had regained control and suppressed dissent, but the student body of South Korea remained radicalized. Underground film clubs emerged wherein agitated students and amateurs could make angry, socially relevant, artistically ambitious short films outside the purview of the government-sanctioned film industry. By definition, these filmmakers were criminals, and they developed an outsider's outlaw aesthetic. Eventually, the political scene would resolve itself, but the underground short film culture remains to this day a vital proving ground for new talent.

1988 turned the tide. With the advent of the 1988 Seoul Olympics, Hollywood studios finally won a long-sought concession from the South Korean government: permission to open a film exchange to distribute American movies in Korea.

This is a big deal, and to understand the role this decision played in the creation of what is now the most vibrant and robust cinema outside the United States, we need to go back in time, to the birth of the movies. Or rather, 1919, the birth of the movies in Korea. By 1919, motion pictures had been around in the rest of the world for over a generation. ***The Cabinet of Dr. Caligari*** had already introduced German Expressionism, Fritz Lang was making the first of his massive multipart epic pulp thrillers, Louis Feuillade had already given the world Fantomas, Judex, and the Vampires, Charlie Chaplin had already made some of his best works, Buster Keaton was about to launch his solo career, and D.W. Griffith had already made both ***Birth of a Nation*** and ***Intolerance***. And only now did the first Korean film appear. By our understanding, ***Uirijeok Gutu*** barely even counts as a "movie," being in fact a stage play with occasional filmed inserts.

The first Korean talkie was not until 1935, seven years after ***The Jazz Singer***, the first color film not until 1949, the first onscreen kiss not until 1954! Film historian Hyeon-chan Ho, publisher of *100 Years of Korean Films*, summed it up this way: "The first century of Korean films was simply a history of remorse."

It is almost impossible to pass any more complete judgment on the early years of Korean film because so little of it even exists anymore. All Korean silents have been lost to the ravages of time and war. Of the entire history of Korean film prior to 1953, only eight movies have survived. Turn on a classic movies channel on American cable and you can expect to see all manner of movies from the 1930s and 40s dominating the schedule. Ask the average Korean movie buff about "classics" and they'll think you mean movies made in the mid-1980s.

This sorry state of affairs is especially vexing to fans of J-Horror because it denies us access to the roots of the central icon of the genre: the ghostly girl with long black hair and a white dress. Her appearance in Korean horror films may match the imagery of Japanese films, but not (as we might have supposed) because Korean filmmakers were copying the Japanese template. This figure is actually a central character of ancient Korean folklore. When ***The Ring Virus*** unveiled its spook, "Eunsuh Park," Korean audiences did not see a local equivalent of Sadako, they saw Kumiho, the fox with nine tails.

Fox spirits abound in Eastern folklore, but Korean traditions are distinctive in presenting the fox as an exclusively evil, and female, monster. According to a legend dating back a thousand years, Kumiho is a shapeshifting demon that assumes the appearance of a beautiful woman in order to seduce and destroy men. She is recognizable by her long dark locks and figure-hugging dress, as well as her vixen-like sexuality.

Where Kumiho was a supernatural creature posing as a seductive woman, she had a counterpart in the Virgin Ghost in White. This ghost, as her name pointedly clarifies, has the same appearance as the fox spirit but a different origin. This poor thing died a virgin, and because she failed to fulfill her role as a woman she is stuck between worlds. In olden days, long hair was considered a sign of great beauty, and white clothing was standard attire. Thus, the traditional imagery of the ghost is not especially other. This is just a beautiful woman who happens to be dead, and if you're not paying attention you may not realize she is a ghost.

Contemporary Korean horror makes much of the idea that ghosts can interact fully with the human world without necessarily giving themselves away. The movies we will examine in the chapter are full of examples of ghosts who do not themselves realize they are dead, and who are accepted as real people by the living as well. The "white costume" bit gets stretched, though, more so than in Japanese J-Horror. A few of the long haired ghosts who populate Korean thrillers are dressed in tight black dresses, but the stock iconography is familiar enough to provide a clever gag in ***Bunshinsaba***: a teenage girl who just happens to be in her white pajamas and wearing her hair long over her face gets mistaken for a ghost by her own sister.

The classic story of the Virgin Ghost in White is told in the two-hundred-year-old legend of Jang-wha and Hong-ryeon. This fairy tale received a cinematic adaptation in 1924 back when the majority of Korean films were just Japanese propaganda. The popularity of ***The Tale of Jang-Wha*** inaugurated a cycle of horror films about lady ghosts: ***The Beauty's Public Cemetery***, ***The Daughter-in-Law's Grudge***, ***The Headless Female Killer***.

And there was plenty of Korean mythology to fuel the trend. One curious superstition of old had Korean villagers burying dead maidens in a flat grave in the middle of some well-traveled road. Ordinary deaths would receive more ceremonial burial mounds, but a dead virgin was likely to return as a ghost. So, the thinking went, secret her corpse in the middle of the street so some unsuspecting passing gentleman might happen to need to relieve himself on her unmarked grave. The mere sight of a man's penis would be enough to sate her restless spirit and allow the girl's phantom to pass on to the next world. There are a variety of ghost stories built upon this premise, which vary as to whether the man is blessed or cursed by his urinary encounter with a ghost. To judge from the title alone this would appear to be the subject of ***The Beauty's Public Cemetery***.

The longstanding traditions of Korean folktale, through their earliest cinematic adaptations, consistently portrayed women as dangerous, untrustworthy, and otherworldly. The Confucian proverb "man high, woman low" is a diehard prejudice even in modern-day Korea. One is hard-pressed to find a traditional Korean ghost story that does not reinforce the idea that women are by nature a menace to male society.

During the first true blossoming of a Korean film industry to speak of, director Ki-young Kim made this misogynist attitude the centerpiece of his career as a horror film director. Since his films are largely unavailable today, I will defer to film historian Art Black, who described Kim's creations this way: "Melding excessive B-movie sensibilities with deeply personal psychodramas, Kim created a highly influential body of work that both typifies and surmounts Korean film melodrama. In the typical Kim Ki-young scenario, a family's domestic bliss falls victim to uncontrollable sexual desire and a menacing, vengeful woman. A husband is likely to commit rape; the rape victim is likely to become obsessed with her attacker; the rapist's wife is likely to find herself battling fiercely to keep her family together while the 'other woman' manipulates the weak husband and tears apart the matrimonial bond. In addition to his proto-gothic visuals, Kim made liberal use of rats, poison, shamans, necrophilia, bizarre dialogue, extraordinary characters and an idiosyncratic juxtaposition of styles and generic conventions to create a wholly unique cinematic universe."

Kim's wild and woolly films continued into the 1970s, but by then the horror genre had been discredited and all but abandoned by the rest of the industry. In 1962, the Korean government passed the Motion Picture Law decreeing that film producers had to produce commercial movies. At the same time, firm quotas reserved almost all theaters for domestic productions. Japanese pop culture was universally banned and had been since the end of WWII, but even imports from other countries were severely restricted.

However, this quota system backfired. If the goal had been to promote the development of a Korean film culture, it did no such thing. Theater owners realized that the real money was in popular imports. Since they could only be allowed to screen foreign films if they also ran a slate of domestic films, all that mattered was the creation of "quota quickies," junky films whose sole purpose was to provide the excuse to bring in better films from somewhere else.

Filmmakers who might have harbored ambitions for something more had few opportunities to reach for it. A 1973 amendment to the Motion Picture Law took the already overwhelming censorship and made it worse; now all movies were required to conform with and promote President Chung-lee Park's ideology.

Then, everything changed overnight. Hollywood succeeded in establishing a film exchange in Seoul in 1988 and won the right to allow more or less free and open competition between American films and Korean ones. One day, the Korean film industry is guaranteed by law an audience for whatever crap they crank out, and the next, Korean films have to compete head-to-head against the best Hollywood has to offer, with no safety net. Korean films went from controlling virtually the entire domestic market to a scraggly 16 percent share by 1993.

But that is not the end of our story; it's the beginning. By 1993, a new democratically elected civilian government had taken over in the first-ever peaceful transfer of power in modern Korean history. This new government eased censorship rules (and indeed, by 1996, censorship was ruled unconstitutional). The old guard of Korean filmmakers faced the tough new world of foreign competition and went down with their ship, but there was a new generation of filmmakers waiting in the wings, trained in the world of underground film clubs. And, for the first time ever, there were no limits on what they could do.

By 1999, this New Wave showed what they were made of. The Korean action thriller ***Shiri*** was the top grossing film of the year in Korea, beating out ***Titanic***. Three of the top ten movies were Korean, in fact. By 2001, domestic productions had fully 50 percent of the market, and with overall box office figures growing across the board. By 2004, Korean films claimed 72.8 percent of the market.

Not only did Korean films perform phenomenally well with Korean audiences, they became a powerful export commodity as well. Between 1999 and 2000, Korean film exports jumped a whopping 60 percent. And then the next year, they leapt again by 56 percent. Although Korean films sold poorly to the United States, this new Korean cinema found a hungry audience in Japan, Hong Kong, and across Europe, one of many signs that the role of Hollywood in global film was diminishing (see Chapter 10 for more on this).

By that point, no one could deny that South Korea's film industry was among, if not *the*, most robust in the world.

The full scope of Korea's film renaissance far exceeds the scope of this book. The horror boom is but one component of an industry-wide commercial explosion across multiple genres. I say this so you don't think I am misrepresenting the role of horror films in the new Golden Age of Korean cinema just because it's the component that concerns us here. However, the J-Horror format did find a perfect niche in Korean film. Compared to action films and other genres with proven international appeal, J-Horrors are relatively cheap to make. Furthermore, while the excess-addicted contemporary Japanese had to restrain themselves to develop the minimalist aesthetic of J-Horror, Korea's censorial aversion to overt sexuality and graphic violence overlapped ideally with J-Horror's conventions.

As we have just seen, however, the Korean version of J-Horror arose from a different and independent set of cultural, historical, and economic forces. Korean J-Horror and Japanese J-Horror are like the triceratops and the rhinoceros, two similar looking animals identically adapted to their environment but of unrelated species with no common ancestor. Since Korean J-Horror evolved separately, it has certain distinctive features distinguishable from the Japanese species. Chief among them is the fact that, in broad strokes, the roughly two dozen or so Korean ghost movies made since 1998 all tell the same story.

The standard-issue Korean ghost story follows this pattern: A child or young woman is harmed due to the negligence or cruelty of a person who should have been its or her protector. The guilty party or parties desperately cover up the crime, to such an extent that in many cases they suffer memory loss and/or undergo a personality change to invent a new, guilt-free, persona. Supernatural events (usually a string of murders) force the living to confront the hidden or forgotten past and to come to grips with the lost memories. Don't expect Oprah-style "closure," expect a bloodbath.

The pattern is so ubiquitous, once you've seen a few of these movies it becomes child's play to guess the final reel's "twist" every time. Just look for the character with memory problems or unexplained personality changes.

To some extent, this enduring pattern reflects the influence of ***Shiri***: not just any blockbuster, but *the* blockbuster that set Korean cinema on its path to renaissance. ***Shiri*** uses the Jekyll-Hyde split personalities of its characters, their secret identities and buried secrets, as a metaphor for the situation of Korea as a divided nation. As long as Korea remains cleaved in two, its history pockmarked by shame, its culture is certain to respond to stories that question identity and dig out hidden guilt.

Since Korean horrors tell the same basic story, and almost all of them do so with a uniform set of J-Horror symbols, outsiders (especially Western critics) have been quick to call them "derivative." This is partly due to the mistaken belief that Korean J-Horrors ape the Japanese ones but also comes from a false set of expectations.

The Korean horrors that try to innovate, even if only a little bit, may win international accolades and film festival prizes, but those that stick closest to the formula tend to do best in the domestic market. Korean audiences obviously have not minded about the "derivative" nature of these movies, many of which have broken box office records, launched careers, dethroned American imports, and generally been overwhelming commercial hits. Korean audiences respond more emphatically to the horror films that stay within the conventions of the genre. Their familiarity is their strength, like a popular song on the radio, or a comfy pair of slippers—what outsiders see as unoriginality is actually a form of intimacy. These are the modern equivalent of folktales in which cultural traditions and morals are encoded into repetitive stories whose common features make them easy to remember.

In other words, there is something about the fundamental Korean horror story paradigm that speaks loudly to contemporary Korean culture, enough so that audiences do not grow tired of its restatement year after year. As with the underlying themes of Japanese horror, we will find it provides a platform for the patriarchal, even macho Korean society to grapple with women's growing independence and rejection of traditional gender roles. Some of these films will be more conservative and misogynist, some will be more progressive and feminist, but all of them will be concerned with what it means to be a woman, wife, or a mother.

The modern manifestation of Korean horror first appeared, well before Don-bin Kim's ***Ring Virus***, in the summer of 1998. Its astonishing success would launch Korea's own preeminent horror franchise, ***Yeogo Kueidam***, known in English as ***Whispering Corridors***.

A "kueidam" is the Korean cognate for what we've already encountered in Japanese as "kaidan." These are traditional ghost stories about souls whose violent or unhappy deaths leave behind angry spirits. Since "yeogo" means school, we have the functional equivalent of ***Gakkou no Kaidan***, or "Haunted School" (flip back to Chapter 3 if you need a refresher). Indeed, its producer Choon-yun Lee, founder of the Cine2000 film company, admits he was inspired by the box office success of the Japanese ***Haunted School*** films to try his hand at a Korean version. It would be many years yet before the Japanese film would be screened in Korean theaters (Japanese films were still banned), but Lee knew of its popularity and figured Korean audiences would cotton to something similar. There were certainly plenty of school-based ghost stories and urban legends from which to draw, and with horror films basically abandoned long ago the form would feel fresh.

But there was something more, something that distinguished ***Yeogo Kueidam*** from ***Haunted School***, something inherent in that word "yeogo." These are not just any old schools, you see, but specifically all-girl high schools. To top it off, the gender-segregated school system is a controversial remnant of Japanese colonialism.

That, and they are literally nightmarish.

Contemporary Korean high schools put manifold stresses on their students in ways almost unfathomable to outsiders. Competition is ruthless, the workload crushing. It is not unknown for students to remain at their desks until midnight. Bullying is severe.

Ki-min Oh had a screenplay that used the context and structure of a supernatural horror story to indict this system. He had tried shopping it to the major production houses but found rejection at every turn. Then he brought it to Lee, who personally abhorred the school system and saw an opportunity to make some money while expressing a serious social concern.

"Korean secondary education was geared toward suppressing individuality and creativity and turning students into these 'good boys and girls,' punched from cookie-cutter molds, you know?" Lee explained to interviewer Kyu-hyun Kim in 2006. "I suppose the competition is easy enough to understand on an abstract level, but I want non-Koreans to understand that competition in real life can sometimes be very stifling. If everyone competes for the same goals, the same goods, then it becomes stifling."

Lee happily agreed to produce the film, and turned to a novice talent to direct. Ki-hyung Park had won various film festival prizes for his 1996 short film ***Great Pretenders*** but had never handled a full-length feature. That thirty-minute short, though, experimented with horrific imagery and suspense enough to demonstrate to Lee that here was the man for the job. With few contemporary Korean horror movies to look to for guidance, Park took his inspiration from Ki-young Kim. But where Kim's work reveled in misogyny, Park reinvented the traditions of Korean ghost stories for a new generation.

Whispering Corridors opens with the suspicious suicide of a teacher cruelly nicknamed "Old Fox." Calling a woman a fox in Korea is fightin' words—an appropriate English equivalent would probably involve profanity. But "Old Fox" earned her epithet; her vicious treatment of her charges led to the suicide, long ago, of misfit student Jin-ju.

Decades after Jin-ju's tragic death, her onetime best friend Eun-yung Hur has returned to the school, as a teacher. She finds that the school has in no way improved since she was last there. The teachers alternate between hitting and hitting on the students, handing out good grades in return for sexual favors, brutally beating those they dislike, and exhorting all students to consider one another their mortal enemy. Those teachers are now dying, but Miss Hur has trouble parsing out how many of the suicides are actually the work of Jin-ju's poltergeist. The dead girl is not the only one with an axe to grind. Angry ghosts are one thing, but this school is such a nasty piece of work that violent death seems preferable.

As with many of its Japanese counterparts, ***Whispering Corridors*** finds escape only in self-sacrifice and compassion. As the walls of the school weep with blood, the audience cannot possibly see Jin-ju as a villain; she is rather the victim of an inhuman school system. The teachers are so callous and indifferent, they do not even notice that the dead girl keeps re-enrolling, forever repeating the worst day of her life.

Whispering Corridors opened on May 30, 1998 to considerable controversy. The conservative National Teachers Association of South

Korea lobbied to have the film banned, calling it libel. The protests only brought more public attention to the film, which became a runaway hit. Made in just two months for the ridiculously low sum of $500,000, ***Whispering Corridors*** thrilled some two million viewers and became the second highest grossing Korean film of the year. More significantly, it landed as the seventh-highest grossing film overall, a sign of the growing box office clout of Korean films.

Such hits demand sequels.

"From the very beginning I wanted ***Whispering Corridors*** to be a brand name," Lee explains of his decision to mount a sequel in name only. "Different directors, different stories, different settings, different schools—different *types* of schools if possible. We tried very hard to avoid repeating the same thing again."

So, for ***Whispering Corridors 2***, Lee brought in the team of Tae-yong Kim and Kyu-dong Min to write and direct a different and arguably superior follow-up. It was released in Korea as ***Tubonjjae Iyagi***, but the filmmakers admitted they preferred the international title ***Memento Mori***.

A richer and more lush cinematic experience than its predecessor, ***Memento Mori*** opens with a moment of unexpected discovery: a high school girl finds a diary on her way to school. The book is an elaborate scrapbook, dense with pictures, keepsakes, and flowery writing. It is literally a labor of love, a token of the torrid romance between two of Min-ah's classmates.

Ah, but you see, since Korea's schools are segregated, a schoolhouse affair is by definition a lesbian one.

Teenage love is always a fragile thing, apt to end in hot words and tears, but the taboo nature of homosexual liaison only increases the stress—this affair ends in death. And if J-Horror has taught us anything, it is that nothing good comes from psychic girls dying in unhappy circumstances. The diary now holds the key to it all, not just the hidden secrets of the taboo romance, but the accumulated psychic energy of the dead girl, the talisman by which she will make her grievances most assuredly known.

The diary is also the centerpiece of the movie as a whole, which is structured, like a scrapbook, as a collage of images imbued with more psychological meaning than a mere cursory reading could fully unpack. The extravagantly visual film unfolds in a non-chronological fashion, as if we the viewers were flipping through the diary, assembling the full story out of fragments.

"There are various kinds of shared diaries. Usually it's just for two persons. And it's a secret," explains Kyu-dong Min. "We found a story about a girl who began to sell her body to a man, because he gave her money to buy a cell phone, etc. If someone had discovered the truth, she couldn't have stayed in the school, she would have been kicked out, because this is illegal in Korea. And she got pregnant, she got an abortion. She just confessed everything to her friend. So this must be very secret."

The filmmakers managed to collect examples of these secret shared diaries from actual students and handed them over to the film's art designer, who based the film's book on these true-life inspirations.

As secrets go, homosexuality is an extremely taboo subject in South Korea, where traditionalist attitudes about sex stubbornly hold their ground. Tae-yong Kim and Kyu-dong Min were university students at the Korean Academy of Film Arts in 1995 when Min met an openly gay man for the first time. Min knew almost nothing about homosexuality, but, being a student radical, was drawn to the situation faced by this young man whose daily life was a chronicle of violence and prejudice. Min started working on a short film called ***Her Story***, about a romance between two high school lesbians. But the gay activists that Min turned to for advice urged him to abandon the project, convinced that a straight man could never accurately portray a gay relationship.

Min didn't give up, and the finished ***Her Story*** went on to considerable acclaim at international film festivals and became a rallying point for Korea's gays. It also became the rough draft, more or less, of what was to become ***Memento Mori***. Min read a newspaper article about two girls caught kissing in a school corridor. One was summarily expelled, the other endured so much ruthless hazing she killed herself a few weeks later.

In the end, the film that Min and Kim developed from such true-life inspirations differs from the one they had hoped to make. Although both men are straight—and happily married—their close-knit friendship and collaborative partnership was so intimate they came to empathize with gay couples and saw the ***Memento Mori*** project as an opportunity to craft a metaphor for their own relationship. The producers feared a public backlash, however, and urged the filmmakers to tone down the homosexual content of the film dramatically.

The filmmakers even faced resistance from their own cast. "At first, they were people with homophobia," says Min. "They hated the characters. They just acted to be stars, because they believed they would be stars after this film." But the experience of making the movie, of enacting their characters' pain, changed them, Min adds. "After they saw the edited film, they regretted so much what they had done before."

Audiences, too, had to face up to their prejudices in order to watch the movie. Min notes that "in Korea, the response from the audience was...either a craze or hatred, because it dealt with something not normal in Korea." To Min's surprise, foreign audiences "got" the film in ways Koreans did not, despite cultural barriers. "I thought it would be different, because you don't know the Korean school, the fashions, the metaphors, you don't know that, but... I think they are more focused than the Korean audience, they try to get more things from Asian films."

Memento Mori was not a hit at home, where audiences rankled against its controversial subject matter and muted scares. Elsewhere, though, it was a standard bearer for all that was good and exciting about Korea's New Wave. It racked up awards across international film festivals and was embraced around the world as one of the signature Asian horror films of recent times. In his survey of Korean cinema, film historian Anthony Leung cited it as one of the ten most important Korean films ever made. This is a delirious sensual experience, full of visual symbolism, ripe cinematography, a gorgeous soundtrack, and a dreamlike stream-of-consciousness structure.

Kim-tae Yong and Kyu-dong Min were now well on their way. On their way, that is, to making melodramas and documentaries. They had no further use for horror.

This became a discouraging pattern. ***Whispering Corridors*** initiated a horror boom but did little to lift the stigma of this long disreputable genre. You could make money with horror flicks, but you weren't likely to get any respect from the conservative film establishment and Korean movie critics.

New Wave Korean cinema is driven by youth. Some 70 percent of the movies made on the peninsula hail from first-time directors. These novice talents find horror a useful tool: show your stuff playing with the outsize cinematic tools of special effects and gimmicky editing, in a proven commercial genre. But once these first-timers make their names, they drop horror like a hot potato.

For the next few years, Korean horror was dominated by this trend: call it "dilettante horror." Half-measures and pulled punches all, the handful of "horror" movies made during this period would appropriate the basic elements of J-Horror, but with no desire to scare the audience. Horror movies that do not scare, these supernatural dramas won few friends at the box office but got high marks from horrorphobic critics.

It begins with Ki-hyung Park. With the white-hot success of ***Whispering Corridors*** under his belt, he announced his intention to abandon straight horror for something he called a "supernatural romance."

Park's ***Secret Tears*** is as much a J-Horror as his first film, nonetheless. If ***Whispering Corridors*** was Park's answer to Japan's school-based chillers like ***Phantom of the Toilet*** and ***School Mystery***, his ***Secret Tears*** is the Korean ***Tomie***.

So we get teenage sex doll Mi-jo, played by the petite Mi-jo Yun. With eyes as big and soupy as teacups, Yun's role is largely a blank slate onto which the other characters (and the audience) project their own desires and fears. Mi-jo Yun's eyes are so cartoonishly big, she seems like a flesh and blood anime character, a manga come to life. Like Junji Ito's villainess, Mi-jo is reborn in an act of violence for a half-life whose only purpose is death.

Mi-jo enters the story at the moment that she appears to be leaving the world, run down by a speeding car. Inside the car are a group of callous jerks led by one of those insurance agents whose job it is to tell bereaved survivors that their dearly departed's policy won't be paying out, for this reason or that. He deals with death every day, in the most disaffected way possible. One dark and stormy night, he and his equally unappealing friends take to the road three sheets to the wind and promptly run into a passing teenager .

They don't just hit her. They hit her so hard, her body is flung into the sky. They have time to stop the car, get out, and look up before her body starts to come back down.

There is much about Mi-jo that is...mysterious. For starters, she emerges from this accident unscathed. She doesn't have so much as a bruise—and her mind is equally blank. She has no memory of the collision, or herself, or her past. It's as if she only started to exist immediately after being struck.

Eager to keep his drunken driving secret, Gu-ho ignores all reasonable advice to the contrary and takes the girl home, where he strikes up a very ill-advised sexual affair.

The only reason she's with him at all is that he kidnapped her in order to conceal his involvement with a drunken hit and run. He's keeping from her vital information about a family tragedy of which she is the only survivor. She is the prime suspect in a possible insurance fraud involving arson and murder, designed to rip off his company.

She's only a ninth grader, for Chrissakes. Oh, and did I mention she's got psychic powers.

Gu-ho and his friends are not good people. They are deeply flawed, human but not admirable. And Mi-jo enters their world, mistaken for a wide-eyed innocent, but she may well be a force of divine justice bringing supernatural retribution for their various sins.

The Japanese films of the Haunted School see their characters victimized by a spirit world that is all around us and which can become threatening to anyone who happens to be in the wrong place at the wrong time. The characters of ***Secret Tears*** trigger their problems by their own bad behavior. Compared to the Shinto-inspired attitude of something like ***Ring***, ***Secret Tears*** shows a decidedly Christian philosophy, reflected in pronounced Christian symbolism. Mi-jo is revealed to have been a "church nut" (in the words of her neighbor) obsessed with apocalyptic fantasies. Unlike Jesus, though, for all her godlike powers, Mi-jo has no capacity for forgiveness.

The character of Mi-jo also has hints of the Korean fable of the little match girl. In this fairy tale, a pauper is constantly refused earthly comforts or kindness by those around her until she dies alone in the snow, to be taken to Heaven. A few years after ***Secret Tears***, the story of the little match girl was used as the basis of a South Korean variant on ***The Matrix***, called ***Resurrection of the Little Match Girl*** (2002). In between CGI effects and martial arts mayhem, that film followed much the same path as ***Secret Tears***: a vulnerable girl falls romantically for the very men who are so badly misusing her.

Park is greatly benefited by a strong cast—Seung-woo Kim, Hyeon-woo Jeong, and the gorgeous Eun-suk Park—whom he then tasks with playing mean, selfish characters who show only their worst selves, yet still come across as sympathetic (the Seinfeld Syndrome). This isn't easy acting, to make such unpleasant people likable, and these three performers are pitch perfect.

Secret Tears was a commercial flop, but nevertheless signaled the direction Korean horror would take. Some would be similarly restrained and dramatic in focus, some would be more outlandish and horrific, but all Korean horror would ruminate on the same theme: the search for lost memory and the painful consequences of finding it.

Let's face it: Korea entered the civilized world late in the 20th century after a wasted century of repression and stunted cultural growth. Some of that sorry history can be blamed on the likes of Japan, the United States, the Soviet Union, and other outside forces that deprived the Koreans of their sovereign destiny. But it can't all be pawned off on foreigners. Koreans have to face up to their own complicity in their fate, but that means they have a hefty backlog of unhappy memories and a history they'd rather rewrite.

It is no accident that so much of Korean horror is about questions of identity and memory. Almost all of them build towards a nearly identical climax. The main characters suddenly realize to their shattering horror that they are not who they thought they were, but had created a phantom identity to conceal from themselves their own past sins. Although it is not a J-Horror per se, the extraordinary science fiction drama ***Nabi: The Butterfly*** deals with the very same theme. Seun-wook Moon's film posits a near future where Korea is afflicted with a virus that erases people's memories. But it turns out this plague is actually a boon for the tourist industry. The world is full of people who'd happily use up their vacation days to have their unhappy memories taken away. South Korea and voluntary amnesia go hand in hand.

In nearly all of these films, the act of retrieving memories is a mistake. Remembering the past only opens up unhealed wounds and sets off a cycle of tragedies.

There are some memories left forgotten.

Consider Jong-chan Yoon's arthouse hit ***Sorum*** ("Gooseflesh"), Korea's only "horror" film released in 2001. Like ***Secret Tears***, it may be peppered with the familiar ingredients of J-Horror—family tragedies begetting supernatural curses, sensitive women seeing the red-clad ghosts of dead children, flickering lights, lots and lots of dark water—but it is not actually a scary movie at all. It never even tried. Instead, Jong-chan's debut feature uses the ghost story premise as a backdrop to a romantic tragedy in the vein of Masato Harada's ***Inugami*** (with which ***Sorum*** shares much of the same taboo subject matter—see Chapter 7).

Jin-young Jang won the Blue Dragon Award for best new actress of the year for her portrayal of Sun-young, an abused wife suffering from the death of her son. She turns to various forms of self-destruction, like prostitution, to blunt the pain. Enter lonely taxi driver Yong-hyun (Myung-min Kim), a drifter with his own dark secrets. He takes apartment 503, next door, site of a fatal fire that links everyone in a chain of hidden tragedies, cruelty, and death. The dilapidated building, decaying, poorly lit, and soaked by angry rain, is as haunted as a home can be. But these sad people don't need the grudges of past heartbreaks to curse them, they bring their own curses ready-made.

Notwithstanding its haunted house roots, this thing cleaves closer to the cool thrillers of Claude Chabrol, of the ***Le Boucher*** variety. A sad bunch of doomed losers are brought together, and their lives inevitably devolve into murder(s), fade to black. Director Yoon says his film features only "people who are pitiful, foolish, and hopeless." In the end, the tragic accumulation of all the characters' pain is more haunting than any ghost can hope to be.

Yoon studied film in the United States, making a series of short films in Syracuse before returning to South Korea to helm this. It predates Hideo Nakata's ***Dark Water*** but covers much of the same iconographic territory—this is one seriously f***ed-up piece of real estate.

Yoon admits that his approach ran in the opposite direction of the typically high-octane aesthetic of modern Korean cinema, but the experiment paid off. Critics hailed ***Sorum***, which garnered serious attention at international film festivals and did decently well at the box office despite competition from ***Harry Potter and the Sorcerer's Stone*** and ***Shrek***.

In the summer of 2003, another dilettante-horror made its appearance, with the same emphasis on empty souls unable to find redemption for past sins. Indeed sin is the operative word here, as Su-yeon Lee's ***4 Inyong Shiktak*** plays with the same Christian notions that flowed through ***Secret Tears***. The Korean title translates to "Table for Four," but the film is marketed under the blander English title ***The Uninvited***. It is one of the rare movies discussed in this book directed by a woman. Lee's auspicious first film may be slack in pace and short on conventional scares, but it is among the most haunting and upsetting modern horror movies. It is close in theme to Kiyoshi Kurosawa's ***Pulse***, but I wouldn't recommend running them back-to-back unless you want your guests to start committing suicide in despair.

Sin-yang Park stars as Jung-won, an interior decorator so disconnected from the world he might as well already be dead. Park is playing against type: better known for strong performances as gangsters or romantic leads, here he is called upon to play a hollowed-out shell of a man. Early in the film, he yanks on an electrical cable in the ceiling, only to have the plaster give way and the room above come crashing down on him. One feels Jung-won is every bit as fragile himself—one good tug on the right emotional cord and his soul will come spilling out.

Although he was raised in a church by a pastor, he seems to be lacking in the Christian notion of charity. Time and again he spies people in need but lifts not a finger to help them. Eventually this selfishness starts to catch up with him, and he is haunted by the ghosts of two little girls whose deaths he might have prevented.

Enter Jung-yun, a woman of many problems. Her newborn son is dead, her worthless husband blames her for the loss, and she suffers narcoleptic fits. That, and she has psychic gifts that allow her to see the ghosts of the dead girls in Jung-won's apartment. As his psyche starts to fall apart, he turns to Jung-yun in the hopes that her spiritual insight can reach into his mind past the memory block that has erased his childhood. Something happened back then, something so awful his father suspiciously has no photographs with which to fill in the details. Maybe if he can reconnect to his lost past, he can find a way towards his increasingly uncertain future.

But Jung-yun has troubles of her own. In between falling asleep on cue and helping Jung-won retrieve lost memories that he will be very unhappy to have back, she has to testify as a witness in the murder trial against her best friend, Jung-sook.[1] Perhaps Jung-sook was tormented by mental illness, perhaps she just was not cut out to be a mom, but under the strict gender expectations of her society, there's little difference between the two. Either way, she didn't stay a mother for long. One fine day she dropped her baby off the ledge of her apartment building.

Now Jung-yun has no choice but to sit in open court and swear on a stack of Bibles that her friend was a killer, a crazy bitch, *a bad mother*. But Jung-yun's testimony will only ruin Jung-sook's already ruined life further; she won't be much help to Jung-won either. Sure, she'll dig out his buried past, but odds are those memories were lost for a reason. In the world of ***The Uninvited***, discovering the truth about yourself only makes life insufferably worse.

As the psychic Jung-yun, actress Ji-hyun Jeon has also been conspicuously cast against type. Jeon is one of the biggest stars in Korea, the toplining lead of one of the biggest hits of modern Korean film, ***My Sassy Girl***. In this film, no sassiness is required. Instead Jeon gets to play the human equivalent of a "mute" button.

In 2003, Ki-hyung Park returned with another slow-burn tragedy in the dilettante horror mold. ***Acacia*** revolves around the Kim family, a childless couple with communication issues. She's an infertile working woman with no interest in motherhood, and he's a jerk with overbearing parents who demand a male heir forthwith! He pressures her to adopt, but the son she picks out from the orphanage ain't what the in-laws had in mind.

Little Jin-sung is old enough to have clear memories of his biological mother, and he adapts poorly (read: not at all) to his new home. He rejects his new family name, carries around a dead bug like Linus has his security blanket, and insists his mother has been reincarnated as the acacia tree in the backyard. When his stepmother becomes unexpectedly pregnant with her own biological son, the family tensions are brought to the breaking point. Someone's going to get hurt.

One by one, the Kim family is slaughtered. Ki-hyung Park deserves kudos for staging this story without resorting to any of the familiar approaches. No long-haired ghosts here, just a malevolent tree and a lot of string. Never thought spools of blood-red yarn was scary? You will.

Park's innovative visualization, however, merely serves a familiar story: in the universe of K-Horror, if you kill a kid, don't expect to live happily ever after. Why this needs saying—so often!—is beyond me, but folklorist Heinz Insu Fenkl has an idea: "In Korea, the most frightening ghosts are the ghosts of young women who have not fulfilled their feminine potential," he writes, "in other words, women who have died without marrying and having children."

This is certainly the horror of ***The Uninvited***: unwanted and unloved children, dropped off balconies, abandoned on trains, left to play in traffic by the women who failed to be their mothers. In ***Acacia***, the father is a useless presence, insensitive to the needs of his family and emotionally unable to fulfill them if he were to notice. He's quick to blame his wife. "Drop your ridiculous work and pay attention to the kid," he barks at a woman enduring unimaginable grief. ***Memento Mori*** too belongs to this category, with its lesbian lovers rejecting their heterosexual roles entirely.

Even as South Korea takes lengthy strides into the modern age, ancient value systems are hard to shake off. A Korean woman's primary role is to produce a male heir. If she should fail to do this, she dishonors her ancestors.

This has resulted in a dangerous skewing of the population. In 1961, South Korea joined Pakistan and India in establishing firm population control policies. Laws mandated smaller family sizes and made contraception widely available to ensure compliance. Abortion had long been illegal, but in the face of the population explosion the government decided to simply stop bothering to enforce the laws prohibiting it. From time to time, lawmakers attempted to officially lift the ban but faced stiff opposition from the country's Catholic leaders. Since the laws weren't being enforced anyway, there was little reason to force the issue. The abortion bans stayed on the books, but Korean women continued to use abortion as a form of birth control. A cottage industry emerged of private health clinics whose primary form of income came from cash-only undocumented abortions, and polls found that the majority of women who used these services were unaware they were illegal.

Which brings us to the part about dangerously skewing the population. Since ancient tradition demanded male heirs and valued women only as vessels for providing them, and since the laws placed strict limits on family sizes, Korean society started to inexorably tilt male. Female fetuses were being aborted. In 2003, the government had to officially prohibit sex selection, but since abortions were already "illegal," the only way to do this was to ban finding out a fetus' sex in utero.

I assume the reader is well familiar with the wrenching debate on abortion in America, with its uncompromising passions on both sides. The Korean debate is perhaps more difficult: along with the Christian opposition to the practice is the Buddhist belief that each aborted fetus is a soul demanding to be remembered, and these religious concerns are thrust up against the practical limitations of population control and the cultural devaluing of female babies.

As this issue heated up in the legislature, and with abortion being discussed openly in Korea for the first time in ages, along came Korean horror to dramatize the taboo and directly address the double standards placed on women in Korean society. Chang-jae Lim's ***Unborn but Forgotten*** (2002) is not only a timely work of social commentary but a welcome return to full-blooded horror after all the toothless dilettante horrors before it. ***Unborn but Forgotten*** went on to enormous success in both South Korea and Europe as one of the more stylish and suspenseful genre entries. It is not, however, unpredictable.

TV journalist Soo-jin and her buddy in the cyber-crime unit of the police department are following a bizarre case in which pregnant women die exactly fifteen days after viewing a particular web site. The site itself seems innocuous enough—it advertises the St. Mary Woman's Clinic—but women who have visited the web page appear distorted in the viewfinder of Soo-jin's camera. Making matters worse, Soo-jin is herself pregnant and has been to the St. Mary Clinic! Her pregnancy must be kept secret, since it is the product of an illicit affair with an up-and-coming news anchor at her station and their adulterous actions could cost them their jobs. He is desperate that she abort the child before their affair is discovered, but Soo-jin is worried that her difficult dilemma all-too-closely parallels the one that sits behind the cursed web site and the ghostly plague racking up so many dead moms-to-be.

Unborn but Forgotten feels like a Korean answer to ***One Missed Call***: both pictures are coldly calculated to mimic the story structure of ***Ring***, down to its pairing of a girl reporter with a male colleague to investigate the tragedy behind a viral curse propagated through modern technology. But the connection is merely coincidental. Chang-jae Lim was not aping ***One Missed Call*** because that Japanese film would not be permitted into Korean theaters for another year.

By the turn of the millennium, Korea had a firmly established horror film franchise all its own, a few homegrown horror auteurs, and a distinctive local flavor to their domestically manufactured genre pictures. Only now would the world of Japanese horrors finally begin to creep across the border into once-forbidden theaters. The initial stage had come with the announcement in 1998 that President Dae-jung Kim would begin loosening the age-old restrictions on Japanese cultural imports. As a first baby-step of this new openness, Korea would permit co-production arrangements between Japanese and Korean film companies. The first ever such co-production we have already encountered:

The Ring Virus, made and released in the time between ***Whispering Corridors*** and ***Memento Mori***.

Various political controversies between the two countries temporarily derailed the plan to fully open Korean doors to Japanese pop culture. That would not come until 2004. In the meantime, it took high-level negotiations to arrange for permission for selected Japanese films to be, belatedly, distributed in Korean theaters. In 2001 the first slate of J-Horrors made it to limited engagements in Seoul. ***Don't Look Up***, ***Phantom of the Toilet***, ***Clairvoyance***, and ***Haunted School*** made their rounds thanks to the third Korean-Japanese Cultural Product Trade. Eventually, in years to come, ***Ju-On***, ***Ju-On 2***, ***Ring 2***, and ***One Missed Call*** would arrive and take their places in the Top 20 Japanese films in the Korean box office.[2] By then, Korea's homegrown version of the form had fully taken root.

And for that, much credit goes to the man they call the Korean Alfred Hitchcock: Byung-ki Ahn.

This is a bit unfair to Hitchcock's memory, and to Ahn, who deserves to be considered on his own strengths. But Ahn does share with Hitchcock a peculiar distinction, namely, an unabashed embrace of genre filmmaking. When so many Korean directors drop horror like a hot potato and struggle to escape any perceived residual taint of having once deigned to touch such a disreputable style, Ahn proudly flies his horror colors.

Ahn also stands out from the pack in that he is a seasoned professional. Most of the other filmmakers we encounter in this chapter are brash young wunderkinds leaping directly from film school shorts to feature-length horrors. Ahn, however, spent a decade in the trenches as an assistant director to Ji-young Jung. Working on such films as ***White Badge*** and ***Life and Death of the Hollywood Kid***, Ahn cut his teeth before the New Wave was even a ripple. By the time Korean cinema started to take off, Ahn was ready to make his mark.

We encounter the cinema of Mr. Ahn for the first time in the summer of 2000, with the low-budget shocker ***Gawi***. For no good reason, some sources cite the English title of this as ***The Horror Game Movie*** (although it contains no game). Even more off-point are the sources that call it ***Scissors***, a mistake stemming from the fact that the word "gawi" can also mean scissors. The intended title (and the one which actually appears onscreen in English on the original Korean print) is ***Nightmare***.

Ahn's debut introduces several aspects that will come to be characteristic of his style. He has an aggressive, traditionalist approach to horror, in which scares are punctuated by loud music, blood and enough lightning flashes to induce an epileptic fit. Ahn is also partial to highly

BIG BROTHER

Back in the heyday of cult auteur Ki-young Kim, a film critic wrote in The Economist: "A Korean movie in which the heroine is not routinely stripped and ravished by the third reel can be quite refreshing." Were he writing today, he might be inclined to offer up similar sentiments about camcorders.

To some extent, the ubiquitous appearance of video cameras in Korean horror can be blamed on ***Ring*** and ***The Ring Virus***. Video technology often is used here as a window into the spirit world, with inanimate pixels reacting to spectral influences overlooked by the human eye.

This is not the whole story, though. The revealing videotape in ***Nightmare*** has little to do with ***Ring***'s notions of spirit photography and everything to do with electronic surveillance. Koreans lived for decades under the ruthless eyes of various military dictatorships all too happy to use intelligence services to quash dissent.

Recently, the Korean government installed video cameras throughout the streets of Seoul. The highly contentious policy claimed to reduce crime: crooks would be disinclined to ply their trade if they knew they were on camera. But statistics discredited the CCTV system thoroughly. Aside from a minor and temporary drop in petty crimes like jaywalking, the cameras did nothing to reduce the violent crime rates. The administration refused to dismantle the system despite the public outcry and the lack of any proven benefit.

In the fall of 2005, the Korean privacy advocacy group Jinbonet invited Privacy International to hand out their uncoveted Big Brother Awards in the Republic. Jinbonet expected the top Big Brother Award to razz the Seoul CCTV surveillance system, but there were so many privacy violations in South Korea the organization found plenty of worse invasions to highlight. "Actually, a lot of what invades personal privacy has already become part of our daily lives," said Jinbonet's policy coordinator Jeong-woo Kim. "It's the remnants of the dictatorial government," wrote Privacy International's judges.

complicated plots in which secrets from the past come back to haunt present-day situations. Additionally, Ahn shares with most of the writers and directors of Korean J-Horrors the notion that, in the end, the ghosts may not be the real problem; their supernatural mischief can help reveal the greater crimes of the living.

Nightmare introduces a group of college students who have banded together in a club they call "A Few Good Men." The name is misleading. These are both men and women who value their friendship with one another above all else. As for the "good" part, well...

One dark and stormy night, things went very wrong. It seems one of their number is not who she says she is, and the act of unmasking her true identity opens up ancient wounds. What happens next is obscure, but when the dust settles, one is dead, another is in a mental institution, and the remaining friends are variously crippled, haunted by nightmares, or (oddly) very successful in life.

Two years later, and one by one, the friends start to die. It might be the curse of the dead girl, finally taking her revenge. Then again, it might be something else—it all depends on what actually happened the night she died. So it's a mighty lucky thing that one of the friends was always toting around a camcorder, methodically documenting every second of his life. Somewhere on that tape is the answer, the proof of what has since been forgotten, suppressed, and covered up.

Nightmare freely mixed ***Ring*** with ***I Know What You Did Last Summer*** (albeit with higher achieving characters). As much as Ahn's love affair with lightning, this became his calling card. His films follow in the path cleared for them by other, more original, filmmakers, but what he lacks in innovation he makes up for with enthusiasm and conviction. ***Nightmare*** was an overnight sensation, easily one of the most popular of the new breed of Korean horror films. Thanks to its success, Ahn was able to form his own company, curiously named Toilet Pictures, and begin production on a second, more ambitious feature.

Pon ("The Phone" is its onscreen English monniker) became the first Korean movie ever to bring in over $15 million at the box office, cementing Ahn's position as Korea's preeminent horror auteur. Ahn brings back actress Ji-won Ha to play the lead (also named Ji-won). And like ***Nightmare***, ***The Phone*** sports a ludicrously complicated plot. Ji-won is a courageous reporter who has recently broken a story on a wide-ranging underage sex scandal, ruining the careers and reputations of many powerful men. To protect herself from their threats of revenge, she goes into hiding, and changes her cell phone number.

The new number, though, is cursed. She routinely receives phantom calls which are a) incomprehensible, b) terrifying, and c) not recorded by the phone company as actual calls. The previous owners of this particular cell phone number all died mysteriously, which would be troubling enough if it weren't for the fact that Ji-won's best friend's daughter Young-ju happened to answer one of these ghost calls and has since been acting possessed.

But wait, there's more. Young-ju isn't really the daughter of Ji-won's best friend. Ji-won's friend was infertile, and secretly conspired with Ji-won to use one of Ji-won's donated eggs. Young-ju is actually Ji-won's biological daughter. Oh, and by "acting possessed," I mean Young-ju has developed a severe sexual obsession with her father and wants to replace her (step)mother in his affections and bed.

All that, and you get a ghost with the most exceedingly long hair in the history of long-haired ghosts. So long, in fact, that her locks have actually replaced the electrical wiring in the house where Young-ju is strutting her creepy stuff. As this unsettlingly oversexed preschooler, Ahn has cast Seo-woo Eun, easily the creepiest child actor in the history of movies.

Incest and statutory rape are hinted at, but do not figure overtly, in Jae-woon Kim's extraordinary ***A Tale of Two Sisters***. With Korean horrors already conspicuously obsessed with women's issues, ***A Tale of Two Sisters*** goes even further in crafting a chick-flick horror opus. The lone man in the cast, played by Kap-su Kim, is an emotionally-withdrawn father so distant he barely registers at all; the ghosts that crawl out from under his sink have more personality. The show is stolen by its trio of lead actresses, especially Jung-ah Yum, whose standout performance changed the direction of her career.

"Analyzing it as a feminist film that uses the 'male gaze'—I don't understand that," said director Kim. "I didn't make it as a female or a male film. It's just the protagonist's point of view. I'm just following the protagonist. It's not a film about any big ism."

As with its J-Horror cousins a few miles south, this film was more popular with women than with men, redirecting the usual marketing strategies of horror pictures. Korean critics, traditionally hostile to horror films as such, grumbled that ***Tale of Two Sisters*** had at best a weak and confused plot. Kim mocked their complaints as being like Placido Domingo berating Eminem for not singing properly. Critics be damned, audiences loved this modern masterpiece and turned it into the third highest grossing movie of 2003, knocking away the likes of ***The Matrix Reloaded***. Festival crowds and foreign audiences too rallied around this sumptuous, voluptuous cinematic experience. Director Jae-woon Kim likened the film to the effect of watching a bowl full of overripe flowers rot—an apt description if there ever was one. These people blew their budget on red.

A Tale of Two Sisters was Kim's third feature, and he had already distinguished himself as one of Korea's most audacious talents. He first came to prominence in 1998 with the sublime horror comedy ***The Quiet Family***, which plays a bit like the slasher version ***Fawlty Towers*** meets Hitchcock's ***The Trouble with Harry***. Then, in 1999, Kim's comic ***The Foul King*** radically changed the way the Korean film industry worked (see box). With ***A Tale of Two Sisters***, Kim took that finely honed sense of comic timing and arch wit and put it to use on something different, swapping terror for laughs.

Variety raved, calling it "a director's piece." Kim agreed with this assessment: "I'm the protagonist of this movie."

In one infamous image, a menstruating ghost straddles a teenage girl's bed. A faint trickle of blood leaks down the phantom's leg, followed by a hand of something *reaching out from between her legs*! This is but one fleeting image, a second's worth of film, in a production that has filled every second of its 115 minute long running time with startling and unexpected ideas.

A Tale of Two Sisters adapts the ancient folktale of ***Jungwha and Hongryeon*** (and in fact, that is the Korean title of the movie). Something like a crossbreed of ***Hansel and Gretel*** and ***Cinderella***, the legend had already been filmed some five times since 1924, with minor variations on the basic story of a cruel stepmother who abuses and ultimately kills her two stepdaughters, leading to the usual back-from-the-grave revenge.

Jae-woon Kim reworked this fable for a modern audience. In Japanese films of the same stripe, child abuse is often linked with Multiple Personality Syndrome (see Chapter 7). Likewise, Kim uses the concept of multiple personalities to twist the familiar tale into a new, unfamiliar

THE NETIZEN WORLD

Between making ***The Quiet Family*** and ***A Tale of Two Sisters***, Jae-woon Kim made history.

The occasion was a satire called ***The Foul King***. What made this movie special was its innovative financing. The $77,500 budget was raised online by Intz.com. Originally, Intz.com wanted only to energize audiences and generate buzz, but they ended up selling shares in the picture to 464 private investors. Think ebay, with folks from all walks of life buying part-ownership in a movie. ***The Foul King*** became the fourth highest grossing picture of 2000, and its investors took home a staggering 97 percent return.

With that explosive success story, "netizen funds" became the name of the game. In 2001, the gangster flick ***Friend*** needed some quick cash just two weeks out from its release, and 190 netizens invested $77,000. In one minute. A few months later, and the market had only gotten hotter. The producers of ***Kick the Moon*** netted $115,000 for their action comedy in just ten seconds. Today, all Korean movies are at least partially financed in this way.

Netizen financing became so prevalent, services like Simmani.com and Daum.net emerged to allow investors to trade netizen shares like a movie-only stock market. Worried that this provided too great an opportunity for investors to get fleeced (not every film is a blockbuster), the government announced that the Financial Supervisory Service would start regulating netizen funds and trading.

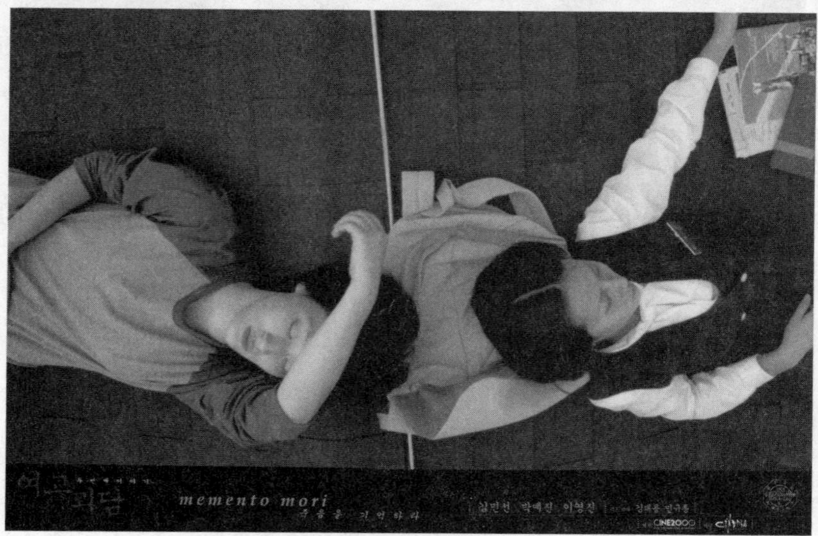

Scenes from Memento Mori

Japanese poster for A Tale of Two Sisters

form. Densely layered with memories, hallucinations, dreams, and flashbacks, it is hard to summarize the plot of ***A Tale of Two Sisters*** without getting bogged down in too much detail or giving away its most thrilling revelations.

Two teenage sisters return home after an ambiguous hospital stay. Their names are Su-mi and Su-yeon (which mean "Rose" and "Lotus," just like the traditional names Jangwha and Hongryeon). Their stepmother Eun-ju is a wicked piece of work whose manic behavior and abusive treatment of them appears invisible to their useless father. Eun-ju tosses around accusations of insanity as casually as one would paper airplanes, while a ghost with long black hair patrols the house at night.

As with ***Ju-On***, once the film has put all of the pieces of the puzzle together and revealed the origin of this cascade of horrors, the anguishing tragic truth is more frightening than any of the scares that have derived from it. ***A Tale of Two Sisters*** succeeds in creating what the director called a "pure horror movie." While watching it, you are engrossed in the opulence of the imagery and soundtrack; when it has finished, you're haunted forever.

When Jae-woon Kim offered the role of the wicked stepmother to actress Jung-ah Yeom, she fairly jumped at the chance. Yeom had already distinguished herself in some genre pictures like ***H*** and ***Tell Me Something*** but knew too well how she was becoming typecast. The role of Eun-ju was something unlike she'd ever been offered before, and pretty much unlike anything anyone else was writing in any other kind of movie, period. "If I do this right," she thought, "I could change my career."

It called for a degree of scenery chewing that made her uncomfortable. Constantly fretting that her over-the-top performance was going to get her fired, she had to trust in Kim's directorial confidence that the end result would cohere as a convincing and emotionally resonant whole. As ***A Tale of Two Sisters*** started to rack up international acclaim as one of the finest horror films to come out of all of Asia, Yeom reaped the benefits of her gamble. As she'd hoped, the experience did open up new doors for her.

Meanwhile, no less than 3,000 actresses flooded into Cine2000's offices to audition for roles in the third ***Whispering Corridors*** entry, ***Yeowoo Gyedan*** ("Wishing Stairs"). First-time director Jae-yeon Yun had her pick of performers both neophyte and experienced. She whittled the selection down to two, Ji-hyo Song and Han-byeol Pak, but was not sure which actress to cast in which part. So she proceeded to begin rehearsals with the question still unsettled, waiting to see which role clicked with which girl.

There was plenty of time, since both Song and Pak were obliged to spend the next two months in intensive ballet training to prep them to play ballerinas on screen. Yes, you read that right. Jae-yeon Yun had the luxury of spending as much time on ballet classes as Ki-hung Park had to complete the first ***Whispering Corridors*** in its entirety.

The setting this time is an arts-focus boarding school where So-hee and Jin-sung are studying ballet. Their friendship runs deep—at times they seem closer and more romantic than the lesbian lovers of ***Memento Mori***. As students they must compete for a prize only one of them can win, a dancing scholarship abroad, the launching point for a serious career.

School legend has it that the cracked and dilapidated steps leading to the dormitory have magical powers. Close your eyes, and walk the stairs slowly, counting each step aloud. If a phantom twenty-ninth step appears, you may ask the fox spirit to grant a wish.

The girls discover that this legend is true. But asking favors of mischievous fox gods is a dangerous game. One of them will win the scholarship, but it will cost them both—and the school—more than anyone was willing to pay. Cue the ghost with the long black hair, turn on the faucets of blood, and let the party begin.

The producers at Cine2000 had seen a short film by a student at the Korean National University of Arts. ***Psycho Drama***, a claustrophobic comedy set in a mental institution, won its maker Jae-yeon Yun her feature debut at the head of Korea's biggest film franchise. Her immediate concern stepping into such auspicious shoes was how to stay true to the established formula while still bringing a fresh perspective. She decided to stage the action at an arts school like the one she herself attended.

"It centered around the students' competitive nature and their desire for acknowledgment," Yun explains. "The setting really helped us to accent these things in the film." Star Ji-hyo Song adds, "She told us that tragedy occurs when many people look toward reaching the same goal."

Audience reaction was split. Like ***A Tale of Two Sisters***, women turned out strong, but men generally stayed away in droves. As the first woman director in the ***Whispering Corridors*** series and one of the few woman directors in the industry overall, Yun pondered the role her gender played in the tone of the film: "I am not sure about the visible changes in terms of reflecting 'women's perspective.' However it is a good thing that people's standard image of a 'film director' is breaking down due to the greater participation of women." She adds, "It can be somewhat burdensome when all others see in me is that I am a woman filmmaker... I still think, though, the most important issue is diversity. I think the empowerment comes when we recognize that we have multiple voices, and try not to pigeonhole one another into easily identifiable categories."

Ironically, recognizing women's voices is the central theme of the fourth ***Whispering Corridors***, ***Moksori*** ("Voice," but inexplicably retitled "Voice Letter" for the English speaking market). This time around, the producers had their pick of 4,500 auditioning actresses for a tale once again set in an arts-focus high school.

Music students Young-eon and Sun-min are best friends 4 ever, so tight that not even death can separate them. When Young-eon dies mysteriously, no one can see her ghost but Sun-min can still hear her voice. This is the power of friendship, but weird girl Cho-ah can hear Young-eon's disembodied voice because she has psychic gifts. Exactly what happened to Young-eon is unclear: the ghost is foggy on the details, as the incident itself is missing from her increasingly inaccurate memory.

"It's time for the truth to be hidden. Or the other way around," cautions Cho-ah. This means, of course, the usual Korean horror game of unblocking lost memories and unmasking fake identities in order to expose truths too terrible to accept.

Director Equan Choe had served as assistant director on the previous ***Whispering Corridors*** entries. He came to the set fully aware of the challenges ahead. "Of course, I found it really hard to make a film for the series as I had to be able to put my own characteristics and my own style within the limitations of the traditions of the original," Choe told *The Korea Times*. To this end, Choe sampled familiar elements from the preceding installments: from ***Whispering Corridors***, a central character who is a ghost unwilling to accept the fact of her own death; from ***Memento Mori***, a furtive lesbian romance; from ***Wishing Stairs***, an arts school in which differences in talent drive wedges between friends. What Choe added to this mix was a viral curse, familiar from Japanese films but largely unknown in Korean horror.

Japanese J-Horror populates its landscape with protagonists who stumble ass-backwards into supernatural problems that had not been previously any of their business. By contrast, Korean J-Horror connects the dots with meticulous specificity. There's always a reason why this ghost targets that victim. The you-get-what-you-deserve Christian morality underlying Korean horrors does not fit well with the everybody's-screwed logic of Japanese ghosts. Chew on this: ***The Uninvited*** depicts a crushing loneliness that destroys the lives of a handful of lost souls; ***Pulse*** depicts a crushing loneliness that eliminates all life on earth.

CELLO, HOW ARE YOU

Not every Korean horror flick has the good fortune to manage either the ethereal arthouse sophistication of ***Voice Letter*** or the exploitationist entertainment value of Byung-ki Ahn's concoctions; some fall awkwardly in between. Witness Woo-chul Lee's 2006 ***Cello***. Like the instrument that gives it its name, it is pretty on the outside, hollow on the inside, and capable of generating entertainment if played properly.

The plot is a been-there done-that mish-mash of other, better, Korean horrors, primarily ***Voice Letter*** plus ***The Ghost*** plus ***Acacia*** plus ***The Phone***, stitched together haphazardly like Frankenstein's monster. You'll also find fragments of ***A Tale of Two Sisters*** and ***The Wig*** in this Stone Soup of a movie.

However, ***Cello*** does highlight a curious fact about Korean J-Horror: an abundance of artists populate these tales. It is somewhat easy to fathom why Korean horror obsesses on buried guilt and repressed memories; you don't have to look hard to find reasons why stories of split personalities would enthrall a nation divided into "good" and "bad" halves struggling to negotiate their common heritage and hopefully a united future. But why should it also be the case that nearly every Korean ghost story involves an artist—a musician, a singer, a painter, a sculptor, you name it?

Artists are engaged in the act of conjuring, creating and preserving an illusion of life. You could say that art is a socially acceptable form of communing with the spirit world. Art leaves behind a tangible artifact of a specific moment in time, a relic of the past that endures into the present, and ghost stories are all about the past encroaching into the present.

And then there's this: with the isolated exceptions of folks like Byung-ki Ahn, most of the filmmakers responsible for the wonderful world of Korean horror were ambivalent about it. The genre has yet to shake off its ill repute on the peninsula. Perhaps the depiction of artists on screen represents a sort of vicarious self-flagellation for the artists behind the screen, troubled and sullied by their association with horror.

Voice Letter bucks that trend. It establishes a repeating pattern that seems certain to produce an unending cycle of voiceless ghosts and broken hearts. Many Korean horrors borrow ***Ju-On***'s jumbled non-chronological structure; ***Voice Letter*** taps its notion of a perpetual-ghost-machine.

"I don't particularly like horror films," admits Choe, placing himself squarely in the majority of Korean directors. Whatever his proclivities, Choe gave ***Voice Letter*** his all. With extravagant CGI work (the budgets for these things just kept on getting bigger), ornate sound design, and experimental editing techniques, Choe used every trick at his disposal. The film opened strong, debuting at fourth place in the box office.

The ***Whispering Corridors*** franchise represented such a powerhouse that other films not actually part of its brand sought to crash the party. The summer of 2004 found not one but two movies, separated by scarcely a month, that followed the pattern of the first ***Whispering Corridors*** so closely as fall just this side of unauthorized remakes.

First in theaters was Tae-kyeong Kim's ***Ryeong***. Marketed under the disappointingly bland title "The Ghost" in America, and the equally uninspiring title "Dead Friend" in other places, this really *ought* to have been called "Hide and Seek," for the children's game that dominates the flashbacks and informs the film's structure. Once again, a memory-impaired person is provoked by ghostly apparitions and supernatural murders to uncover the hidden secrets of a long-forgotten crime.

English games of hide-and-seek generally kick off with a call, "Ready or not, here I come!" This Korean version of the game has kids chanting, "Hide well, or your hair might show!" This is critical since, as we all know by now, ghosts love hair. The two little girls playing this game long ago are unwittingly well on their way towards creating a ghost, or two, in the usual manner of drowning. Dead wet girls unite!

As small children, Ji-won and Su-in can be friends, but only because kids don't pay much mind to class divisions. By high school, the rift between rich and poor is a yawning chasm. Su-in is poor, socially maladroit, and unceasingly forgiving and generous. Ji-won is the alphabitch at the head of a clique of cruel bullies.

Or, rather, she was.

Years have passed, Su-in has not been seen for a long time and her fate is unknown, and amnesia has taken away all that once was Ji-won. One by one, Ji-won's former friends (bullies all) are dying—drowned in empty, dry rooms. Seeking to understand what is happening, and hoping maybe to stop it, Ji-won has to unlock her lost past. Whatever it is that she's forgotten is the key to answering what happened to Su-in, and who really Ji-won is.

The plot is familiar to the point of being shopworn, and director Tae-kyeong Kim trades only in the most conventional J-Horror imagery. Long-haired ghost? Check. But these statements of fact are not criticisms, per se. Korean audiences, far from minding that ***The Ghost*** offered up cinematic seconds, turned it into the top horror film of the year.

Dimension Films in Hollywood took one look at ***The Ghost***'s overwhelming box office numbers and immediately bought remake rights. Thus, if you've seen one Korean horror movie, you've seen ***The Ghost***, and if you haven't seen ***The Ghost***, *you're sure gonna.*

Meanwhile, Byung-ki Ahn decided he wanted to do his own cover version of ***Whispering Corridors***. He hadn't even started rolling cameras when he managed to sell remake rights to his ***Bunshinsaba*** to Japanese producers at Happinet Pictures for a record-setting $3 million, with nothing but a one-page synopsis to show them. By the time he'd finished shooting, but had not yet even released the film to theaters, he sold American remake rights to producer Samuel Hadida for a Hollywood redo called ***The Spell***.

Setting aside the illogic of buying, sight unseen, remake rights to a movie that is itself something of a remake and is largely identical to another film which is already slated for a U.S. remake, the notion of an American version of ***Bunshinsaba*** fairly boggles the mind. Ahn's strength is as a director, not a writer, and ***Bunshinsaba*** appeals primarily on the basis of his sure hand behind the camera, even when the convoluted plot starts to strangle itself. That plot depends on audience acceptance of rural communities so unsophisticated that they still believe in—and fear—witchcraft. When was the last time someone in America was burned as a witch? ***Bunshinsaba*** is set just a generation after—in real honest-to-gosh life—Korea's government had to officially ban superstition and exorcisms.

The title refers to the spell invoked by the main character to sic evil spirits on the bullies who torment her (shades of ***Eko Eko Azaraku***, see Chapter 3). She succeeds in conjuring up an angry ghost, complete with hair extensions, to wreak vengeance on the school's mean girls, but things take a turn for the worse when she realizes the ghost has an agenda of its own.

Ahn directs the film with his usual flair, and his usual dependence on others' past hits. If ***The Phone*** was Ahn's ***Ring***, this is his ***Whispering Corridors***. Although ***Bunshinsaba*** was adapted from a novel by Jong-ho Lee, its bodycount storyline of school bullies, dead girls possessing other victims to claim revenge, séances gone wrong, and people struggling to come to grips with their own guilt steers very close to ***The Ghost*** at times, even down to coincidentally sharing a few scenes._

Having already turned out in record numbers for ***The Ghost***, Korean audiences were lukewarm towards ***Bunshinsaba***. Ahn had already cleaned up on it, however, having presold remake rights before the tepid box office figures started rolling in, and having made the film for a much lower budget than usual. Although the movie looks gorgeous, its deceptively rich cinematography was not in fact shot on expensive 35mm film. Ahn was the first Korean filmmaker to use cutting-edge technology called "Digital Intermedia" to achieve film-like results with inexpensive videotape.

In the summer of 2005, ***Ghost*** director Tae-kyeong Kim returned as director of photography on another psychological horror story, also photographed using the Digital Intermedia process. Filmmaker Yong-gyun Kim, used to directing melodramas, felt out of his element on a horror project and turned to Tae-kyeong Kim to bring a little "been there done that" magic to the set. Although Tae-kyeong Kim's digitally-enhanced photography is superb, his suggestions to Yong-gyun Kim for how to "horror it up" were less thrilling. Thanks to Tae-kyeong, some arbitrary and generic digressions were tacked into a film that didn't need them: long-haired ghosts, creepy kids in red dresses, flickering lights in crummy apartment buildings, and ghouls in the attic. Even without these extra seasonings, ***The Red Shoes*** is among the most visually arresting modern Asian horror movies, with a host of more bizarre surrealist visions revealing a true painterly eye. Just wait until you get to the blood-red snowstorm, or the flashback involving a troupe of ballerinas in Japanese military uniforms doing an interpretive dance number that ends with a multiple hanging!

Director Yong-gyun Kim also tapped the services of composer Byung-woo Lee, whose extraordinary soundtrack to ***A Tale of Two Sisters*** added considerably to its luxurious atmosphere. Lee's soundtrack to ***The Red Shoes*** is another standout credit on his increasingly impressive resume.

Yong-gyun Kim felt the need to turn to such battle-hardened horroristas because he did not in his heart see ***The Red Shoes*** as a standard ghost flick. Instead, he wanted to make a psychological thriller in which people, not spooks, were the true menace. Meanwhile, the producers had watched with keen eyes how Hollywood kept hungrily coming to town to throw money around for remake rights for the most conventional and predictable Korean horrors. Kim struck a compromise. For the theatrical release, he would agree to fit his vision into the traditional format, with the usual memory problems and last-minute "gotcha" twists now de rigueur for Korean ghost movies. But for the DVD release, he would be allowed to recut the film as the psychological thriller he envisioned.

The alternate DVD cut of ***The Red Shoes*** is only slightly longer, but for once the DVD exclusive director's cut doesn't simply shove back in censored clips of graphic violence, as is so often the case with American horror movies, but uses the platform to reimagine the film as a suspense thriller about people.

People with memory problems and crippling guilt about their failure to conform to traditional women's roles, that is. Either way it is still a Korean horror movie, with or without the long-haired ghost.

Writing the script along with co-writer Sang-ryeol Ma, Yong-gyun Kim took as his most overt (and clearly acknowledged) inspiration the fable by Hans Christian Andersen. This classic tale, first published in 1845, involves a tempting pair of red slippers that arouse greed, vanity, and other earthly urges in whoever wears them until the heroine ultimately redeems herself by cutting off her sinful feet and the shoes that have possessed them. About a century later, Emeric Pressburger produced a landmark film adaptation of ***The Red Shoes***, which didn't make it to Korean theaters until 1954, on the heels of the Korean War. Fearing war-weary audiences would shy away from something so evocative of gore, the Korean distributors decided to change the title to…The Pink Shoes. And so, forever after, Koreans have known Andersen's fable by this altered name. Thus, the actual Korean title of Yong-gyn Kim's picture is ***Bunhongshin***, "The Pink Shoes."

Sure enough, the shoes are pink. We're talking about a compelling pair of pink pumps which have the power to make the wearer feel a surge of womanly self-confidence, sexual allure, and overpowering jealousy. That, and the shoes sometimes eat the feet of the lady above.

Sun-jae Hun (played by Hye-soo Kim) is a woman who could use a shot of self-confidence. Her loveless marriage dissolved thanks to her husband's infidelity, which she only discovered during a panic attack—she thought she'd allowed something terrible to happen to her grade-school daughter Tae-soo, played by extraordinary child actress Yeon-ah Park. She's aging, she's a divorced mother, her life is a joke, and the only thing she enjoys is collecting shoes, so these supernatural heels fill a very urgent need. But Tae-soo wants them, too, and the power struggle over the shoes will bring mother and daughter into other conflicts as well. Especially about men. If Sun-jae is going to use the shoes to get back into the dating scene, she's going to have to come to some kind of grips with, ahem, what happened to her cheatin' hubby.

"Desire and selfishness are the focus of this film," explains director Yong-gyun Kim. In addition to adapting Hans Christian Andersen's story, Kim also took inspiration from a Tolstoy short story about an adulterous husband plotting to murder his unfaithful wife. And then, of course, the whole thing was mapped on to the usual Korean horror template of a person spinning off an alternate identity to cover up their guilt—guilt to be forced into the open by a ghost's vengeance.

Within this heady mix of influences, Kim also found time to root his phantoms in something that in point of fact actually does haunt Korean culture: Japanese colonialism. The origin of the red shoes (or the pink shoes—cinematographer Tae-kyeung Kim did spend a lot of time making these things look preternaturally pink) is set in 1944 with

Japanese fascists the source point of all the pain that follows.

Yong-gyun Kim's discomfort with toeing the line on conventional horror reflected an increasingly difficult challenge facing the Korean horror movie industry. While the likes of Byung-ki Ahn had no occasion to sweat their reliance on convention, and the makers of the ***Whispering Corridors*** franchise had a brand name to protect, everyone else was feeling the tension between the fairly predictable entertainment favored by audiences and remake-deal brokers, on the one hand, and the anti-horror sentiments held by so many directors and critics alike on the other.

In response to this tension, the genre began to intermix with other genres, to produce a mini-cycle of what could be termed "Horror-Plus" movies. In the summer of 2004, while ***The Ghost*** and ***Bunshinsaba*** went after the ***Whispering Corridors*** fans, San-gon Yoo directed a ghost story that cleverly disguised itself as a police procedural. The opening titles of ***Face*** include the ominously corporate-sounding credit "scenario developed by Needle Film." As one would expect from a movie written by committee, ***Face*** sticks close to the tried and true. It wants to be seen in the same company as high-profile Korean detective films like ***Memories of Murder*** or ***Tell Me Something***, but its buddy-cop setup is as generic as they come. The ghost story is likewise familiar stuff, with the usual revelations of lost memories, forgotten crimes, and ghosts that successfully pass as human. It broke no new ground, other than performing an addition of "cop movie" and "ghosts," but did well enough to warrant its own imitators. In the summer of 2006, Sang-hun Ahn made his debut with ***Arang***. ***Face***'s star Yun-a Song returned for yet another police procedural-cum-horror adapted from an old Korean folktale.

The summer season of 2005 found ***The Ring Virus***' Dong-bin Kim making a long-awaited return to the genre. ***Red Eye*** has several ironic coincidences to its name. It came out in Korea at the same time that, in the U.S., Wes Craven's film of the same name debuted. Also, while Dong-bin Kim was following up his work remaking ***Ring*** with a film about a ghostly carriage commingling past tragedies with present calamities, Gore Verbinski in Hollywood was following his ***Ring*** remake with a film about a ghostly vessel... You get the idea. All that, and Dong-bin Kim's ***Red Eye***, set on a train, is also the same old Korean ghost story.

The setting makes a huge difference, though. The familiar moments (some scary hair, a videotape that shows things people can't see, a psychic girl who sees dead people, and some ghosts who don't realize they're dead) somehow feel a little less shopworn when sitting on a different shelf. Kim does a good job of recreating the vibe of 1970s-era disaster movies like ***Bullet Train*** and ***The Cassandra Crossing*** and has a star-studded cast to hold the somewhat shaky plot together: ***Wishing Stairs***' Ji-min Kwak, ***H***'s Eol Lee, ***Old Boy***'s Dae-yeon Lee, ***Uninvited***'s Won-sang Park.

Red Eye finished as the tenth highest grossing domestic production of the year, but failed to crack the top ten overall. Still, it was a solid showing for Dong-bin's highly anticipated homecoming.

By far the most accomplished, exciting, and commercially successful of these "Horror-Plus" approaches came from writer-director Su-chang Kong. He had already made an international name for himself at the helm of the slasher thriller ***Tell Me Something***, but with ***R-Point*** he showed his range. This is a war movie. A war movie, plus ghosts.

The R-Point of the title (a title given, by the way, in English in the original print) is a sacred swath of land in the jungles of Vietnam where, centuries earlier, Chinese invaders slaughtered a village and dumped the bodies into the lake. I'll say that again slowly: the brutal murders of countless innocent women and children, tossed into the lake. Once more with feeling: dead wet girls, and lots of them.

The year is 1973, and a squad of Korean soldiers are sent into R-Point under the guidance of a psychopathic lieutenant with the mission of discovering any trace of the previous mission. They don't have to worry about the Viet Cong, because the Vietnamese consider R-Point sacred, but dumb ass soldiers aren't much for respect. And while their lieutenant's killer instincts are useful in war, they aren't admirable character traits anywhere else.

In case you didn't know, South Korean forces were the second-largest group of foreign troops fighting in the Vietnam War, after Americans. But the sucker punch of ***R-Point***, its greatest distinguishing feature, is that which side you're on doesn't matter. The ghosts of R-Point don't give a damn if you're Yankee or Viet Cong or Chinese or Korean or whatever. As the doomed soldiers succumb to the relentless horrors of ***R-Point***, they rightly ask, "Why us?" Other Korean ghost movies punish the guilty for specific crimes, like the murder of a child, but the soldiers here are punished for the simple crime of being soldiers. Killing in wartime is still murder, and all soldiers have blood on their hands.

R-Point opened at the very top of the box office on its debut weekend, shoving ***The Bourne Supremacy*** down to third place. Hollywood came calling, for the usual remake requests...and then noticed something. Audiences back home in the States were reeling from their own Vietnamesque military misadventure, with scandals like the Haditha

Massacre calling into question all the virtues one would want to associate with soldiers. ***R-Point***'s thoughtful pacifist message, not to mention its pitch-perfect suspense and clever storytelling, fit exactly the American public's mood. Perhaps Su-chang Kong's thriller could stand on its own, as a universal statement, even without the usual remake intervention.

On January 13, 2006, ***R-Point*** got a limited theatrical release in America, one of very few Korean horrors to merit such, its disquieting message every bit as evocative for audiences here as there.

R-Point also deserves note for being the only all-male horror film in this book. There are plenty of all female, or mostly female, ghost stories, but it takes a sure hand to put men in jeopardy and not elicit chuckles from macho Koreans.

"No matter which horror film you're watching, if it's a man getting scared, it doesn't have the same impact on people," opines Byung-ki Ahn. "In a recent Korean horror film, there's a scene where a male character is scared, but people ended up laughing. It wasn't just the actor's fault."

Ahn had reason to consider this issue carefully. As the summer of 2006 approached, he was putting finishing touches on ***APT***, which had originally called for a male lead.

After ***Bunshinsaba***, Ahn had intended to switch gears entirely and make a big-budget spy thriller called ***Eye of the Dynasty***. Years passed, delay followed delay, and Ahn had to ultimately admit he couldn't raise the necessary funds. So he sat down, scribbled out a one-page synopsis of another J-Horror-styled scare-fest, and snagged his production funds in an instant from a Japanese distribution company.

Whereas Japanese J-Horrors had long been looking to manga for direct or indirect inspiration, the Korean world of graphic novels ("manhwa") had not similarly intersected with filmed entertainment. The Internet age started to change that, with Korean web surfers increasingly interested in online manhwa. Like a dam bursting, the 2006 season found no less than a dozen manhwa adaptations rushing into production.

Among the most popular manhwa artists is Do-young Kang, or Kangpool to his many fans. While Ki-hyung Park adapted one of Kangpool's stories into the controversial ***Timing***, Ahn selected a story Kangpool had titled "A Chilly Psychological Mystery Thriller." In addition to rewriting the story to change the protagonist from a man into a more vulnerable woman, Ahn set his mind to bleaching out Kangpool's oddball comedy (although, for Ahn, as we discovered, removing the male lead was step one in avoiding comedy).

The story involves a cursed apartment building whose automated lights shut off every night at 9:56 pm. In the darkness, bad stuff happens.

A simple setup, perhaps, but adapting the manhwa to Ahn's cinematic needs required more than a dozen separate rewrites, with new drafts coming in as they filmed. "It's been the most difficult script I've worked on," complained Ahn, joking he was likely to continue rewriting even after releasing the film.

Over at Cine2000, Choon-yun Lee faced his own concerns about striking the right tone. He had hoped to follow ***Voice Letter*** with the fifth ***Whispering Corridors*** entry in 2006, but as the summer began he had yet to make any firm announcement. Finding the right idea, and the right people to realize it, was more important than arbitrary deadlines.

"I want ***Whispering Corridors*** films to be strong horror films, but 'pretty' films too. Beauty is an important factor. Excessive cruelty and gore are definitely not good," Lee explained, adding that he saw this as a principal distinction between his kind of horror and the kind of entertainment made in Japan. "I understand that this is a matter of stylistic choice in a way, and perhaps an effect of living in a more sexually open culture, with pornography as a cinematic genre much better developed than in Korea, but that is not what my movies are about. Of course, the ***Whispering Corridors*** series are horror movies so not everything is picking daisies in a flower garden, you know. They are supposed to be scary. That's fine, but I do want to keep making movies whose primary audience remain high school girls or young women who just stepped out of that all-girls environment. It is important that there are Korean movies that can be appreciated by them, and give these people a voice, so to speak."

In the end, this is the greatest accomplishment Lee and Ahn and all of the Korean horror-makers have achieved: to give voice to the voiceless. Japanese colonialists forced Korean culture underground; Korean dictators displaced the Japanese but kept some of their stifling restrictions. Filmmaking emerged in the tumult of the 1980s as an expressly political and rebellious force. Horror filmmaking was the ghetto of the industry, the underground within the underground. The rise of Korean J-Horror brings all of these elements together in an expression of defiance and triumph: Korean filmmakers use the techniques of J-Horror to sell Korean culture back to the Japanese, to demonstrate their mastery of the form while emphasizing how *their* iteration of J-Horror is uniquely Korean in origin.

The ghosts of the past have finally found justice.

1. I do not know enough about Korean names to determine if there is any significance to the fact that eleven of the main characters are named "Jung-something." But it sure seems curious, doesn't it?
2. ***Tomie: Replay*** and ***The Spiral*** would be forever kept out by censors due to their unacceptable levels of gore and nudity.

Sources:

"Ahn Byung-Gi Talks," www.twitchfilm.net, January 27, 2006.
"Making of A Tale of Two Sisters," A Tale of Two Sisters DVD Edition, Tartan Video USA, 2005.
"The Making of Wishing Stairs," Wishing Stairs DVD edition, Tartan Video USA, 2005.
"The Red Shoes DVD Review," www.twitchfilm.net, November 10, 2005.
Black, Art, "Coming of Age," Fear Without Frontiers, FAB Press, July 2003.
Buruma, Ian, "Inventing Japan: 1853-1964," Modern Library (Random House), New York, 2003.
Fenkl, Heinz Insu, "Fox Wives and Other Dangerous Women," Realms of Fantasy Magazine, 1999.
Gatto, Robin and Yannis Polinacci, "Interview with Memento Mori Director," www.filmfestivals.com, February 2, 2001.
Gwak, Gyeong-Hee, "The Ring Virus," www.asiandb.com, February 5, 2000.
Joon, Soh, "Horror Thriller R-Point a Hit With Audience," www.asiandb.com, August 28, 2004.
Kim, Kyu-Hyun, "An Interview with Actress Cha Ye-Ryun and Producer Lee Choon-Yun," www.koreanfilm.org, February 9, 2006.
Kim, Kyu-Hyun, "An Interview with Yun Jae-Yeon," www.koreanfilm.org, November 2003.
Kim, Mi-Hee, "Japanese Horror Flicks to Invade Korean Local Theaters," www.asiandb.com, February 21, 2001.
Kim, Tae-Jong, "Director Gives New Voice to Popular Horror Film Series," www.asiandb.com, July 15, 2005.
Kim, Tae-Jong, "High School Horror Film Sends Actress Through Ceiling," www.asiandb.com, March 13, 2005.
Kim, Tae-Jong, "Summer for Korean Horror Film Buffs," www.asiandb.com, June 5, 2006.
Korean Film Observatory Number 15, Korean Film Council, Seoul, Spring 2005.
Lee, Min-A, "Korean Workers Protest Against Video Surveillance," Joon Gang Daily, December 15, 2005.
Leong, Anthony, "Korean Cinema: The New Hong Kong—A Guidebook for the Latest Korean New Wave," Trafford Publishing, Victoria, Canada, 2002.
Paquet, Darcy, "Netizen Funds," Screen International, November 2, 2001.
Rist, Peter and Donato Totaro, "Corridors That Whisper Dark Secrets: An Interview with Director Park Ki-Hyung," Off-Screen, March 6, 2001.
Rist, Peter, "An Introduction to Korean Cinema," Sequences #198, September-October 1998.
Tadesco, Frank, "Rites for the Unborn Dead: Abortion and Buddhism in Contemporary Korea," Korea Journal Volume 36 Number 2, Summer 1996.
www.buddhapia.com
www.koreanfilm.org
www.twitchfilm.net

CHAPTER 9

EYE ON HONG KONG

Cissy (Gigi Lai) is an intrepid girl reporter, investigating allegations of supernatural events. She receives an unmarked videotape in the mail. Curious, she pops it into the VCR, and watches in spine-tingling anxiety as the weird images unspool: abstract images of ominous foreboding, a kanji character for someone's name—Sada something, a well...and then a man, his face obscured by a white cloth... He pulls off the cloth, looks into the camera, and invites Cissy to dinner.

Gotcha!

Tony Leung's 1999 ***Saan Chuen Liu Shut*** (or as it is known internationally, "A Wicked Ghost") is emblematic of the Hong Kong response to ***Ring***. Which is to say: befuddled and schizophrenic.

First, a word or two about ***A Wicked Ghost***, so as to relieve you of the burden of actually watching it. A group of teenagers gather to play at a séance, jokingly conjuring up ghosts. They succeed all too well, unleashing a specter on themselves that kills them off one by one. That's where Cissy comes in, hoping to figure out where her brother and his pals went wrong. The chap on the video, poking fun at ***Ring***, is her romantic interest Mr. Mo (Francis Ng), a drama teacher who for no evident reason looks and acts like a monk. Together, they trace the problem through the city's water supply to its haunted source: an abused actress whose corpse was dumped in an unmarked grave under a pond, turning her into a proverbial Dead Wet Girl.

A Wicked Ghost remains steadfastly self-conscious about following in the footsteps of ***Ring***. Not only does it pay joking homage to its source, but the character and appearance of the Dead Wet Girl is decidedly Sadako-esque. Only crappier. And herein lies the rub: if the sole vice of ***Wicked Ghost*** was its ramshackle production values and lack of imagination, it might have passed as a minor and forgettable also-ran in the J-Horror sweepstakes. But writer-director-producer Tony Leung has little patience for the brooding atmospherics and quiet suspense of J-Horror, and so what he has taken from ***Ring*** he has grafted awkwardly onto a goofy teen comedy. Thus, the film veers drunkenly from broad slapsticky farce to (semi)serious scares, trying to punctuate its sudden mood changes with *ta-daa!*-music stings. Case in point: Cissy and Mr. Mo encounter the ghost of one of their friends in one of the few scenes Leung more or less stages effectively, yet the tension is ruined by the fact that both characters constantly call out the boy's nickname, "Rubbish!" over and over.

Fans of Hong Kong cinema may think they recognize the name Tony Leung, since an actor by that name is one of the brightest stars in Hong Kong today, with such illustrious credits as ***Chungking Express***, ***Hero***, the ***Infernal Affairs*** trilogy, and ***2046***. That's Tony Leung Chiu-Wai, and he's not a part of our story. No, the director of ***A Wicked Ghost*** is Mr. Tony Leung Siu-Hung, Vice Chairman of the Hong Kong Stuntman's Association, director of ***Satin Steel*** and ***Vampire Controller***, and actor in such films as ***The Untold Story: Human Meat Pies*** and ***Enter the Fat Dragon***.

Fans of Hong Kong cinema will certainly recognize Francis Ng, whose previous credits include ***The Bride With White Hair 2***, ***Gen X Cops***, and ***Raped by an Angel 2***. His costar Gigi Lai also appeared in ***Raped by an Angel 2***, as well as ***The Three Lusketeers*** and ***A Wicked Ghost 3***.

Wait, did that say, ***A Wicked Ghost 3***?

Yessiree, it did. Tony Leung had enough success with the first one to turn it into a mini-franchise, revealing that the schizophrenia evident in the first film is not Leung's alone, but perhaps endemic to the entire HK film industry.

The late 1990s, around 1997-99, was a moment of transition for the film industries of Asia, but the exact nature of that transition varied from country to country.

As we've seen, Japan had a once vibrant film industry in the 1960s that fell on hard times. By the 1990s, it had grown insular and moribund, struggling to make ends meet, limited in its ability to reach beyond Asia to a larger international audience. The South Korean film industry prior to the 1990s barely merited the name. Thanks in part to the international commercial popularity of J-Horror, both of these countries experienced a cinematic renaissance, with film festival wins, blockbuster hits, and the attention of Hollywood producers seeking remake opportunities.

But Hong Kong was and is a different story altogether. Through the 1980s, when Japanese and Korean directors struggled mightily, Hong Kong enjoyed a powerful presence in global cinema. High-octane action pictures from the likes of Jackie Chan, John Woo, and Tsui Hark filled screens across Asia and abroad. Movies were made fast, cheap, and out of control. Hong Kong stood with America and Bollywood as one of the top three motion picture industries in the world, and the second largest exporter of filmed entertainment.

Let's linger on those numbers a little longer. Hong Kong was the world's third largest manufacturer of films and the world's second largest exporter of films. In other words, Hong Kong movies were even more popular abroad than at home. This, at a time when Norio Tsuruta's mom and dad were telling him he'd have a sunnier future if he were to pursue lint farming or door-to-door anvil sales than if he tried to ply his trade as a filmmaker. Hong Kong already had the prize that the rest of Asia was vying for.

They had it, then they lost it.

It all fell apart in the late 1990s. Some of the blame can be pinned on the Asian Stock Market Crash of October 27, 1997—the third worst crash in history.

CHINESE GHOST STORY

One of the reasons that Chinese J-Horror movies are so scattershot is that compared to their cousins in Japan or Korea, they lack a straightforward grounding in folklore. China shares with Japan and Korea the ancient iconography of girl ghosts in white dresses and long black hair; indeed, folklorists believe that the image has its roots in Chinese culture and from there was adapted into neighboring cultures. But the lines of connection between this history and contemporary media have been tangled, severed, or blurred.

Hong Kong cinema is especially voracious in sampling ideas and imagery from its movie-saturated culture and regurgitating them back into HK films. One cannot look at the hodgepodge of global influences in HK film and conclude that these movies present a coherently Chinese cultural vision. Hong Kong movies have global reach in part because they are already so cosmopolitan in origin.

Some, but not all. The crash coincided with the ascendancy of the Japanese and South Korean film industries, so other factors must surely have been at work as well.

At issue was the impending handover of Hong Kong to Chinese control in 1997. The glory days of Hong Kong cinema flourished in an independent state, and the men and women who'd done well in that system worried about the future under the domination of Mainland China. Many of the biggest names in Hong Kong cinema (Jackie Chan, Jet Li, Michelle Yeoh, Chow Yun-Fat, John Woo, Tsui Hark, Sammo Hung) left Hong Kong to seek employment in Hollywood.

The 1997 changeover turned out to be less traumatic than feared, and Chinese censorship has not been as big an issue as anticipated, but the damage had already been done: the precipitous departure of the tentpoles of the film industry had left behind a shaky foundation. It would take a few years for Hong Kong's movie business to rebuild itself.

It was during those transitional, and formative, years that ***Ring*** exploded onto Asian screens. Similarly styled horror movies from both Japan and South Korea competed for attention. A new style had announced itself.

Hong Kong's film culture had always thrived on eating itself: a relentless process of sequels and remakes and rip-offs of anything and everything that showed a glimmer of popularity. There was no way the success of J-Horror could pass by unnoticed. But, Hong Kong's film culture also had thrived on an orgy of excess, with extreme stunts, broad physical comedy, and over-the-top intensity the rules of the game. The low-key aesthetics of J-Horror would be an awkward fit at best with the maximalist aesthetics of Hong Kong cinema.

Tony Leung was among the first to jump on ***Ring***'s bandwagon, with ***A Wicked Ghost*** and its sequels, but his inability to capture the essence of what he was trying to mimic would be a characteristic dilemma for Hong Kong's moviemakers. To truly make a Hong Kong J-Horror would mean to fight against all established traditions and audience expectations.

Curiously, one of the best examples of early Hong Kong J-Horror emerged prior to ***Ring***. The film in question was produced and directed by Wellson Chin in 1997 and is known in China as ***Si Yu Si Ri***, which means "April the 4th." That Chinese title however appears onscreen with an alternate English title, under which it was distributed worldwide: ***Temegotchi***.

1997 was the year of the Tamagotchi—an interactive toy pet marketed by the Japanese toy giant Bandai. The name was a sort of Japanese pun, fusing words that simultaneously evoke "loveable egg" and "friendly watch." The egg-shaped toy, which you wore like a watch (and was, I guess, both friendly and loveable) had a primitive digital display where the Tamagotchi creature appeared. It was your duty as a Tamagotchi keeper to care for the thing: to feed it, to give it loving attention, and to help it grow up into a well-adjusted digital thingumajig. If you were an irresponsible parent, the neglected or abused Tamagotchi would grow up to be, well, a bad egg.

Wellson Chin's movie is not an authorized tie-in with the toy. Indeed, the misspelled title pretty much botched the idea of piggy-backing on the popularity of the toy. ***Temegotchi*** does however involve, in a way, a similar premise: bad parenting has bad consequences. Although ***Temegotchi*** predates the J-Horror boom, it hits all the key notes: true horror arising from negligent or abusive parenting, split personalities, ghostly girls in white dresses, a female hero, haunted schools and hospitals. As J-Horror scholar Mandi Apple noted, ***Temegotchi*** pioneers some scenes and images that would later appear in the likes of ***Ring***,

Dark Water, ***Acacia***, and ***Cursed***.

Child actress Wong Man Yee makes her screen debut as Tintin, an orphan girl touched by unending suffering. She is being raised—and abused—by her aunt and uncle, who die under mysterious circumstances. Tintin's grade school teacher is found at the scene, stark raving bonkers, and is accused of the crime. But social worker Sam (Ruby Wong), herself an orphan, suspects there is more to the story than that. She enlists the reluctant help of her policeman boyfriend Wan (Dayo Wong). Together they discover that Tintin is the focal point of a supernatural force determined to avenge all the injustices the poor girl has endured in her short life.

Temegotchi is a distinctly HK sort of movie: a generic premise executed with cleverness, enthusiasm, and style. It is a stunt-addled police procedural full of frantic action and, not infrequently, goofball silliness. Wellson Chin also made such typical HK fare as ***The Inspector Wears Skirts*** (the original and its sequel) and ***Tsui Hark's Vampire Hunters*** and was associate producer on Stephen Chow's ***Kung Fu Hustle***. Like Tony Leung, he had to fight his instincts in order to craft such a low-key chiller, but he succeeded better than Leung in marrying that restrained approach to horror with the loonier characteristics of HK film. ***Temegotchi*** is not a particularly scary or memorable movie, but it is a decent and sincere effort.

By far the strongest part of ***Temegotchi*** is the realistic and touching relationship depicted between the two stars, Dayo Wong and Ruby Wong. That thoughtfully scripted, well-acted love affair grounds the film in material that, like the stunt-packed finale, affords Chin some familiar ground. The spooky ghost stuff, however, is almost an afterthought to a movie that never quite settles on an intended audience.

By 2002, Hong Kong's filmmakers had yet to work out how to make J-Horror their own. On the theory that HK-Horror was still too inflected with the usual HK rowdiness, writer-director Steve Cheng turned out one of the quietest and most introspective ghost stories yet. ***Cham Bin Hung Leng*** ("Sleeping with the Dead") stars Jordan Chan (of ***Biozombie*** fame) as a sadsack doctor whose marriage is disintegrating. At the moment of his birth, he had officially "died" of meningitis, only to be miraculously revived within the hour. Since then, he has had the ability to see ghosts—which hasn't helped his mood any. One by one, his old college buddies are being murdered on their birthdays. As his own birthday approaches, he searches for the answer. This leads him back to a forgotten, repressed crime, a misused young woman, and an angry grudge. But solving that puzzle is perhaps just a distraction from the main show. He has fallen in love with a ghost.

There is much here to like. Curiously, and certainly coincidentally, the setup mirrors the Japanese horror novel *Strangers* by Taichi Yamada. Originally published in Japan in 1987, and available in an English translation from Vertical (Koji Suzuki's American publisher), Yamada's book tells the tale of a sadsack writer in the midst of an acrimonious divorce. He falls in love with a ghost but is too distracted by dealing with a different set of ghosts to realize it at first. In each story, the hero is quick to feel at home with the dead because he is himself all-but-dead, so emotionally shut down as to be cut off from living life fully. The same theme permeates much of Korean horror (see Chapter 8). Like ***Temegotchi***, the relationship drama in the film is stronger and more fully realized than the horror aspects.

Steve Cheng had previously made exploitationist fare along the lines of ***Rape Trap*** and ***Biocops***. Yet he delivers moderation and quiet solemnity here. Producer Raymond Wong is a prolific writer, actor, director and producer whose credits include ***The Bride With White Hair***. ***Sleeping with the Dead*** was never destined to win awards or break box office records, but it is a dignified film that did respectable business. ***Sleeping with the Dead*** earned a $352,000 in its theatrical run, but it was overshadowed two months later by the international hit ***Inner Senses***, which brought in $417,600 in domestic tickets but made a much bigger global splash.

Back in September of 1999, director Lo Chi Leung came out of the screening of ***The Sixth Sense*** thinking he had just seen a most remarkable film. He quickly added M. Night Shyamalan's name to his internal roster of great moviemakers, along with Martin Scorsese, Steven Spielberg, and Akira Kurosawa. Oh, to make a movie like that…

Leung sat down with screenwriter Sinling Yeung (one of the rare women in J-Horror's backstage) to develop a similar story. Leung was himself a scriptwriter, accustomed to writing his own material, but he wanted a woman's perspective for ***Yee Do Hung Gaan*** (what we know as "Inner Senses"). In Hollywood and Japan, producers develop a property and hire a director to make it, whereas in Hong Kong directors conceive of their own projects and seek out producers to back them. Leung cannily noted the J-Horror pattern, so successful at the box office but not yet fully accomplished by Hong Kong directors, and decided to stay true to the formula. Gotta have a strong heroine. With the finished screenplay, he attracted producer Derek Yee, and ***Inner Senses*** was set into motion.

In the lead, Leung cast ingénue Karena Lam as Yan Chueng, a young woman tormented by visions of the dead. Unable to function in society normally because of her affliction—and given to occasional suicidal impulses—she sees psychiatrist Dr. Law (Leslie Cheung). He is a skeptic, convinced that people "see" things only because the accumulated weight of folklore and ghost stories in the media prime us to. Perhaps he can help her...unless *she* changes *him*. Because the thing of it is, Dr. Law's seeing ghosts, too, and his aren't so easy to explain away.

As the English title signals, the filmmakers took their cues quite directly from ***The Sixth Sense***, down to the setup of a patient who sees dead people seeking help from a psychiatrist with secrets of his own. In a sharp break with the rest of Hong Kong attempts at J-Horror to date, Lo Chi Leung presents ghosts that are indeed truly scary but not actually dangerous. Leung knew from Shyamalan's film that the mere sight of ghostly apparitions was unsettling without the need for the spooks to be explicitly hostile. This was the mistake made by ***Sleeping with the Dead***: allowing the most touching aspects of the script to be sidetracked by heroes-vs-ghosts intrigues. Freed of such clunky plot requirements, Leung allows his film to focus on the true heart of the story, the relationship between two wounded souls finding strength in each other. As Leung noted of ***The Sixth Sense***, "It is presented as a horror movie but it is a film about family relationships."

Lo Chi Leung populates his film with exquisitely realized visions, some of which evoke memories of ***Dark Water*** and ***Ju-On***, while telling a story that, like ***A Tale of Two Sisters*** or ***The Ghost***, is about owning up to your own sense of guilt and confronting your own worst memories. While Leung was the first Hong Kong filmmaker to perfectly capture the queasy vibe and anxious suspense of J-Horror, he did so within an honest and realistic portrayal of a very human romance.

"I read an interview in which [Alfred] Hitchcock said what makes his films interesting is not what or who are hiding at the other side of the door, but to make the audience walk at the same pace and open the door together with the character," Leung told interviewer Rudy Joggerst in 2004. "It might be nothing behind the door, because what is inside is not important at all; what is important is the process of opening the door. I tried to execute this idea in ***Inner Senses***... In my perspective, a horror movie is just a way to seek audience attention coming to the theater, but there is always something more that I want to tell the audience."

Producer Derek Yee had spotted Canadian actress Karena Lam in a music video and cast the novice actress earlier that year in the romance ***July Rhapsody***. He liked her so much he selected her for the ***Inner Senses*** lead—her second screen role. New to movies and new to Hong Kong as well, Karena Lam soon found herself thrown into even more disorienting circumstances. Lo Chi Leung took her to a mental institution to observe the patients as research for her role as a psychologically tortured person. Leung and Lam agreed that the key to her character was that she did not think she was insane. So, Lo Chi Leung snuck her into the clinic and left her there to wallow in feelings of discomfort and alienation.

Sadly, the psychological pain suffered by her costar was not so artificial. Leslie Cheung was among the greatest talents of his generation. His boyish good looks, his easy charm, and his sheer skill made him one of the most popular stars in Hong Kong for two decades. He first rose to prominence in John Woo's breakout thriller ***A Better Tomorrow*** in 1987. From there, his career went only up: ***The Bride With White Hair***, ***Days of Being Wild***, ***Happy Together***, and the Oscar-nominated ***Farewell, My Concubine***. Cheung was openly gay—even flamboyant—when Hong Kong sexual mores still chafed at such taboos. He never hid his sexuality, but used it to his advantage in creating complex, multilayered characters. Time Magazine's Richard Corliss described Cheung as "James Dean with a mean streak, a deeper Johnny Depp."

Throughout the production of ***Inner Senses***, Cheung had behaved erratically, and costar Teresa Mo Shun-Kwun said that Cheung had become a "changed man" by the end of the shoot. He continued to struggle afterwards, walking off the sets of two other films and allegedly attempting suicide later in the year. But his coworkers and friends did not see the warning signs until it was too late. In the final scene of the film, Cheung's character contemplates suicide, saved only at the last minute by the loving embrace of Karena Lam. In a heartbreaking example of life imitating art, Cheung went to the roof of the Mandarin Oriental Hotel in Hong Kong on the evening of April 1, 2003. There he repeated the actions his character took at the end of ***Inner Senses***, without hesitation and with no one to stop him. Cheung died that night, at the age of 46.

Despite the attendant tragedy, ***Inner Senses*** enjoyed tremendous success both commercially and critically at a time when Hong Kong cinema sorely needed such a comeback. Leslie Cheung was nominated for the Golden Horse Award for Best Actor, while the Hong Kong Film Awards nominated Karena Lam for Best Actress. Lo Chi Leung took home the Hong Kong Film Award for Best Director.

Inner Senses would have stiff competition for horror fans' attention that year. Two months after it hit theaters, Hong Kong found it biggest hit in years and minted some new celebrities in the process.

Meet Danny and Oxide Pang. Twins, born in Hong Kong, who began their movie careers in Thailand, the Pang Brothers soaked up cinematic influences from across the globe. Think Quentin Tarantino plus the Wachowski Brothers plus Byung-ki Ahn. They got their start in advertising, where their instincts for fast, loud, aggressive aesthetics were honed to a razor-sharp point.

In 1997, Oxide Pang assembled a selection of his own short films into an experimental feature with a premise that prefigured Norio Tsuruta's ***Premonition*** (see Chapter 7). The hero gets a copy of a newspaper from the future and tries to use his premonitory knowledge to alter the destinies of people he knows are doomed. Although ***Who is Running*** was not a commercial hit, it garnered critical raves from foreign film festivals. The Pang Brothers were off to a promising start.

For the next few years, Oxide and Danny collaborated on a variety of projects. By 2002, they had won a slew of festival awards but had yet to achieve much commercial success. Peter Chan of Hong Kong's Applause Pictures had taken note of their prodigious talents and wisely sussed that it was preferable to be with them when they first hit it big rather than wait until after they had become the blockbuster stars they were destined to be. Chan invited the brothers to return to Hong Kong for a Thai-Hong Kong co-production.

Co-written by the Pang Brothers and Jojo Hui, ***Gin Gwai*** ("The Eye") tells the story of Wong Kar Min (Angelica Lee), a woman blind since childhood, who receives a cornea transplant that restores her sight. She starts falling in love with her psychotherapist Dr. Lo (Lawrence Chou), assigned to help her adjust to her newly regained sense of sight. He has his work cut out for him, because not only must she get used to seeing things she's never seen before, she's also now seeing things *nobody else is seeing*. Her eyes were once the property of a psychic little girl, abused and murdered for her prophecies of catastrophe. Wong now sees a world of ghosts, hallucinations of a life that isn't hers, and ominous visions of coming disasters.

EYES OF BOLLYWOOD

On the eve of the release of its horror thriller ***Naina***, the Indian production company IDreams puffed that this was a major step forward for Indian cinema into uncharted territory. "Its concept, theme, and treatment are totally untried," gushed the press release. Which was odd, given that the film is in fact a shot-for-shot remake of the Pang Brothers' ***The Eye***.

Setting that inconvenient fact aside, this rehash of one of the contemporary classics of Asian horror certainly did push the envelope of contemporary Bollywood. For one, there are no songs (!), a single star (Urmila Matondkar), and an un-Bollywood focus on women characters—the only meaningful male actor in the cast has at best a thankless and minor role.

As daring gambits go, these may seem like baby steps, but IDreams confidently expected blockbuster success.

Naina is an honest enough Indian name (one that has already graced a few Indian movie titles), but it is also the Hindi translation of ***The Eye***. So we get Urmila Matondkar as Naina Shah, the unhappy recipient of a cornea transplant that allows her to see ghosts and premonitions of doom. Matondkar is a genuine and deserving Bollywood star and earned her Scream Queen status at the head of the 2003 horror flick ***Bhoot*** ("Ghost"); however, a career spent competing with epic choreography has imbued the lass with the wrong skillset for the kind of restrained atmospherics that made the original ***Eye*** an international hit.

Matondkar flails about this film in full-on panic mode so acute she probably went home each night with muscle cramps. This is especially odd given that, as with the original Hong Kong film, the ghosts she sees may be unsettling to look at but do not actually threaten her with any harm.

The producers ponied up for location shooting in London and a U.K. based effects crew to fill the screen with CGI nightmares (I mean, what else is Ms. Matondkar supposed to be hysterically screaming about?). Director Shirpal Morakhia dutifully copies all of the tricks and techniques of the Pang Brothers' version but seems to distrust that such stuff alone will entertain an audience, so he slathers over the top of it with enough excess to choke a horse. Morakhia also takes pains to duplicate key scenes from Japanese horrors like ***Dark Water*** and ***Spiral***.

It probably would have worked better as a movie if they'd gone ahead and put in the songs after all; the filmmakers so clearly want those big moments and don't quite know what to do without them. In the end, the tropes of Asian horror just do not fit the expectations of Indian cinema very well and is as awkward a fit as the risibly fake bald wig worn by one of the characters.

To complicate ***Naina***'s chances at the box office, it just so happened that the very same day also saw the release of a rival thriller with a markedly similar plot. ***Nazar*** also had going for it the notoriety of having a Pakistani actress in the lead, and ethnic rivalries being what they are, advance reports that this Pakistani star would perform an onscreen kiss with her Indian costar (gasp!) was enough to steal much of ***Naina***'s thunder.

By the time the dust settled, ***Naina*** had handily bested ***Nazar*** in ticket sales, but that was small comfort for a film whose returns were but a fraction of the more conventional ***Bhoot***'s. So much for trailblazing.

In its narrative structure—woman and her shrink see ghosts—***The Eye*** resembles ***Inner Senses***, and its Big Finale cops a handful of ideas from the American thriller ***The Mothman Prophecies*** (released earlier that year). Along the way, nods to ***Parasite Eve***, ***Ju-On*** and ***Ring*** pass by as well. But for all it cribs from others, ***The Eye*** stands on its own as a coherent and confident modern horror classic. The Pang Brothers put

The Eye *franchise*

J-Horror into a blender and came out with something quite tasty—a J-Horror smoothie. Audiences went gaga. By way of comparison: ***Inner Senses*** was a solid commercial hit with a Hong Kong box office take of $418,000; ***The Eye*** shoveled some $13.7 million into its makers' pockets from Hong Kong alone—it then proceeded to swagger its way through the rest of the world, including a theatrical release in the United States.

For her starring role as the harassed victim of a haunted cornea transplant, Angelica Lee was rewarded with the Best Actress award from the 2003 Hong Kong Film Awards. Ironically, her rival in the category was Karena Lam for her performance in ***Inner Senses***. With a canny eye for talent, Lo Chi Leung cast both of them together in his follow-up ***Koma***, a taut suspense thriller about illegal organ transplants. Meanwhile, the Pang Brothers reunited with producer Peter Chan in 2004 for ***The Eye 2***, without Angelica Lee.

Chan and the Pangs noted the difficulties faced by the makers of the ***Ring*** sequels, compared to the clever strategy employed by the folks behind the ***Whispering Corridors*** series (see Chapters 2 and 8, respectively). Following this lead, they opted to let the ***Eye*** name become a brand identity for scary movies about different ways to encounter ghosts, but without plot interconnectivity.

Oxide Pang entered the project with no illusions: "It is a sequel after all. It has already lost the kind of freshness the first one had."

Because they knew that the audience would come with certain expectations based on the first film, the Pangs could afford to loosen the pace a little. The second film is more of a character study compared to the first one's roller-coaster ride chock-full-a-scares approach.

Joey Cheng (Qi Shu) is a wayward young woman whose foolish love affair with a married man has left her discarded, alone, pregnant, and suicidal. Like Dr. David Tsang of ***Sleeping with the Dead***, Joey's near-death experience with a fistful of sleeping pills returns her to the world of the living with the "gift" of being able to see the world of the dead. As if her life wasn't unhappy enough, she must now navigate her way through a clutch of ghosts—and scenes "borrowed" from ***Ju-On*** and ***Pulse***. As with other pregnancy-themed horrors like ***Ju-On 2*** and ***Unborn but Forgotten***, Joey is going to learn the hard way that the fact she is pregnant and surrounded by ghosts is no mere coincidence.

Even more than the first ***The Eye***, this movie is an actor's piece, dependent on the performance of its female lead. Thankfully, the Pang Brothers cast the lovely Qi Shu in the role. A striking beauty, Qi Shu has a tendency to play her roles with emotional volatility and a panic-tinged intensity that suits her character here better than in some of her other performances (Jackie Chan's ***Gorgeous***, the absurd action thriller ***So Close***, and the kung-fu coming-of-age drama ***Just One Look***).

As the main ghost bedeviling poor Qi Shu, the Pangs brought in Eugenia Yuan. Although Qi Shu is without question the star of the show, Yuan got better billing in publicity because she is the bigger international star. Yuan is daughter of the old school kung-fu superstar Pei Pei Cheng. She trained as a rhythm gymnast and was selected for the United States Olympic Team, although in the end she did not compete. Yuan started her acting career in American television, appearing on ***Beverly Hills 90210***, ***Baywatch***, and ***NYPD Blue*** before showing up in Hong Kong feature films like ***The Eye 2***. Her role as a ghost won her a Hong Kong Film Awards nomination for Best Actress—not bad for a role performed mostly mute in front of a special effects green screen.

Although the sequel slipped in terms of audience and critical response compared to the first film, it was still a hit and attracted the attention of Hollywood's remake mongers. Vertigo Entertainment has bought the first ***Eye*** for an American remake, to be directed by Hideo Nakata (the mouth waters at the idea). While Vertigo's producers developed that property over at Paramount, they also snapped up remake rights to ***The Eye 2***, arranging with New Line to distribute the American cover version. Vertigo's producers hired screenwriter Todd Smith to adapt the unrelated plot of ***The Eye 2*** into ***In Utero***, with the odd possibility that the remake of the sequel might appear in theaters before the remake of the original. Gold Circle Films, the company behind ***My Big Fat Greek Wedding***, put up a $25 million budget for ***In Utero***, more money than the Pang Brothers' version made in revenues.

Emboldened by such heady sums, the Pangs returned to the ***Eye*** franchise for the third installment, bizarrely called ***The Eye 10***. The title refers to the ten different ways that a person could summon ghosts, according to the (wholly fictional) "Ten Encounters" book discovered by some vacationing teenagers. Actively and self-consciously courting a teen audience, the Pang Brothers collected ten photogenic young stars, boys and girls, to be put into harm's way, including Wilson Chen, Kate Yeung, Kris Gu, Isabella Leong, and Ray MacDonald.

Like the setup of ***A Wicked Ghost***, these kids set out to conjure up some ghosts out of a sense of boredom and teenage daredevilry, only to regret what they set in motion. And, like ***A Wicked Ghost***, the film juggles serious scares with ironic jokes. Sometimes the juxtaposition of the joking and the scary produces startling and memorable effects. Sometimes it is just jarring: a breakdance contest with a poltergeist, farting to repel attacking ghouls, a hide and seek game gone very wrong.

Although the book and the movie's title promise ten different ways to encounter ghosts, the script by the Pangs and co-writer Mark Wu does not tally up that far. The first two ways, "The Condemned Cornea Transplant" and "Attempting Suicide While Pregnant," are not the sort of thing some disaffected teens could try in a single evening anyway; they're winkingly presented to the audience with clips from the first two films. ***The Eye 10*** has a refreshing irreverence to it that is more satisfying than the similarly parodic ***Cursed*** (see Chapter 7), and if anybody is going to make fun of the genre it ought to be someone who at least knows what they are doing. To date, no American company has shown much interest in remaking ***The Eye 10***, nor has a fourth film in the series been announced.

After all those years of a ruthlessly commercial pop-will-eat-itself pulp culture in Hong Kong cinema, the self-reflexive self-parody of ***The Eye 10*** seems an apt metaphor for the state of Hong Kong's film industry. In the Pang Brothers, we find a pair of filmmakers whose art resides in rehashing the ideas of others in their own idiom; their movies, in turn, are snapped up by outsiders to be rehashed all over again.

We can put some numbers to the issue, if you like. At the transitional moment in the late 1990s, when the movie industries of Japan, South Korea and Hong Kong were all in roiling flux, the combined total of films produced in Asia vastly exceeded that of any other region, including Hollywood. However, as industry analyst Ying-Ming Chang notes in his work at the New School, a quick glance at a chart of global box office proceeds seems to belie this fact. The top ten best-selling movies in the world were American, and Asian films barely cracked the top 200 (!). So when we spoke earlier of Hong Kong being the world's second-largest exporter of movies, that was true but not a full accounting. Consider a golf tournament between Tiger Woods and a bunch of five year olds. Someone has to come in second place, but it doesn't mean the game was close.

Hong Kong generates about 200 movies a year, down from around 250 at the top of the 1990s. The primary markets for these films (aside from Hong Kong itself) are Taiwan, Singapore, Malaysia, and Thailand. These are crucial markets, because HK films only claim 40 percent of domestic ticket sales, with mostly American imports dominating.

Over the course of the 1990s, the Taiwanese market has steadily eroded away from Hong Kong's reach. At the start of the decade, Hong Kong productions commanded between 30 to 50 percent of the Taiwanese marketplace. But when Taiwan lifted import restrictions on Hollywood films, American fare started to muscle their way in. Now, Taiwan is one of the top ten outlets for Hollywood productions, which is great news for American studios but has been devastating for Hong

Kong filmmakers. With Hollywood hoarding 96.6 percent of the Taiwanese audience, there's all but nothing left for Hong Kong.

DOUBLE VISION

The Heirloom was by no means the first Taiwanese horror film to probe the possibilities of commercial success. In 2002, internationally acclaimed director Chen Kuo-Fu made the festival circuit with his slick Hollywood-style serial-killer thriller ***Shuang Tong***, or "Double Vision." The contrast between ***Double Vision*** and Kuo-Fu's existing arthouse reputation was so stark, he could scarcely have shocked the crowd at Cannes more if he had stripped naked and posed in the fountain for the paparazzi.

Back in 1998, Kuo-Fu was feted for his tender romantic drama ***The Personals*** about a woman seeking love through personal ads. Himself a professional film critic, he made ***The Personals*** with a film critic's sensibility. One reviewer called the result a "Godardian film essay." Like much of contemporary Taiwanese film, it was hailed by Western critics but was a commercial sinkhole.

So Kuo-Fu decided to try his hand at something *really* daring: a straightforward genre thriller. "It's nothing that Taiwanese cinema has tried before," Kuo-Fu defensively explained to an audience at Yale University, "but I know that the audience is there for this kind of entertainment film."

Mixing elements of ***Se7en***, ***The X-Files***, and ***The Hypnotist***, Kuo-Fu's ***Double Vision*** is an almost standard-issue buddy-cop/culture-clash/serial-killer flick. A burnt-out hard-boiled detective (played by yet another Tony Leung, this one Tony Leung Ka-Fai) joins forces with fish-out-of-water FBI profiler Kevin Richter (David Morse) to investigate a bizarre string of seemingly impossible murders that follow the pattern of the Taoist Five Visions of Hell.

In a way, ***Double Vision*** is sort of Taiwan's answer to ***Suicide Club*** or ***The Hypnotist***. American audiences tended to rankle at what they saw as an awkward juxtaposition of science fiction and supernatural horror, with the police procedural gradually giving way to irrational mysticism. Yet J-Horror has combined detective stories and ghost stories before—witness ***Cure***, or ***Face***. Ever since ***Ring***, characters in J-Horror have consistently turned to the tools of scientific investigation to explore encounters with the spirit world. If supernatural forces are real, they must admit to rational inquiry, even if they ultimately escape it. At its most reductionist, ***Double Vision*** can be seen as a double-down remake of ***Se7en*** and ***Ring***.

The production was an unprecedented risk for Kuo-Fu. He spent lavishly, on bringing in minor American star David Morse, on extravagant CGI effects, on a showstopping sword fight of epic scale. In the final tally, he'd spent more to make ***Double Vision*** than any other Taiwanese production in history. The risk was handsomely rewarded, with a record-breaking $1.2 million box office take.

But what of Taiwanese films?

There is, actually, a Taiwanese film industry. Like any animal forced to evolve in the footprint of giants, the Taiwanese film industry has become highly specialized, eking out an existence in a niche uncontested by Hong Kong or American producers. Unable to seriously compete for box office presence, Taiwanese films basically stopped trying. Taiwanese films are low-budget, state-subsidized art films modeled on the Italian neo-realist movement, concerned primarily with documenting authentic visions of Taiwanese life.

Which is to say, they don't make movies like ***Raped by an Angel***, ***Biozombie***, or ***Kung Fu Hustle*** in Taiwan.

They do however make films like ***Ring***.

Here's how it happened. Since Taiwanese filmmakers were all but locked out of their own movie theaters, they began to cater to film festival audiences in the hopes of cultivating niche audiences abroad. Thus, events like the Golden Horse Film Festival became increasingly significant. This annual festival of Chinese language films of varying origins in 2004 singled out a raunchy gay sex farce called ***Formula 17***. To say this was an anomaly for Taiwanese cinema is a gross understatement. Directed by a brash young woman colorfully named DJ Chen, ***Formula 17*** went on to become the second highest grossing Taiwanese film of the year. Brazen in both its sexuality and its commercial aims, it signaled a turning point for Taiwanese film.

The producers of ***Formula 17***, Michelle Yeh and Aileen Li, could barely believe their good fortune. Daring to think that investing in youth-oriented genre films might actually be a good business move, they put into production a slate of commercially-minded pictures including ***Zhaibian*** ("The Heirloom").

Sumptuously photographed, packed with camera-friendly young talent, with a devil-in-the-details approach to production design that could just as well have come from the mind of Heironymous Bosch and M.C. Escher, it comes as no surprise to learn that screenwriter Dorian Li and director Leste Chen were both design majors. Together with art director Shun-Fu Luo and cinematographer Pun-Leung Kwan, they had exhaustive preproduction discussions to work out all of the nuances of the film's elaborate visual scheme. The result of all these efforts, ***The Heirloom*** is among the best J-Horrors of any country and a standout piece of commercial cinema from Taiwan.

Pointedly, Leste Chen mentioned in press tours for the film that he felt that the likes of ***Ring*** and ***One Missed Call*** were not atmospheric *enough* (he cited them by name) and that his ambition was to *truly* evoke suspense through subtlety. Perhaps he succeeded too well. The filmmakers became convinced that the shoot was actually haunted and that real "others" might have been captured on film at certain points!

The disturbing tale takes as its premise a genuine Chinese folk tradition of worshipping dead babies. According to the fictional mythology of the film, if you were to purchase a dead baby on the black market and feed it human blood, its ghost would become your slave, granting you godlike powers. Of course, bargains with supernatural forces always come with strings attached.

Jason Chang stars as James Yang, last of the once proud Yang clan, whose prosperity was the result of their secret occupation, i.e., raising ghosts for fun and profit. James inherits the sprawling Yang estate (Bruce Wayne would be jealous) and convinces girlfriend Yo (the stunning Terri Kwan) to move in with him. No sooner does she than *weird stuff* starts going down. Such as: their friends constantly reappear magically within the house when they fall asleep elsewhere. Video surveillance, to determine the cause of such occurrences, reveals the place is lousy with ghosts, hanging from the rafters.

Since Yo is now pregnant with the Yang heir, she is anxious to learn just how and why James came to be last of the line. What happened here so long ago, and why does it still seem to be happening today?

The Heirloom features a story structure distinctive to J-Horror. Old school ghost flicks, whether as old as ***Ghost Story of Yotsuya*** or as modern as Kiyoshi Kurosawa's ***Sweet Home***, all follow a linear path as the heroes deduce the cause of the phantoms and resolve the problem somehow. J-Horror understands that figuring out the world of specters is a vexing challenge prone to confusion, and so employs a dual climax. The heroes guess at what needs to be done, do it, fail, and then have to try again.

The Heirloom is a near-perfect fusion of the three primary variants we've so far encountered: the gimmicky idea-driven Japanese approach, the Korean focus on repressed guilt, and the relationship drama of Hong Kong horrors. That this film, inexpensively made by young filmmakers in a struggling industry, could become a rare commercial success for Taiwan speaks to the international power of the J-Horror form.

J-Horror has thrived in a wide variety of Asian countries, adapting to the local culture and different economic conditions of its varied hosts. But what about outside Asia, removed from the folklore that gave it birth?

Now, at last, we are ready to find out.

TWINS EFFECT

A Tale of Two Sisters*, *One Missed Call*, *St. John's Wort*, *Double Vision*, *The Heirloom, why even the Pang Brothers themselves—it seems as if Asia must be crawling with twins!

In fact, twinning is especially rare in Asia. There are two kinds of twins, with separate rates of occurrence. Identical, or monozygotic, twins occur when a single egg splits into two zygotes after it has been fertilized. Around the world, this happens an average of 4 times out of every 1000 births, regardless of race or culture. Fraternal, or dizygotic, twins occur when two eggs happen to be fertilized simultaneously, but rates of this vary widely by region.

In the United States, 12 out of every 1000 births result in twins, and 2/3 of these are dizygotic (fraternal) twins. Asia has the lowest incidence of dizygotic twins in the world—and in a curious fact, Asian-Americans have twins (either kind) just 3 times out of every 1000 births, a lower percentage than the worldwide average for just monozygotic twins!

According to the movies, all those Asian twins are in some way connected to spirits from the afterlife. I have been unable to compile statistics to confirm or deny this.

Sources:

"A Conversation with Karena Lam," www.cinemasie.com, April 29, 2003.
"Can the Roaring Youth Save Taiwan Film?" China Daily, November 26, 2004.
"The Making of the Heirloom," The Heirloom DVD edition, Tartan Video USA, 2005.
Chiang, Ying-Ming, "Taiwan and Hong Kong's Film Industries in the Context of Globalization," Globalization and the Media, homepage.newschool.edu/~chakravs/YMCessay.html.
Dow, Jason, "The Pang Brothers—Twin Talents," www.yesasia.com, 2005.
Interview with Oxide Pang, www.cinespot.com, 2006.
Joggerst, Rudy, "Invasion of the Organ Snatchers," www.hollywoodvideo.com.
Kelly, Stephen, "Why Does It Have to Be Like This?" www.morphizm.com, May 14, 2003.
Kozo, "The Eye 10 review," www.lovehkfilm.com, 2005.
Kozo, "The Eye 2 review," www.lovehkfilm.com, 2004.
Kraicer, Shelly, "The Personals review," www.chinesecinemas.org, 1999.
Toro, Tamas, "Taiwanese Film Comes Alive at WHC," Yale Daily News, November 7, 2003.
Wilson, Staci Layne, "10 Questions with Lo Chi Leung," www.horror.com, March 2, 2005.
www.hkmdb.com
www.urbandharma.org

CHAPTER 10

J-HORROR AMERICAN STYLE

When all was said and done, Kiyoshi Kurosawa had to tally 2001 as a wasted year. He had come to Los Angeles with guarded optimism, though. Kiyoshi Kurosawa goes Hollywood... Perhaps this was the opening of a new door.

At issue was ***Pulse***, his latest, as scary a nightmare as had ever been conjured up by Japanese cinema. Ever the intellectual, Kurosawa had noted J-Horror's fixation on technology: cursed cell phones, cursed videotapes, and so on. But what of the ultimate marvel of modern technology—the internet? "In one home," says Kurosawa, "there would be four separate rooms with four people all doing something of their own on the internet." The web promised to bring people all over the world together, but only at the cost of keeping them physically apart. Look at all the lonely people, he said. All their aggregated loneliness—what will that wreak?

Thus, ***Pulse***, another notch in the belt of arguably Japan's most interesting and enigmatic filmmaker. ***Pulse*** was fêted at Cannes and the Toronto Film Festival, while audiences queued up for tickets back in Japan. And so, Kurosawa was invited to Hollywood to discuss a remake. Guarded optimism indeed.

What followed was a joke, a textbook study in development hell. Kurosawa had faced more than his share of frustration before—he'd once been blackballed, obliged to fight his way back into the industry (see Chapter 5)—but this was something else altogether. Those Hollywood types had a way of stabbing you in the back while looking you in the eye.

Meeting followed meeting. Kurosawa was to direct the remake, now Wes Craven will direct, now Craven wants out... Kurosawa flew back to Japan with nothing to show for his efforts.

Flash forward five years: in the dog days of summer 2006, the Hollywood version of ***Pulse*** finally appears in theaters. Kurosawa had nothing to do with it and is careful to point this out. "It didn't have my permission," he says. If Kurosawa tries to distance himself from the remake, the remake tries to cozy back up to him. In an odd and possibly unique circumstance, footage from Kurosawa's film was used in the trailers for the remake. As if Hollywood's CGI magicians could not top what Kurosawa wrought on his meager budget back in 2001, a climactic plane crash from the original ***Pulse*** adorns the previews for the Americanized cover version, and rightly so, as it stands as one of the most harrowing moments in contemporary Asian cinema.

Piggy-backing on the promotion of the remake, Magnolia Pictures trotted out the real deal for a limited theatrical run and subsequent DVD edition. The posters proudly boasted "Before ***The Ring***, before ***The Grudge***..." Movie distributors have never felt bound by truth-in-advertising laws, but this particular claim requires some qualification. The intended audience for the Japanese version of ***Pulse*** might be forgiven for thinking first of the *Japanese* versions of ***Ring*** and ***Grudge***, but the chronological fact is that ***Pulse*** only predates the U.S. remakes of these films.

By that point, the world of J-Horror had become a tangle of influences, references, and remakes, enough to warrant jokes: Takashi Shimizu's segment of ***Dark Tales of Japan*** features a Japanese tourist in LA scoffing, "All they do now is remake Japanese films!"

Say what you will about the aesthetic value of these remakes, but one thing is indisputable: they propped up Japanese and Korean filmmakers at a time when otherwise the genre threatened to piffle out. The extraordinary success of the Hollywood versions of ***The Ring*** and ***The Grudge*** changed everything. The original ***Ring*** pulled in $6.6 million in Japanese ticket sales—a sum that made fortunes and set records—but the U.S. version made $8.3 million in Japan just in its first two weeks. In its wake, J-Horror became the Japanese Filmmaker Full Employment Act. Suspense-driven ghost stories were all but guaranteed to find an appreciative Western audience on DVD, perhaps even make it to theaters, while a lucky few would win big-budget remakes; the truly select few would be granted entry into Hollywood itself. The remakes are the most obvious examples of how Hollywood co-opted J-Horror, but they are merely the visible part of the iceberg. Americans started financing the production of Japanese horror films, while Japanese filmmakers started making J-Horrors directly within Hollywood, intermingling the Japanese and American film industries in unprecedented ways.

The rise of J-Horror in Hollywood—and by extension the broader international phenomenon—can be attributed in large part to the actions of just one man. He is not Japanese, speaks only English, and is not in any conventionally understood sense of the word a "filmmaker." Yet his role in this story is at least as significant as any of the directors and producers we have thus far met. You are reading this book because of what he did. His name is Roy Lee.

Born in Brooklyn in 1969 to Korean immigrant parents, Roy Lee

MY RING CAN BEAT UP YOUR RING

I know that I am expected in these pages to offer up my opinion on which is better—the Japanese originals or the American copies. I also know that I risk credibility as a serious student of film if I choose the American ones. But you will not catch me out slamming the remakes simply to prove something. I think this book serves as my credentials as an impassioned fan of Asian cinema without my having to posture. Truth be told, I embarked on this project because of the remakes—I saw the American ***Ring*** and ***Grudge*** first, and fell in love with J-Horror from there.

It is worth questioning why remakes are made at all, instead of letting these wonderful films reach American audiences unadulterated. But that is sadly the answer: Americans don't like subtitles, and the usual arthouse crowd willing to spend an evening with an imported flick tend to dislike horror movies.

The Japanese ***Ju-On: The Grudge*** toured the country at the same time as ***The Grudge*** played multiplexes. The same would have been true of ***Pulse*** had Dimension not delayed the release of the Jim Sonzero version by six months just as Magnolia shipped prints of the original to arthouses. In both cases, the Japanese imports received almost universal critical praise and were often picked out as "must see" selections by local papers. In both cases, the marketing of the remakes served as indirect publicity for the originals. And, in both cases, the box office draws of the originals were anemic—best considered as loss leaders for the eventual DVD editions. I can say from personal experience that the Japanese ***Pulse*** could not have expected better promotion in the Washington, D.C. area, yet when I attended an opening weekend screening at the *only* theater showing it, I was 1/6 of the audience.

Time and again the American public has been given access to the full-strength Japanese originals and has consistently voted with its feet to support only those J-Horrors mediated by Hollywood blondes: Naomi Watts, Sarah Michelle Gellar, Kristen Bell (perhaps we've found here the true cause of ***Dark Water***'s poor performance—Jennifer Connelly's raven locks!).

Before you are tempted to call it racism, consider this: American pop culture is steeped in the cult of celebrity, reinforced on all sides by supermarket tabloids, Us and People, ***Entertainment Tonight***, red carpet award show spectaculars. American movie stars sell American movies, and no amount of critical praise for some subtitled import will get past the fact that audiences here do not know and do not recognize the likes of Koji Yakusho, Ren Osugi, or Miho Kanno.

never harbored any particular desire to go into show business, but he does recall very vividly some early experiences at the movies. His earliest memory of going to a theater is when his uncle took him to ***The Exorcist***, what he recalls as "almost a traumatic experience." Not much

AMERICAN GOTHIC

As in Hong Kong, American pop culture is now in a state of hyperactive self-consumption: whatever role older artistic traditions or American folklore once held in the culture has long since drowned in the torrent of remakes, sequels, rip-offs, and wannabes. Thus it matters little if the Long Haired Ghost has any cultural relevance in the West—***The Ring*** was a hit, and so anything that apes ***The Ring*** isn't totally foreign. The tropes of J-Horror then fit on American screens: long-haired ghosts and creepy kids, gimmicky curses and haunted technology, dark water and dead wet girls, spooks that descend from the rafters above.

But this is not merely a case of Hollywood copying Asian ghosts. This stuff was already percolating in American culture. Ask the filmmakers themselves and you'll hear Taka Ichise, Norio Tsuruta, Hideo Nakata, Kiyoshi Kurosawa, Takashi Shimzu and others list their influences: Sam Raimi's ***Evil Dead*** movies, Robert Wise's ***The Haunting***, William Friedkin's ***The Exorcist***... Sometimes they let those influences float awfully close to the surface—for example, Lo Chi Leung, who openly fashioned ***Inner Senses*** as a Chinese answer to M. Night Shyamalan's ***The Sixth Sense***.

If Taka Ichise wished to repay the favor and have a Japanese director remake some American horror flick, he could hardly have done better than to revamp John Irvin's ***Ghost Story***, a 1981 thriller that is America's earliest authentic Dead Wet Girl. In fact, Ichise is having Hideo Nakata remake the Hollywood chiller ***The Entity*** and has already produced a Japanese version of ***The Blair Witch Project***, Koji Shiraishi's ***Noroi*** ("The Curse").

While Japanese filmmakers increasingly turn to explicit remakes of Hollywood horrors, the imagery of J-Horror has started to become part of Hollywood's stock: ***Gothika***, ***Darkness***, ***White Noise***, and ***The Skeleton Key*** are all recent examples of mainstream Hollywood horror that borrow scare techniques from the playbook of J-Horror.

later, his mother became the bane of the neighborhood for taking him and his sixth grade friends to ***The Fog***. His mother tried to explain she didn't know what MPAA ratings were; his friends suffered bad dreams; Lee merely remembered the lingering power of cinematic nightmares.

He did not immediately pursue a path in that direction. He attended high school in Bethesda, Maryland, then George Washington University as an undergrad. He took an internship at Fried, Frank, Harris, Shriver & Jacobson and became a lawyer. For all outward appearances, it seemed Roy Lee was destined for an ordinary sort of button-down life.

But the day came when Lee left his D.C. firm to go west, where he took a job with a production company called Alphaville, to work as a tracker. At the time, trackers were a lowly breed tasked with reading all the spec scripts floating through Hollywood and communicating their opinions of their commercial merits. This they did, by calling each other up, and talking. Lee was a law firm refugee accustomed to elaborate online databases organizing complex litigation among lawyers spread across the country. He realized he could adapt the kind of software he'd used back at Fried for the tracking field. What if trackers didn't just waste their time on the phone but traded notes online in a database that could be easily searched, with each tracker's opinions tagged with some marker of their individual track record?

The consequences of Lee's Scriptshark service were many. One affected the industry as a whole. Time was, big name writers like Joe Eszterhas or Shane Black could shop scripts around on the pretense of offering their wares on an exclusive basis. Prospective buyers, that is producers, would have no way of knowing if the script was a fresh offering or something already rejected elsewhere and were prone to being bullied into paying exorbitant amounts. Scriptshark made it the simple matter of a mouseclick to identify a screenplay's history and to glean the opinions of readers whose reliability could be easily checked.

There was another consequence, of a more personal nature. As the administrator of the system, Lee had a big-picture view of the trackers' notations scurrying back and forth. And so when he saw readers at many houses all gushing with enthusiasm for a script called ***American Beauty*** by Alan Bell, he figured it had to be hot even if he'd never laid hands on the thing himself, much less read it. Lee called his friend Mark Sourian, then an assistant at DreamWorks Pictures, and advised him of the buzz. DreamWorks bought the property, and the film went on to win the Best Picture Oscar.

Success opens doors. Sourian was promoted to producer at DreamWorks, and Lee surfed the wave of his success to become a producer at Benderspink, a talent management-cum-production firm run by Chris Bender and J.C. Spink.

Lee's job at Benderspink was to acquire and/or develop short films that would be distributed on the internet—an idea that, long before YouTube came along, promised little shelf life as a serious professional career. But no matter, since during his brief tenure at Benderspink, Mr. Lee would play a pivotal role in the launching of the ***Ring*** remake.

Or at least, that is the official story: Roy Lee attends the Puchon International Film Festival, where ***Ring*** wins the Best Picture Award. Noting its awe-inspiring box office return in Asia, and that it is crackerjack entertainment, he calls up Mark Sourian at DreamWorks—a man already inclined to give Lee more than the benefit of the doubt.

Out comes the checkbook and a $1 million check to buy the rights.

The trouble with legends is that good storytelling sometimes trumps facts, and along the way the truth gets fudgy. History has decreed that Roy Lee is the man who brought ***Ring*** to Hollywood, just as history has appointed Hideo Nakata the creator of the form. We have already seen how Nakata must share that credit with others. What of Lee?

Back in 2001, while Kiyoshi Kurosawa was meeting with Wes Craven to set up the ***Pulse*** remake, Fine Line Features was developing an Americanized revamp of ***Ring***. Like ***Pulse***, the project stalled, and Fine Line executive Mike Macari left the company, taking ***Ring*** with him. He had high hopes for the thing, though, and called Benderspink to help represent it for him. ***Ring*** was passed down to Benderspink employee Roy Lee, who sold it to Mark Sourian at DreamWorks, getting himself—but not Macari—named as producer.

It is said that a cycle of mutual threats and angry messages flew between the two men as they warred over their competing versions of the story, and the credit that would come as a result of which story won out. Eventually, both men were listed as executive producers on ***The Ring***.

I mull over this tale of jealousy not to tarnish anyone's reputation but to highlight the curious role of Roy Lee in modern Hollywood. He has a job that, to readers of this book, may sound like Heaven: he watches movies, tells people which ones he likes, and makes a fortune doing just that. And in case that sounds too cushy, bear in mind that for the most part Mr. Lee doesn't even watch the films himself, he has a staff for that, and only concerns himself with watching the ones they think are worth his time. And he has this job in large measure on the basis of his part in suggesting the remake of ***Ring***, a commercial juggernaut of epic proportions—yet he may not even have done that.

Roy Lee succeeds by projecting a vision of himself. He is scrupulous about maintaining his public image, controlling his reputation. He excels at negotiating with Asian companies, thanks to his Korean looks, despite being as American as American gets. He has become the go-to guy for Asian movie remakes because of his enormous track record—a track record which, mind you, actually counts only a handful of films so far, only two of which are unqualified mega-hits, and of those one may not have been his baby so much as is believed. Yet he has sold no less than seventeen remake projects to various studios: ***The Grudge***, ***Dark Water***, ***Chaos***, ***Old Boy***, ***Infernal Affairs***, ***The Eye 2***, ***Infection***, ***Turn***, ***My Sassy Girl***... The mind fairly reels. Along with Doug Davison, Lee founded Vertigo Entertainment, where his job is to tell other producers, "You should remake [fill in blank with Asian movie title]," and then take home a $300,000 check if the movie indeed is made.

To an outside observer, his intermediation may seem superfluous. There is nothing stopping a man like Taka Ichise from approaching a Hollywood company directly. Ichise is a seasoned pro and a hard-headed negotiator with one of the strongest CV's in foreign cinema, and he'd likely do just fine on his own without Lee. The studios could substantially cut their costs by dispensing with Lee's services—why pay him a finder's fee for what anyone with a DVD player and an internet connection could do themselves? Yet Lee remains the pivot point of almost every remake deal.

Roy Lee is unusually good at what ought to be anybody's game. He scarcely has any competition. They come to him, time and again, because he's *better* at it than they could be if they tried to cut him out.

Lee is the beneficiary of a unique moment in film history. Globalism had brought the film industries of East and West closer together than ever before, but someone had to figure out how to establish that final bridge. Lee just happened to be the one to see it before anyone else.

For Asian producers, Lee's offer was simple and direct: You guys are fighting the good fight in competing with Hollywood, and as a result you're making some fantastic movies. But Americans don't go to foreign films, so you're stuck mopping up crumbs in other markets. You could compete for American audiences, but only if your films are in English with American actors. You've already made your film, anyone can see it's good, so why not get it remade in Hollywood and pocket the cash from that, basically selling the same movie twice over? You could try selling the idea yourself, but I know the right guys, I speak English, I live in L.A., and I won't take a dime of your money—I'll be paid by the studio if they make the movie. Do we have a deal?

To the studios in Hollywood, Lee's pitch is more complex, but it is powerfully compelling. There is a reason why studios will happily shell out five or six figures for what he's selling. It's worth ever so much more.

The facts are these: ticket sales in the United States amounted to $9 billion in 2005; the foreign box office tallied $12 billion. These numbers have been cleaving apart for years; the foreign markets become more important every year. With budgets climbing higher, it is now the case that few American-made movies can make a profit in the domestic market. Without foreign sales, Hollywood would collapse.

"The decision to greenlight a film is now often based on the potential for international sales," Lionsgate International President Nicolas Meyer explained to the Washington Post. "Everything about the movie business today is about the global market."

According to Peter Bart, editor of Variety, "Now nobody in their right mind running a studio would make one of these incredibly expensive films until they had convinced themselves that it would play well overseas."

This explains much about Hollywood that is otherwise perplexing. Take a ludicrous overbloated piece of sci-fi cheese like Michael Bay's ***The Island***. A flop in the U.S., rejected by critics and audiences alike, it pulled in just $35 million here, but grossed $124 million abroad—of that, $22 million came just from South Korea. Or consider Chris Tucker, the most valuable movie star in the world. He has but a few movies to his name, and no one in America would rate him above Tom Hanks or Tom Cruise, but his ***Rush Hour*** films with Jackie Chan earned a boggling $600 million around the globe. He will get a $25 million salary to appear in ***Rush Hour 3***, making him Hollywood's highest paid star.

Hollywood is in the business of selling movies to foreigners—Asians chiefly among them—and in that they are primarily competing against Asian filmmakers. While Hollywood is the world's predominant film industry, to the extent it has competition, that competition comes from the East, especially Hong Kong and India. The most vital secondary markets for Hollywood outside America are in Asian nations—Japan, Hong Kong, Taiwan, South Korea—and these countries have their own film industries making increasingly competitive motion pictures.

Figuring out what Americans want to see is tough enough, but deducing what the world wants to see?

Traditionally, Hollywood has used every gimmick and contrivance to hedge their bets—the marquee value of a star name, an adaptation of a popular book or TV show, a sequel to a blockbuster hit, a remake of a fondly remembered classic—anything and everything to minimize the risk of investing millions upon millions of dollars in the manufacture of a film nobody particularly wants to pay to watch.

On top of that, there is the preview process, in which a group of random folks are roped by the studio's marketing department and shown an early version of the film to test their reactions. They say that Harold Lloyd first invented the notion back in 1919. Since then it has become an essential feature of the Hollywood landscape.

It is both ruthlessly calculating and inexact. Making changes to a movie based on the reactions of a mere handful of people does not necessarily make the movie better. History is full of legendary examples of flicks that tested poorly but were huge hits when released—without changes. The reverse is also true: films with strong test screenings can yet tank. And then there are those movies revised by test screenings that end up alienating their target audiences… We could discuss ***Pulse*** here, if we were not getting ahead of ourselves.

Enter Roy Lee, with the following logic: Forget evaluating pitches or spec scripts, trying to envision a movie from words on a page. Here are finished films which are already proven big in Japan, demonstrated commercial hits around the world, but are still new to Americans. And you can consider the extant versions a form of rough draft. Keep what you like, change what you don't.

And where this concept might once have run aground over concerns that Japanese entertainment could not be readily translated into an American idiom, this is no longer true. Perhaps in response to the global pressures on its makers, American pop culture has gradually become Asianified.

Asian imports used to be drastically altered to efface their foreign origins. At the very least, they would be dubbed; in some cases, new footage of American actors would be crudely inserted into the films so as to spare American audiences the pain of having to watch and identify with foreign characters. Consider the ***Mighty Morphin Power Rangers***. This is a long-running series made in Japan, but for U.S. distribution it is hacked to pieces. Only the special effects sequences are kept, while new scenes of American stars are substituted into the holes.

The situation is in the process of reversing itself. Increasingly, American-made entertainment tries to establish Asian bona fides: huge chunks of ABC's top-rated drama ***Lost*** are shown in Korean without so much as subtitles. Or Quentin Tarantino's epic ***Kill Bill***, in which Uma Thurman and others deliver extended sequences of Japanese dialogue. Imports like ***Kung Fu Hustle*** and ***Ong Bak: The Thai Warrior*** play in ordinary multiplexes without dubbing, sent out by distributors unafraid that mall-going teens might object to the subtitles. Children's television was once a platform by which to expose kids to equal measures of civics lessons and toy commercials but is now increasingly a venue by which to give children ancient Chinese wisdom and martial arts techniques: ***Jackie Chan Adventures***, ***Avatar: The Last Airbender***, ***Sagwa the Chinese Siamese Cat***…

One last piece of the puzzle: horror has evolved into a mainstream, mass-market genre in the United States. For years, horror was a ghetto for low-budget shockers aimed at gore-hungry boys. Only rarely would a production company dare to pony up for a theatrical release of a horror picture; most were junked out directly to video. 1999 proved a pivotal year, with the one-two punch of ***The Sixth Sense*** and ***The Blair Witch***

Project. It was for Hollywood a paradigm shift similar to that caused in Japan by ***Ring*** and ***Cure*** the previous year, a pair of commercial and critical hits that redirected horror entertainment away from cheap scares and into inexpensive suspense.

"Horror used to be a dirty word for studios," Peter Block of Lions Gate Films told USA Today. "We'd make a dozen horror films for the straight-to-video market and maybe release one commercially. Now it's hard to find a weekend free for your horror film. [It's become] part of the establishment."

As in Japan, Hollywood found that teenage girls and young women were key to the fortunes of New Horror. In the wake of ***The Ring***, studio analysts found that women and girls had come to comprise 60 percent of the horror audience. According to Revolution Studios founder Tom Sherak, the change came about when and because horror moved "away from the slasher stuff a bit and more toward suspense. They don't want to be grossed out. That's more for the guys. Girls want to be scared in a more realistic way."

With the rise of female audiences came another curious development. Consumer research data showed that the primary factor to get women interested in any particular horror offering was simply: does the trailer look scary? It did not matter whether there were huge movie stars or a connection to some established franchise or what the plot was—none of the traditional marketing factors applied. A scary trailer and the girls will go in droves.

In practical terms, this meant that whereas the creation of an action blockbuster or some fantasy epic relied on massive outlays of cash for big marquee names and CGI trickery, you could put more modest funds into a suspense thriller and stand a good chance of making a windfall.

However Roy Lee ended up representing the ***Ring*** remake, and regardless of whether he even fully realized what it was he was selling, he came to DreamWorks with exactly the right idea at exactly the right moment. It would be the most successful horror remake in Hollywood history, and if that sounds like a minor triumph, we can parse out the two achievements: it was among the most successful horror films of all time and among the most successful remakes of all time. It cost a mere $40 million to make (sounds huge, but these days that counts as fairly low-budget by Hollywood studio standards) and recouped $249 million worldwide—$129 million of that at home. It went on to be the top-selling horror DVD ever at a time when sales of horror discs were constantly increasing.

It would make the careers of nearly everyone involved. Premiere

Magazine named producers Walter F. Parkes and Laurie MacDonald #26 of the Fifty Most Powerful People in Hollywood thanks to their association with ***The Ring***. Ehren Kruger was the up-and-coming screenwriter hired to localize Hiroshi Takahashi's script. Previously he was notable mainly for writing ***Scream 3***, and afterwards would be earning seven figures for his stories about monsters. To direct, Parkes and MacDonald hired Gore Verbinski, the young man who had filmed ***MouseHunt*** for the studio. He would soon be among Hollywood's top tier of directors, riding high on the ***Pirates of the Caribbean*** series.

To woo Verbinski onto the project, Parkes sent him a VHS dub of Nakata's 1998 film. The director was surprised by the austere, anti-Hollywood slant of the idea. "Emotionally the film is inherently on the cold side, yet it deals with the relationship between mother and child," he said.

"It's a simple premise but not exactly a 'studio picture,'" Verbinski also remarked. "I think that is what interested DreamWorks as well. It's both pulp and avant-garde." Verbinski was on.

Parkes, MacDonald and Verbinski were agreed that for a modestly budgeted horror thriller aimed at women, built around an emotionally intense story about parenting, the lead role demanded a solid actress whose skills as a performer were of more importance than her star value. When Jennifer Connelly, Gwyneth Paltrow, and Kate Beckinsale turned the part down, the role of Rachel Keller went to the then-largely unknown Australian actress, Naomi Watts.

Watts had been struggling in the margins of the industry for years and had just enjoyed something of a breakthrough with her role in David Lynch's ***Mulholland Drive***. Thanks to ***The Ring***, she too would win her place as a major Hollywood star. When Premiere Magazine recognized Parkes and MacDonald as top power brokers, the magazine also placed Naomi Watts, Ehren Kruger, and Gore Verbinski on the runner-up list. Such are the rewards of a blockbuster hit.

Joining Watts in the cast were Martin Henderson, a talented veteran of New Zealand's film industry yet unknown to Americans, as Watts' ex-husband Noah, and David Dorfman as her preternaturally mature son Aidan. Dorfman is one of Hollywood's most impressive child actors; his maturity beyond his years has startled the directors for whom he works. When approached to star in ***The Ring***, Dorfman sniffed that "the horror genre is getting a little out of style, if you know what I mean," and added that in his opinion, "the last great horror movie was ***The Shining***."

When Hideo Nakata visited the set of Verbinski's remake, he was pleased with what he saw. Verbinski took Nakata aside and told him how much he admired the original, and especially Nakata's distinctive directorial style. Verbinski explained he was keen to maintain that feel for the American revamp. Even if the seasonings had to be adjusted here or there, the meal was to remain substantially the same.

"I tried to maintain the minimalism of the original," Verbinski later explained. "The film is a study in abstraction. Devoid of clutter. It takes on a sort of inner dream logic."

When Nakata saw the finished film some months later, he was struck by how well Verbinski lived up to his word. "I loved it," Nakata told J. Lopez of the website theringworld.com. "To be honest, I was expecting something more gory, but he kept the similar kind of feeling which ***Ring*** had, and it seemed kind of faithful to the original. So I really liked it a lot."

Ehren Kruger says that the main difference between Nakata's approach and that of Verbinski was pacing. The American version is zippier and more energetic, in part because Verbinski wanted to distract audiences from the less logical aspects of the storyline.

"I found there to be a Dream logic vs. Emotional logic issue. The Western desire for linearity and resolution are so destructive to a film like this," Verbinski said. It was a tightrope Verbinski and Kruger had to walk, maintaining the mystery without alienating Americans accustomed to having their stories meticulously mapped out.

The cursed video itself is a fine case in point. Over the years and the different film versions of the story, there have been a number of cursed videos, each with its own character. In Koji Suzuki's novel, the images are carefully described, each one a specific clue to the events of Sadako's unhappy life and death. The most faithful screen adaptations (1995's TV version and the South Korean ***The Ring Virus***) follow Suzuki's descriptions closely. When Hiroshi Takahashi and Hideo Nakata made their 1998 version, they altered Sadako's backstory and thus were able to change the video's imagery into something that they felt worked better on screen. Kruger and Verbinski once again rewrite the history of the girl in the well (named Samara Morgan in the U.S. version) and yet again change the content of the video—but here, they make the video vastly more abstract and oblique. No longer is the video so directly a roadmap to the dead girl's past. Reviewers raved about the "scary video" in the remake, comparing its surreal imagery to the work of Luis Buñuel.

Verbinski was prepared to take the remake even further into abstraction. Indeed, the emphasis on logic and linearity in ***The Ring*** is as much a consequence of Verbinski's respect for Hideo Nakata as a response to American audience expectations. When ***The Ring*** appeared on DVD, Verbinski added to it a short film called ***Don't Look At This***, a clever approach to presenting "deleted scenes." Verbinski took some fifteen minutes' worth of excised material and compiled it into a mini-film whose experimental editing and fractured chronology hints at the daring direction ***The Ring*** *could* have gone had its makers not felt constrained to stay close to Nakata's original vision.

Meanwhile, Nakata was becoming big business in Hollywood. Roy Lee sold remake rights on Nakata's ***Dark Water*** for $55,000 and convinced Universal Studios to begin developing a remake of Nakata's Hitchcock-meets-***Memento*** noir thriller ***Chaos***, with Robert DeNiro in the lead. Time Magazine named Nakata one of the 100 Most Influential People of 2004. All this without him actually making a film in Hollywood.

At first, Nakata was hobbled by low expectations. His star was certainly rising in Hollywood, but he did not have anyone close to him who knew how to capitalize on that. Roy Lee recognized Nakata's growing star power, but his agenda and Nakata's were not necessarily aligned.

In his extraordinary essay "Remake Man" for The New Yorker, journalist Tad Friend recounts a particularly telling incident. The year was 2003, and Taka Ichise had come to the U.S. seeking backing for his ***J-Horror Theater*** package: six horror films budgeted at $1 million apiece, to be made in Japan by the cream of the crop of the current generation of Japanese horrormeisters (see also Chapter 7).

The very next day, Lee turned around and pitched the idea to a select group of movers and shakers, careful to single out the one name certain to light up the room: "We can get Hideo Nakata to do a film in Japan, with American actors, for one million dollars."

That's all he needed to say. "That's a no-brainer," said one exec. "Hideo Nakata? One million? Done. Done," said another, before adding, "But why would the director of ***Ring*** and ***Dark Water*** make a movie for us for a total of one million dollars?" The first exec had the ready answer, "They haven't figured it out yet. He's a Japanese director and they haven't figured it out yet."[1]

Lee then moved on to the task at hand. The real reason he'd brought this group together was to sell them Takashi Shimizu's ***Ju-On: The Grudge***.

Ichise had come to town multitasking. He hoped to secure financing for ***J-Horror Theater***, but his main objective was to sell remake rights on ***Ju-On***. He'd sent out some screeners of Shimizu's chronologically jumbled haunted house thriller (see Chapter 6) but without much success. It would take Roy Lee's special genius to seal the deal, with just two hours' work.

Lee, you see, knew something Ichise didn't. The blockbuster sensation ***Spider-Man*** made its director Sam Raimi into an A-lister but did nothing to change his roots as a maker of low-budget grindhouse horror. You can take the boy out of B-horror but you can't take B-horror out of the boy. Raimi reconciled the two parts of his professional identity by joining with Robert Tapert in May 2002 to form Ghost House Pictures, a company dedicated to making and promoting small-scale horror films. Ghost House had a special interest in seeking out promising talent from overseas. And Lee was friendly with Nathan Kahane, one of the hungry young wolves at Ghost House charged with realizing Mr. Raimi's ambitions.

The screening was, ahem, a "hit." Raimi came out of it raving that he'd just seen one of the twenty best horror movies, ever. "Now I'm being schooled in horror!" he marveled. Lee made the sale.

In keeping with the "small scale" edict, Raimi only paid $250,000 for the rights, a quarter of what Taka Ichise got for rights to ***Ring***. Raimi then made a startling but brilliant decision: since the strength of ***Ju-On*** came from its director more than a clever screenplay, he would keep Takashi Shimizu on as director of the remake and let him work as before, at home in Japan, with his Japanese cast and crew—augmented by some Americans in key roles in front of and behind the cameras. Shimizu would bring the project in for just $10 million—again, a quarter of what ***The Ring*** cost.

Sarah Michelle Gellar may have been a TV star at the head of ***Buffy the Vampire Slayer***, but she had never been asked to topline anything save for those ***Scooby-Doo*** movies. After ***The Grudge***, her manager would boast that she had finally become a true movie star—Gellar got herself a new manager less inclined to speak such inconvenient truths in public.

2004 proved to be a goofy year at the movies. A number of expected blockbusters sank, while dark horses like ***The Grudge*** became huge hits. Thanks to its small budget, ***The Grudge*** was one of the few genuinely profitable movies of the year and helped propel Sony Pictures to a $1.3 billion domestic box office tally. ***The Grudge*** made $110 million worldwide, $39 million of it at home, and was the twenty-first top grossing film of 2004.

If Shimizu's remake helped solidify the box office clout of J-Horror, it helped prove a different point in Japan. Taka Ichise and Takashi Shimizu went from competing against Hollywood to working with Hollywood, without actually changing what they were doing.

Or, not changing it much.

Roy Lee's first reaction to seeing the original ***Ju-On*** was skepticism. It lacked the clearly delineated rules that drove ***The Ring***. "We need films with rules. Rules and hooks," Friend quotes Lee in The New Yorker as telling Ichise. Taka was unmoved. "Japanese horror movies are not logical," Ichise answered. "Logical horror movies fail."

But Sam Raimi and his producers had the same reaction as Lee. As the lights came up on the screening of Shimizu's Japanese ***Ju-On***, they agreed: they'd liked it, they'd been well spooked, but they didn't actually understand any of it. Lee, worried that their confusion would be a stumbling block for the deal, tried to explain that since ***Ju-On*** was actually the *third* film in a series, Shimizu had not felt much obliged to (re)explain all the details of the premise. Some of the film's stranger moments make more sense, he said, if you've seen the previous two videos.

Raimi was not sure it made good business sense for an American movie to intentionally baffle its audience. The deal was contingent on getting Shimizu and his English screenwriter Stephen Susco to retrofit that material from the earlier videos back into the script to help it make more sense.

These were the watchwords of Americanized J-Horror: the most attractive remake opportunities were those with high-concept gimmicks, and in all cases the ambiguity and illogic that Ichise rightly identifies as endemic to the form would be flattened out in the American versions.

Instead of violating the spirit of ***Ju-On***, as might have been expected, however, Stephen Susco's adaptation combines elements of the preceding four (!) films into one best-of compilation. Actress Takako Fuji, one of the series' two lead ghosts and a veteran of the cycle since its earliest manifestations, noted that the American film "took the best of all the parts." And then, onto that highlights reel, Susco grafted an entirely new subtext—culture shock. It was perhaps an unavoidable consequence of shoving a gaggle of American expatriates into a Japanese movie, but culture shock actually fit nicely into Shimizu's scheme. He had already been using his adroit sense of horror to render visions of Tokyo foreign and alienating in the earlier films; here, he allows audiences to see Japan through the eyes of terrified, homesick blondes.

No one could accuse the American ***Grudge*** of being a traditional story, the dots all connected and laid plain. The story is still as disorderly as ever, and this time around the chapter indexing has been dispensed with. The makers trust their audience to keep up and figure out on their own that the events are not told in sequence.

Screening the original ***Ju-On***, Raimi noticed that although it was a Japanese film it was not especially culturally specific. It just *happened* to be Japanese, but could be anywhere. It was this aspect that attracted him to the remake and convinced him that he should retain the original director for the update. Raimi asked Shimizu to sign on for the remake, to which Shimizu replied, "What the hell are you talking about?"

For the first time in his life, Takashi Shimizu would have to leave Japan—to make ***The Grudge*** he would be obliged to go get a passport.

Shimizu braced himself for the prima donna attitudes he expected from his American stars. Those stars, in turn, were perplexed by the traditions of Japanese filmmaking and struggled with learning their Japanese lines, while the Japanese cast were discomfited to perform in English. The American producers demanded splashy CGI effects, while Shimizu stood firm in his belief that "special effects actually reduce the horror." While they respected his achievements with the previous films, the American members of the production team were startled to see Shimizu's seemingly loosey-goosey approach: filming scenes that were not written, shooting entire sequences in the time normally reserved for warming up, and generally showing little respect for the corporate style of American film production. Sam Raimi may have thought this a "low-budget" endeavor, but it was still millions of dollars of somebody's money at stake. For people like Takako Fuji, who had been with Shimizu since the early days of the more DIY ***Ju-On*** videos, the whole thing seemed bizarre: "Look at where we've come with this."

It was, in short, an experiment with no right to succeed.

Yet succeed it did. Shimizu found his American stars to be warm, generous, and hard-working, and they in turn found him to be a kooky cut-up who put them at ease. The American producers found Shimizu to be remarkably efficient and constantly imaginative, whose instincts, even when controversial, always proved right, while Shimizu found the producers to be smart operators with the project's best interests at heart, whose suggestions frequently improved the product. True, Shimizu could not understand why an American student in a funk would wear jeans, since they are so dressy (!), and the cast could rarely remember to remove their shoes and were put off by meals with too many eyeballs. Yet, what culture shock they found on the set working together tended to enhance their ability to transfer it onto the screen.

There were other side-benefits to the experience, too. Takashi Shimizu had long been a fan of Raimi's ***Evil Dead*** movies and had even incorporated homages to them in past films. When Raimi's brother Ted was cast in a small role, Shimizu was enough of a fan to note that Ted Raimi had, in heavy makeup, once played a zombie in ***Evil Dead 2***. Meanwhile, Sam Raimi was delighted to discover the soundstage they would be using was located at Toho Studios, home of Godzilla. When

Sarah Michelle Gellar and Takashi Shimizu

Ryo Ishibashi arrived on the set to play the detective, the Americans all hailed the star of Takashi Miike's ***Audition***. It was a veritable love-fest.

In the end, ***The Grudge*** was more than the sum of its parts. Its various constituents all worked hard, and worked together, to craft one of the finest works of J-Horror—and a true American/Japanese hybrid at that. Shimizu was thus in a position to take all of those J-Horror symbols and place them, intact and untranslated, squarely into American pop culture: long-haired ghosts, murky bathtubs, ghostly kids, defaced photos, spooky cell phone calls, wraiths that emerge from videotapes, viral curses built around family tragedies and murdered children. ***The Grudge*** confidently mixes Japanese in with the English, and not always with subtitles. The opening title sequence first renders the title in Japanese, and only then appends the English translation. This was, for all intents and purposes, the realization of the idea that Roy Lee pitched on Ichise's behalf: an American-financed Japanese horror film with American stars, made in Japan.

Shimizu had found the perfect marriage between Hollywood and Japan. He could stay busy, even preternaturally so: ***The Grudge***, ***Ju-On: The Grudge 3***, ***The Grudge 2***, ***J-Horror Theater Volume 3: Reincarnation***, and ***Marebito*** sandwiched in between. Shimizu is the kind of director who can make an entire feature in the time it takes most people to commute to work, and then make another feature in the time it takes you to watch the first one.

Meanwhile, Hideo Nakata suffered the opposite fate, still shuffling through Hollywood looking for a movie. DreamWorks had been developing the ***Ring*** sequel for a while; just weeks into the first film's run, its popularity had been enough to prompt sequel talks. Ehren Kruger was happy to return, and Naomi Watts was contractually obligated to return whether or not she was happy, but Gore Verbinski turned them down. Parkes and MacDonald all but begged him, but Verbinski averred that he didn't actually like horror all that much. Verbinski pointed out how many remakes of Hideo Nakata's films were in the pipelines at various houses and expressed hope that Nakata could maybe take one of those gigs himself.

Nakata was already otherwise occupied, though. He landed at MGM developing ***True Believer***, but then Dimension came along and swallowed that, only to drop it into turnaround and leave Nakata out of a job. Meanwhile, having been turned down by both Gore Verbinski and ***Donnie Darko***-auteur Richard Kelley, DreamWorks turned to a young unknown named Noam Murro, a neophyte promoted from the ranks of commercials. Murro didn't pan out—the proverbial "creative differences" reared their head—and suddenly DreamWorks found itself with a headless ***Ring*** sequel on their hands at the same moment that Hideo Nakata was looking for something to do.

Have your people call my people...

Somewhere in someone's head the lurking thought: Nakata has already made a ***Ring 2*** and it was no great shakes. Of course, that cannot be blamed on Nakata, nor on Hiroshi Takahashi, nor Taka Ichise. It is the inherent challenge of concocting a sequel to ***Ring*** (see Chapter 2). Koji Suzuki did it, with *Spiral*, but DreamWorks had only bought remake rights to Hideo Nakata's film version, nothing more, and they had paid handsomely for it. There was no question of paying again just to extend those rights deeper into the source texts. Making ***The Ring Two*** as an adaptation of *Spiral* might have been a creatively sound notion but it was practically impossible. Instead, Ehren Kruger and Hideo Nakata would be asked to write something new, using only the previous ***The Ring*** as its basis.

"We chose not to duplicate any of that," said Walter Parkes of the sundry Japanese sequels. "None of those movies worked as well as the first film did. And because we had put a lot of additional emphasis on Rachel and her son, we thought it would be most interesting to explore that further. When you have an actress as good as Naomi Watts associated with a franchise, you want to put her right at the heart of things."

Nevertheless, ***The Ring Two*** would bear more than a passing resemblance to ***Ring 2***. The cursed video is still circulating among teenagers, its evil spreading. Samara (or Sadako) wants to live again by possessing the body of little Aidan (or Yoichi). Rachel (or Asakawa) is doing everything she can to protect her son, even though her efforts are misidentified as acts of child abuse. Newcomer Max (or Mai) wants to help, but must go through the same process of discovery all over again. Meanwhile Rachel (Asakawa) explores the secrets of Samara's (Sadako's) true parents. Ultimately, the heroine enters a bathtub (or a pool) by way of penetrating Samara's (Sadako's) world for a final confrontation with the drowned girl in the well.

"There are some thematic similarities," avers Ehren Kruger. "Just by the material's very nature, it's going to deal with a videotape and it's going to deal with this vengeful little girl. It's going to deal with this mother and her son, but story-wise it's an entirely different story than the Japanese sequel."

"These films are completely different," adds Nakata, "so it's safe to say there's no influence from ***Ring*** or ***Ring 2***."

Maybe, but there is a line of influence extending from Nakata's ***Dark Water***: both pictures involve a climactic act of parental self-sacrifice from a women coerced into being a mommy to a lonely ghost.

ATTACK OF THE DEER

"I know it's silly, because I like the woods and camping, but deer make me nervous, especially when they're just looking at you. They're scary." So says Hideo Nakata. Unfortunately, audiences did not agree with him, or, at least, they did not generally find his herd of CGI deer in ***The Ring Two*** to be anything other than laughable.

It was a painful moment, since Nakata had tried to eschew the familiar scares of his past works and develop new images. Don't expect deer to join the dependable tropes of the genre alongside murky bathtubs or ringing cell phones.

Oddly, the crew found the deer to be scarier than the audience did. The production was plagued by a number of incidents paralleling the imagery of the film. The set was repeatedly flooded, and a member of the crew was actually attacked by a deer. Reporters noted that Hideo Nakata had arranged a Shinto ceremony to purify the production and assumed he was reacting to the specifics of these occurrences. In fact, it is not uncommon in Japan for the makers of horror movies to feel their sets are haunted; purification rites are a regular first-day tradition on such films. Nakata is by no means alone among the filmmakers in this book to suggest genuine ghosts attended the making of their films.

The emphasis on Naomi Watts' Rachel and her troubled relationship with David Dorfman's Aidan gives ***The Ring Two*** emotional depth, but at a cost. Much of the mystery has dissipated—the viewers have Samara's number by now. Watts has to play her role with greater anguish and grief than before. Coupled with Nakata's more subtle approach, and it all makes for some heavy going.

Parkes and MacDonald had seen fit to pour 50 percent more money into ***The Ring Two***'s coffers—a budget of $60 million, compared to $40 million for the first film. It was a daring act of defiance of sequelitis. Most horror sequels report a drop in attendance from their parents, but the makers of ***The Ring Two*** expected to break the pattern.

They were disappointed.

The Ring Two opened in the United States to sluggish box office returns, falling behind ***The Grudge***. Overseas, it opened on the slowest weekend to date of the year. It was top of the pack, of a fairly anemic pack. In most foreign markets, ***The Ring Two*** had better per weekend ticket sales than the first film, but it did not have the same "legs," and so brought in less money overall. In the end, ***The Ring Two*** earned just $76 million at home, $143 million total worldwide.

This was still profitable. It had performed below industry expectations, but at a time when most everything was underperforming as well. ***The Ring Two*** may not have been the runaway hit its predecessor was, but still managed to make a decent showing under the circumstances. Talks were soon afoot for ***The Ring Three***, with Nakata (but not the increasingly expensive Naomi Watts) invited back.

To an extent, the lackluster showing of ***The Ring Two*** can be blamed on ***The Grudge***. Takashi Shimizu dallied in all the same images and themes, but did so within the context of a novel premise and a renewed sense of mystery. Audiences accepted ***The Grudge*** as an ersatz ***Ring*** sequel, which left the authentic Nakata sequel with a palpable been-there-done-that air.

Between them, Shimizu and Nakata had managed to make Japanese style J-Horrors within the Hollywood system, combing American movie stars and long-haired ghosts for sale to American and Japanese audiences alike. However, whereas J-Horror in Asia is a vibrant and expansive genre with dozens of movies competing for the same audience using the same bag of tricks, Americans were introduced to these images only through ***The Ring***. Without the deeper cultural context and folkloric basis for these images, their use in American films would be limited by American audiences' willingness to watch what they would perceive as copycats.

It was at this point that another foreign filmmaker tried to break into Hollywood, choosing J-Horror as the safest, most commercial venue in which to make his studio debut. He was neither American nor Japanese, and took for granted that murky bathtubs, viral curses, and dark-haired ghosts were authentic parts of American pop culture, ripe for reinterpretation and revision from a foreigner's perspective.

Walter Salles is a young Brazilian hotshot, a multilingual son of a diplomat whose ***The Motorcycle Diaries*** won awards at Cannes, BAFTA, the Independent Spirit Awards, and the Academy Awards.

SAMARA NEVER DIES

The Ring Two had no premiere. The official story was that Naomi Watts was "unable to attend." Whatever the reason, the lack of the usual gala celebrations sent a clear signal to the press that the studio was losing faith in the sequel's prospects.

This is not to say that the producers gave up on promotion. In one publicity stunt, thousands of video copies of the "cursed video" were scattered in various public places for people to find, and watch, with the film's web site helpfully advertised after Samara's abstract visions. Along with the authorized movie web site, DreamWorks put up a few other sites as well: one purported to collect emails and video clips posted by people who'd seen the video and made copies before dying; another site alleged to be the real estate agent for the house where Samara grew up.

Britain's The Guardian named him the twenty-third best director in the world. Hungry for new talent, Hollywood came calling. Salles initially demurred, fearful that working in Hollywood was akin to "selling out." Further complicating matters was Hollywood's cultural myopia. They figured the way to woo Salles was to offer him opportunities to remake South American films for American audiences.

To Salles this was anathema. He felt that translating South American culture into American idioms was wrong, untruthful to both cultures. And then they offered him ***Dark Water***. This time, staying true to Japanese or North American culture did not seem to weigh on his mind.

Roy Lee had sold remake rights on Hideo Nakata's 2002 hit within months of its opening in Japan. Up until this point, all of Lee's J-Horror remakes had been handled by people who saw themselves as careful stewards charged with translating these Asian thrillers into English with as little alteration as necessary—to the extent of including the original Japanese creators when possible. Walter Salles' ***Dark Water*** would break tradition and be the first time the Japanese roots of the material would be blithely ignored.

This was not necessarily a problem. Indeed, the ***Dark Water*** project seemed extraordinarily promising. The original had been hailed as one of the very best modern Asian horror had on offer. Salles was as hot a young director as any on the planet, and he was attracted to the story's themes of "abandonment and urban solitude." For the lead role, he cast Jennifer Connelly, who had been the original top-pick to star in ***The Ring***. Connelly is an Oscar-winning actress who has worked with Sergio Leone, Dario Argento, Jim Henson, Darren Aronofsky, Ron Howard, and Ang Lee. She came to the set already a fan of Nakata's original, cautious to do it justice.

"We were doing our version of it out of respect rather than disrespect," she said. "I think if we were trying to mimic it, or weren't respectful of it or really changed the tone of it that would be one thing. But while it is different in some ways, where it is similar to the original ***Dark Water*** is that balance it strikes between having emotional depth and being a thought-provoking film, while also hopefully quite scary too."

Backing her up would be arguably the finest ensemble of character actors in a contemporary horror film: Tim Roth, John C. Reilly, Pete Postlethwaite...a cast normally gathered in the service of Shakespeare, not Japanese ghosts.

What could go wrong?

The Grudge succeeded by bringing together a disparate collection of elements in service of a common goal, creating a true team effort. ***Dark Water*** collects an extraordinary roster of talents and misuses them. Salles clearly has no feel for this kind of material, distrusts the idea of making big studio pulp thrillers, and so tries too hard to make a Serious Drama.

Taka Ichise's conviction that J-Horror is fundamentally illogical bears repeating here. Ichise co-wrote the original ***Dark Water*** screenplay (see Chapter 2). The Japanese film admits no single definitive answer to what is happening; instead, it keeps open three competing and equally compelling possibilities. We see a woman struggling with a messy divorce, her child bearing too much of the burden and seemingly haunted by the ghost of a dead child. It could be she is imagining her poltergeist as she cracks under the crushing psychological pressure of her circumstances. It is also possible she is the victim of a hoax perpetuated by her cruel ex-hubby in order to discredit her in court. Or, maybe she really does live in a building with a haunted plumbing system.

The ambiguity of the premise is precisely what holds it all together. From the uncertainty comes the fear.

It is also the case that from the uncertainty comes the drama. Nakata gets to have his cake and eat it, too. The film is scary because we are not sure what is true, and sympathize with the heroine's paralyzed non-reaction; the film is haunting because the supernatural shenanigans provide a framework for dramatizing an all-too-real situation. Nakata manages to wring maximum suspense out of the set-up while using the more conventional ghost story histrionics as a metaphor for the painful human relationships at the heart of the film.

Salles squanders both. His version includes the script material positing real-world explanations, but the cinematic presentation does not keep those ideas alive as plausible alternatives. In the American version, the ghost is decidedly real and is never in any serious doubt. This robs the movie of its suspense, and cheapens the metaphor. Walter Salles provides a suitably Big Hollywood Climax, but sheer water pressure alone does not equal drama, and the sucker-punch impact of Nakata's carefully restrained original drowns in Salles' soggy delivery.

Dark Water is not a bad movie, merely one that is serious and austere without being scary. The result is much like certain Korean horrors such as ***Sorum*** or ***The Uninvited*** (see Chapter 8)—sincere dramas that just happen to have ghosts in them. In the current pop culture climate, this is a commercial mistake. The ladies who want their scares aren't going to find them here.

Disney, the studio behind the debacle, finished out the year 2005 so badly off they had to close some divisions, and decreed they were never going to make an R-rated film again. For all its merits, ***Dark Water*** was a bomb, and it suggested the bloom was off the J-Horror rose. Roy Lee found Hollywood a colder place.

Which brings us neatly to the story of Roy Lee and Dimension Films. The legendary Bob and Harvey Weinstein spun Dimension Films off from Miramax as a small studio specializing in teen-oriented pulp. Horror has always been big with Dimension, and Roy Lee signed them up as one of Vertigo Entertainment's first clients. The "first look" deal had Dimension paying Lee's overhead and salary in return for first crack at whatever he was selling.

The Weinsteins were no fools. They had been pursuing the Asian horror remake market on their own with little success and were happy to have Lee's services. At first. The brothers soon realized Lee was selling an admixture of fanboy enthusiasm, a smattering of Asian film industry contacts, and snake oil. If they could connect directly with those contacts, what did they need him for?

Lee became furious, incensed that Vertigo was tied into a contract with a company that seemed to have no intention of actually making his movies and was end-running around him to make those same movies without him. For example, there was that ***Pulse*** remake that Wes Craven still had in his back pocket…

Craven's interest in ***Pulse*** had cooled, and the Weinsteins had pulled him off of it to work on ***Cursed*** (not the J-Horror spoof discussed in Chapter 7, but the werewolf movie with the same name). Meanwhile, the Weinsteins were similarly moving Jim Sonzero around from unproduced development deal to unproduced development deal, looking for the right fit. Sonzero was a former commercial director with a jones for horror, but the first handful of titles fizzled. So, Bob Weinstein suggested the long-dusty ***Pulse***. "They asked me if I was interested and I said yes, so I watched the original," explains Sonzero. "I thought the pace of it was…off for American audiences. It's a little slow. I mean, I loved it and I was patient, but I thought it could be goosed and made a little more energetic."

Pacing would prove the bane of Sonzero's tenure on ***Pulse***. To take back all those years of inactivity, both for the remake and for its director, everything suddenly had to happen yesterday. Rushed into production by Bob Weinstein to meet a predetermined release schedule, Sonzero did not yet have a final script. He did however have a photogenic cast of teenage heartthrobs: Kristen Bell (star of TV's ***Veronica Mars***), Ian Somerhalder (the first of ***Lost***'s castaways to be killed), and pop singer Christina Milian. Rolling cameras without a net, Sonzero decided to hedge his bets and film additional unscripted material.

"My strategy was to shoot what was on the page as well as several additions to the storyline we could follow through on later," said Sonzero. "When you approach a film like this, a director has to have enough foresight to create as many options for himself as possible, so I created several things that weren't in the script that we could just choose to expand on regarding the characters and plot."

As the original release date approached, test screenings of ***Pulse*** indicated problems. Bob Weinstein decided to send Sonzero back in to follow up on some of those flailing plot threads and revamp the movie. The release date was shoved back, to March 2006, to provide time for the rejiggering.

Trailers for ***Pulse*** started to appear in theaters, and Magnolia Pictures trotted out the original to capitalize on the publicity, only to have Dimension once again yank the film back for retooling and once again delay its release. The second test screening went better than the first, but not well enough; Sonzero was sent back to the field one more time to shoot yet more alterations. By this point, Sonzero was working with cast members who had not even been a part of the original shoot. Special effects technicians were told that, having faithfully duplicated some key moments from Kiyoshi Kurosawa's original, their work was going to be discarded since the film no longer would include those scenes.

Test screenings and MPAA censors had kept enough extra chefs in the kitchen to all but guarantee a ruined soup, but Sonzero took a deep breath and decided to be zen about the whole thing. As ***Pulse*** stumbled towards its August 11, 2006 release, Sonzero announced he would go back to making commercials, where life was a little simpler. Dimension dumped the movie into theaters with muted fanfare and no press screenings, as if embarrassed by it. Which they would have a right to be: it is a tawdry piece of work, loud and aggressive where the original was anguished and tentative. The ambiguity and abstraction that gave the original its power has been replaced by dunderheaded explanations and explicit missions for the characters. Fans of the American remakes of ***Ring*** or ***Grudge*** could go back to their respective Japanese originals and enjoy them on the same terms, but anyone who happened to actually like the Dimension ***Pulse*** (hard to credit it to Sonzero, it's clearly a corporate product) would find the original a jarring, disorienting experience.

Three times Bob Weinstein had slammed on the brakes on the ***Pulse*** remake, already so long in coming. At the root of his concern was not the indifferent test screenings, nor the troubling box office of ***Dark Water***. He worried, simply, that ***Pulse*** was a little too much like ***The Ring***. Considering that the original ***Pulse*** was commissioned by producers who explicitly tasked Kurosawa with hewing closer to the ***Ring*** paradigm, this is telling.

The larger cultural resonance of J-Horror's ingredients in Asia allows filmmakers there to continue to experiment with the form without being branded (there) as mimics. There are market pressures on filmmakers to stay close to the style of ***Ring***, the biggest commercial hit in the genre, but this is common sense. In America, the symbolism of long-haired ghosts and gimmicky viral curses runs no deeper than ***The Ring***'s box office success, and so additional American J-Horrors cannot escape being compared back to that film as the all-important point of reference.

It is impossible at this stage to fully gauge the extent of the J-Horror remake boom: it's hard to tell if the explosion is on the wane or not when you're still in the middle of all the smoke and noise. A great number of remakes remain on the boards for manufacture and release in the near future. Some are promising (Hideo Nakata's ***The Eye***, Takashi Shimizu's ***The Grudge 2***), some less so (an American ***Bunshisaba***? a Hollywoodized ***One Missed Call***?), some may already have been abandoned (***Don't Look Up*** seems to have stalled). Only time will tell what may come of these.

Either way, we have been witness to a unique moment in global pop culture. Asian cinema has been full of fads that never penetrated

THE GRUDGE 2

In the dreary winter months of 2006, Takashi Shimizu returned to the ***Grudge*** world for the second film in the American cycle, the sixth overall. Sarah Michelle Gellar returned, briefly, as a blonde-haired ghost, while Amber Tamblyn (a minor player in Gore Verbinski's ***The Ring***) took center stage as Gellar's onscreen sister. Takako Fuji returned as Kayako, and Japanese superstar Ryo Ishibashi came back as well. Virtually the entire offscreen team reunited on Toho's lot for round two.

Takashi Shimizu, ever the goof, smiled broadly as he pondered his place at the head of a franchise so healthy, and so singularly *his*: "I'd like to do other movies, as well. I tried to make other films, but the timing is a little bit strange. I asked to do the next *Grudge* so I've been missing the opportunity to do others. But I really like to make other films, as well."

Although Shimizu's career has been built on sequels, remakes, remakes of sequels and sequels of remakes, he is well aware of the dangers. "We shouldn't continue to do remakes because otherwise we're not going to create something new. When we run out of ideas, then Hollywood is at risk. Doing a remake is a very sensitive decision business-wise, but I don't think it is the only way to make films. I also have to think about new ideas and new movies, and that's what Hollywood should do."

the American consciousness: Tora-san, anyone? Americans do not line up to listen to Japanese music, nor is Japanese food wildly popular (save for sushi). But at least for a moment at the turn of the millennium, these two cultures from opposite sides of the planet came into alignment on one thing: a common set of nightmares.

1. In the end, Lions Gate bought the entire six film package for $6 million, but whichever studio wrote the check, the fact remains that although I discussed ***J-Horror Theater*** in Chapter 7 as Japanese movies, they are being financed by American companies for distribution to American audiences. The boundaries between Hollywood and abroad blur.

Sources:

"Don't Watch This," short film directed by Gore Verbinski and written by Ehren Kruger, "The Ring" Special Edition DVD edition, DreamWorks, 2003.

"Hollywood's 50 Most Powerful," Premiere Magazine, June 2005.

"Jennifer Connelly: The Dark Water Interview," www.futuremovies.co.uk, 2005.

"Rings," short film directed by Jonathan Liebesman and written by Ehren Kruger, "The Ring" Special Edition DVD edition, DreamWorks, 2005.

"Roy Lee: King of the Asian Box Office Smash Remake," Goldsea, 2006.

"The Grudge 2 Begins Filming in Tokyo," www.GhostHousePictures.com, February 21, 2006.

Booth, William, "Hollywood Caters to a Ravenous Global Appetite," The Washington Post, May 27, 2006.

Chute, David, "The Fellowship of the Ring," Premiere Magazine, March 2005.

Douglas, Edward, "Kiyoshi Kurosawa on Pulse," www.comingsoon.net, October 21, 2005.

DuFoe, Terry and Tiffany, "Kadee Strickland On Killer Snakes and Nasty Grudges," Videoscope, Winter 2005.

Epstein, Daniel Robert, "Interview with Walter Salles," www.suicidegirls.com, September 29, 2004.

Fischer, Paul, "Takashi Shimizu Interview," www.darkhorizons.net, September 24, 2004.

Friend, Tad, "Remake Man," The New Yorker, June 2, 2003.

Heianna, Sumiyo, "Interview with Roy Lee, matchmaker of the macabre," Kateigaho International Edition, Winter 2005.

Lopez, J. "Gore Verbinski Interview," www.theringworld.com, 2002.

Lopez, J., "Interview with Nakata Hideo," www.theringworld.com, 2005.

Mes, Tom, "Kiyoshi Kurosawa Interview," www.midnighteye.com, August 20, 2003.

Murray, Rebecca, "Takashi Shimizu Talks About The Grudge 2," www.movies.about.com

Nguyen, J.D., "Interview with Roy Lee," KFC Cinema.com, July 8, 2002.

Otto, Jeff, "IGN Interviews Ehren Kruger," www.filmforce.ign.com, February 2, 2005.

Rich, Joshua, "10 Big Surprises," Entertainment Weekly, January 28, 2005.

Rotten, Ryan, "Director talks Pulse reshoots etc." Fangoria Online Edition, July 13, 2006.

Shapiro, James Emanuel, "Emerging Cinema Master—Kiyoshi Kurosawa," www.dvdtalk.com, 2005.

Snider, Mark, "Girls Just Wanna Scream," USA Today, February 10, 2005.

www.ring-themovie.com

CHAPTER 11

THE J-HORROR ROUNDUP

Now that you have read this book, you have become a J-Horror expert. You know the difference between ***Spiral*** (Rasen) and ***The Spiral*** (Uzumaki), between ***Ring 2*** and ***The Ring Two***, between ***Doppleganger*** and ***Ikisudame*** (Doppleganger), between ***Ju-On***, ***Ju-On: The Grudge***, and ***The Grudge***—not to mention between ***Ju-On 2***, ***Ju-On 2: The Grudge***, and ***The Grudge 2***. You know the identity of the phantom of the toilet, you know why Tomie will not die, you know the secret of the Green Monkey. You can distinguish the different cinematic styles of Norio Tsuruta and Higuchinsky, of Oxide Pang and Byung-ki Ahn, of Hideo Nakata and Kiyoshi Kurosawa.

And after reading about (or having watched) all these movies, you have probably come to the conclusion that all buildings in Japan are haunted schools, haunted hospitals, or haunted houses. You would never watch an unmarked videotape or answer a cell phone call from yourself in the future. You would not participate in séances, ESP experiments, or attend high school in South Korea. You would not visit a web site that promised personal connections with the dead, nor would you collect objects with spiral patterns. You would not water killer trees, raise killer jellyfish, or feed human blood to naked women you find under the subway. And if you see a girl in a white dress with loooong black hair… Run.

But what does it all mean?

After watching the cursed video and researching its history, Asakawa and Ryuji were finally in a position to ask the Big Question: *Why?* This is now our task. We've seen the videos, we've researched their history, now it is time to ask *why*.

The first step is to accept this cohort of highly commercial horror movies as a legitimate art movement.

The Japanese films (and to an extent their American remakes as well) were created by a network of friends and colleagues who came from similar backgrounds with similar influences. Together they took familiar imagery and put it in the service of dramatizing modern fears and concerns, which turned out to be more universal than they had expected. This, at a time when global competition was forcing the film industries of the world closer together. Because these influences, issues, and pressures were universal, the same kind of movie evolved more or less independently in places like South Korea and Hong Kong as well—parallel movements to the one begun in Japan.

People who write about film are constitutionally inclined to resist the most baldly commercial expressions of cinema: remakes, sequels, franchises, genres. They generally prefer to believe in a strict dichotomy: original works of film worthy of serious attention on the one hand, and lesser compromises made only for profit on the other. This is of course balderdash, but it is popular balderdash.

On top of that, horror filmmaking has always struggled for respect. Horror evokes the baser emotion and does so by trading traditional narrative drama for impossible visions and nightmare scenarios.

Straightforward dramatic fiction is the cinematic equivalent of representative art: it is what it appears to depict. A portrait, let's say, of a seventeenth century duchess cannot easily carry any additional meaning beyond the subject at hand—hey, here's a picture of a duchess. Modern art's abstraction defies easy interpretation, however. A surrealist's painting of a headless nude coated in ants or a Dadaist collage of newspaper clippings do not represent anything specifically real and therefore open themselves to a wider array of possible meanings. This is the power of genre film. By exploiting extremist imagery and fantastical situations, such movies are capable of carrying deeper meanings and broader cultural resonance than mere drama can.

J-Horror is a tapestry of images and ideas capable of serving double duty—to tell a ripping yarn and deliver pure entertainment to the masses, yet also to suggest a deeper dimension of fears too abstract or intense to dramatize directly.

When a film like ***Ring*** enjoys massive commercial success, we should not view that as a sign that it has "sold out," but rather that its content had special meaning to large numbers of people around the world. Other filmmakers rush to repeat its success out of a purely financial motive, yes, but their ability to do so is contingent on their ability to connect with the same audience needs and desires. A gold rush can only happen if there is actually gold there to be had.

The gold rush analogy is apt. The traditional way of thinking about movies wants to see a single creator, an origin point, and the copycats that follow in its wake. But we have had little success identifying a true father of J-Horror. Instead we find many fathers, at different times and places, each of whom played a seminal and decisive role in developing the genre. It is as if J-Horror was always already there, waiting to be discovered, and a select group of pioneers happened upon it first. The host of filmmakers behind the movies discussed in this book represent different claims—some bigger than others, some older than others, some a matter of dispute and contention—but there is no one single true claim looming above all others. And there appears to be territory yet undiscovered, nooks and crannies of the genre yet to be claimed.

In olden times, folklore was an oral tradition. Stories passed down over generations evolved in the mouths of countless different storytellers, adapting to the needs of each new audience. Those stories that held the most relevance and power changed the least over time and endured the longest—Darwinism as applied to fiction.

Motion picture franchises and genres serve a similar function in modern society. Characters and situations with special cultural importance endure retelling and more retelling, through sequels and remakes and all those allegedly impure commercial forms of media. Certain characters prove to be especially "sticky" in the cultural sense, and thrive as genres unto themselves. Batman and Superman have lasted since the 1930s, Sherlock Holmes first appeared in 1887, Frankenstein was born in 1818, while Romeo and Juliet trace their roots back to 1476! Their endurance is proof of their relevance.

Just as I've looked back into folkloric history to find the roots of the long-haired ghost, I can foresee a future, maybe hundreds of years from now, when researchers will ponder the resurgence of the image and look back to these movies—our modern folklore, the myths of the twenty-first century—to understand their enduring appeal.

It is too soon to lay such honors on J-Horror, but we can begin to track their cultural power. Since Koji Suzuki first wrote *Ring*, there have been five books, a few manga adaptations, a TV movie and two television miniseries, seven theatrical movies (in three countries) and yet more in the works. These are just the official authorized permutations, too. Since Junji Ito first drew ***Tomie*** there have been several original manga, a TV movie, and six theatrical features. Takashi Shimizu made two short films for a TV anthology, which has spun off ***Ju-Ons*** in two countries in the form of two videos and at least five theatrical features.

When horror movies started chasing the most overt scares, they traded away their role as modern myths. J-Horror reclaimed that status by connecting ancient images of terror with contemporary and very real fears.

We have seen how the roots of these franchises extend into dusty traditions deep into the past. Yet, as a coherent whole, J-Horror does not appear before 1990. It is a phenomenon that arose from a certain special coincidence of factors.

The first of these conditions is technological progress. Old-school horror is a strictly supernatural affair, but there is a reason why so much J-Horror revolves around haunted technology. Arthur C. Clarke said that "any technology sufficiently advanced would be indistinguishable from magic"—this is the world in which we live. Few people can profess to genuinely understand how computers work, but a great many people use them nonetheless. Anyone with a cell phone or a VCR can now claim everyday powers once reserved for shamans. The more we accept magic into our daily lives, the closer the spirit world comes to us, whether or not we share Japan's Shinto beliefs.

Secondly, both Asia and the Western world are facing pitched battles over the proper social structures to support families. There can be no "winner" of the mommy wars, but there are losers. Regardless of what position you may take on who should bear the responsibility for child rearing, the economic facts of life in our century oblige most moms to be working moms, both in Japan and in America. Giving children what they need is sometimes profoundly difficult for families, who find themselves in the most painful of compromises. From abortion to adoption to gay marriage to day care to the quality of schools, our common societies are preoccupied with figuring out how to structure society to best serve children. This presupposes an agreement that we do not yet have such a system and that our children are not yet best served. These issues can be debated with both cold logic and rhetorical fury in various public forums, but there remains a deeper reserve of guilt and emotional intensity that defies easy expression in words. Films like the ones mentioned in this book give voice to such emotions at a time when audiences on both halves of the globe find them pressing.

Finally, thanks to the increasingly global nature of movie competition, films that invoked such universal themes were especially valuable. Filmmakers in Asia and the West are jockeying for the same international audience. Within that audience, young women and teenage girls are increasingly critical. To reach young men and boys costs lots of money, while targeting young women and girls is substantially less expensive and offers greater potential rewards. Horror movies aimed at girls would be made and marketed on a different nexus of scare tactics—not the strong stuff of gore and violence, but the quiet ruminations of dread, the queasy afterburn of anguish, the unshakable pallor of an irrational nightmare.

At the turn of the millennium, low-budget suspense-driven thrillers that can appeal equally to Asian and American audiences were of critical importance to filmmakers regardless of their location.

As a result, the film industries of Asia and Hollywood have started to intertwine, the delineations between them growing foggy. As I write this, the ability of Hollywood remakes to trump the popular appeal of the Japanese versions has begun to falter. The opportunity now exists for Japanese filmmakers, perhaps with American backing and American actors, to beat Hollywood at the J-Horror game, and in so doing give Japanese films a competitive edge in the global market. We may be on the cusp of a radical change in the relative position of Hollywood against foreign competitors.

I will leave you with the thoughts of three of J-Horror's masters on the relative strengths of the Asian film industries against Hollywood and the possible future of the genre.

Lo Chi Leung: "Asian cinema do not have much resources compared to Hollywood cinema. We cannot handle too much and difficult special effects, that's why we have to put effort on designing characters. For horror movies, if special effects cannot help much, then the other way is to go deep into the character's inner thoughts... I believe this is the distinct difference between these two cinemas and also the answer for this trend."

Kiyoshi Kurosawa: "I think that, in general, it is impossible for the sensibilities that these Japanese films have to be remade inside the Hollywood system."

Hideo Nakata: "There are many great films being made right now in Japan—and in spite of the fact that the Japanese film industry is sometimes described as ailing. By the same token, there are a lot of flashy, dramatic looking films coming out of Hollywood that aren't any good."

FILMOGRAPHY

HONTO NI ATTA KOWAI HANASHI (1990)
Official English Title: SCARY TRUE STORIES
Directed by Norio Tsuruta
Screenplay by Chiaki Konaka
Starring: Genda Tetsuaki (Narrator), Junko Asanuma (Mariko), Mai Moriguchi (Akemi), Yumi Goto (Masayao), Masakazu Tanaka (Kabashima), Akiko Hoshino (Akemi's gradmother), Emi Tarada, Arisa Ogasawara, Akane Aizawa, Hitomi Yamanaka, Shinobu Kosakai, Hisako Yamada
Produced by Satoru Ogura and Naokatsu Itou
Cinematography by Yoshiya Tatsuno, Hirohiko Kimura, Tomoyoshi Nakamura, and Takashi Suga
Music by Kit Cut Club
Running time 42 minutes, 49 minutes, and 47 minutes
Released in Japan on video as three separate videos between 1990-1991

HONTOUNI ATTA KOWAI HANASHI: JUSHIRYOU (1992)
Official English Title: CURSE, DEATH AND SPIRIT
Directed by Hideo Nakata
Screenplay by Hiroshi Takahashi (episodes 1 and 3), Akihiko Shiota (episode 2)
Starring: Michiko Hada (Satomi), Maiko Kawakami (Etsuko), Kim Kumuko (Ghost), Oka Mitsuko (Taskako), Yasuyo Shirashima (Kyouko), Yuma Nakamura (Akemi)
Produced by Takahiro Obashi and Akira Ozeki
Cinematography by Haruhisa Taguchi and Takeshi Hamada
Music by Katsuo Oona
Running time 65 minutes
Released in Japan on TV Asahi, 1992

EKO EKO AZARAKU (1995)
Official English Title: WIZARD OF DARKNESS
Directed by Shimako Sato
Screenplay by Junki Takegami from a story by Shinichi Koga
Starring: Kimika Yoshino (Misa Kuroi), Miho Kanno (Mizuki Kurahashi), Miho Tamura (Maki Yoshida), Kanori Kadomatsu (Kazzumi

Tanaka)
Produced by Yoshinori Chiba, Shunichi Kobayashi, Tomoyuki Imai
Cinematography by Shoei Sudo
Music by Mikiya Katakura
Running time 82 minutes
Released in Japan on April 8, 1995

TOIRE NO HANAKO-SAN (1995)
Official English Title: PHANTOM OF THE TOILET
Alternate English Title: HANAKO IN THE TOILET-ROOM
Directed by Joji Matsuoka
Screenplay by Takuro Fukuda
Starring: Yuka Kouno (Saeko), Ai Maeda (Natsumi), Takayuki Inoue (Takuya), Etsushi Toyokawa (Yuuji), Nene Ootsuka (Yuriko), Koutaro Santou (Katou), Naoto Takenaka (Katou—father)
Produced by Shigehiro Nakagawa, Toshiaki Nakazawa, Nozumo Enoki, Haruo Umekawa
Cinematography by Norimichi Kasamatsu
Music by Kuniaki Yakura
Running time 90 minutes
Released in Japan on July 1, 1995

GAKKOU NO KAIDAN (1995)
Official English Title: HAUNTED SCHOOL
Alternate English Titles: School for Ghosts, School Ghost Stories
Written and Directed by Hideyuki Hirayama
Starring: Ayako Sugiyama, Hironobu Nomura, Masahiro Sato, Kasumi Toyama, Shiori Yonezawa, Junichiro Tsukada, Hajime Atsuta, Shohei Machida
Produced by Yasuhiko Higashi, Mikihiko Hirata, Sumiji Miyake, and Tsutomu Tsuchikawa
Cinematography by Kouzou Shibazaki
Edited by Akimasa Kawashima
Music by Fuji-Yama
Running time 100 minutes
Released in Japan on July 8, 1995

RINGU: KANZEN-BAN (1995)
Official English Title: RING: THE COMPLETE EDITION
Directed by Chisui Takigawa
Screenplay by Joji Iida from the novel by Koji Suzuki
Starring: Katsunori Takahashi (Asakawa), Yoshio Harada (Ryuji), Ayane

Miura (Sadako), Mai Tachihara (Shizuka Asakawa), Maha Hamada (Mai Takano), Tomorowo Taguchi (Jotaro Nagao), Akiko Hinagata (Tomoko Onishi), Shigeyuki Nakamura (Yoshino)
Produced by Endo Ryunosuke
Cinematography by Iwata Kazumi
Music by Ike Yoshihiro
Running time 95 minutes
Released in Japan on television by Fuji TV on August 11, 1995

JOYU-REI (1996)
Official English Title: DON'T LOOK UP
Alternate English Title: GHOST ACTRESS
Directed by Hidco Nakata
Screenplay by Hiroshi Takahashi
Starring: Yurei Yanagi (Tashio Murai), Yasuyo Shirashima (Hitomi), Kei Ishibashi (Saori),
Produced by Sento Takenori
Cinematography by Takeshi Hamada
Edited by Shuichi Kakesu
Music by Akifumi Kawamura
Running time 73 minutes
Released in Japan on video on March 2, 1996

CURE (1997)
Directed by Kiyoshi Kurosawa
Screenplay by Kiyoshi Kurosawa
Starring: Koji Yakusho (Detective Takabe), Tsuysohi Ujiki (Sakuma), Anna Nakagawa (Fumi Takabe), Masato Hagiwara (Mamiya)
Produced by Tsutomu Tsuchikawa, Atsuyuki Shimoda
Cinematography by Tokusyo Kikumura
Edited by Kan Suzuki
Music by Gary Shiya
Running time 111 minutes
Released in Japan on January 1, 1997

PARASAITO IBU (1997)
Official English Title: PARASITE EVE
Directed by Masayuki Ochiai
Screenplay by Ryoichi Kimizuka from the novel by Hideaki Sena
Starring: Hiroshi Mikami (Toshiaki Nagashima), Riona Haduki (Kiyomi), Tomoko Nakajima (Asakura), Kenzou Kawarasaki (Kiyomi's father), Tetsuya Bessho, Ayako Oomura, Noboru Mitani, Ren Osugi

Produced by Yuu Ookawa, Jirou Komaki, and Tadamichi Abe
Cinematography by Ryouichi Kimiduka
Music by Joe Hisaishi
Running time 120 minutes
Released in Japan on February 1, 1997

KOKKURI-SAN (1997)
Official English Title: KOKKURI
Directed by Takahisa Zeze
Screenplay by Takahisa Zeze and Kishu Izuchi
Starring:
Ayumi Yamatsu (Mio), Hiroko Shimada (Hiroko), Moe Ishikawa (Masami), Rika Furukawa (Asaka), Saki Aoshima (Midori/Mio)
Produced by Shigehiro Arake and Minoru Yokote
Cinematography by Shogo Ueno
Edited by Shinichi Fushima
Music by Goro Yasukawa
Running time 87 minutes
Released in Japan on May 21, 1997

SI YU SI RI (1997)
Official English Title: TEMEGOTCHI
Directed by Wellson Chin
Screenplay by Lawrence Lau
Starring: Dayo Wong, Ruby Wong, Wong Man Yee, Law Lan, Cheung Joe, Chow Chi Fai, Mui Fun, Kan Shui Chiu
Produced by Daniel Lam and Danny Wang
Cinematography by Tsang Tat Sze
Edited by Ng Wang Hung
Music by Yan Lok
Running time 88 minutes
Released in Hong Kong in 1997

RINGU (1998)
Official English Title: RINGU [RING in this book]
Directed by Hideo Nakata
Screenplay by Hiroshi Takahashi from the novel by Koji Suzuki
Starring:
Produced by Takashige Ichise, Takenori Sento, Shinya Kawai
Cinematography by Junichiro Hayashi
Edited by
Music by Kenji Kawai

Running time 96 minutes
Released in Japan on January 31, 1998 on a double bill with Rasen (The Spiral)

RASEN (1998)
Official English Title: THE SPIRAL
Directed by Joji Iida
Screenplay by Joji Iida from the novel by Koji Suzuki
Starring: Koichi Sato (Andou), Miki Nakatani (Mai Takano), Hinako Saeki (Sadako), Shingo Tsurumi (Miyashita), Hiroyuki Sanada (Ryuuji)
Produced by Shinya Kawai, Takashige Ichise, Takenori Sento
Cinematography by Watanabe Makoto
Music by La Finca
Running time 98 minutes
Released in Japan on January 31, 1998 on a double bill with Ring

YEOGO GOEDAM (1998)
Official English Title: WHISPERING CORRIDORS
Alternate English Title: SCARY STORY IN A GIRLS' HIGH SCHOOL
Directed by Ki-Hyung Park
Screenplay by Ki-Hyung Park and Jeong-Ok In
Starring: Mi-Yeon Lee (Eun-Yung Hur), Kyu-Ree Kim (Ji-Oh), Se-Yeon Choi (Jae-Yi), Young-Su Park (Mad Dog), Yong-Nyeo (Mrs. Park), Jin-Hee Park (So-Young), Jy-Hye Yoon (Jung-Sook)
Produced by Ki-Min Oh
Cinematography by Jeong-Min Suh
Edited by Sung-Won Ham
Music by Sung-Heon Moon
Running time 105 minutes
Released in South Korea on May 30, 1998

SHINSEI TOIRE NO HANAKO-SAN (1998)
Official English Title: SCHOOL MYSTERY
Alternate English Title: THE REBIRTH OF HANAKO IN THE TOILET-ROOM
Directed by Yukihiko Tsutsumi
Screenplay by Hiroshi Takahashi
Starring: Ai Maeda (Satomi), Maya Hamaoka (Kanae), Ayako Oomura (Etsuko), Hideyuki Kasahara (Kousuke), Reiko Takashima (Reiko), Shinichi Ogishima (Asaoka), Hiroshi Nagano (Yabe), Ichiro Ogura (Takeo), Miyako Yamaguchi (Eiko)
Produced by Hirofumi Ogoshi, Shigeyuki Endou, Man Itou

Cinematography by Satoru Karasawa
Music by Akira Mitake
Running time 95 minutes
Released in Japan on July 4, 1998

TOMIE (1998)
Written and Directed by Ataru Oikawa
From the manga by Junji Ito
Starring: Miho Kanno (Tomie Kawakani), Mami Nakamura (Tsukiko Iszumisawa), Yoriko Douguchi (Dr. Hosono), Tomorowo Taguchi (Detective Harada), Kouta Kusano (Yuuichi Saiga), Kenji Mizuhashi (Yamamoto)
Produced by Yasuhiko Azuma, Tatsuhiko Hirata, Youichiro Onishi, Shun Shimizu, Tsutomu Tsuchikawa
Cinematography by Akira Sakoh and Kazuhiro Suzuki
Music by Hiroshi Futami and Toshihiro Kimura
Running time 95 minutes
Released in Japan on October 6, 1998

RINGU: SAISHUU-SHO (1999)
Official English Title: RING: THE FINAL CHAPTER
Directed by Hiroshi Nishitani, Hidetomo Matsuda, and Yoshihito Fukumoto
Screenplay by Kouji Makita and Naoya Takayama
Starring: Toshirou Yanagiba (Asakawa), Tomoya Nagase (Ryuuji), Hitomi Kuroki (Rieko), Kotomi Kyouno (Akiko), Akiko Yada (Mai Takano)
Produced by Kenji Shimizu and Sousuke Osabe
Music by Toshiyuki Watanabe
Running time 12 45-minute episodes
Released in Japan on television by Fuji TV on January 7, 1999

RINGU 2 (1999)
Official English Title: RINGU 2 [RING 2 in this book]
Directed by Hideo Nakata
Screenplay by Hiroshi Takahashi
Starring: Miki Nakatani (Mai Takano), Daisuke Ban (Dr. Ikuma), Kyoko Fukuda (Kanae), Kenjiro Ishimaru (Oomuta), Nanako Matsushima (Reiko Asakawa), Hiroyuki Sanada (Ruyuuji), Katsumi Murumatsu (Kouichi Asakwaw), Hitomi Satou (Masami)
Produced by Takachise Ichise
Cinematography by Hideo Yamamoto
Music by Kenji Kawai

Running time 95 minutes
Released in Japan on January 23, 1999 on a double bill with Shikoku

SHIKOKU (1999)
Alternate English Title: LAND OF THE DEAD
Directed by Shunichi Nagasaki
Screenplay by Kunimi Manda and Takenori Sento from the book by Masako Bando
Starring: Yui Natsukawa (Hinako), Michitaka Tsutsui (Fumiya), Chiaki Kuriyama (Sayori Hiura), Toshie Negishi (Teruko), Ren Osugi (Yasutaka), Taro Suwa (Oda)
Produced by Masato Hara
Cinematography by Noburo Shinoda
Edited by Yoshiyuki Okahara
Music by Satoshi Kadokura
Running time 101 minutes
Released in Japan on January 23, 1999 on a double bill with Ring 2

SAIMIN (1999)
Official English Title: THE HYPNOTIST
Alternate English Title: HYPNOSIS
Directed by Masayuki Ochiai
Screenplay by Masayuki Ochiai and Yasushi Fukuda from the novel by Keisuke Matsuoka
Starring: Goro Inagaki (Saga), Miho Kanno (Yuka Irie), and Ken Utsui (Sakurai)
Produced by Touru Shibata and Toshiaki Harada
Cinematography by Osamu Fujiishi
Music by Kuniaki Haijima
Running time 110 minutes
Released in Japan on June 5, 1999

RING (1999)
Official English Title: THE RING VIRUS
Written and Directed by Dong-Bin Kim
Starring:
Eun-Kyung Shin (Sun-ju), Dun-Na Bae (Eun-Suh), Jin-Yeong Jeong (Choi Yeol), Seung-Hyeon Lee (Sang-Mi), Chang-Wan Kim (Prof. Ikuma), Ggoch-Ji Kim, Yeon-Su Yu
Produced by Mauricio Dortona
Cinematography by Chul-Hyun Hwang
Music by Il Won

Running time 102 minutes
Released in South Korea on June 12, 1999

TOMIE: ANAZA FEISU (1999)
Official English Title: TOMIE: ANOTHER FACE
Directed by Toshiro Inomata
Written by Shoutarou Oikawa from the manga by Junji Ito
Starring: Runa Nagai (Tomie), Akira Shirai (Oota), Chie Tanaka (Miki), Nobuaki Kaneko (Takashi), Atsuishi Okuno (Mori), Tomonori Yoshida (Yasuda), Eriko Odaira, Mayumi Yoshida, Hiroaki Muroi, Tomomasa Ono, Takara Harada,
Produced by Yasuyuki Uemura, Shun Shimizu, Naokatsu Itou
Cinematography by Naoki Kayano
Music by Hideaki Hayashida
Running time 72 minutes
Released in Japan on October 25, 1999

YEOGO GOEDAM 2: TUBONJJAE IYAGI (1999)
Official English Title: MEMENTO MORI
Written and Directed by Tae-Yong Kim and Ky-Dong Min
Starring: Min-sun Kim (Min-Ah), Yeh-Jin Park (Hyo-Shin), Young-Jin Lee (Shi-Eun), Jong-Hak Baek (Mr. Goh), Min-Hie Kim (Yeon-An), Hyo-Jin Kong (Ji-Won)
Produced by Choon-Yeon Lee
Cinematography by Yoon-Soo Kim
Music by Sung-Woo Cho
Running time 98 minutes
Released in South Korea on December 24, 1999

SAAN CHUEN LIU SHUT (1999)
Official English Title: A WICKED GHOST
Written and directed by Tony Leung
Starring: Francis Ng, Gigi Lai, Gabriel Harrison, Edward Mok, Celia Sie
Produced by Tony Leung
Cinematography by Stephen Wong
Edited by Ng Wang Hung
Music by Simon Leung
Running time 85 minutes
Released in Hong Kong in 1999

KOUREI: USHIROWO MIRUNA (1999)
Official English Title: SÉANCE

Alternate English Title: Spiritualism: Don't Look Behind
Directed by Kiyoshi Kurosawa
Screenplay by Tetsuya Ooishi from the novel by Mark McShane
Starring: Koji Yakusho (Satou), Jun Fubuki (Junko), Tsuyoshi Kusanagi (Hayasaka), Kitarou (Kashiwabara), Ittoku Kishibe (Professor), Ren Osugi (Customer)
Produced by Yasuyuki Uemura, Tomo Jinno, Takehiko Tanaka, Atsuyuki Shimoda
Cinematography by Takahide Shibanushi
Music by Gary Ashiya
Running time 118 minutes
Released in Japan in 1999

RINGU 0: BAASUDEI (2000)
Official English Title: RING 0: BIRTHDAY
Directed by Norio Tsuruta
Screenplay by Hiroshi Takahashi from the short story "Lemon Heart" by Koji Suzuki
Starring: Yukie Nakama (Sadako), Seiichi Tanabe (Hiroshi), Yoshiko Tanaka (Akiko), Atsuko Takahata (Kaoru), Kumiko Asou (Etsuko), Takeshi Wakamatsu (Shigemori), Daisuke Ban (Dr. Ikuma)
Produced by Shinji Ogawa, Masao Nagai, Masato Hara and Taka Ichise
Cinematography by Takahide Shibanushi
Music by Shinichiro Ogata
Running time 99 minutes
Released in Japan on January 22, 2000 on a double bill with Isola

ISOLA: TAJUU JINKAKU SHOUJO (2000)
Official English Title: ISOLA
Alternate English Title: ISOLA: MULTIPLE PERSONALITY GIRL
Directed by Toshiyuki Mizutani
Screenplay by Toshiyuki Mizutani from the novel by Yuusuke Kishi
Starring: Yoshino Kimura (Yukari), Yuu Kurosawa (Chihiro) , Ken Ishiguro (Kazuhiko), Satomi Tezuka (Hiroko), Mariko Watanabe (Yayoi)
Produced by Shunsuke Yamada, Fumio Inoue
Executive Producer Masato Hara
Cinematography by Shuji Kuriyama
Edited by Noboyuki Takahashi
Music by Takeo Miratsu and David Matthews
Running time 93 minutes
Released in Japan on January 22, 2000 on a double bill with Ring 0: Birthday

TOMIE: REPLAY (2000)
(The Japanese title screen uses the English title in romanized letters)
Directed by Fujiro Mitsuishi
Screenplay by Satoru Tamaki, inspired by the manga by Junji Ito
Starring: Mai Hosho (Tomie Kawakani), Sayaka Yamaguchi (Yumi Morita), Yosuke Kubozukai (Fumihito Sato), Masatoshi Matsuo (Takeshi), Kenichi Endo (Dr. Tachibana), Makoto Togashi (Atsuko Kinoshita), Shun Sugata (Dr. Kenzo Morita)
Produced by Yasuhiko Higashi, Mikihiko Hirata, Sumiji Miyake, and Tsutomu Tsuchikawa
Cinematography by Hideo Yamamoto
Edited by Ryuji Miyajima
Running time 95 minutes
Released in Japan on February 11, 2000 on a double bill with Uzumaki

UZUMAKI (2000)
Official English Title: UZUMAKI: THE SPIRAL
Alternate English Title: VORTEX, WHIRLPOOL
Directed by Higuchinsky
Screenplay by Takao Niita from the manga by Junji Ito
Starring: Eriko Hatsune (Kirie Goshima), Fhi Fan (Shuuichi), Hinako Saeki (Kyouko), Shin Eun Kyung (Chie Maruyama), Keiko Takahashi (Yukie), Ren Osugi (Toshio Saitou), Taro Suwa (Yasuo Goshima), Denden (Futada)
Produced by Yasuhiko Higashi, Mikihiko Hirata, Sumiji Miyake, Man Kurosawa and Tsutomu Tsuchikawa
Cinematography by Gen Kobayashi
Music by Keichi Suzuki and Tetsura Kasibuchi
Running time 91 minutes
Released in Japan on February 11, 2000 on a double bill with *Tomie: Replay*

JU-ON (2000)
English Title: JU-ON: THE CURSE
Written and Directed by Takashi Shimizu
Starring: Yurei Yanagi (Kobayashi), Chiaki Kuriyama (Mizuho), Takako Fuji (Kayako), Ryota Koyama (Toshio Saeki), Takashi Matsuyama (Takeo Saeki), Hitomi Miwa (Yuki), Asumi Miwa (Kanna Murakami), Taro Suwa (Yue Kamio), Yumi Yoshiyuki (Noriko), Denden (Detective), Yoriko Douguchi (Nakamura), Ryota Koyama
Produced by Yasuhiko Higashi, Mikihiko Hirata, Sumiji Miyake, and Tsutomu Tsuchikawa

Produced by Takashige Ichise, Masaaki Takashima, and Kazuo Kato
Planner Producer Man Kurosawa
Supervised by Hiroshi Takahashi
Music by Shiro Sato
Running time 70 minutes
Released in Japan on video on February 11, 2000

KARISUMA (2000)
Official English Title: CHARISMA
Written and Directed by Kiyoshi Kurosawa
Starring: Koji Yakusho, Hiroyuki Ikeuchi, Ren Osugi, Yoriko Douguchi, Jun Fubuki
Produced by Satoshi Kanno, Atsuyuki Shimoda
Cinematography by Junichiro Haya
Edited by Junichi Kikuchi
Music by Gary Ashiya
Running time 104 minutes
Released in Japan on February 26, 2000

JU-ON 2 (2000)
English Title: JU-ON 2: THE CURSE
Written and Directed by Takashi Shimizu
Starring: Yuuko Daike (Kyoko Suzuki), Makoto Ashikawa (Tatsuya Suzuki), Kahori Fuji (Yoshimi Kitada), Mayuko Saito (Clerk), Dankan (Deliveryman), Yurei Yanagi (Kobayashi), Chiaki Kuriyama (Mizuho), Hitomi Miwa (Yuki), Asumi Miwa (Kanna Murakami), Tomohiro Kaku (Nobuyuki Suzuki), Takako Fuji (Kayako Saeki), Ryota Koyama (Toshio), Denden (Detective Yoshikawa), Taro Suwa (Kamio), Reita Serizawa (Iizuka), Taizo Mizumura (Taiji Suzuki), Harumi Matsukaze (Fumi Suzuki), Takashi Matsyuama (Takeo Saeki)
Produced by Yasuhiko Higashi, Mikihiko Hirata, Sumiji Miyake, and Tsutomu Tsuchikawa
Produced by Takashige Ichise, Masaaki Takashima, and Kazuo Kato
Planner Producer Man Kurosawa
Supervised by Hiroshi Takahashi
Music by Shiro Sato
Running time 75 minutes
Released in Japan on video on March 25, 2000

TAJUU JINKAKU TANTEI SAIKO: AMAMIYA KAZUHIKO NO KIKAN (2000)
Official English Title: MPD PSYCHO

Directed by Takashi Miike
Screenplay by Eiji ootsuka from his manga
Starring: Naoki Hosaka (Kazuhiko Amamiya/Yosuke Kobayashi), Tomoko Nakajima (Machi Isono), Ren Osugi (Tooru Sasayama), Saduharu Shiota (Masaki Manabe), Yoshinari Anan (Kikuo Toguchi), Rieko Miura (Chizuko Honda), Nae yuuki (Tomoyo Tanabe), Tomonori Masuda (Tatsuya Ueno)
Produced by Naoki Abe, Yoshihisa Nakagawa, Toshihiro Satou
Cinematography by Naosuke Imaizumi
Music by Tsugutoshi Gotou and Yumi Shirakura
Running time 6 individual 54 minute episodes
Released in Japan on TV on May 2, 2000

BIMIL (2000)
Official English title: SECRET TEARS
Written and Directed by Ki-Hyung Park
Starring: Seung-Woo Kim (Gu-Ho), Mi-Jo Yun(Mi-Jo), Hyeon-Woo Jeong (Hyeon-nam), Eun-Suk Park (Do-kyung), Ye-Jin Son, Seon-Hwa Jeon, Young-Hwan Kim
Produced by Yo-Jin Lee, Ki-Hyung Park
Cinematography by Yong-Shik Mun
Edited by Seong-Weon Ham
Music by Kyu-Yang Kim
Running time 105 minutes
Released in South Korea on June 3, 2000

NAGAI YUME (2000)
Official English Title: LONG DREAM
Written and Directed by Higuchinsky
Based on the manga by Junji Ito
Starring: Shuuji Kashiwabara (Mukoda), Masami Horiuchi (Dr. Kuroda), Eriko Hatsune (Kana Sakurai), Kenjiro Tsuda (Dr. Yamauchi), Tsugumi (Mami)
Produced by Kenshi Kinoshita, Choji Miyake, Dai Miyazaki, Ryoichi Sato, Asao Tsunoda
Cinematography and Editing by Higuchinsky
Music by Zuntata
Running time 58 minutes
Released in Japan on television by TV Asahi on July 7, 2000

GAWI (2000)
Official English Title: NIGHTMARE
Alternate English Title: HORROR GAME MOVIE
Written and Directed by Byung-Ki Ahn
Starring:
Gyu-Ri Kim (Hye-Jin), Ji-Won Ha (Eun-Ju), Jeong-Yun Choi (Seon-Ae), Ji-Tae Yu (Hyun-Jun), Jun-Sang Yu (Jeong-Ok), Jun Jeong (Se-Hun), Hye-Yeong Jo (Mi-Ryeong)
Produced by Hyeong-Wook Goh, Stanley Kim, and Min-Ho Lee
Cinematography by Seok-Hyeon Lee
Edited by Seong-Weon Jo
Music by Tae-Beom Lee
Running time 97 minutes
Released in South Korea on July 29, 2000

SENRIGAN (2000)
English Title: Clairvoyance
Directed by Manabu Iso
Written by Keisuke Matsuoka
Starring: Miki Mizuno, Hitomi Kuroki, Toshirou Yanagiba
Produced by Shigeyuki Endou
Running time 100 minutes
Released in Japan in 2000

INUGAMI (2001)
Written and Directed by Masato Harada
From the novel by Masako Bando
Starring: Yuki Amami (Miki Bonomiya), Atsuro Watabe (Akira Nutahara), Eugene Harada (Seiji Doi), Shiho Fujimura (Tomie Bonomiya), Kazuhiro Yamaji (Takanao), Kanako Fukaura (Momoyo Bonomiya), Shion Machida (Sonoko Bonomiya), Kenichi Yajima (Michio Bonomiya), Masato Irie (Hirofumi Bonomiya), Makoto Togashi (Hide), Torahiko Hamada (Old Man), Myu Watase (Rika Bonomiya), Keiko Awaji (Katsuko Doi), Koichi Sato (Mimoto the Hunter)
Produced by Yasuhiko Higashi, Mikihiko Hirata, Sumiji Miyake, and Tsutomu Tsuchikawa
Cinematography by Junichi Fujisawa
Edited by Soichi Ueno
Produced by Masato Hara, Fumio Inoue, Hisao Nabeshima, Shunsuke Yamada
Running time 106 minutes
Released in Japan on January 27, 2001

OTOGIRISO (2001)
Official English Title: ST. JOHN'S WORT
Directed by Ten Shimoyama
Screenplay by Goro Nakajima and Takenori Sento from the book by Shukei Nagasaka
Starring: Megumi Okina, Yoichiro Saito, Koji Okura, Reiko Matsuo, Minoru
Produced by Masato Hara
Cinematography by Kazuhiko Ogura
Music by Asako Yoshida
Running time 85 minutes
Released in Japan on video on January 27, 2001

TOMIE: REBIRTH (2001)
Directed by Takashi Shimizu
Screenplay by Yoshinobu Fujioka from the manga by Junji Ito,
Starring:
Miki Sakai (Tomie Kawakami), Satoshi Tsumabuki (Takumi Aoyama), Kumiko Endou (Hitomi Kitamura), Masaya Kikawada (Shun Hosoda), Shuugo Oshinari (Hideo Kimata), Mia Murano (Rie Ayoama), Yuri Hachisu (Yumiko), Yutaka Nakajima (Tomoko Hosoda)
Produced by Tsutomu Tsuchikawa, Tooru Ishii, Ken Takeuchi
Cinematography by Yoichi Shiga
Edited by Ryuji Miajima
Music by Gary Ashiya
Running time 101 minutes
Released in Japan on March 24, 2001

KAIRO (2001)
Official English Title: PULSE
Alternate English Title: CIRCUIT
Directed by Kiyoshi Kurosawa
Screenplay by Kiyoshi Kurosawa
Starring: Koji Yakusho
Produced by Shun Shimizu, Seiji Okuda, Takeshi Inoue, Atsuyuki Shimoda
Executive Producer Yasuyoshi Tokuma
Cinematography by Junichiro Hayashi
Edited by Junichi Kiku
Music by Takeshi Haketa
Running time 119 minutes
Released in Japan on May 23, 2001

IKISUDAMA (2001)
Official English Title: SHADOW OF THE WRAITH
Alternate English Title: DOPPELGANGER
Directed by Toshiharu Ikeda
Screenplay by Masaya Ozaki and Setsu Yamaguchi from the manga by Nanaeko Sasaya
Starring: Koji Matsu (Ryoji), Yuichi Matsuo (Kazuhiko), Hitomi Miwa (Asaji), Asumi Miwa (Naoko), Yuma Nakamura (Kyoko), Yuriko Hirooka (Kimie), Asami Katsura (Ako), Kozue Ayuse (Mariko), Makiko Fujii (Kazumi)
Produced by Man Kurosawa, Yoshihisa Nakagawa, Yoshihiro Yuuki, Masami Kubota
Cinematography by Haruhisa Taguchi
Edited by Akimasa Kawashima
Music by Tomohiko Kira
Running time 117 minutes
Released in Japan on June 23, 2001

SORUM (2001)
English Title: Goosebumps
Written and Directed by Jong-Chan Yun
Starring:
Jin-Young Jang (Sun-Yeong), Myeong-Min Kim (Yong-Hyun), Ju-Bong Gi, An Jo, Young-Hoon Park
Produced by Jong-Hyak Baek and Pil-Seon Hwang
Cinematography by Seo-Shik Hwang
Edited by Min-Ho Kyeong
Running time 100 minutes
Released in South Korea on August 4, 2001

KAKASHI (2001)
English Title: The Scarecrow
Directed by Norio Tsuruta
Screenplay by Satoru Tamaki from the manga by Junji Ito,
Starring: Maho Nonami (Kaoru), Kou Shibaski (Izumi), Grace Yip (Sally Chen), Yoshiki Arizono (Noji), Shunsuke Matsuoko (Tsuyoshi)
Produced by Yoichiro Onishi
Cinematography by Wataru Kikuchi
Edited by Hiroshi Sunaga
Music by Shinichiro Ogata
Running time 86 minutes
Released in Japan on November 16, 2001

TRICK (2002)
Directed by Yukihiko Tsutsumi
Screenplay by Mitsuharu Makita
Starring: Yukie Nakama (Naoko), Hiroshi Abe, Katsuhisa Namase (Detective Yabe), Yoko Nogiwa, Naoto Takenaka
Produced by Junichi Kimura, Kenji Kazano
Cinematography by Shigetomo Madarame
Edited by Nobuyuki Ito
Music by Yoh Tsuji
Running time 119 minutes
Released in Japan on January 11, 2002

HONOGURAI MIZU NO SOKO KARA (2002)
Official English Title: DARK WATER
Directed by Hideo Nakata
Screenplay by Hideo Nakata and Takashige Ichise from the novel by Koji Suzuki
Starring:
Hitomi Kuroki (Yoshimi), Rio Kanno (Ikuko at age 6), Asami Mizukawa (Ikuko at age 16), Mirei Oguchi (Mitsuko), Fumiyo Kohinata (Kunio), Yu Tokui (Real Estate Agent), Isao Tokui (Apartment Manager), Shigemitsu Ogi (Lawyer)
Produced by Takashige Ichise
Cinematography by Junichirou Hiyashi
Edited by Noboyuki Takahashi
Music by Kenji Kawai
Running time 102 minutes
Released in Japan on January 19, 2002

JISATSU SAAKURU (2002)
Official English Title: SUICIDE CLUB
Alternate English Title: SUICIDE CIRCLE
Written and Directed by Sion Sono
Starring: Ryo Ishibashi, Masatoshi Nagase, Yoko Kamon, Kimiko Yo, Hideo Saka, Akaji Maro, Rolly
Produced by Tomita Toshikazu, Kawamata Masaya, Yoshida Seiji
Cinematography by Kazuto Sato
Edited by Onaga Akihiro
Music by Hasegawa Tomoki
Running time 94 minutes
Released in Japan on March 9, 2002

CHAM BIN HUNG LENG (2002)
Official English Title: SLEEPING WITH THE DEAD
Directed by Steve Cheng
Screenplay by Simon Loni, Steve Cheng, Kelvin Lee and Isis Lam
Starring: Jordan Chan, Kelly Lam, Cheng Tat Ming, Simon Loni, Sharon Chan, David Lee, Ricky Fan, Elena Kong, Li Fong, Rani Wong
Produced by Raymond Wong and Peter Chin
Cinematography by Tony Cheung
Edited by Choi Hung
Music by Kwok Chi Yin
Running time 95 minutes
Released in Hong Kong on April 7, 2002

YEE DO HUNG GAAN (2002)
Official English Title: INNER SENSES
Directed by Lo Chi Leung
Screenplay by Lo Chi Leung and Sinling Yeung
Starring:
Karena Lam (Yan Cheung), Leslie Cheung (Dr. Jim Law), Maggie Poon (Siu Yu Cheung), Waise Lee (Wilson Chan), Valerie Chow (Mrs. Chan), Norman Chu (Mr. Chu), Samuel Lam (Professor Fong), Li Wen Sun (Yan's Father), Hong Dou Liu (Yan's Mother)
Produced by Derek Yee
Cinematography by Kwok-Man Keung
Music by Peter Kam
Running time 100 minutes
Released in Hong Kong on March 28, 2002

GIN GWAI (2002)
Official English Title: THE EYE
Directed by Danny and Oxide Pang
Screenplay by Danny and Oxide Pang and Jojo Hui
Starring: Angelica Lee (Wong Kar Mun), Lawrence Chou (Dr. Wah), Chutcha Rujinanon (Ling), Yut Lai So (Yingying), Candy Lo (Yee), Yin Ping Ko (Mun's Grandmother), Edmund Chen (Dr. Lo), Wai-Ho Yung (Mr. Ching), Wilson Yip (Taoist)
Produced by Peter Chan
Cinematography by Decha Srimanta
Edited by The Pang Brothers
Music by Orange Music
Running time 98 minutes
Released in Japan on May 9, 2002

TOMIE: SAISHUU-SHO—KINDAN NO KAJITSU (2002)
Official English Title: TOMIE: FORBIDDEN FRUIT
Alternate English Title: TOMIE: THE FINAL CHAPTER
Directed by Shun Nakahara
Screenplay by Yoshinobu Fujioka from the manga by Junji Ito
Starring: Nozomi Andou (Tomie Kawakami), Aoi Miyazaki (Tomie Hashimoto), Jun Kunimura (Kazuhiko Hashimoto), Yuka Fujimoto (Kyoko), Ayaka Ninomiya (Megumi), Chiaki Outa (Tomoko), Tetsu Watanabe (Suzuki)
Produced by Toru Shimizu, Tsutomu Tsuchikawa, Junichi Matsushita, Sun Shimizu
Cinematography by Kazuhiro Suzuki
Edited by Ryuji Miyajima
Music by Tatsuya
Running time 91 minutes
Released in Japan on June 29, 2002

PON (2002)
Official English Title: THE PHONE
Directed by Byung-Ki Ahn
Screenplay by Byung-Ki Ahn and You-Jin Lee
Starring: Ji-Won Ha (Ji-Won), Yu-Mi Kim (Ho-Jeong), Woo-Jae Choi (Hang-Hoon), Ji-Yeon Choi (Jin-Hie), Seo-Woo Eun (Yeong-Ju)
Produced by Yong-Dae Kim
Cinematography by Yong-Sik Moon
Music by Sang-Ho Loe
Running time 102 minutes
Released in South Korea on July 26, 2002

THE RING (2002)
Directed by Gore Verbinski
Screenplay by Ehren Kruger from the book by Koji Suzuki
Starring:
Naomi Watts (Rachel Keller), Martin Henderson (Noah Clay), David Dorfman (Aidan Keller), Brian Cox (Richard Morgan), Jane Alexander (Dr. Grasnik), Daveigh Chase (Samara)
Produced by Laurie MacDonald and Walter F. Parkes
Cinematography by Bojan Bazelli
Edited by Craig Wood
Music by Hans Zimmer
Running time 115 minutes
Released in the United States on October 18, 2002

HAYANBANG (2002)
Official English Title: UNBORN BUT FORGOTTEN
Alternate English Title: The White Room
Directed by Chang-Jae Kim
Screenplay by Hyeon-Geun Han
Starring: Jun-Ho Jeong (Seok), Eun-Ju Lee (Su-Jin), Ji-Yu Kim, Seong-Yong Kye, Kan-Hie Lee, So-Yeon Lee, Ji-Yeon Myeong
Produced by Hee-Suk Yu
Cinematography by Hui-Ju Park
Music by Jeong-A Kim
Running time 95 minutes
Released in South Korea on November 15, 2002

SHUANG TONG (2002)
Official English Title: DOUBLE VISION
Directed by Chen Kuo Fu Chen
Screenplay by Chen Kuo Fu and Su Zhao Bin
Starring:
Tony Leung (Huo-Tu), David Morse (Kevin Richter), Rene Liu (Ching-Fang), Wei-Han Huang (Mei Mei), Leon Dai (Feng-Bo)
Produced by Chen Kuo Fu Chen, Ricky Strauss, Huang Chih Ming
Cinematography by Arthur Wong
Edited by Wen Ze Ming
Music by Lee Sin Yun
Running time 110 minutes
Released in Taiwan on December 5, 2002

JU-ON (2003)
English Title: JU-ON: THE GRUDGE
Written and Directed by Takashi Shimizu
Starring: Megumi Okina (Rika Nishina), Misaki Ito (Hitomi Tokunaga), Misa Uehara (Izumi Toyama), Yui Ichikawa (Chiharu), Kanji Tsuda (Katsuya Tokunaga), Yuya Ozeki (Toshio), Takako Fuji (Kayako Saeki), Takashi Matsyuama (Takeo Saeki), Kayoko Shibata (Mariko), Yukako Kukuri (Miyuki), Shuri Matsuda (Kazumi Tokunaga), Yoji Tanaka (Yuji Toyama), Chikara Ishikura (Hirohashi), Daisuke Honda (Detective Igarashi)
Produced by Takashige Ichise
Creative Consultant Kiyoshi Kurosawa
Supervised by Hiroshi Takahashi
Cinematography by Tokusho Kikumura
Editing by Nobuyuki Takahashi

Music by Shiro Sato
Running time 92 minutes
Released in Japan on January 25, 2003

SAINNYONG SIKTAK (2002)
Official English Title: THE UNINVITED
Alternate English Title: Table For 4
Written and Directed by Su-Yeon Lee
Starring: Shin-Yang Park, Ji-Hyeon Jeon, Yeon Yu, Yeo-Jin Kim, Won-Sang Park
Produced by Jeong-Wan Oh and Hun-Tak Jeong
Cinematography by Yong-Gyu Jo
Edited by Min-Ho Gyeong
Music by Yeong-Gyu Jang
Running time 126 minutes
Released in South Korea on May 1, 2003

JANGWHA, HONGRYEON (2003)
Official English Title: A TALE OF TWO SISTERS
Written and Directed by Ji-Woon Kim
Starring: Su-Jeong Lim (Soo-Mi), Geun-Yeong (Soo-Yeon), Jung-Ah Yum (Eun-Joo), Kap-Sun Kim (Father)
Produced by Jeong-Wan Oh
Cinematography by Mo-Gae Lee
Edited by Hyeon-Mi Lee
Music by Byung-Woo Lee
Running time 115 minutes
Released in South Korea on June 13, 2003

YEOGO GOEDAM 3: YEOWOO GYEDAN (2003)
Official English Title: WISHING STAIRS
Alternate English Title: WHISPERING CORRIDORS 3
Directed by Jae-Yeon Yun
Screenplay by Jae-Yeon Yun and Su-Ah Kim
Starring: Ji-Hyo Song (Ji-Seong), Han-Byeol Park (So-Hio), An Jo (Hye-Ju), Ji-Yeon Park (Yun-Ji)
Produced by Chun-Yeon Lee
Cinematography by Jeong-Min Seo
Music by Myeong-Ah Gong
Running time 97 minutes
Released in South Korea on August 1, 2003

JU-ON 2 (2003)
English Title: JU-ON 2: THE GRUDGE
Written and Directed by Takashi Shimizu
Starring: Noriko Sakai (Kyoko Harase), Chiahru Niyama (Tomoka Miura), Kei Horie, Yui Ichikawa (Chiharu), Shingo Katsurayama, Takako Fuji (Kayako), Yuya Ozeki (Toshio)
Produced by Takashige Ichise
Cinematography by Tokusho Kikumura
Editing by Nobuyuki Takahashi
Music by Shiro Sato
Running time 93 minutes
Released in Japan on August 23, 2003

DOPPERUNGENGAU (2003)
Official English Title: DOPPELGANGER
Directed by Kiyoshi Kurosawa
Screenplay by Kiyoshi Kurosawa and Ken Furusawa
Starring: Kouji Yakusho (Michio Hayasaki), Hiromi Nagasaku (Nagai), Yusuke Santamaria (Kimishima), Masahiro Toda (Aoki), Hitomi Sato (Takano)
Produced by Motoo Kawabata, Takayuki Nitta, Atsushi Sato and Atsuyuki Shimoda
Cinematography by Noriyuki Mizuguchi
Edited by Kiyoshi Kurosawa and Masahiro Onaga
Running time 107 minutes
Released in Japan on September 27, 2003

ACACIA (2003)
Official English Title: ACACIA
Written and Directed by Ki-Hyung Park
Starring: Hye-Jin Shim (Mi-Sook Choi), Jin-Geun Kim (Do-Il Kim), Oh-Bin Mun (Jin-Seong Kim), Na-Yoon Jeong (Min-Ji)
Produced by Sungkyu Kang, Ki-Hyung Park, and Yeong-Shik Yu
Cinematography by Hyeon-Je Oh
Edited by Seong-Weon Ham
Music by Man-Sik Choi
Running time 102 minutes
Released in South Korea om October 17, 2003

CHAKUSHIN ARI (2003)
Official English Title: ONE MISSED CALL
Directed by Takashi Miike

Screenplay by Yasushi Akimoto and Minako Daira from the novel by Akimoto Yasushi
Starring: Kou Shibasaki (Yumi Nakumura), Shinichi Tsutsumi (Hiroshi Yamashita), Anna Nagata (Yoko Okazaki), Kazue Fukiishi (Natsumi Konishi), Mariko Tsutsui (Marie Mizunuma) Karen Oshima (Mimiku Mizunuma)
Produced by Yoichi Arishige, Fumio Inoue, Naoki Sato
Cinematography by Hideo Yamamoto
Edited by Yasushi Shimamura
Music by Kouji Endou
Running time 113 minutes
Released in Japan on November 3, 2003

SHIBUYA KAIDAN 1 & 2 (2004)
Official English Title: THE LOCKER 1 & 2
Directed by Kei Horie
Screenplay by Kazunari Shibata and Osamu Fukutani
Starring:
Asami Mizukawa (Erika), Shuuji Kashiwabara (Ryouhei), Chisato Morishita (Yuuna), Mayuka Suzuki (Ai), Tomohisa (Keitarou), Toshihiro Wada (Akihiko)
Produced by Kazunari Shibata, Kengo Kaji, Youichi Iwasa
Cinematography by Naohiro Momotsuka
Music by Youhei Tsukazaki
Running time 72 & 72 minutes
Released in Japan on February 7, 2004

JU-REI GEKIJOU-BAN: KURO JU-REI (2004)
Official English Title: JU-REI: THE UNCANNY
Directed by Koji Shiraishi
Screenplay by Naoyuki Yokota
Starring:
Chinatsu Wakatsuki, Miku Ueno, Eriko Ichinohe, Ichirou Ogura, Hiromi Senno, Kenji Shio, Yasuko Mori, Kurumi Sawaki, Yuurei Yanagi
Produced by Wataru Suzuki, Hajime Harie, Takashi Oohashi, Natsuko Kitani
Cinematography by Kazuyuki Sakamoto
Music by DRA
Running time 76 minutes
Released in Japan on March 27, 2004

GIN GWAI 2 (2004)
Official English Title: THE EYE 2
Directed by Oxide and Danny Pang
Screenplay by Jojo Hui
Starring: Shu Qi (Joey), Eugenia Yuan (Yuen), Jesdaporn Pholdee (Sam), Philip Kwok (Monk), Rayson Tan (Gynaecologist)
Produced by Peter Chan, Lawrence Cheng and Jojo Hui
Cinematography by Decha Srimantra
Music by Payont Term Sit
Running time 95 minutes
Released in Hong Kong on May 17, 2004

FACE (2004)
Official English Title: FACE
Directed by sang-Gon Yoo
Screenplay by Hie-Jae Kim and Cheol-Hie Park
Starring:
Yun-Ah Song (Seon-Yeong), Hyeon-Jun Shin (Hyeon-Min), Seung-Wook Kim, Seok-Hwan An, Won-Hui Jo
Produced by Yong Han
Cinematography by Ji-Yeol Choi
Edited by Gok-Ji Park
Music by Han-Na Lee
Running time 92 minutes
Released in South Korea on June 11, 2004

RYEONG (2004)
Official English Title: THE GHOST
Alternate English Title: Dead Friend
Written and Directed by Tae-Kyeong Kim
Starring:
Ha-Neul Kim (Ji-Won), Sang-Mi Nam (Su-In), Bin (Eun-Seo), Yi-Shin (Mi-Kyeong), Hie-Ju Jeon (Yu-Jeong), Yun-Ji Lee (Eun-Jeong)
Produced by Oh-Young Jeong
Cinematography by Yong-Sik Mun
Edited by Yong-Su Kim
Music by Wan-Hee Choi
Running time 98 minutes
Released in South Korea on June 18, 2004

BUNSHINSABA (2004)
Official English Title: OIJA BOARD

Alternate English Title: Witch Board
Written and Directed by Ahn-Byung Ki
Starring:
Gyu-Ri Kim (Eun-Ju), Se-Eun Lee (Yu-Jin), Yu-Ri Lee (In-Suk), Seong-Min Choi (Jae-Hun), Jeong-Yun Choi (Ho-Kyeong)
Produced by Yong-Dae Kim
Cinematography by Dong-Cheon Kim
Edited by Sun-Duk Park
Music by Sang-Ho Lee
Running time 92 minutes
Released in South Korea on July 30, 2004

ARPOINTEU (2004)
Official English Title: R-POINT
Written and Directed by Su-Chang Kong
Starring:
Woo-Seong Kam, Byung-Ho Son, Tae-Kyung Oh, Won-Sang Park, Seon-Gyun Lee, Nae-Sang Ahn, Byeong-Cheol Kim, Kyeong-Ho Jeon, Yeong-Dong Mun
Produced by Kang-Hyeok Choi
Cinematography by Hyeong-Jing Seok
Edited by Na-Yeong Nan
Music by Pa-Ian Dal
Running time 107 minutes
Released in South Korea on August 13, 2004

SUIYOU PUREMIA: SEKAI SAIKYOU J HORAU SP NIHON NO KOWAI YORU (2004)
Official English Title: DARK TALES OF JAPAN
Written and Directed by Masayuki Ochiai, Norio Tsuruta, Takashi Shimizu, Yoshiro Nakamura, and Koji Shiraishi
Produced by Takachise Ichise and Jeremy Alter ("Blonde Kaidan" segment)
Running time 82 minutes
Released in Japan on TBS Television on September 22, 2004

KANSEN (2004)
Official English Title: INFECTION
Alternate English Title: J-HORROR THEATER VOLUME 1
Directed by Masayuki Ochiai
Screenplay by Masayuki Ochiai from the story by Ryochi Kimizuka
Starring: Koichi Sato, Masanobu Takashima, Mari Hoshino, Michiko

Hada, Kaho Minami, Shiro Sano
Produced by Takachise Ichise
Cinematography by Hatsuaki Masui
Edited by Yoshifumi Fukazawa
Music by Kuniaki Haishima
Running time 98 minutes
Released in Japan on October 2, 2004 on a double bill with Yogen (Premonition)

YOGEN (2004)
Official English Title: PREMONITION
Alternate English Title: J-HORROR THEATER VOLUME 2
Directed by Norio Tsuruta
Screenplay by Noburo Takagi and Norio Tsuruta
Starring: Hiroshi Mikami, Noriko Sakai, Maki Horikita, Mayumi Ono, Kei Yamamoto, Kazuko Yoshiyuki
Produced by Takachise Ichise
Cinematography by Naoki Kayano
Edited by Hiroshi Sunaga
Music by Kenji Kawai
Running time 95 minutes
Released in Japan on October 2, 2004 on a double bill with Kansen (Infection)

MAREBITO (2004)
English title: THE STRANGER FROM AFAR
Directed by Takashi Shimizu
Written by Chiaki Konaka
Starring: Shinyua Tsukamoto (Masuoka), Tomomi Miyashita (F), Kazuhiro Nakahara (Arei Furoki), Miho Ninagawa (Aya Fukumoto), Shun Sugata (MIB)
Produced by Tatsuhiko Hirata
For Eurospace: Kenzo Horikoshi, Atsuko Ono
Series Supervisor Hiroshi Takahashi
Cinematography by Tsukasa Tanabe
Edited by Masahiro Ugajin
Music by Toshiyuki Takine
92 minutes
Released in Japan on October 23, 2004

THE GRUDGE (2004)
Directed by Takashi Shimizu
Screenplay by Takashi Shimizu and Stephen Susco
Starring:
Sarah Michelle Gellar (Karen Davis), Jason Behr (Doug), William Mapother (Matthew Williams), Clea Du Vall (Jennifer Williams), KaDee Strickland (Susan Williams), Grace Zabriskie (Emma Williams), Ted Raimi (Alex), Bill Pullman (Peter Kirk), Rosa Blasi (Maria Kirk), Takako Fuji (Kayako Saeki), Yuya Ozeki (Toshio Saeki), Takashi Matsuyama (Takeo Saeki)
Produced by Doug Davison, Takashige Ichise, Roy Lee, and Robert G. Tapert
Executive Producer Sam Raimi
Cinematography by Lukas Ettlin and Hideo Yamamoto
Edited by Jeff Betancourt
Music by Christopher Young
Running time 91 minutes
Released in the United States on October 22, 2004

GEKIDAN KOGANEMUSHI (2004)
Official English Title: MARRONNIER
Directed by Hideyuki Kobayashi
Screenplay by Hideyuki Kobayashi, inspired by the manga by Junji Ito
Starring: Mayu (Marino), Misao Inagaki (Mitsuba), Hiroto Nakayama (Numai), Hoshino Haruna (Ichiyo), Miyako Takamiya (Mitsuko), Hime (Kaori), Tetsuya Shibata (Tetsuji), Masakazu Yoshida (Masaya), Yuriko Anjho (Sayoko), Hideyuki Kobayashi (Kitawaki), Junji Ito (Painter)
Produced by Junji Ito
Cinematography by Hideyuki Kobayashi
Edited by Hideyuki Kobayashi
Running time 80 minutes
Released in Japan *in 2004*

REDEU-AI (2005)
Official English Title: RED EYE
Written and Directed by Dong-Bin Kim
Starring:
Shin-Yeon Jang (Mi-Sun), Ji-Min Kwak (So-Hee), Dong-Kyu Lee (jin-Kyu), Hye-Na Kim (Hee-Joo), Eol Lee (Jong-Hyun), Hyeon-Suk Kim (Jin-Sook), Dae-Yeon Lee (Prof. Kim), Won-Sang Park (Jung-Ho)
Produced by Nam-Hie Kim and Yong-Guk Kim
Cinematography by Hee-Seong Byeon

Edited by Min-Kyeong Shin
Running time 96 minutes
Released in South Korea on January 28, 2005

CHAKUSHIN ARI 2 (2005)
Official English Title: ONE MISSED CALL 2
Directed by Renpei Tsukamoto
Screenplay by Minako Ooyoshi from the novel by Akimoto Yasushi
Starring: Mimura (Kyoko Okudera), Asaka Seto (Takako Nozoe), Yuu Yoshizawa (Naoto), Peter Ho
Produced by Kazuo Kuroi, Naoki Satou, Youichi Arishige
Music by Kouji Endou
Running time 105 minutes
Released in Japan on February 5, 2005

SHIRYOUHA (2005)
Official English Title: DEAD WAVES
Directed by Youichiro Hayama
Screenplay by Youichiro Hayama and Kayo Kanou
Starring:
Toshihiro Wada, Shihori Kanjiya, Masaki Miura, Shigenori Yamazaki, Akiko Esaki, Asuka Kurosawa, Yukimi Tanaka, Yuki Outake, Kanji Furutachi, Mari Sakai, Miho Hirata, Meikyou Yamada, Akihiro Nakatani
Produced by Takeshi Moriya and Toshinori Nishimae
Cinematography by Masahito Nakao
Music by Hajime Yamane
Running time 77 minutes
Released in Japan on February 5, 2005

GIN GWAI 10 (2005)
Official English Title: THE EYE 10
Directed by Danny and Oxide Pang
Screenplay by the Pang Brothers and Mark Wu
Starring: Bo-Lin Chen (Tak), Yu Gu (Ko Fai), Kate Yeung (May), Isabella Leung (April), Bongkoj Khongmalai, Ray MacDonald (Chongkwai)
Produced by Peter Chan, Lawrence Cheng, Jojo Hui, and Eric Tsang
Cinematography by Decha Srimantra
Edited by Curran Pang
Music by Payont Persmith
Running time 81 minutes
Released in Hong Kong on March 24, 2005

TOMIE: BEGINNING (2005)
Written and Directed by Ataru Oikawa
From the manga by Junji Ito
Starring:
Rio Matsumoto (Tomie), Kenji Mizuhashi (Kenichi), Akifumi Miura (Inoue), Takashi Sugiuchi (Yoshino), Yuka Iwasaki (Naoko), Asami Imajuku (Reiko), Nahana, Fujiyama
Produced by Ken Takeuchi, Shouichi Uemura, Hisaya Narita, Yasuhiko Higashi
Cinematography by Ryuu Segawa
Music by Masami Miyoshi
Running time 74 minutes
Released in Japan on April 9, 2005

TOMIE: REVENGE (2005)
Written and Directed by Ataru Oikawa
From the manga by Junji Ito
Starring:
Minami, Anri Ban
Produced by Naoya Narita and Yasuhiko Higashi
Cinematography by Ryu Segawa
Edited by Izumi Ishida
Music by Masami Miyoshi
Running time 72 minutes
Released in Japan on April 16, 2005

CHOU KOWAI HANASHI A: YAMI NO KARASU (2005)
Official English Title: CURSED
Directed by Yoshihiro Hoshino
Screenplay by Yoshihiro Hoshino and Yumeaki Hirayama
Starring:
Yuouko Akiba (Ryouko), Takaaki Iwao (Komori), Etsuyo Mitani and Osamu Takahashi (Store Owners), Hiroko Satou (Nao), Susumu Terajima (Akira)
Produced by Takeshi Katou, Suguru Matsumura, and Chikao Imagawa
Cinematography by Masahiro Taniai
Music by Kuniyuki Morohashi
Running time 81 minutes
Released in Japan on video on April 26, 2005

THE RING TWO (2005)
Directed by Hideo Nakata
Screenplay by Ehren Kruger
Starring:
Naomi Watts (Rachel Keller), David Dorfman (Aidan Keller), Simon Baker (Max Rourke), Elizabeth Perkins (Dr. Temple), Gary Cole (Martin Savide), Sissy Spacek (Evelyn)
Produced by Laurie MacDonald and Walter F. Parkes
Cinematography by Gabriel Beristain
Edited by Michael Knue
Music by Henning Lohner and Martin Tillman
Running time 110 minutes
Released in the United States on May 18, 2005

NAINA (2005)
Written and Directed by Shripal Morakhia
Starring: Urmila Matondkar (Naina), Anuj Sawhney (Dr. Patel), Shweta Konnur (Khemi), Kamini Khanna (Naina's Grandmother), Sulabha Arya (Parvati Amma)
Produced by Rakesh Mehra
Cinematography by C.K. Muralidharan
Edited by Amitabh Shukla
Music by Salim and Suleman Merchant
Running time 103 minutes
Released in India on May 20, 2005

DARK WATER (2005)
Directed by Walter Salles
Screenplay by Rafael Yglesias from the screenplay by Hideo Nakata and Taka Ichise from the short story by Koji Suzuki
Starring:
Jennifer Connelly (Dahlia), John C. Reilly (Mr. Murray), Tim Roth (Jeff Platzer), Dougray Scott (Kyle), Pete Postlethwaite (Veeck), Camryn Manheim (Teacher), Perla Haney-Jardine (Natasha/Young Dahlia), Ariel Gade (Ceci)
Produced by Bill Mechanic, Roy Lee, and Doug Davison
Cinematography by Affonso Beatto
Edited by Daniel Rezende
Music by Angelo Badalamenti
Running time 103 minutes
Released in the United States on June 27, 2005

YEOGO GOEDAM 4: MOKSORI (2005)
Official English Title: VOICE LETTER
Alternate English Title: Voice
Directed by Equan Choe
Screenplay by Equan Choe and Joon-Seok Sol
Starring:
Ye-Ryeon Chah (Cho-Ah), Ok-Bin Kim (Young-Eon), Seo-Hyeong Kim (Hee-Myn), Hyeon-Kyeong Lim (Hyo-Jung), Ji-Hye Seo (Seon-Min)
Produced by Choon-Yeon Lee
Music by Byeong-Hun Lee
Running time 104 minutes
Released in the United States on July 15, 2005

GABAL (2005)
Official English Title: THE WIG
Alternate English Title: Scary Hair
Written and Directed by Shin-Yeon Won
Starring:
Min-Seo Chae (Su-Hyeon), Hyon-Jin Sa (Ki-Seok), Seon-Yu (Ji-Hyun)
Produced by Dae-Young Heo
Cinematography by Dong-Eun Kim
Edited by Seon-Min Kim
Running time 106 minutes
Released in South Korea on August 12, 2005

CHELLO HONGUMIJOO ILGA SALINSAGAN (2005)
Official English Title: THE CELLO
Directed by Woo-Cheol Lee
Screenplay by Woo-Chul Chung
Starring:
Ho-Bin Jeong (Jun-Ki), Da-An Park (Tae-Yeon), Hyeon-A Seong (Mi-Ju), Yu-MI Jeong
Produced by Seong-Do Park
Cinematography by Yong-Chul Kwon
Edited by Yong-Soo Kim
Music by Han-Na Lee
Running time 94 minutes
Released in South Korea on August 18, 2005

ZHAIBIAN (2005)
Official English Title: THE HEIRLOOM
Directed by Leste Chen

Screenplay by Dorian Li
Starring:
Terri Kwan (Yo), Jason Chang (James), Yu-Chen Chang (Yi-Chen), Tender Huang (Ah-Tseng), Yi-Ching Lu, Kuo-Cheng Cheng, Ching-Ching Lin
Produced by Michelle Yeh
Cinematography by Pung-Leung Kwan
Edited by Ju-Kuan Hsiao
Music by Jeffrey Cheng
Running time 97 minutes
Released in Taiwan on September 16, 2005

PUREI (2005)
Official English Title: PRAY
Directed by Yuichi Sato
Screenplay by Tomoko Ogawa
Starring:
Tetsuji Tamayama (Mitsuru), Asami Mizukawa (Maki), Katsuya Kobayashi, Fumiyo Kohinata, Sanae Miyata, Mitsuyosho Shinoda, Toshiyuki Toyonaga
Produced by Takeshi Moriya and Toshinori Nishimae
Cinematography by Akihiro Kawamura
Music by Kei Yoshikawa
Running time 77 minutes
Released in Japan on October 15, 2005

KIDAN (2005)
Official English Title: INFERNO
Alternate English Title: Strange Story
Directed by Takashi Komatsu
Screenplay by Takashi Komatsu from the manga by Daijirou Motoboshi
Starring:
Ema Fujisawa (Satomi), Hiroshi Abe (Reijirou), Chisun, Yuurei Yanagi, Hiroshi Kanbe, Masami Horiuchi, Minoru Shiraki, Teisui Ichiryuusai, Reiko Kusamura
Produced by Takashige Ichise
Music by Kenji Kawai
Running time 84 minutes
Released in Japan on November 19, 2005

RINNE (2006)
Official English Title: REINCARNATION
Directed by Takashi Shimizu
Screenplay by Takashi Shimizu and Masaki Adachi
Starring:
Yuuka (Sugiura), Karina, Kippei Shiina, Tetta Sugimoto, Shun Oguri, Marika Matsumoto, Mantarou Koichi, Atsushi Haruta, Miki Sanjou
Produced by Takshige Ichise
Music by Kenji Kawai
Running time 95 minutes
Released in Japan on January 7, 2006

MIZUCHI (2006)
Official English Title: DEATH WATER
Alternate English Title: Water Spirit
Directed by Kiyoshi Yamamoto
Screenplay by Kiyoshi Yamamoto from the book by Hirofumi Tanaka
Starring:
Haruka Igawa (Kyoko), Atsurou Watabe (Yuichi), Nanasa Hoshii (Yumi), mami Yamasaki (Misato), Masatoshi Matsuo, Masaki Irie, Shin Yazawa, Hitomi Miwa, Mio Suzuki (Hiromi), Denden, Yuurei Yanagi (Professor Morikawa)
Produced by Takafumi Ohhashi
Cinematography by Tokusyo Kikumura
Edited by Nobuyuki Takahashi
Released in Japan on May 27, 2006

CHAKUSHIN ARI: SAISHUUSHO (2006)
Official English Title: ONE MISSED CALL: FINAL
Directed by Manbu Asou
Starring:
Maki Horikita, Meisa Kuroki, Geun-Seok Jang
Music by Kouji Endo
Running time 103 minutes
Released in Japan on June 24, 2006

ARANG (2006)
Directed by Sang-Hoon An
Screenplay by Sang-Hoon An and Yun-Gyeong Shin
Starring:
Yuna Song, Dong-Wook Lee, Jong-Soo Lee, Su-Young Choo
Cinematography by Gwang-Seok Jeong

Edited by Im-Pyo Ko
Running time 97 minutes
Released in South Korea on June 28, 2006

APATEU (2006)
Official English Title: APT
Directed by Byung-Ki Ahn
Screenplay by Byung-Ki Ahn and Mu-Sang Jo from the manga by Do-Young Kang
Starring:
So-Young Ko, Sung-Jin Kang, Hee-Jin Jang, Ha-Seon Park, Min Yu
Cinematography by Myeong-Sik Yun
Running time 90 minutes
Released in South Korea on July 6, 2006

NOROI (2006)
Official English Title: THE CURSE
Written and Directed by Koji Shiraishi
Starring:
Masafumi Kobayashi, Marika Matsumoto, Kana Yano
Produced by Takashige Ichise
Running time 115 minutes
Released in Japan on August 20, 2006

OYAYUBI SAGASHI (2006)
Official English Title: VANISHED
Directed by Naoto Kumazawa
Screenplay by Naoto Kumazawa, Yukiko Manabe, and Izumi Takahashi from the book by Yuusuke Yamade
Starring:
Ken Miyake, Ayumi Itou, Kenichi Matsuyami, Runa Nagai, Hiroyuki Onoue, Toruu Shinagawa, Shihou Harumi, Shirou Sano
Produced by Taro Nagamatsuya and Kimio Hara
Cinematography by Koichi Saito
Music by Goro Yasukawa
Edited by Ryuji Miyajima
Released in Japan on August 26, 2006

ROFUTO (2005)
Official English Title: LOFT
Written and Directed by Kiyoshi Kurosawa
Starring:

Miki Nakatani (Leiko), Etsushi Toyokawa (Professor Yoshioka), Hidetoshi Nishijima, Yumi Adachi, Sawa Suzuki, Haruhiko Katou, Ren Osugi
Produced by Atsuyuki Shimoda
Cinematography by Akiko Ashizawa
Music by Gary Ashiya
Running time 115 minutes
Released in Japan on September, 2006

PULSE (2006)
Directed by Jim Sonzero
Screenplay by Wes Craven from the screenplay by Kiyoshi Kurosawa
Starring:
Kristen Ball (Mattie), Ian Somerhalder (Dexter), Christina Milian (Isabell), Rick Gonzalez (Stone), Riki Lindhome (Janelle), Jonathan Tucker (Josh)
Produced by Michael Leahy and Joel Soisson
Cinematography by Mark Plummer
Edited by Marc Jakobowicz
Music by Elia Cmiral
Running time 90 minutes
Released in the United States on August 11, 2006

SAKEBI (2006)
Official English Title: J-HORROR THEATER VOLUME 4: RETRIBUTION
Written and Directed by Kiyoshi Kurosawa
Starring:
Kouji Yakusho, Manami Konishi, Tsuyoshi Ihara, Hiroyuki Hirayama, Joe Odagiri, Ryou Kase
Produced by Takashige Ichise
Released in Japan in late 2006